Reach For The Sky

THE BATTLE OF BRITAIN
A Novel of Lt. Corn

Story by Vixyy Fox

Illustrations by Little Napoleon

Hitching for Words

Copyright
Author Vixyy Fox
Title Reach For The Sky

© 2012, Vixyy Fox
(vixyyfox@yahoo.com)

Published 2014 through Weasel Press

Winner of the Coyotl Award for 2012 Best Novella

Table of Contents

This book is dedicated to Anthony Stewart, a fellow aviation enthusiast and furry; without whom I would never have met an English Stag by the name of Lieutenant Archie Corn.

Foreword

*by Gene Wolf friend
and fellow writer*

History fades. Two words that sum up an inexorable truth.

History is like a photographic snapshot. When it's first taken everyone and everything in the picture is familiar. Everyone knows the location and who that was standing and smiling in the background. Over the years the picture yellows but the main characters are still known; though they appear somewhat out of time and unfamiliar. As more time passes the picture becomes indistinct, the characters forgotten, and even the reason the picture was taken no longer known.

History fades. It's a fact. Battles are fought; won and lost, and then forgotten.

Famous and epic history changing battles such as Zama and Marathon are no more than a footnote to history now. The uniforms or armor worn, the weapons used, the texture and lay of the ground upon which people died, even the factors crucial to the decisions on how to wage the struggle, are so faded as to be lost in history itself.

The everyday details are always the first to vanish; forgotten first, lost forever. Those smallest of facts which are lost almost immediately are the most tragic.

The people who fought; what were their thoughts just before the battle they knew was coming? What were their fears? What were their hopes and dreams? What led them to this exact point in time knowing that at any instant they might be no more? What were their thoughts in the maelstrom of battle? What were some of the certainly uncountable heroic acts carried out and instantly lost to history even as the battle raged?

History fades everywhere but here. In these stories history is brought to vivid life from the perspective of those who lived it. The stories in this series are based upon fact but not necessarily upon the dry dates, places and events so easily forgotten. Within these pages a consummate story teller, Vixyy Fox, brings to life history blended with characters all too human yet set apart. You forget they are Fox or Stag or Bulldog or Wolf. The fact they are not human makes you understand more fully the human emotion Vixyy paints them with.

There is the determination of the Wolf; unwavering loyalty expressed as German nationalism. Then again the tenacious Bulldog is shown to be fierce and unrelenting as the leader of England or as an old fighter pilot. Then too the quickness and cleverness of the Fox is brought forward as a sorely needed wingman complimenting the determination and resolve of the English Stag; willing to take on all challenges no matter the cost.

Every story here is based in fact. Every story is grounded in reality and painted artistically on those most able to convey to us the most important thing we have forgotten; what it was like for the individuals who were there.

These stories are enjoyable and memorable. I dare say you might get choked up at times and laugh out loud at others. In either case, you will learn that friends and enemies are sometimes difficult to tell apart. You will also see that tears do not always mean sadness and laughter does not always mean joy. In short, you will learn.

History fades; but not here.

Preface

This book is about a history that is fast disappearing. Those old enough to actually remember the events first hand have, for the most part, passed on; taking that memory with them.

All too often we live our lives with the thought that the times we live in are not that spectacular. Since everyone is living in the same moment, accepting their surroundings 'as is', they never mark that which they do as unique. Thus they never much speak of it except for the occasional 'remember when' conversations held between siblings.

My own parents are a prime example. Having lived through WWII, my father was among the first occupying troops of Tokyo while my mother was an army nurse during the Africa Campaign. They seldom shared their experiences with us.

I ran across an article one time where my father was interviewed about a gun emplacement they'd had to storm. 'I guess I didn't get hit because I was faster the rest of the guys,' he was quoted as saying. His reference was to his being a football player before the war.

My mother actually told me that she'd dated the bombardier of the Enola Gay. I asked her what happened and she said that one day he simply wasn't there any longer. Having received secret orders he'd shipped out.

To her dying day my mother could not eat peanut butter. She did tell me the reason for that one. While she was stationed in Africa an army truck dropped off a 55 gallon drum of peanut butter for the girls at their make shift front line hospital. The nurses were so desperate for anything from home; they quickly popped the lid and dove in up to their elbows.

My grandfather was much the same. Having joined the navy during WWI, he participated in The Great Mine Barrage and the only thing we ever heard about it was that beans were good for you. He had a tattoo of an anchor on his arm but had no idea how he came by it. The tattoo apparently happened while he was on leave in London and had been too inebriated to remember anything.

In 'Reach For The Sky' you will find that the stories, though fictional, are based upon actual history. Though 'we' of the present might view this era as a grand adventure, those who lived through it saw most of it only as life; and it was brutally raw. Bad things happened all the way around and unless we remember, history will certainly repeat itself.

I should like to quote Winston Churchill:

Bessie Braddock: "Sir, you are drunk."

Churchill: "Madam, you are ugly. In the morning, I shall be sober."

Oh… wait… wrong quote…

I have found that history can, indeed, make you smile. Then again, if you embrace the cold hard ugliness of much that has happened, it can just as easily make you cry.

You will have to forgive an old Fox's strange sense of humor. The reason for this particular quote was only to point out that even during the darkest of times humanity never truly leaves us. We will always try to at least allow for a laugh and a smile that might otherwise have disappeared forever.

What these stories are about is best summed up by something told to me by my neighbor's father back in the 1960's; when so many of those who lived through this time were still alive and their memories fresh. He was a very quiet fellow by the name of Mr. Whaley and on that day, as he worked upon his motorcycle, he told me he had been among those who stormed the beaches at Normandy. I asked in my innocence how he was able to face such a thing. He told me in his soft spoken way that it was easy – 'You just made your mind up that you were already dead and then it was all right.'

Courage is what this book is about… courage. In the words of Sir Winston Churchill;

"Courage is the first of human qualities because it is the quality that guarantees all the others."

9

"Why?"

Shadows

by Vixyy Fox

Bearing ourselves humbly before God ... we await undismayed the impending assault ... be the ordeal sharp or long, or both, we shall seek no terms, we shall tolerate no parlay; we may show mercy – we shall ask for none.

Winston Churchill: BBC Broadcast, London, July 14, 1940

The artist, compelled to create, formed the image in oils; filling the blank canvas while the combined colors on her pallet ran like blood. She pulled the image from the dark recesses of her mind where it burned like a torturer's implement. She would have plucked out her own eyes if it would have kept the raw emotions from wracking her; but even blind she would have seen the Wolf's face… or perhaps more properly, just the portion of it that was not shrouded in shadow.

That was the part that scared her the most; the part not seen but known to be. There were so many stories never told… so many that had now passed into history; forgotten for all time.

Waking in London the day before, she had been unexplainably anxious. It was apparently the anniversary of some famous battle and on the radio, as she brewed her morning tea, she heard Winston Churchill's voice giving probably his most famous speech.

'The gratitude of every home in our Island, in our Empire, and indeed throughout the world, except in the abodes of the guilty, goes out to the British airmen who, undaunted by odds, unwearied in their constant challenge and mortal danger, are turning the tide of the World War by their prowess and by their devotion. Never in the field of human conflict was so much owed by so many to so few.'

Clicking the radio off, she muttered some words about dead politicians and wars belonging to other generations. Taking her tea, she stepped ino the small living room only to find her art supplies taken out and standing next to the door. In the corner of her eye she saw the visage of a tall Stag in an aviator's flight clothing looking at her. He had a mustache and his expression was sad. With the specter came the smell of smoke. London had suffered severe devastation during the Blitz of 1940, and she had heard many such tales of this occurring; but never before to her. When she turned to what she thought was there, she saw only the plant she kept in the front window.

The radio in the kitchen turned on again and Winston Churchill was heard to say, 'Bearing ourselves humbly before God ... we await undismayed the impending assault ... be the ordeal sharp or long, or both, we shall seek no terms, we shall tolerate no parlay; we may show mercy – we shall ask for none.'

It was more of a feeling than an actual voice but, she heard it all the same: 'Tell them…'

Her grandmother Chelsea had lived through this time. Though the old Collie had suffered much, she rarely said anything about it. 'We showed'em," she would mutter every now and again with a nod. 'We did… we showed'em good…'

'The stories are being lost…'

This time she looked around for the person who had spoken; but there was no one there. That was when the urge to paint hit her hard and she almost dropped her cuppa.

Calling in sick to work, the young Collie packed the art things into the boot of her car and began driving with no known destination. She never questioned the direction in which she drove, which was towards Bristol, though all along her route she found herself stealing furtive glances at the sky.

Well outside of her imagined destination, she turned off on a secondary road, which led to another, and then another, and still another until the road dead ended at a farm. It looked much as it had for better than two hundred years. Getting out of the car, she felt immediately watched. Glancing to the second story window, she found it open, the curtains moving slightly in the cool breeze; but no one was there.

Things around her suddenly became more focused. With the sound of a low flying aircraft came an even louder sound of a crash which she automatically turned to; only to find the trees undisturbed by the quiet afternoon.

Closing the car door, she walked to the door of the farmhouse and rang the bell. A voice seeming to be very far away yelled they were coming, and so she waited. A cold breeze blew from somewhere and she shivered just as the door was pulled open and a very old Spaniel gazed out at her.

"How might I help you, Miss?" he asked. His quiet yet distinct accent marked him as a dyed in the wool local.

There was the sound of a low flying aircraft passing over them and the chatter of gunfire. Spinning about, she looked skyward, shielding her eyes from the sun. "WHAT IS IT?" she yelled in the frustration of finding nothing. "WHAT DO YOU WANT FROM ME?"

The farmer's paw on her shoulder nearly made her jump out of her skin. "It's all right," he told her, "I understand. I was there, you see."

Holding the door open for her, he nodded reassurance to her. After serving tea, he helped retrieve her things and then led the way to the upstairs bedroom where she set up her canvas and immediately began to paint.

As she feverishly applied the brush stokes, random flash patterns of an event that took place long ago occurred within her thoughts; taking her through the entire story. What she was feeling had happened to someone who was but a small part in a major event that rocked the world.

"Töte mich! Bitte töte mich! Bitte töte mich! Bitte töte mich! "
(*"Kill me! Please kill me! Please kill me! Please kill me!"*)

The scream froze the artist in space and time, riveting her to the stool upon which she sat. Had it been real… or was it only in her mind?

Within the confines of the farmhouse, the only thing heard now was the ticking of the old mantle clock.

§

The following story is based upon true history. In the early days of the Battle of Britain, the Luftwaffe sent out single bombers on daylight raids in the belief they would be able to accurately strike their targets and also be able to single handedly fight off any opposition to their raid.

The names of the pilots involved are unchanged. The Spitfire pilots involved really did land and assist.

Eye-witness Ray Wheatcroft accompanied the severely burned bodies of three dead German airmen to Gillingham Mortuary. He was twenty years old at that time. They were buried on 8 July in graves 1097, 1098 & 1099. The bodies were exhumed (in 1962?) and taken to the German war cemetery, Cannock Chase, Staffordshire.

(Winston Churchill: we may show mercy – we shall ask for none.)
[The author would further; among the warriors there was honor…
among the politicians there was none at all.]

§

Hans looked to his left, and then to the right, checking for the fighters he knew were there somewhere. The Heinkel bomber's glass nose gave him very good visibility in all directions. It was only a pity that the panels were not bullet proof.

"Where are we?" he shouted to his navigator.

"Approaching Bristol," Gerhard yelled back.

"Best get to your bombing position then. Be sure you find us a good target."

"I'll pick it out, but you have to get us there," the Dog shouted back with a smile. Unlike the pilot, who was a Wolf, Gerhard was a German Shepherd. Their lines were close and they were friendly enough to go drinking together, but Hans was still a Wolf; that was why he was the pilot. Being a full Wolf he had much honor and his unreserved loyalty to guide him. He was admittedly proud to do his duty.

§

"Aye, I know of the ghost," old Brian told her while looking over her shoulder at the painting. He smiled a sad smile. "I've lived here in this house for as long as I can remember. When you arrived and asked me if you could stay for awhile to paint, I knew he'd found you. It takes a special person to get that close to the fallen… and so you must be very special indeed."

He nodded slightly and winked.

"I was a lad then," the old Spaniel told her, as he handed over the cup of tea he'd slowly brought up the stairs. The cup chattered on its saucer in the old Dog's paw like a set of bad dentures but his voice was as steady as his paw wasn't. "I remember it as if it were just yesterday. The fellow you've painted died right here in this room. You caught him well enough and good that you didn't show his right side. Gor but there wasn't much left of his face. God knows he begged my mother to kill him. He was in terrible pain."

14

§

The single bomber didn't encounter trouble until after its raid, which in fact did little damage. Gerhard had deliberately dropped their bombs early, ensuring that perhaps only one would make it to the top of the building which was the target he chose. Later it was reported that only slight damage was caused to the roof of the Rodney Works.

It was July of 1940, and Luftwaffe command, in its latest bit of infinite wisdom, felt that single bombers making precision strikes during daylight would cause more damage than many sent groping for a single target at night. In actuality, some of them also hoped to keep civilian casualties to a minimum by doing this. If a bomber could better see its target, they reasoned, thus would be the case. This did not sit well with the bomber crews who had to run the gamut of fighters waiting for them; but all being loyal to their country and its leadership, few were the words spoken in opposition.

"Dogs, dogs, dogs, at eleven o'clock!" the dorsal gunner called out. He had a single heavy machine gun and this started to rattle as he began defending his aircraft if just a little early.

"Call out directions when you can," Hans instructed over the intercom. "Nose, keep watch for a frontal; you know they like that attack. The bomber was presently still over the west coast of England and had a long way to go in order to get home again. If they were to get away from the faster fighters Hans would have to be the best he could be.

Pilot Officer Edwards, Pilot Officer Saunders and Sgt. Fokes belonging to Yellow Section, 92 Squadron, (Pembrey) winged over, beginning their strafing run on the lone bomber.
Edwards called 'Tally-ho' over the radio while Sgt. Fokes was heard to mutter 'fish in a barrel'.

"Stay away from the front if you can," Saunders warned, "They have a 20 mil waiting for you there."

His words were masked by the sounds of Edwards unconsciously pressing his gun button and mike button at the same time.

§

Old Brian looked upon the painting Chelsea had accomplished in such an incredibly short amount of time. The Wolf's single visible eye stared out at him in pain and anger. It was not a look of blame, but one of question. He was angry because he did not understand.

'*Why?*' the face in the painting asked.

"His identification tags gave his name as Lieutenant Hans-Heinrich Delfs," the old Dog told her quietly. He was very brave and a good pilot. He kept flying though the flames were upon him in the cockpit. They were too low to bail out."

Chelsea sat watching the old fellow as he stood gazing upon her work. It was obvious he was reliving the event as he told her about it. In the telling she was pulled along with him; smelling the smells of a farm and of cordite and of burning fuel.

"It had been good weather that summer," Brian told her, "And we were done with the hay early on. The barn was full and there was a huge hay mound to the side of it as well. We kits had great fun climbing in it, though we weren't supposed to. I believe it was around time for tea. As I played in the yard, I heard the sound of engines and looked skyward. The bomber passed over our house at perhaps five hundred feet. That is a guess of course; he could have been higher I suppose. There were three fighters chasing him down and even as I watched shell casings began falling all around me like rain. If they hit you they hurt like hell, so I ducked under the eaves of the house. The larger aircraft began to smoke, as did the fighter in the lead. That one peeled off and headed away towards Bristol while the other two continued on."

He paused, his breath catching in his chest; the painting seeming to breathe in his place. After a moment's strained silence, the farmer pulled in air like a drowning man finding the atmosphere again. He then continued on as if he'd never stopped.

"As I watched, the bomber lost altitude and turned, coming back towards the farm here. As he got close I could clearly see the flames. The left wing was blazing as was part of the fuselage up around the cockpit. His landing gear and flaps came down and it was clear to me that he meant to put down in the field. As it neared our farm, the Heinkel lost more height, cutting through one bank of small elm trees. Those were flexible and gave way so he made it across the road. That's where his luck ended. The aircraft struck a big strong elm tree and skewed round on the bank of the hedge. The impact was so hard that it hurled one engine a long way across the field."

It was mayhem after that. Apparently I was not the only witness, as people came quickly to the spot. The two Spitfires actually landed nearby and the pilots ran to help with the rescue. I'm not sure of the number of the Wolf crew, but two died in the crash, and the pilot, as I told you, died here in this room. Perhaps he will find peace now that you've captured his image. With your permission, I would like to pay you for your work and leave it up here above the mantle."

No money was exchanged between the pair. Instead, a gift was given in remembrance of good deeds done during a dark time by those on both sides of a war no one actually wanted. "Deeds such as these," Brian told her sagely, "are rarely reported for fear of punishment and generally go unnoticed by all save the Creator."

In this final act of charity, peace was finally granted to a soul that had been thought to be lost for simply being on the wrong side in the name of misguided loyalty.

Battles At Angels Ten

Sir Winston Churchill
"Never in the field of human conflict was so much owed by so many to so few."
* Manfred von Richthofen
"The great thing in air fighting is that the decisive factor does not lie in trick flying but solely in the personal ability and energy of the aviator."

Air Vice Marshal Smithe looked down upon the situation board and frowned. Four Collies of the WAAF (Women's Auxiliary Air Force, the ladies of which were respectfully referred to as 'Waafs') presently pushed small aircraft tokens around the map using long pool cue like sticks.

Another four stood in the background wearing large headsets and speaking into microphone like mouth pieces. These four were English Shepherds and were on duty as his communications officers; chosen from the ranks for their calm demeanor and sharp minds. These females were live on the communications grid with hundreds of spotting stations and radar sites all around England. Each of them knew every voice by name, where they were stationed, and their reliability factor. As soon as the reports came in, it was their job to decide on the spot what was put up on the situation board as reliable information. On their instructions the four positioner Waafs would add, take away, or simply adjust the tokens.

The Duty Fighter Control Officer, the position Smithe now filled, would observe their undertakings and then make a threat assessment. If it was warranted, flights of the Royal Air Force would be scrambled to intercept on his command. He personally had control of the entire country's protective prowess; which was extremely thin at best. What pilots he had were suffering from battle fatigue and their aircraft were being pushed to a limit never envisioned by their designers.

As he watched, one of the talkers said something to her positioner and a token was placed upon the board over Dover. "Inbound fighters at Angel's ten," the talker said loudly.

"It's confirmed?" Smithe asked her from his seat above.

"Pukka Gen, sir," (good information) she replied. "Anthony caught them on the RDF (radar), and it was confirmed just now by a visual from the bell tower at Western Heights. Reginald's a Sheltie of the Old Guarde, sir. He might be aged but he has the eyes of a hawk. He calls them as 109's with yellow noses."

"I could use the talons of a hawk right now," the Air Marshal muttered. A yellow painted nose designated an ace, and there were four of them flying together. Looking at the board, he saw no one and nothing available to throw at this threat. To be sure, they were on a Free Hunt [Freie Jagd] strafing run. It was much easier to kill aircraft on the ground when they were not moving. Hit fast, hit hard, and then fly home again.

"What's their incoming direction?"

"Direct route towards London, sir," the talker reported. As she spoke, one of the positioning Waafs pushed the token six inches further along the board. "Estimated arrival is ten to fifteen minutes."

"Scramble 92 Squadron at Biggins Hill."

"92 has just landed from a bomber intercept, sir," the talker re-

sponsible for that section reported. "They are out of fuel."

"The Polish 302 out of Duxford is also not available, sir," added a third, "They're north on intercept."

"Bloody hell!"

The fourth talker quietly said something and a positioner on the other side of the table placed a single aircraft token on the board, carefully pushing it to a position directly over London. "We have one maintenance ferry up and in the area, sir," she reported. "He's coming from 759 Spitfire Maintenance, HMS Herron en route to the 92."

"A ship?" he asked, not being familiar with the 'HMS' designation named. "Shore station, sir, at Yeovilton."

"Who is it?"

The Waaf notifying the Duty Fighter Controller consulted her note pad. "A Stag by the name of Lieutenant Corn, sir. He is flying the Egham Spitfire."

"Lord Beaverbrook was an absolute genius suggesting communities purchase Spits for our boys," the old Bulldog rumbled. "Get him on the radio!"

> [*Note: Lord Beaverbrook (yes that really was his name) was placed in charge of fighter production by Sir Winston Churchill and in this role he personally invented ways to increase fighter inventory; one of which was for communities to purchase an aircraft and then donate it to the RAF. Another idea he had was an appeal for aluminium, stating to the country, 'We will turn your pots and pans into Spitfires and hurricanes']

From a third battery of Waafs, a radio operator picked up her microphone and pressed the key. "Egham Spitfire, this is RAF Command, do you read, over?"

There was a crackle, of static and then a voice came clearly over the radio speakers, "Hows'it I rate a call in from Command? Is that you Mable? Do you fancy a brandy tonight m'dear? No pun intended of course."

"Bloody cheeky ex-Auxiliaries," the Air Vice Marshal grumbled. Moving to the radio operator's table, he held out his hand for the microphone. "Lieutenant Corn, this is Air Vice Marshall Smithe. Please do maintain proper radio decorum. We have four 109's coming your way. They are estimated over 'Sacred Ground' (a pilot's home base) in ten minutes time most likely to strafe. 92 Squadron is in between and bloody well stark naked. I need you to fly intercept. Direction will be from Dover at Angels Ten. Over."

"Well why didn't you just say so?" the pilot called back. "Wilco, AVM. I'm bangers fuel (half full) and three hundred ammo. (full load - three hundred rounds for each of the eight .303 machine guns) Clearing guns – fangs out. Be sure you inform Archie (London's anti- aircraft batteries) that's there's a friendly among the Wolves. Over."

"Chase them away, and I'll buy the brandy tonight," Smithe responded.

"And if I shoot them down?"

"A bottle for each smoking hole," the AVM called back. When the radio operator looked at him, he asked her, "What?"

"Proper radio decorum, sir?"

"As good as it gets under the circumstances," he responded grimly. "Oddly, I believe I served with this fellow's father during the first war."

§

Lieutenant Archie Corn held a thumb up to eclipse the sun in order to view that area of sky. He knew the enemy was coming so that gave him the advantage. If he could gain enough altitude, he would dive on them and at least have a running start towards a chance of survival. 'Yellow Nosed Bastards' were no one to fool with. One rookie mistake and they would have you dead on the bull's eye; actuality - not a pun. His eyes made a quick circle of his instruments looking for anything amiss, but so far the old girl was ticking along like a living, breathing race horse.

With solid information such as was given, he normally would have found a convenient cloud to skirt in and around while lying in wait. Unfortunately, and oddly for English weather, the sky was devoid of any cover at all. This was a detriment but not a stopping point; he would simply have to out fly the adversary.

In the distance, four small dots appeared, heading in his direction. The splash of yellow on their noses made them easy to identify. "Tally-ho," the Lieutenant called over the radio.

The wit and playful sarcasm were now gone from his voice as he became all business. Pulling on his oxygen mask, he banked slightly to the left, wanting to move more to the side of the incoming fighters. With a major amount of luck, they might not see him and he would be in position to rake all four as he passed broadside to them. They were flying finger four (Finger-four) formation, however, so it was doubtful he would be allowed that pleasure. This formation made things extraordinarily difficult as the tail always afforded cover for the lead. That, and the fact he would undoubtedly be spotted long before he could intercept, turned the odds directly against him. Pushing the throttle to full power, Lieutenant Corn rolled the dice in this Devil's crap shoot and hoped for a seven.

Within a minute, at a combined closing speed of some seven hundred miles per hour, the dots became well defined outlines. The Spit pilot, tipping his yoke over spun his aircraft around on its axis and began a diving attack. Even as he did so, however, the four Messerschmitts began their evasive manoeuvres.

Maintaining their lead/wingman positioning, the Schwarm split into pairs with the forward most unit continuing on to the intended target. The rearmost pair turned into him and climbed to the attack. The hope and theory was simple: that the lone aircraft would consider the odds and run away. In breaking off, the roles of attacker and defender would reverse, and a victory would be scored if the Germans could catch up. In the meantime, they were free to raid without the threat of another aircraft present.

The Stag, with his eyes on the two other fighters, left his throttle at max, braced himself, and pressed in as he had to do.

Closure to range flying head to head took only seconds. The lead Messerschmitt began firing long before the Spitfire could even think of it, but the burst was high by a scant foot. All noise within the Spitfire's small cockpit flattened out and joined together as, with tracers flying all around him, the pilot pressed his own firing button, and the Egham Spitfire physically jittered with the recoil. He too missed and the two aircraft, in a flash of yellow and green, flew past each other head to belly.

As soon as the first enemy fighter was past, the Spitfire was again subjected to a hail of fire from the following wingman. This was at more of an angle so there was no response to be made other than an involuntary duck of the head. Ten of the German's heavier machine gun bullets and

one cannon shell punctured the Spit's fuselage just behind the cockpit. Miraculously, they did no damage other than the holes they created.

"Command," the Lieutenant called calmly, "Two of the Bandits have broken off and are behind me. The other two are inbound to Sacred Ground. Call up Archie and have them open fire; I'll take my chances. Over."

"Copy, Egham Spit," replied the Waaf radio operator, "Waggle your wings for ID, please."

Immediately with her request black puffs of smoke appeared all around the sky; but especially in front of the two inbound fighters. The Lieutenant quickly did a wing waggle at his friends on the ground and the black puffs around his craft diminished. Archie was obviously abreast of the situation and stood ready and tracking.

With everyone now at full power, the chase was on. Advantage, however, went to the Spitfire as its pilot flew straight into the ugly black clouds with little thought to his own safety. The Messerschmitts, however, slowed considerably to effect evasive manoeuvring.

By the time the airfield was in sight, Lieutenant Corn had a choice to make. Having overtaken the pair, he was sitting in a prime position to easily pick off the trailing fighter. This then left the lead aircraft to rake his fellows on the ground, taking a good many of them out of action, perhaps permanently. To attack the lead aircraft, however, would place him directly in front of a very angry wingman.

Pulling back on his stick slightly, he raised the nose of his aircraft and pressed the fire button as he overflew the rearmost aircraft and the leader came into his sights. Smoke began to flow back from the yellow nose. The attack on the airfield was immediately broken off as this fighter broke left and climbed trying to escape his attacker.

The young Stag, mindful of the situation he'd placed himself in, broke sharp right and did the same just as a stream of tracers shredded his left wingtip. He had no time to rubberneck as he corkscrewed back up to altitude, but he did spy a telltale plume of smoke and a parachute.

There was no celebration in his heart over this... there was simply no time as he again scanned the skies for enemy aircraft. In this case, Archie was a good indicator, as his black puffs of death readily pointed to where the pilot should look.

Lieutenant Corn removed his oxygen mask and throttled back his engine at the sight of two retreating specs in the distance. There was a third closer on that he might have chased, but the pilot knew he would never catch up. Moving his throttle back further to cruise, he toggled his radio button.

"Command, this is Egham Spitfire," he called, "They've had enough I suppose; they're headed back to the Channel. Might we be expecting bombers, over?"

There was a silent moment with but light static and then the radio operator called back, "No inbound reports Egham, what is your situation?"

Archie looked around his aircraft and then made a quick observation of his instruments. The engine was still running rock solid. "The Spit's a bit shot up but nothing that can't be fixed. Twenty minutes fuel remaining. Shall I stay cover for a bit?"

"Negative Egham, you are instructed to land forthwith... AVM's regards, he says 'good job'.

And so it was, through the quiet bravery and selflessness of a people as a whole, a nation was saved and the tide was turned upon something unspeakably evil. Though they flew, and they achieved some victories; there were also defeats, anguish, and much pain.

In the end, as a whole we celebrate just the fact that we are still free. With patches over holes made in an attempt to kill, and a fresh marker on the hull indicating the same having been done to the one who tried. The victor is awarded a promised bottle of brandy and then is ordered aloft once again.

Through this we can live...

We have lived...

We do live...

Lieutenant Terrance Chrysanthemum

This is not a time when women should be patient. We are in a war and we need to fight it with all our ability and every weapon possible. Women pilots, in this particular case, are a weapon waiting to be used. - Eleanor Roosevelt, 1942.

The RAF recognizes seven aircrew personnel who were from the United States of America as having taken part in the Battle of Britain. American citizens were prohibited from serving under the various US Neutrality Acts. If an American citizen defied these strict neutrality laws, there was a risk of loss of their citizenship and imprisonment. Because of this, Americans either misled the British authorities about their origins, claiming to be Canadian or other nationalities at war.

For this reason, the true number of Americans serving in the RAF may never be known.

- Wikipedia, 2011.

The pilot stood at attention in front of Wing Commander Stewart Falstaff, a Bulldog who'd won his wings in the first war. She was a Fox in her early twenties and hardly looked even that. The old warrior grumped and harrumphed as he read and re-read the introduction letter on his desk. The initials 'E. R.' at the bottom of the letter were very compelling… if they truly belonged to whom he thought they did.

"And you are to tell me that you flew here alone and of your own accord?" he finally asked.

"Yes, sir."

"What aircraft?"

"Twin Beech, sir."

"You stole this craft?"

"It was given to me for my use. Now that I have arrived, I plan to donate it to the Royal Air Force. It's a good ship, sir, fresh out of overhaul. It got me here without trouble."

"Possession being 99 percent of the law, I'm sure you can do with it what you please. I will, however, gratefully accept your gift on behalf of the Crown. What route did you fly?"

"New York, to Nova Scotia for fuel, over Greenland, slept and refueled in Ireland, then on to Scotland. I would mention, sir, that I also flew across your border without discovery until I set down here; though I'm sure word was sent from Ireland."

"That does not speak well for our defenses," he grumbled, "I shall have to have a word with the watchers and the gunners who most certainly were asleep." He folded up the letter of introduction, reinserted it back into its envelope, and passed it back to her. "I'm sorry, but we cannot use you. You are an American, and it is illegal for you to help."

He expected the Fox to be crushed by this announcement but, oddly, she stood before him unruffled.

"Did you hear me?" he barked at her.

"Yes, sir," she responded, but I think if you will re-read my letter, you will see that I am Canadian."

"It said American."

Taking the letter from its envelope she spread it out upon his desk. Removing a pen from its holder she lined through 'American' and wrote in 'Canadian'. When this was done she slid the paper across the desk for his re-inspection.

"You are a female," the old Dog growled at her without looking at the paper.

"Let's not mince words sir," she countered, "You need pilots. The Germans have bled the RAF dry, and if you can't hold the skies the big show's over. After your country is overrun, the hero won't ride off into the sunset and there'll be nothing left but yesterday's news reels and coming attractions for movies that won't ever happen. I am a fully qualified fighter pilot. My father flew in the first war and he damned well taught me everything he knew. The rest I learned on my own with my mother's blessings."

The weekly report stared at the old soldier from the corner of his desk. The folder containing it was marked 'classified' and for good reason; it contained the names of the dead, the wounded, and the numbers he was lacking. He had pilots sleeping in their aircraft he was so short.

"Where is your father now?" he asked her.

"Dead."

"I'm sorry," he said softly.

"Don't be, he lived a good life. He was a test pilot; crashes happen. It was how he would have wanted it."

"And your mother?"

"She asked a personal favor and the letter you just read was written. She has no son to send to her ancestral home land… there is just me."

Rising from his seat, the Wing Commander placed his hat upon his head. Taking his time, he adjusted it to a proper and regulation angle. He then faced the Fox with finality. "You're still female and we can't change that with a strikethrough on a piece of paper; can we?"

"I can pee standing up," she told him non-pulsed.

He smiled at that. "I'm sure you can. Do you have a girlfriend too?"

"If it's a requirement," she responded, "But don't expect it to go past paw holding." She smiled back. "Will I have to fly a Hurricane, or do I get a Spit?"

"Young lady," he began, but she cut him off, extending her paw.

"Please call me Terrance, Sir, or Terry if you wish. I am a young man wishing nothing more than to help protect your country from a terrible fate. I have flown over a hundred hours in the Brewster Buffalo, twenty more in the Curtis P-40, as well as hundreds more in a whole slew of lesser craft… don't ask me how I arranged the war birds because I'll be required to lie again and that's getting off to a bad start. I have a light paw on the controls and I can make them dance to my tune. You need me."

"I can still see the roundness of breasts underneath your flight jacket," he told her, not taking the proffered paw. "You'll need some padding. Did anyone other than the officer who showed you in happen to see you?"

"Only the ground crew."

The Bulldog snorked a chuckle. "So only about fifty or so males and all of them downwind of your perfume I'm sure. How does your aircraft fly?"

"Stable and quick."

"Good… I need you to fly me to London. When we get there… Terrance…" he waved a paw waiting for a last name.

"Chrysanthemum," she replied, looking at the vase of flowers on his desk.

"Yes," he replied, "I suppose that it is. When we get there I will speak to the Air Vice Marshal. I will make no promises, but know that I am grateful you have come. When we arrive, I expect you will spit and scratch like any other of my pilots, yes?"

"Of course, sir…with the best of them… and thank you."

§

Flight Lieutenant Archie Corn sighed and looked over at the intel officer who was to debrief him. He felt totally done in... emotionally drained as he had never been before.

"There were fifty of the blighters, Fred."

He breathed in and out deeply, suddenly feeling as unstable as a Spit missing one wing. His heart was breaking, and it was not something he could even discuss with his debriefing officer, even though the interview would be held in the strictest confidence. He suddenly felt more emotional than he'd ever felt in his life.

"They had fighter escorts close in," he finally managed, "But that was to our advantage since they couldn't jump us from that position. We were flying finger four, diving down from angels thirty. Harry was lead followed by Carter, followed by me, and I was followed by Terrance."

The Lieutenant made a sudden retching sound and then ran for the door. As soon as he was out the big Stag doubled over the banister and threw up.

§

Archie looked above and saw the 'student' pilot he was tasked to instruct looking back down at him through the clearness of his Perspex canopy. He was about to say something caustic over the radio but the fact was; he'd never seen anyone so absolutely adept at flying before. Pushing forward on his control stick, he gently nosed his aircraft down. The relative positions of the two aircraft never changed even though the altimeter was now creeping earthwards.

Pressing the 'speak' button, he called out, "Your face is turning red."

The other aircraft executed a half roll and lined up neatly on his right wing tip no more than three feet away. "Is that better?" his student called back.

"Much," the Stag replied, giving a thumbs up of approval. "Your turn to hide and then I'll come after you. What say to that cloud just ahead? When we go in you break right, and I'll break left. When you come out on the other side, begin."

"Wilco Teach," was the call back. "Cheerio, pip pip, and all that other cute Brit talk. Watch your backside, because you won't see mine."

Coming out of the cloud, the Stag was still muttering about the impertinence of 'Yanks' in general when he heard, 'Tacatacatacataca...' over the radio in the tenor voice of his student. This was followed by a buffeting as the one aircraft passed precariously close to the other but in a way for which there was no defence.

"I say Archie, old fellow," called a baser voice somewhat clustered in static, "Did you just get trounced again?" There was a burst of following laughter by the rest of his mess mates. It was obvious they were all clustered around the airfield's command radio as if listening to an episode of 'The Shadow'. "You're costing me a lot of money Terrance," the voice called out. "I've been consistently betting on the Stag, but it would seem the Fox is up to chewing off his ankles."

"You can afford it, sir," the youngster called back, "I've watched you play cards. Tell whoever's taking your money that they owe me a share for doing their dirty work for them."

The mike was again keyed in preparation to a humoured return, but the 'alert klaxon' was clearly heard over the airwaves. "Combat frequency Archie," Harry instructed, "Incoming bombers."

"Switching," the training leader called back and then dialed the radio knob over. Looking around, he found Lieutenant Chrysanthemum already formed up on his wing. As a pair they began a slow corkscrew climb. "Base, Green Two," he called, using their training designator, "Up and ready."

"Stand down Green Two. Return to Sacred Ground via the loop. Wing waggle twice over the Thames for ID."

"Wilco, Base," he called back.

Looking over at his wingman, he saw him point at his ear and then hold up a thumb motioning upwards followed by two fingers. Reaching forward, Archie dialed his radio up two clicks. "Do you read me Teach?" came the tenor voice over the airwaves.

"Loud and clear."

"Why don't we join the battle?"

"Our orders are to return to base," he replied flatly, though he felt the same urge.

"But we have at least another thirty minutes in the air and we're fully loaded."

"Did you learn nothing in ground school?" was the reply. "Discipline is the key to survival. Without discipline you have chaos and with chaos you have no direction with which to fight the enemy. Ground Control conducts the chess game; we are but the pieces on the board."

"You're boring as hell, did you know that?"

"Boring but alive," he retorted in his British calm. "Tune back to battle frequency now and stay off the radio."

§

"Boredom, however, is a fickle bitch," Archie told the debriefing officer later, "One moment you're flying along minding your own business and the next she kicks you square in the chops. We came back via the loop as instructed and there right in front of us are six Messerschmitt 110's making a bombing run on the field. We dove on them, of course. Tail gunners not withstanding, I got one, and Terrance gets two... bing bang boffors. The other three dropped their bombs in the river and, as Terrance put it, 'skeedaddled back to Kraut land'."

"You think he's ready then?" the officer asked him.

The stag smiled, thinking the question totally ignorant. The other officer, reading the expression for what it was, added, "I ask this in my official capacity, Lieutenant; you were assigned as his teacher, and he is now listed to be your wingman. The entire squadron is aware you were trounced four out of five times by this beginner during your training session." Archie cleared his throat at the jibe. "Ah… yes, of course. I think he is more than ready, sir. It's a pity we don't have more like him."

"You don't have a problem that Lieutenant Terrance is… smallish?"

"And what's that supposed to mean?" the pilot bristled. "You been watching him in the loo or something?"

The intel officer chuckled and then wrote a note upon his clipboard. "The Wing Commander already told me we'll have the pinning ceremony at the pub tonight. For now, Flight Lieutenant Terrance will be stationed here with us. Next week, they'll probably send him further north."

"Why?"

"Why not? Jerry does bomb other targets than 'just' London." He looked at the Stag in a strange way. "Do you have something to add, Lieutenant?"

"No sir."

"Congratulations, then… three more to go and then you're an ace."

§

The pinning ceremony happened at the Froth and Gill Pub amongst as many pints of beer as the presently off duty pilots could afford. Archie watched his mates from a quiet corner, discretely drinking as little as he could get away with. In particularly, he watched his new wingman. He was confused by his feelings for this new fellow. He found himself oddly attracted and beginning to doubt his sanity because of it. Mind, there was always a feeling of camaraderie amongst the pilots in general, but this time...

Someone began banging a teaspoon on his beer mug and everyone's attention was drawn to the front of the small room.

The Group's Executive Officer stood and raised his drink. "To those who have gone before," he said simply. A chorus of voices sang out in the refrain of 'Here, Here'. Glasses were drained and there was a moment's silence after which the Group Commander stood.

"I have now," he called out loudly, "the honour of welcoming the newest member of 92 Squadron… Flight Lieutenant Terrance Chrysanthemum, front and center, please."

The lithe Fox stood and though the pilot staggered slightly coming forward, Archie observed that he navigated the tables better than most sober people. The Commander, a very tall Sheep Dog, bent slightly and pinned a cloth patch to the sleeve of the Lieutenant's tunic. "I expect," he said, his words slurring slightly, "that the next time I see you, this patch will be properly sewn in place."

"Yes, sir."

"Congratulations on your victories this afternoon, Terrance," he added, shaking the Fox's paw briskly, "The people of England thank you.

I am happy, at least, that some of our cousins have not forgotten us."

"Of course, sir."

After the applause died down, another round of drinks was served. Someone began banging away on the pub's old piano to bad effect but everyone sang none the less. During this fracas, Archie observed his new wingman quietly excuse himself and slip out the side door into the night. This wasn't all that unusual as they had the following day off and sleep was a priority for some; but something told him he should follow. The Stag remembered his first kill and the emotional rollercoaster he went through because of it was not all that pleasant. Sliding his mug over to the pilot sitting next to him, he winked. "Off to have a pee, Harry. Hold down the fort, will you?"

Harry slapped him on the arm and winked back, knowing the Stag was not much of a drinker. "Good night, Archie. We'll see you in the morning, eh? Good flying today."

Slipping out the door, he was somewhat surprised at the coolness of the night. Present, too, was the smoke of a multitude of fires burning around London. It pulsed and flowed like a living thing as it reflected the moon and the intermittent search lights. It also shrouded the lone figure walking slowly down the street.

The pilot stood for a moment, considering why he'd followed the Fox outside. His thought process suggested that perhaps he should not intrude, but the ever present smoke goaded him forward. It reminded him of why he flew… why they all flew, except perhaps the Yank. That was a puzzle to him. As far as he knew Terrance had no relatives in the country. The thought that he was in it just for the thrill of killing didn't fit either. There was much about this fellow that unsettled the Stag and he wanted to understand why; especially since they were to fly together.

"Terrance," he called out, "Wait up, and I'll walk with you."

The smallish figure turned and tucked his paws into pants pockets that seemed too big. No reply was shouted, but he did wait. Archie's largish gait brought him quickly alongside.

"Are you all right?" the Flight Lieutenant asked, true concern in his voice.

"I suppose so."

"'Suppose so' doesn't come close to answering the question," he shot back and then burped. "Pardon… the beer upsets m'gut when I've had too many."

"I had just one and it was more than enough," Terrance replied quietly. "I think it's stronger than American brews."

"But… I saw you drink at least six."

The Fox chuckled. "You were watching me? Perception is everything, Teach. I'd have a few sips and then change it out with someone else at the table who was more done than I was. Drinking makes me sick and that's not something I need."

"You're right, of course," the Stag replied. "Perhaps I should call you Teach, eh?" He waited a bit and then said, "Now tell me what you're feeling."

"Relief that I saw at least three parachutes today," was the simple reply.

"There was none from mine," Archie muttered in true sadness, "He was a flamer."

"Is it wrong to kill?" the Fox asked him softly.

"I suppose it depends on the circumstances," the Stag responded. "What are the alternatives? We did not ask the Germans to come over and bomb us, now did we?" He waited a moment and then, in a gentler tone, said, "I wish to ask you a question as your wing man. You don't have to answer it, but do, please, give it some thought. Why did you volunteer to help us?"

"I don't know," Terrance answered quickly. "I mean… I do know superficially, which is all the reasons you might suggest or have heard. Deep down, though, I'm not really certain of the why… I was simply driven to do so. I suppose it was for the same reasons Chennault and his Tigers are in China?"

"I see," the pilot responded, though he didn't really.

They walked in silence for a few minutes, the music from the pub fading behind them; each lost in their thoughts.

"Archie," Terrance finally said, looking up at him. It was the softness of the other pilot's voice that caught the Stag's attention. "We both have the day off tomorrow; would you stay with me tonight?"

The Lieutenant, caught by surprise, choked for a second and then politely coughed to cover his embarrassment. "Um… I do have some reading to undertake yet… ops orders and such."

Terrance stopped walking and looked at him, the darkness hiding both their expressions. The Stag heard a feminine sounding giggle and his embarrassment quickly changed to sudden panic. What brains he had left went into a nose dive at being approached like this by a fellow pilot. In the near darkness, he watched wide eyed as Terrance began undoing the top buttons of his tunic.

"Steady there big fellow," the smaller pilot told him. "You taught me that the trust of your wingman is as important as breathing in a combat situation. I ask that you trust me now. Do that and your questions will be answered in short order, though what you learn… well, it's a rather large secret; fair enough?"

"Yes… well, I suppose it would be… ahhh… certainly for you I'll do that Terrance… trust, that is."

Reaching out, she grabbed his large paw and stuffed it down her tunic. As the Stag's fingers found soft flesh and a roundness that belied anything male, he sucked in his breath without even realizing it. His thumb and forefinger next found an erect nipple and he pulled his paw back out as if he'd received a shock from an engine magneto.

"Bloody hell," he muttered, "You're female."

"Give the fellow a cigar," she whispered. "But that information is just for our time off. The day after tomorrow I become just as male as any of the other pilots in the squadron, agreed?"

"Why me?" he managed to ask.

"Because you're my wingman," she replied. Reaching out she took his paw again, "Because you're the best damned pilot I've flown with yet… and because I need you."

Moving closer, she hugged him around his middle. He, in turn, hugged her around the shoulders. Relief flooded over him with the understanding that what he'd been feeling… and was still feeling for this other pilot, was perfectly normal.

"How many others know?" he whispered in her ear.

"Only the Wing Commander. It's all very hush hush."

In the darkness of the night, shrouded by the smoke of a city struggling for its very survival, he kissed her between the ears and just for a little while things with the world became right again.

§

When Archie was done heaving his guts out, he stood straight, took a deep breath, and wiped his mouth with the back of a paw.

"I find," said a voice next to him, "that in times of high stress and sorrow, it does me good to go out and shoot down a bomber or two. Trounce a fighter and you feel much relief, though it does takes a while for the anger to go away. The emptiness of a lost love, however, takes a long long time to fade."

Archie turned to the voice and found Wing Commander Falstaff standing next to him. Taking a flask from his coat pocket, the Bulldog handed it to the flyer. "If it's empty when I get it back, I won't be angry," he told the Stag.

Taking him back into the airfield shack, he retrieved the Intel Officer's pad from him. "I'll handle this one Fred. Why don't you go have a cuppa. Do me a favor before you leave, though, and place a guard on the door; I don't wish us to be disturbed."

When the fellow was gone, he settled himself behind the desk, motioning for the Stag to sit in the chair opposite him. "Tell me everything," he instructed in a soft voice.

And then the story began… bombers everywhere… fighters of all sorts… an aerial ballet of death and destruction to no logical purpose a sane mind could ever conceive.

Harry was the first to go down after no less than three bombers preceded him. His parachute blossomed, tangled, and then spiraled down in a bad fashion.

Carter left the area trailing smoke. No flames were spotted though he was losing altitude. (Intel would later report that he crash landed in a farmer's field.)

Terrance bagged one bomber, and wounded a second before his aircraft simply nosed over into a spin from which it never recovered. Their talk on the radio had been all business to the point where it simply stopped.

And then the chatter stopped and Archie was alone among the bombers. He bagged four and sent fifth home with smoking engines before running out of ammunition. The fighters were pulled away by a flight of Hurricanes and another group of Spitfires roared through what was left of the bomber formation.

(Intel later reported only ten bombers made it to their target and of those only seven left for home. The numbers, however, were really fifteen and ten.)

"She said you knew, sir," Archie added when he was finished.

"I did; and I can assure you no one else must know."

"Why?"

"Because that's just the way it is," the old Bulldog growled. "Terrance shall be properly mourned. Since you were his wingman, I will request of you a letter to his mother?"

Archie sat straight in his chair, though his heart was breaking. "I will take care of it, sir."

"Give it to me personally when it's finished, and I will see that it is addressed and sent," the Commander told him as he finished writing his notes. Looking up from the pad, he furthered, "I would also request that you compose a similar letter detailing your time 'as a pilot' with Terrance. This is to be addressed solely to a person of the initials E.R., and it shall contain as many details as you can recall; including today's action. I will also see to the mailing of that personally."

"Of course, sir."

There was a moment of silence and then the pilot asked, "Might I ask what her real name was, sir?"

"I'm sorry," the Wing Commander replied softly, "But if she didn't tell you, then I am not at liberty to pass on the information. You were friends, were you not? Odd she didn't share that information with you."

"It was an unspoken understanding, sir. We had but the moment, so I never asked."

Taking a final swallow from the flask, Flight Lieutenant Corn stood, handed it back to his Commander and then asked to be excused.

§

Two years later, while flying cover for returning American B-17's, Squadron Leader Corn sidled up to a bomber with a feathered engine. He had just chased off a Messerschmitt 110 that was stalking the big aircraft and the crew were all smiling and giving him the 'V' for victory sign. As he came alongside, just below the co-pilots cockpit window he noticed a very familiar picture of a young Vixen in the sexiest of poses... one that he was quite familiar with; though her breasts were very much larger than he remembered.

Calling up the bomber's pilot on the radio, greetings were exchanged and he asked about the image painted on the ship's hull.

"She was my flight instructor," the pilot told him happily.

"And she is waiting for her hero at home I suppose... good woman, eh?" Archie asked him.

There was a dead moment on the static of the airwaves and then the pilot responded that he didn't know where she was. She had flown off one day without a goodbye and never returned.

"I had her painted on the ship for luck," he told the Squadron Leader, "and with hopes that someone might recognize her. Maybe they'll be able to tell me where I can find her."

"Aren't Foxes known rather for their... ummm... smaller physical attributes?" Archie asked.

There was a pause, and the Stag could see the pilot and co-pilot talking. Finally, with a little bit of static on the radio, the pilot called back with an apology. "I'm sorry, sir, but I don't understand Brit all that well. Could you please say what you mean in American English?"

His accent was exactly that of Terrance's, and Archie choked for a second. "Her tits," he finally managed, "They're much too big for a Fox."

"Oh! That! That's not accurate at all, and I'm pretty pissed about it. The rest of the boys thought it would be a good joke and paid the artist three times his fee to do it. I'm getting her fixed next paycheck. She was a beautiful vixen and a wonderful flyer. Everything I know about flying I owe to her."

Archie nodded silently in agreement, he owed her a great deal as well. Looking at the image, it almost felt as if they were again flying together.

After a moment's quiet contemplation he asked the other pilot, "Please... could you tell me her name?"

Blind Stray

Lt. Corn found himself alone in a low cloud cover upon coming back from across the channel. He was flying a special reconnaissance mission for which a call of 'volunteer' had sounded.

The Spitfire was the chosen aircraft for the flight, though it was a tad slower than the Mosquito; the usual choice for such things. The object was to get in and get out quickly and unseen if that too was possible. If seen, he was to make the mission appear as a 'seek and destroy' shooting up anything on the ground he might find as a viable target. He rather liked that idea.

His instructions were simple, fly a roundabout route to position X and complete a low altitude flyover. He was to fly exactly as if on a bombing run, the only difference being that the bomb attached to his aircraft was actually an automatic camera device. It had enough film for only one pass and to keep things at the best possible focus, he was to fly over at exactly 1500 feet.

"When you're ready to film," the intelligence officer told him, "just push your bomb release button. The camera will then operate until it's out of film."

Everything seemed simple enough, and of course, the entire mission was classified so he was forbidden to speak of it. His mates in his Wing, however, knew he was going; just not where or why. They were not blind or deft. Before he'd gone, everyone had shaken his hand and wished him luck.

And now… now he was lost in the low hanging cloud cover with a compass that was turning lazy circles. He had no idea how far off course he'd strayed, or even where he might be.

Keeping an eye on his artificial horizon and another on the small bolt he'd hung from a string as a superstitious backup to this, he flew ever lower hoping for a breakout to occur. In keeping with the mission requirements, he was not allowed to call on his radio until he was back over Hallowed Ground… but where was he exactly?

40

The altimeter showed one thousand feet and still there was no sign of an opening in the cloud layer. England's weather was notorious for such conditions. Normally, in a situation like this, he could always trust to his parachute should he run out of fuel; but with this mission, the images he carried on film beneath the belly of his aircraft were critical; and that would be lost.

Feeling the hair on the back of his neck prickle, he looked up from his instruments and swept the sky around him. A vague shape appeared off his starboard wing that he realized was the wingtip of another Spitfire. Reaching down, he flicked on his running lights, back off, then on and off again. The other craft returned the signal and slowly continued in on its converging course until it was right alongside and clearly visible.

The stag stared, his hand on the stick keeping him perfectly in place three feet off of the other aircraft's wingtip. Through the Perspex of the other fighter's canopy, Flight Lieutenant Terrance Chrysanthemum smiled back at him.

Wiggling her fingers at him, the Fox made a small circle with one finger, pointed to him and then to herself, and then off in a direction slightly to their left.

This was impossible. He had seen his friend shot down… had attended the funeral… had personally written the letters of condolence passed over to Wing Commander Falstaff.

His mind raced, and then a complete calm came upon him. If it was his time to go, he reasoned, or if, indeed, he had already barreled it in and she was to be his escort to something better; then he would gladly accept his fate. His heart ached at the sight of her.

He nodded and gave a thumbs up.

The two aircraft changed course slightly. Terrance in the lead, they flew on for approximately fifteen minutes. Archie never took his eyes off of her, until she held a finger up pointed to her eyes and then forward. Turning to look at what she was indicating, he saw a small hole in the cloud layer… sweet heaven and earth meeting right at the fringe of his home airfield.

His reaction was immediate; throttle back, flaps and landing gear down, flare out, chop power. There was the jarring thud as the wheels kissed the grass and his tail came down, bouncing slightly at the impact.

As soon as the aircraft stopped rolling, he switched off the engine, pulled his canopy back and attempted to rise, forgetting that he was buckled in. Struggling with this, he finally managed to stand erect in the cockpit. Ripping off his flight helmet, he looked to the sky and strained to hear anything at all.

Like a ghost, the fog moved in on him and quashed any sound at all.

Presently, there was the soft purr of a motor and the ground crew arrived to handle the 'special' package and his aircraft.

The intelligence officer in charge came to stand next to the aircraft, and even though he was two ranks higher, saluted the pilot. "My God, that was marvelous!" he shouted at the aviator. "We've been zero/zero ever since you left. I never thought I'd actually see you again old man. How did you do it?"

"I had help," Archie called down to him softly.

The fog almost took his words away. Without another word to anyone, the Stag unbuckled his parachute and let it fall back into the cockpit. When he was free of this burden, he climbed down and walked off into the fog.

Birdmen

Author's note: Through the internet we are able to see glimpses of what used to be. We should learn from these glimpses, and try to see what it was truly like in times that happened before we were born. They shaped who we are today, and it's always good to know from where you came.

Vixyy Fox

Memories of the Plough Inn: (from an eyewitness description)

The pub had a central door at the front which opened into what was the "off-licence", just a counter three feet wide.

Author's note: premises licences, in as far as they concern the sale of alcohol during those times, were categorized to include on-licences (allowing consumption of alcohol on the premises) and off-licences (alcohol must be removed from the vendor's premises and drunk elsewhere).

On each side there were doors, the left to the bar where you could hear the rattle of dominoes going on incessantly and on the right the smoke room which always seemed quiet. Each room could only hold about twelve people before it became overcrowded.

From the web site of Geoff Sandles:

There is a wartime story about the Plough that recalls how a young pilot crashed his Tiger Moth into the rear of the pub. Struggling from the wreckage, he staggered into the pub to order a stiff drink - and was told by the landlord he'd have to wait his turn to be served, just like all the other crashed pilots who came into the bar.

"Corn! … did you read my last, over." "Negative, Flight Leader."

"Best have your radio checked when we get back then," the veteran flyer instructed. His voice was clipped and terse; somewhere between kind understanding to Corn's sense of loss and pissed as a wet rooster that he did not put it aside in good British fashion. The fact he'd called the Lieutenant by name rather than call number was indicative of his feelings.

"I said, we shall have some company coming up and you should keep an eye out for him, over."

"Friend or foe, over?"

"Friend, you silly ham handed stick gripper." This new voice was markedly different and yet all too familiar. "Last I saw of you was after that cock-up you had in the Moth trying to do your circuits and bumps. Bloody well pissed drunk you were too; not that I blame you none. You're lucky I let you sleep it off."

"No friend of mine," the Stag calmly replied over the air waves. He smiled under his oxygen mask and added, "Just an old 'bad advice' flight instructor come back to haunt me. You come up here so I could shoot you down, Henry? That's right nice of you if you did."

"Actually, I'd thought to do you that favor m'self just to put you out of your misery; except word was passed you needed a new wing man. There I was in a cushy position advising the uppers when Top looks at me and mentions this fact; so I wiped my lips, swallowed, and volunteered to cover your hairy arse. Congratulations on becoming an ace, by the way."

"You get any yet?"

"They finally just now released me from instructing snot nosed kiddies; so what do you think?"

"You two can kiss your hellos later," the Flight Leader called over the radio, "Cut the chatter now and watch for the Boche." There was a pause as the Flight Leader gave the radio time to settle before giving a fresh call out. "Control, this is Blue Flight, climbing to Angels Twenty Five, anything known to be coming our way?"

"Clear sky Blue Flight, turn ninety right and begin your descent back to Hallowed Ground."

"Wilco," the leader responded, and as a group the four aircraft

turned.

"Let go of the bloody stick!" the instructor yelled from the back cockpit. There was no intercom in the little aircraft except for a rubber hose that went from a funnel mouth piece in the back cockpit to the student's headset in the front. Even with that, the engine noise made it near impossible to be understood clearly. The Bulldog was just about to take out the 'student control cudgel' he carried with him to (cough cough… ahem…) tap his student on the head for attention when the young Collie released his death grip on the forward stick, allowing the instructor to assume control. In short order, the craft's coming approach into a rather large looking tree was redirected with but a few leaves attaching themselves to the landing gear. This was accompanied by a stall and a nose down recovery which bounced the craft off of the ground with a bone jarring thump.

Upon landing back at the airfield the sage mentor quickly took matters in paw as he unstrapped himself from his seat.

"GET OUT OF THE COCKPIT AND STAND AT ATTENTION YOU MORON! IF YOU MOVE A MUSCLE TO ESCAPE BEFORE I CAN GET OUT I WILL HUNT YOU DOWN AND KICK YOUR ARSE FROM HERE TO LONDON!"

Flight Cadet Archie Corn stood at 'parade rest' watching as his soon to be instructor berated the student whose turn it was to fly before him. Near frothing at the mouth, the flyer bellowed his discontent with the fellow. By the time he was done, all that was missing from the poor cadet's face were the tears.

"YOU ARE A SODDING WASH OUT!" Lieutenant Henry Badcock yelled. "IF I EVEN SEE YOU AROUND AN AIRCRAFT EVER AGAIN I WILL PERSONALLY KICK YOUR TAIL TO ANGELS TWENTY! NOW GET BACK TO THE BARRACKS AND PACK YOUR KIT ON THE DOUBLE!"

As the cadet ran off the instructor made to leave back to the flight shack, but seeing Corn standing like a statue, stopped in front of him.

"And what do you want?" he growled.

"To fly, sir."

"I'm sure you do, but with a rack of antlers like yours you'll be causing too much drag. Sorry… won't do, and it's time for a beer in any case."

Archie was calm in his outward appearance, but inside he was almost having an epileptic fit. Flying was the only thing he'd ever wanted to do. Now to be turned away just for being the creature he was hardly seemed fair. He held his orders out at arm's length as if holding up a broadside for a circus.

"It says here, sir, that I am to be trained to fly fighters. This order has been signed by the Royal Air Force's Air Vice Marshal personally. I don't think you should disobey his orders."

The Bulldog snatched the paper from the Stag's hand, tore it into little pieces and then ground them under his boot. Looking at Archie, he said softly, "It's not his signature, Miss Prissy, it's a bloody rubber stamp. He hasn't got enough ink in his pen to sign all the orders for the booger brains they've been sending me to train; which leads me to question the sanity of those in charge. Now you tell me why I should risk my life and limb trying to teach you some respect for the sky."

The Stag thought for a moment, and then told him, "One day you will be flying alongside me, sir, and you will need me to be competent as your wingman."

"Like that's going to happen," the Lieutenant muttered gruffly.

The Stag, wondering at the intent of the muttering, added, "Have you not paid attention to world news, sir?"

"No… should I have?"

"Germany is on the move again. They are rearming and they have a fighter already ruling the skies in Spain."

"The Messerschmitt?"

"Yes, sir."

"And if I train you… do you think you'll be better than me?"

"I'm not sure I could be better," Archie replied honestly, "But I will be doing my damnedest to be the best in the sky, bar none. If I surpass you it will only be because of that."

"What's your name?" the Bulldog asked, cocking an eyebrow at the cadet's mettle.

"Flight Cadet Archie Corn, sir!" he replied sharply with an accompanying salute.

"Have you flown before?"

"Only gliders, sir, but I have had my ground school and was top of the list."

"What's the first thing you do when arriving to your aircraft?"

"You do a walk-around inspection, sir. That's to make sure there are no obvious defects…"

"That's not what you do," Badcock said, interrupting him, "You address the ship by name and you give her a bloody big kiss."

"Where, sir?"

"Anywhere you want, I suppose. On the bloody old stick if you're that sort of fellow, but I prefer on the cheek of the engine cowl like I would my Mum. Get on good terms with the old girl, that way she's less likely to let you down." He motioned to the aircraft he'd just flown in. "Her name is Margaret."

§

Henry took a long pull from his mug and then set it down on the bar top, taking the time to wipe his lips on the back of his other paw. "And that was my first introduction to your Lieutenant Corn," he told the pilots gathered at the Froth and Gill. "He was undoubtedly the best student I ever had. I pressed him to become a trainer, of course, but his heart was on the Spit, not the Tiger Moth."

"You might as well have asked him to fly transports," chuckled a Corgi at the end of the bar. "Nothing quite so boring as going from point A to point B and only having to pay attention to your defensive maneuvers; except perhaps having to teach piss heads how to take off and land."

"Here now," the Bulldog chastised, "We mustn't poke fun at the 'low and slows'. We all wear the same pilot's brevet and they do bring us our mail and Vees." (*Vees: a brand of wartime cigarette.*)

"No offense meant Old Chum, but perhaps you should 'get some in' before you tell your grandmother how to suck eggs," the Corgi countered arrogantly, " I've got three to your none; so if I wish to poke fun of anyone, I believe I might just do so."

The Bulldog's reaction was immediate, though measured. While the rest of the group chuckled, himself included, he calmly went over, grabbed his fellow pilot by the front of the shirt and lifted him from his barstool.

"This is how you take off," he said softly and then threw the fellow to the floor. "And that's how you land. Now then, that wasn't so boring, was it?" Spreading his legs apart, he glared down at the other pilot. "You could say I've had a bit of experience teaching piss heads, eh? Now then, if you want to make something of it, I would suggest you get up off your arse and give it a go; but do be warned, I don't play fair. One kick to the goolies and you'll be singing soprano for a while... and I seldom miss."

The door opened and Lieutenant Corn walked in. There was a moment's pause as he assessed the scene before him. "Up to your old tricks I see, Henry."

The Corgi scrambled up from the floor. "That's going to cost you," he hissed, "Raise your fists now."

"Don't lose your wool, Andras," Corn advised the fellow, "You do that and you'll regret it. Henry's a middle weight champion boxer. I've seen him take down an opponent nearly twice his size."

"Why thank you Archie," the former instructor began, but the Stag cut him off. "What started this?"

Henry pointed at the Corgi, "The half-pint hero here was disparaging transport pilots and flight instructors. I merely gave him a little advice on takes offs and landings."

"That's true," chimed in one of the other pilots, "Andras forgot his mouth again and had it coming sure enough."

"You'll find, young fellow," the Bulldog said, looking at the Corgie, "That I really am an old lag; even though I haven't any Hun. Crosses on my aircraft… yet."

The Corgi looked at Corn and told him, "I say Flight Officer Prune here is S.O.C. (S.O.C.: Signed off Charge. Aircraft no longer usable or wanted by R.A.F.) and Top sent him here so he could be gotten rid of as 109 bait."

There was a hushed moment around the bar. The pilot had stepped way over the line and was now on his own.

"Take it outside," Corn told the two of them. "The winner comes back in and buys the next round. The loser goes back to base and will polish the winner's boots each morning for the remainder of the week… agreed?"

The Corgi nodded and the Bulldog smiled. "Now you're whistling a tune I can dance to," he growled.

Less than a minute later, Flight Lieutenant Henry Badcock strode back into the bar and ordered another round of drinks.

About half way through his beer, the former flight instructor began the tale Archie had been expecting, and dreading, as soon as he heard who his new wingman was to be.

§

"OK then," Henry told his prize pupil, "You have flown the required hours without mishap, so it's time for your test. I will be watching you as much as possible, and I will also be your radio handler. Do you have any questions?"

"Which aircraft, sir?"

"You'll take Margaret, of course. I gave her the day off yesterday for maintenance so she's all ready for you. Are you familiar with the failure policy?"

"Failure policy, sir?"

"Well of course. If you don't pass the exam there have to be penalties just as in all of life. In this case, the penalty reflects back upon the offer I made you, but with a time limit. If you pass, which is highly likely, you will go on for advanced training with upgrade to Spitfires. Being that you are my best student, and this was your one wish, I called in a few favors and arranged it."

The Stag blinked; it was everything he had hoped for. "Why... thank you, sir."

"Call me Henry and don't thank me just yet. Should you fail... which you would have to severely prang your kite to do so, you will be assigned here at Starverton for a period of six months helping me teach piss head flying cadets."

Archie saluted the Bulldog. "It would be an honor to do so, sir... Henry."

"You're such a liar," the instructor growled with a smile.

§

Strapping on his parachute, Archie strode to the little Tiger Moth and straight away kissed it on the engine cowl. "Good morning Margaret, I am here on behalf of the Crown to take my flying exam. Flight Instructor Badcock has given me permission to use you for said exam. I do hope you don't object." He took the craft's lack of response as a yes and proceeded with his walk-around. Nothing was amiss.

Checking to see the aircraft's chalks were in place, he climbed into the cockpit where he buckled in and continued with his preflight check.

Starting

Check sufficient fuel, oil, batteries
External and internal checks satisfactory
Chocks in place
Slipstream vector clear of delicate items (keep the odd things from blowing away in the prop wash)
Trim aft, Stick aft (keeps the tail on the ground after start – prop wash over the control surfaces)
Switches Off Fuel On
Tickle until fuel dribbles (hand pump to fill the carburetor)
Throttle set for suck in (pulling raw fuel into the cylinders by rotating the engine)
Suck in over six compressions, and then
Choose a good compression to be next
Switches on (at least the rear [impulse] ones)
Start

Looking out and to the front on both sides, he yelled 'CONTACT' indicating the mechanic, (in this case another student pilot) should swing the prop for start.

With a puff of black smoke, the engine caught and immediately revved, whereupon Archie adjusted his throttle and then continued with his check list.

Pre Taxi

Four minutes at 1,000 rpm Mag check at 1,600 rpm
Full power check giving at least 1,900 rpm
Check intercom and radio
Radio call to ground control

"Flight 23 radio check," the Stag called out.
Henry's voice came back, "Loud and clear 23."

Pre Takeoff

Trim neutral
Throttle Friction nut tight (loose in front cockpit)
Fuel on and sufficient

Engine happy and lubricating ok
Set Compass heading
Harnesses tight and hatches closed
Stick full and free movement
Consider E.F.A.T.O. fields (*'engine failure at take off' alternate landing sites*)
Radio call to Ground Control asking permission to take off

Following his check list to the letter, the young Lieutenant called up Ground Control and asked permission to take off.

"Jolly good show so far 23," his Flight Instructor called back, "You are cleared for takeoff, God speed and good luck."

Archie advanced the throttle and was rewarded with a throaty sound of a healthy engine. All gauges were in the green and within seconds, his tail came up as the agile little aircraft became airborne.

§

Henry thumped his mug to the bar's countertop after draining the last of its contents. "And that was as good as it got, the rest of the flight was balls on buggered."

There was a chorus of 'What happened?' from all of those present and the Bulldog smiled at his former student, waiting for him to finish the story.

"I crashed," the Stag told the group quietly. He quickly took a drink of his beer to cover his smile.

"Gor, Archie, tell'em the rest of the story. It's not like it was some huge scandal, though it could have been. A true pilot is selfless, and that was you, sure enough. I'd have passed you regardless, except I really needed the help."

Again there was the chorus of voices urging him on.

The Stag sighed. "Losing an engine is not a big deal on a Tiger, as you all know. She'll fly like a nose heavy glider fine enough. The problem was the field I'd chosen for my 'efato'. Normally it was quite empty, but wouldn't you know it wasn't that morning, eh? One of the local school teachers decided it was a lovely day for an outing and that nice grassy field was filled with children. With the engine out, I was silent as a diving hawk so there would have been no warning at all. Not much I could do except turn to the closest patch I saw. This caused me to lose airspeed. A stall followed, and I pranged her in."

"Pranged her hell," Badcock laughed, "He bloody well barreled right into the wall of the Plough Inn…" With that he burst into ribald laughter at the obvious irony of the crashed into pub's name; as did all the other pilots. When he could talk again, he added, "And that's not even the best part, please tell'em, Archie, because I can't; it's too darned touching and I might cry."

With another sigh, the Stag looked at his mess mates and told them, "I was so distraught over ruining Margaret that I climbed out of the wreckage and went straight in and ordered three fingers of whisky. The barmaid, who was busy picking up the pieces of what I'd caused, coolly told me I would have to wait in line like all the other crashed aviators that came into the pub. When I looked up at her, and I am sure it was a look that indicated sudden death at making fun of my plight, she nodded to those behind me in the bar. One old fellow stood up. He was a French Poodle, and he tells me in that funny accent they have, 'My name is Jacques, and I flew with the Lafayette Escadrille… shot down three times, crashed five. We are all birdmen here.' Another of the old fellows stood up and he tells me his name in Ernst and he piloted a 'Brisfit' F2B artillery spotter over the lines during the Great War. He had been shot down by none other than Manfred von Richthofen." He began ticking them off on his fingers. "Fred flew Spads, Bruce flew Sopwith Triplanes, and one very old fellow was a former dirigible Captain with the burn scars to prove it."

"Tell'em what you did Archie," Henry said, his face now dead pan serious.

"I damned well waited my turn."

In the midst of the laughter that erupted, the door to the pub opened and Flight Lieutenant Andras Connah came back in. Striding directly to Badcock, he stood at attention and saluted.

"I would like to apologize, sir," he near cried out.

Archie looked at his former instructor and raised an eyebrow.

Henry winked at him and said softly for the Stag's ears only, "I never really struck him while we were outside, Arch, I merely bob'd and weaved a bit while tapping him five or so times on the cheeks so he could think about it a bit. You know my theories on teaching: lessons are not learned by force… they are taught by making your sprog (*student*) think for 'imself."

Turning to the other flyer, the Bulldog stuck out his paw. "Accepted," he said loudly, "But you still have to polish my boots."

"Of course, sir."

With that, Archie signaled the barkeep and another round was ordered for everyone.

Every Day

Archie watched the yellow nosed Messerschmitt as it slowly circled him like a protective angel. He was lazily swinging in his parachute, pistol drawn and held in his left hand as his right was having some trouble.

He'd been jumped while ferrying a Hurricane from Dover to the 401 Squadron in Northolt. That squadron, largely consisting of volunteers from the Royal Canadian Air Force and flying the slower aircraft, had suffered a fairly high loss rate as they'd battled against the German formations over South London. To help, some of the pilots from 92 Squadron were 'volunteered' to ferry aircraft to them on their down day. As the Stag floated towards the earth, he could hear his Commander's voice, 'Come on Archie, it's not like we do this every day... just one flight down and back, then you can rest, eh? I'll even buy the next round at the pub.'

As the pilot watched his enemy's aircraft, he began to wonder if his mind was working right, or if the shock of his bailout had damaged his capacity for thinking. The fellow had saved his life.

He was lucky to be alive.

§

"ACHTUNG!"

The pilots in the small room all stood in the same motion, turning their attention to the Wolf who had just entered.

"At ease," the gray muzzle gently commanded. The room loosened up considerably; but they did not yet sit. This was their Staffel Commandant Oberst Dierk Locke, an ace many times over and extremely respected by the entire Luftwaffe. Through his rank alone the Wolf should have been in charge of a Gruppen, but he chose to remain and lead his staffel. Having earned two Iron Crosses for his victories, he was entitled to this choice and it was so honored.

He looked at his pilots, taking in the measure of the Wolfs flying under him. Most were green rookies, fresh out of the flying schools. From his expression they could tell he was not pleased about something.

"Sit."

The command, like the first, was softly spoken, but to a Wolf, they all knew the depth of strength behind the single spoken word. As one, they sat in the plain wooden chairs that had been provided.

"I am told that my staffel is a bunch of drunken latrine diggers not suited to even flying cargo. This word was whispered to me from higher up so I must take it seriously and without question."

The Wolf paused a moment to let his embarrassment in front of command sink in before continuing.

"I agree that you flew well yesterday," he told them, his face poker straight serious, "But that is no excuse for you to drink yourself to stupidity. What if we had to scramble? The British will eventually go on the offensive and will wish to bloody our noses, ya?"

He left that hang in the air for everyone's benefit and then, when the timing was perfect, furthered, "You all have a responsibility to each other and to our country. The understanding as a pilot is what?"

"Fly alone… die alone…" the pilots said together, "Fly as a unit and you will survive."

"Goot … zo… If this happens again, I will have the entire staffel digging latrines for the mechanics, am I clear? Like a good Staffel that stays together; you will be punished together, no?"

In the distance there was an explosion, but no one seemed to notice.

"Yesterday," the Commandant began, "our Royal friends doggedly tried once again to force us to submission."

There was a group chuckling at this comment, as it was the German Luftwaffe attempting to force the submission of the R.A.F.

"I would like to say that we showed well for ourselves, having shot down three Spitfires to the loss of only one Messerschmitt, but the loss of anyone or any aircraft is a matter of somber reality. It is true they left with their tails between their legs; but we also lost Gerold."

There was a quiet pause as Locke began to slowly pace before his pilots. His uniform was immaculate and his posture ramrod straight.

"There is a new order that I received just an hour ago. At last we will be allowed to once again operate as the Wolf fighters we are and not nurse maid guardians to a wing of bombers. Our Gruppen has been authorized a Freie Jagd [*Free Hunt*]. The objective Headquarters wishes us to concentrate on is the destruction of British fighter aircraft. Once we have thinned out their pack they will not be able to so well defend against our bombers; and I need not remind you of the terrible losses our brothers suffered at the hands of the Spitfires and Hurricanes. Beginning at dawn tomorrow, we will sally two aircraft at a time. Your hunting area is up to you, but I will remind you to conserve your fuel as much as possible for better time over target. Are there any questions?"

One of the fighter pilots stood. He was a Baltic Wolf, thick bodied with a course accent and showing little pedigree. His name was Günter and he'd gained his position flying fighters more from his political connections as a 'good Nazi party member' than for his ability at flying aircraft. Among the other pilots of the staffel it was a given that you did not openly speak your mind in his presence. It was whispered he'd also been friends with the mechanic who had known ties to the Gestapo. That one had 'accidently' walked into a spinning propeller two weeks previously during a raid by the British.

"I have heard," the large Wolf said, "that this order also instructs that we are to disarm our enemy's fighter forces by any means necessary." There was a pause as the two Wolfs momentarily locked eyes. Then hesitantly the one called Günter added, "Mein Herr."

"You may sit, Leutnant," Locke told him, intentionally using his rank and letting him know he was but a junior officer no matter whose friendship he had curried.

When the other Wolf did as instructed, the commandant addressed his entire staffel, though he never took his eyes from this particular pilot.

"What Leutnant Meyer is referring to is the shooting of enemy pilot's in their parachutes. (The use of his family name was a marked reference to the pilot's family history as farmers) I will make my feelings on this subject very clear and you may consider this a standing order. If a pilot is in his aircraft he is fair game. If he has bailed out; it is the same as if he has waved a white flag. Disobedience to this order will result in a court-martial and I will personally command the firing squad. Both of our sides take prisoners every day. How our brother pilots are treated when captured is predicated on how we treat those whom we in turn capture.

This staffel will not be the one responsible for changing that."

The pilot named Meyer blinked and then nodded. At this small signal of submission, the Oberst turned his attention to the entire group. "If you begin shooting prisoners, then there is no chivalry left in a world that desperately needs such a thing. When this war is over and we have won; this same world will need to heal itself. Even more importantly, if you become nothing more than a raging brute during battle, there would be no reason for your enemy to ever surrender. Because of that, a crucial battle could be lost to one who would otherwise have given up."

The Oberst gave this just enough time to sink in, before instructing his men to check the roster to see who had which duties and at what times. Their base still required defense against their counter parts doing the same thing to them.

§

By the luck of the draw a discrete whisper into the ear of the Oberst's adjutant, the Wolf named Günter was assigned to fly wing to his commander during the Freie Jagd. This was not unusual, as Locke made sure to fly with all of his pilots, giving them valuable training as he did so. Already, three of the new pilots had two kills each and more than that showed great promise in their flying abilities and leadership.

On this day, he allowed the junior Wolf to fly lead while he trailed behind in the 'six' position. As they broke through an upper cloud cover over England, Oberst Locke was pleased to see a single Hurricane flying five thousand feet below them on a straight and level course heading north towards London. The sun, almost directly overhead, made it near impossible for the British flyer to see them.

The lead Messerschmitt appeared to be blind, and this did not please him. Throttling up and maintaining radio silence, he came next to the Baltic Wolf. Using hand signals he conveyed the find, instructing the other Wolf to attack. With a nod and a thumbs up, the other pilot winged his aircraft over into a dive, executing a classic 'slash' attack to perfection. Within moments, his unsuspecting prey was riddled with bullets.

Nosing over, the Hurricane turned onto its back, the canopy rolled back, and a small figure fell away, followed shortly by the blossoming of a parachute. For the downed enemy aircraft, Locke was genuinely happy. This would be Günter's first victory and reason for a well earned meal of potatoes and sausage with one of their special dark beers.

That was when the junior pilot, either forgetting who his wingman was or belligerently performing a defiance of standing orders, pulled a high 'G' turn and came back around, opening on the floating pilot with his machine guns.

§

Lt. Corn was taken completely by surprise. The ferry aircraft, albeit repaired and ready for duty, had developed an oil pressure problem. He was watching the gauge rather than the sky when things fell suddenly apart around him. Still suffering from the shock of having to take to his silk, he now found tracers flying past him with the sound of angry bees. His right arm was struck, and though the bullet passed through the fleshy part of the muscle, it still hurt like the Devil had bitten him. The attacking Messerschmitt flashed past in a roar of propeller and engine as his dangling body was buffeted in the wind that it caused. The Stag's reaction was one of rage rather than fear. If he was to die, he determined he would do so giving fight.

Reaching over with his left hand, he managed to draw his service revolver, a weapon with an effective range of little more than a hundred yards. Kicking his feet, he managed to spin himself about to face his attacker.

Günter, further slowing his aircraft as he circled back around, dropped his flaps and landing gear so he could line up on his intended target easier. He actually smiled as the British aviator came into his sights. With no reason to even lead the target; this would be an easy kill.

Raising and sighting his pistol, the British pilot found a stream of tracers raining down upon the approaching aircraft like the wrath of God. With deadly accuracy the bullets and cannon shells riddled the cockpit of the fighter which blew apart as the fuel tank torched.

There was a flash of yellow and a second Messerschmitt roared past, deftly half rolling to avoid the shrapnel from the fire ball. A moment later, it was back, slowly circling the parachute. Its flaps and landing gear were down in the same way as the first aircraft, though it did not do anything other than circle. On its last time around, it came close enough that the Stag could see the pilot. The Wolf saluted him as he passed close; then tucked his gear and flaps back up and departed for home.

§

61

Historical research: Though both sides in the war were known to shoot at parachuting aviators, this was generally the exception, not the rule.

There were acts of chivalry...

This event occurred in December of 1943 when Charles Brown and the crew of "Ye Olde Pub" were nursing their badly damaged B-17 back home. They happened to fly directly over Oberleutnant Franz Stigler's fighter base. Stigler had already shot down two other B-17s that day and quickly taking off, caught up with "Ye Olde Pub" to make it kill number three.

As Stigler moved in to fire, he noticed how badly damaged the B-17 was. There were gaping holes in the fuselage and half the rudder and horizontal stabilizer was shot off. The tail gunner did not fire, so he closed in and could see blood dripping off the .50 caliber tail guns. Inside, Stigler could see the crew members frantically tending to the wounded.

At that point, he felt that shooting down the aircraft would be like shooting men in their parachutes.

Stigler pulled up alongside the B-17 and motioned for Brown to land in Sweden. Brown, however, continued towards home. When they reached the coast, Stigler saluted, pulled up and flew back to base. If his actions had become known, he would have been court-martialed and possibly shot for letting an enemy bomber escape.

Charles Brown and "Ye Olde Pub" made it back to their base in England. Much later, these two former enemies met again and became close friends.

Red and Green

Archie sat in the cockpit of his Spitfire. It was in the hanger which, though not unusual, was strange for him to be sitting in it during maintenance.

The hanger, however, was empty and quiet. This was very odd.

Seeing the cockpit access panel open, he leaned over and pulled it shut. There was a hollow metal on metal sound that reverberated within the emptiness of the building.

He felt cold and a shiver ran through his body. Looking downwards from the latching mechanism, he noticed the emergency pry bar was painted red. That was odd, as it had always been regulation green to match the interior paint. His head felt fuzzy.

From outside the building came the sound of thunder. It was soft and distant sounding, but for the flash through the skylights that lit the entire sky, he would have thought it was an explosion.

Where had he been? More importantly to his soggy mind; where was he now?

"The Spitfire was seen as the backbone of the R.A.F. during the Battle of Britain, though in reality, the Hurricane was responsible for more downed aircraft," intoned a voice sounding as though it came from down a long hallway. There was the rattle of a chain and the sound of a metal barred door sliding open. "Now," continued the voice, "What you are about to see is a prime example of a Spitfire that actually flew during that great battle. I will ask that you do nothing that might mar her finish as many many many hours went into her restoration."

There was the sound of shuffling feet as a small group wandered over to the aircraft led by an old Bulldog whom the stag thought sure must have been Henry Badcock's grandfather.

"Lady's and Gentl'men, I give you the Egham Spitfire which was flown by none other than Battle of Britain Ace Archie Corn."

"He was a Stag," piped up a little vixen. She stood forward from her mother, completely unafraid of the grumpy looking old fellow.

Archie couldn't help but smile. She would make a good pilot... he was sure of it. "That he was," the Bulldog replied affably. "I knew him quite well actually."

"You did?" she asked, her eyes going wide. "But you're so old."

The child's mother snatched at her ear and gave it a tweak. "You be polite," she hissed at her daughter.

"It's quite all right madam," the curator told her, his mirth bubbling like a brook during spring flood. Looking to the little vixen, he told her, "We were all young and so full of life back then mon Cherie. The sky was our battleground, and we knew no limits but those of fuel remaining and the ceiling altitude of our aircraft."

'True to form', the Stag thought to himself, 'the old boy is going to give them a lesson not by lecture, but by letting them figure things out on their own with but a directional nudge or two. Certainly this trait must be inbred to the Badcock family. That would explain why Henry was such a good flight instructor.'

"Did you know that an airplane is a living breathing creature just like you and I?" he asked the child softly, bending slightly to be closer to her as if he was imparting a secret.

"It is not," she replied in her childlike straightforwardness. "It's a machine."

"Oh aye," the Bulldog responded, "True enough, and I see you have done your homework; but when the chips are down and you've only a gallon left by the gage, and yet she flies you clear back over the channel where you manage to dead stick'er into a farmer's field... how do you explain that, eh? When you're up in the middle of that mess they call a dogfight," he paused and stood as if having a sudden thought, "A dogfight," he laughed, "and me a Dog. If you were flying then, would it be a foxfight?"

The child laughed, her voice musical in the emptiness of the hanger. "Yes, yes, yes... a foxfight."

The adults of the group all laughed.

"Well then," the curator continued, "When you're way up in sky

64

all tangled up in a foxfight and for no apparent reason at all your ship flips over on her side into a stall and forces a dive for the deck just as a stream of tracers passes close enough you could light a Churchill cigar on them; then my child, you tell me if she's 'just' a machine."

Archie watched this in wonder. Here he was sitting in the cockpit, and though a few of this odd assortment of camera toting creatures gave him a glance, it was as if he wasn't even there.

"1,030 horsepower!" the little girl near shouted in her exuberance. "Eight Browning machine guns!" the Bulldog shot back.

"Thirty six foot wingspan!" the vixen gave him.

"And an inch," he added, "Thirty one feet and three and a half long! Now how tall was she?"

"Eleven feet five inches," the child replied without even batting an eye. This met with a round of applause from all the adults present, including the curator.

"By God I've never met your equal among any student I ever taught to fly," he told her, "Except perhaps for Archie himself."

"You really did know him?" she asked.

"Taught'im, and then even flew as his wingman," he replied proudly. "Tell you what, how would you like to sit in the Egham's cockpit? I think you've earned it right enough."

The little vixen was overjoyed as were the adults of the group. They'd all been warned 'not to touch' prior to even attending the historical movie before they came in. That the old fellow was allowing for this was a marked privilege to be sure.

Moving around to the back of the wing in preparation to mounting, the Bulldog told them, "You will note that some things have changed over the years. When I open the cockpit access door you will see a pry bar mounted on it. This was to assist a pilot in getting out after a mishap or crash. I will personally attest to its attention catching ability when waved in the face of an angry engineer or other such adversary. I even threw the bloody thing at a German bomber once after running out of ammunition." He paused as he struggled to get up onto the wing. "The bar mounted on this door, you will note, is painted red. This is in accordance with the current air regulations for emergency equipment. Back during the war, however, they were generally painted green to match the aircraft. Trust me; we all knew exactly where it was located."

Turning, he looked down at the vixen. "Just give me a moment to remove this wax likeness of our Stag from the seat – he's only there for show, mind you – and your mother can hoist you up to me, is that fair enough?"

The little Fox clasped her paws to her chest expectantly and nodded.

Turning to the cockpit, Henry Badcock reached in and pulled the latch back, gently lowering the access hatch and exposing the rest of the cockpit.

Archie smiled at him. "Hello Mr. Badcock, is your son Henry about? I think I would like to speak with him."

The old Bulldog stopped in his tracks and looked at the pilot as if he was seeing a ghost. "Archie?" he finally managed.

There was the sound of children's voices then, echoing off the walls of the empty hanger. They were singing a Christmas carol all out of tune and obviously as loud as they could.

"Is it Christmas?" the Stag asked softly.

"No…" the Bulldog replied, "It's mid August and bloody well hot out. Come on now and wake up, I have to get you back to base."

The Stag closed his eyes and it felt as if he were falling. He found himself dangling from a parachute, his pistol clutched in his left hand. The Christmas carol persisted and even seemed to be getting louder.

"QA… what the bloody hell are those children doing?" Badcock's voice demanded. "They're too damned noisy and it's confusing old Arch here."

"That's Captain QA to you, Flight Lieutenant," the nurse corrected him. She sounded hard as nails and the Stag was sure she would be slapping his face presently. 'Nothing to be done but slap her back,' he mused to himself as he floated in his parachute.

"The children wanted to do something to cheer your fellow here," she added, "so I suggested they sing something for him. The only thing they could all agree on was 'Joy To The World' because it's a happy song, they told me. They are doing it for him, you know. He's had a sedative and will be out of touch for a bit longer I'm afraid."

"How is he?"

"A bit banged up on hitting the ground, and a bullet passed through his arm, but he'll do."

"He better do," the Bulldog told her softly, "Word is the Luftwaffe's mounting a huge offensive, and we have to get everything in the air that we can muster."

"Is it the invasion?" she asked him as the children started again from the beginning of the song.

"Perhaps so," was the response.

Archie opened his eyes then. Blinking twice, he sat up and took a stuttering breath. "You have a car?" he asked without looking up.

"The Captain's motorbike," his wingman responded, smiling at the nurse's surprise, "But it has a sidecar."

"Help me stand then," the Stag told him, "I'll sleep on the way."

Looking up, he smiled for the children, though he was in pain and his head was throbbing. "Thank you," he told them, "your singing was very lovely, but I have to go now. Keep your heads down, eh? If you see airplanes flying over you be sure and run to the slit trenches, all right?"

As Henry helped him out of the bed, the children put their heads together and fervently whispered back and forth. As the pilots made it to the hallway, they followed as a group. Once on the front porch, they quickly aligned themselves into two rows, short in the front and tall in the back. As Henry helped his friend into the motorbike's small sidecar, they began to sing…

And did those feet in ancient time
Walk upon England's mountains green?
And was the Holy Lamb of God
On England's pleasant pastures seen?
And did the Countenance divine
Shine forth upon those clouded hills?
And was Jerusalem builded here,
Among those dark satanic mills?

Bring me my bow of burning gold,
Bring me my arrows of desire;
Bring me my spear! O, clouds unfold!
Bring me my chariot of fire!
I will not cease from mental fight,
Nor shall my sword sleep in my hand
Till we have built Jerusalem
In England's green and pleasant land.

'Jerusalem'

By Henry Blake

In war, there is the aggressor and the defender. Once the battle is joined, however, the difference between the actual combatants becomes blurred. Both sides, leaning heavily on nationalism, do what they feel is required of them as individuals to defeat the common enemy.

The leaders, of necessity, remain aloof. They are the players of this deadly game, and everyone under them is but a piece to be moved upon the board. The distinction between right and wrong quickly becomes blurred as the objective is solely kept forefront in their vision. Those who stand in the way of obtaining their goals are, without a doubt, in the utmost of jeopardy. The leaders during the Battle of Britain never hesitated to cross the lines differentiating right from wrong as they saw the need.

The attitude of the opposing leaders during this battle, however, were remarkably different.

Winston Churchill: Battles are won by slaughter and maneuver. The greater the general, the more he contributes in maneuver, the less he demands in slaughter.

§

Adolf Hitler: Generals think war should be waged like the tourneys of the Middle Ages. I have no use for knights; I need revolutionaries.

Of necessity, Winston Churchill was willing to sacrifice the lives under his charge to preserve the freedom of England.
Because all of Europe had easily fallen to him, Adolf Hitler, like a spoiled child, wanted the one thing he could not have. He was willing to sacrifice the lives under his charge in order to take it.

For the men and women fighting the war, those whom this book is a reflection of, humanity departed only when it was required to do so. On both sides of the war, soldiers carried on and did their duty as they must while trying their best to maintain what civility they could.

I recently had the privilege of speaking with Mr. Melvin Brownless, Luftwaffe researcher for the Aircrew Remembrance Society.

http://www.aircrewremembrancesociety.com/luft1939/rommel.html

He kindly sent me a copy of the story book produced by the officers & men of 1./(F)123 Reconnaissance Group which was given to the orphans of those of the unit who had already fallen: the Christmas "Kinderbuch" (Children's Book) was written in 1941.

I also found a photo of RAF Fighter Command pilots entertaining children during this time with one of their own dressing up as Father Christmas.

This book is about people such as these.

The Foe

Their aircraft danced upon light air
In an ocean of sky one cannot see;
Gracefully flying formation in threes
They left white snow like contrails
Exactly marking where they would be.

T'was a heartlessly cold aerial ballet
Where sticks of bombs were dropped,
And multiple guns all round shot;
Both sides died ignominious deaths
But the resolute Hun was firmly stopped.

-Flight Lieutenant Archie Corn

Mind's Eye

Thoughts: Bits and pieces of word pictures flowing in and around the mind during those times when there's nothing and no one to communicate to or with. A self-contained process by which everything and everyone functions.

Advance the throttle and she moves forward.

Tail rising the craft is airborne

Jouncing and floating on unseen air

With the vibrating thunder of an engine

Coupled to a propeller

That chews through the sky

Like starvation through porridge on a cold morning.

"Stag Two, Stag One, follow my course close on. Stag Three and Four follow a league behind."

"Stag Two, roger."

"Stag Three, roger."

"Stag Four, roger."

The radio is scratchy sounding but understandable.

Stick is steady… no vibration…

Rudder a bit kinky; one degree trim

Check left/right/up/down/instruments…

All green – all good – pain in the right arm –

'Work through it old chum'

Round and round we go

"And where does it stop?" questioned a familiar voice in his head set.

Picking out the lead most dive bomber, he adjusted his course to intersect and continued to watch as the aircraft grew closer. The Germans were not unobservant however. As he closed the formation scattered; all of them diving towards the ground. Tracers from the rear gun positions laced the sky.

"Bloody slow bastards," Henry's gravel voice muttered in the Stag's ear.

"Did you call Two?"

"Negative."

"I'm on the lead."

"I've got the two towards the right."

"Yellow Nosed Bastards eleven o'clock," Sammy called out, "Engaging."

Archie watched the silhouettes against the sky through his gun sight. As the angles began to jell in his mind, his thumb switched his weapons button off of 'safe'.

Gun sounds on the radio with a call, "Get out of there Andras, you're smoking... Andras!"

Archie's gun sight was now full of Stuka... his thumb pressed the fire button and his body vibrated with the stutter of eight machine guns. Tracers began floating back at him from the tail gunner's position but they stopped abruptly and smoke began pouring back past the cockpit. The aircraft went completely vertical, slowly spinning in its death throes.

"Scratch one," the Stag called out

"Same, same," responded Henry.

"Bale Andras... Don't be an anchor!"

"Stag flight, Control, help is coming."

"Watch behind Henry... I'm on my way, but you've got a nine trailing you."

"I see silk... Andras is out."

"Five nines heading down Arch, time to bugger off."

Gun sounds...

Gun sounds...

"First flight has jettisoned bombs and they're leaving, second flight still pressing in."

"I'm tailed Arch... where the bleed'n hell are you?"

Look around… look around… sky sky sky specks chasing… bank and throttle full… engine response quick and good….

Tracers bridged the gap between the two aircraft Archie was closing on but the shot was wide. "Hang on Henry…"

"I'm holed! Give'im a squirt right quick or I'm gone for six."

Archie's first attempt was too angular. The deflection as it was only gave him a split second's window of opportunity, and it wasn't enough.

Hard bank left… over compensated… hard bank right… body heavy heavy… vision graying out as the extreme 'S' turn brought the Spit's nose back around and behind…

At the last second, the German fighter broke off and dove, leaving a trail of black smoke from a full on throttle; the one maneuver a Spitfire could not duplicate with speed enough to catch up.

"About bloody time you got here," Henry called over the radio. The relief in his voice was barley contained.

"A friend in need," the Stag called back.

"Is a friend indeed," the Bulldog replied.

"Stag Three… status."

"Andras baled… I think. Winged one and got winged. I'm bleed'n but it's just a nick."

Instruments… sky… ground…

"Tallyho," came a distant call over the airwaves as 32 Squadron found the second flight of Stukas.

Archie looked over at the Bulldog who was now flying off of his left wing. Henry held up two fingers in a 'victory' sign, and though he was wearing an oxygen mask, the Stag was sure he was smiling. As he watched, his wingman then stuck his middle finger through a huge hole in his Perspex canopy, carnally moving it in and out.

Shaking his head, the flight leader called Control. "Stag flight, bingo fuel… heading back to Hallowed Ground."

"Roger Stag Flight, cleared to proceed."

Over the airwaves for just a moment there fluttered the notes of a popular song sung, in actuality, by a German Wolfess. Though Archie knew the song well, he also recognized the tone of the voice as not quite belonging to said German Wolfess.

When you're battered and on the ropes
And you've just about lost hope
A friend in need
To staunch the bleed

Truly is a friend indeed.

"You're messing with me," Archie muttered.

"No I'm not," Henry decried the call out, "You just saved my bloody arse, why would I be messing with you? And why are you singing that silly arsed song?"

"I'm not singing," the Stag called back, "You're hearing things."

"I heard it too," Sammy called back, "Kind of scratchy, but I heard her."

"It wasn't me," Control called up. She was a good looking Collie named Beatrice and Henry was quite fond of her. If she was caught chatting on the radio even in a minor way, she would have been in big trouble; and yet she chimed in.

"You're all three daft," Archie told them, "After we land and debrief the pair of you need to go out and collect Andras. Control; obliged if you could get us a location. Now stay off the radio."

"Yes, dear," he heard her whisper.

"And you stay out of my mind unless I'm asleep," he thought to himself. The voice in his head. the one he heard in such instances, sounded more like it was shouting. "Bad enough they all think I've lost my mind but I'm beginning to think it as well."

Her giggle stayed with him all the way back to base.

Airplane

by
Flight Lieutenant Archie Corn

Note from Archie: Wistfully written upon return from flight while having a cuppa and watching the sky.

Dedicated to the Egham Spitfire

Not alive, as in living and breathing,
Not a creature of mental instability,
She rises from the ground as a thoroughbred
To the sole purpose of her breeding;
Meant to jump high up within the thinness
Of the atmosphere
And I am awed.

This beautiful creature abides my presence
Huddled within her cockpit amidst
Lumens of exactitude and indication.
Like a tumorous lump benign in my existence,
She understands the requirement for my touch.

How much longer until she will be free
To live among the clouds with the ghosts of her ancestors?

As we fly together, I dream for her
Knowing that in the end, when she is worn out,
Much as her pilot she will be laid to rest,
Never to fly again.

We will be but ghosts of what went before then,
Remembered for a generation or two
Until even that is taken by oblivion.

And yet we both shall ever hear the music of children's voices Pretending
they can fly.

Escape

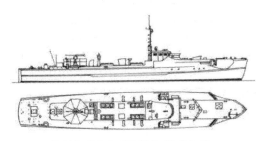

S 30–37 (1939/40) (Mickel)

Archie was enjoying a pint at the Froth and Gill when a runner came in specifically looking for him.

"Commander Fleming's respects, sir," the young private told him after coming to attention at his table, "He says to pass on that you are needed as soon as you can 'hike your arse back to base'. He said to tell you that in exactly those words, sir."

Henry Badcock looked at the stag over his mug. "What do ya suppose found its way up 'is backside? It's not like we get a whole lot of rest these days, is it? I apologized for pinching his motorbike the other week. He was chuffed even though I got you back safe and sound."

Archie gave his friend a look that said he should mind his comments in front of the enlisted and the Bulldog snorted. He'd had a good six pints to Archie's one and was apparently feeling grumpy. Lack of sleep and constant stress were taking their toll on all of them.

"How did you come?" the Stag asked softly.

"I ran, sir," The Dog replied. He was a Whippet and chosen as a runner exactly for that as he was obviously fast. "That's why they call me a runner."

Henry snorted at this, almost choking on his beer. The comment was not made with sarcasm but with the innocence of a young fellow, and it tickled the Bull Dog to no end.

"I suppose I should get going then," the Stag told his wingman. "Please run back and tell the Commander I'm coming, eh?" he instructed the Private. "I'm not quite as fast as you and besides; I'm nursing a wound so running is not too much of an option."

"I'll have to remember that one," Henry chuckled. "I'm sorry Jerry, but while you're attacking, I must only stroll to my aircraft because of an old wound you gave me. Please be a good fellow and wait a moment will you? I'll be up presently to shoot you up a bit."

The Private chuckled at this. When Archie gave him a look, he saluted. "Right away, sir," he said a little too loudly and then was off again out the door and into the night.

"D'ya think it's a night flight Arch?" his wingman asked.

"No, it's something else. Otherwise the 'Old Man' wouldn't have worded the message as he did. He has a dry sort of wit and that's about as funny as he can be under the circumstances."

"Right then," Henry told him with a small two fingered salute, "See you in the morning for kippers and tea. I do wish, however, that for a change they would give us eggs."

When Archie made it back to base the runner was waiting for him at the gate. After the Sergeant of the Guard checked the pilot's papers (even though he knew him quite well) the Private came forward, saluted, and then asked him to please follow.

As they walked, the young Whippet queried, "So how many have you got so far, sir?"

"How many what have I got?"

"How many airplanes have you shot down?"

"Seven."

"Pardon me for saying so, sir, but you don't seem too happy about it. That makes you an ace and so far you're tops in the maintenance pool for kills. The boys there all have the highest respects for you."

"Maintenance pool?"

"It's a friendly wager the mechanics get together on, sir. Actually, it's based upon the aircraft more so than the pilots. Pilots come and go, but the airplanes stay until they're done in."

"Done in?"

"Yes, sir; done in. S.O.C. I mean to tell you I've seen the men work bloody miracles with what's left of a kite. Sometimes they take what's scavenged from different wrecks and piece them together just to make one whole. Mind, I'm just a runner, but I do hope to join up with the maintenance group one day. At the moment they have me helping with the fueling. I drive the bowser (fueling lorry) when I'm not on duty as a runner."

"Then you would know that the Egham Spit has seven Iron crosses painted on her."

There was a moment's pause before the young fellow admitted he'd known this.

"Then why ask?"

"You're famous, sir. Please pardon if I have insulted you, but I just wanted to be friendly. Later I can tell the boys that we had a chat like old chums."

"What's your name, Private?"

"Timmons, sir."

"And your given name?"

"Simon, after my grandfather."

The pilot stopped walking, forcing his guide to stop also. In the darkness he faced the youth, and held out his right paw. "Simon, my name is Archie, though when we are about I expect you will maintain proper military decorum. I am pleased to consider you a chum."

The youth grasped his paw and pumped it up and down. "Thank you, sir… Archie… sir… thank you."

The Stag was led to the field shack which was not so unusual as the Commander used it principally as his office so he could remain closer to the aircraft. Around the entrance were the duty group, some smoking, some sipping at the ever present cuppa which was the life blood of Fighter Command pilots in general. They would remain here all night, some sleeping on the ground under a wing, and yet others in the cockpit; ever waiting for the order to scramble.

There were soft greetings in the darkness which were returned and then Archie was quietly up the wooden steps and opening the door leaving his escort outside. Inside, there was but one light on and that was carefully shrouded. Commander Fleming sat in his chair behind the desk, while on a chair next to the desk was the figure of a flyer he thought to be lost the week before. This pilot, a Fox, was wrapped in a blanket. His uniform and Mae West life vest were in a sodden pile at his feet.

"Bloody hell Marrek, is that really you? We all thought you'd gone for a Burton."

The flyer did not look up.

"It's nice to see you too Archie," Commander Fleming said from behind his desk. "I'm glad you could make it so promptly."

The Stag stopped walking and looked at the Sheltie, puzzlement clearly in his expression.

"We have a bit of a mystery on our paws at the moment," his C.O. informed him. "It would seem that Flight Lieutenant Marrek has been spit back by the sea. He was returned to us not more than an hour ago by the fishery patrol," he stopped to check his watch, "Make that two hours ago, but his only words so far were an urgent request to speak with you. Otherwise… nothing."

"Is he in shock, sir?" Archie asked, pulling up a chair and turning it around backwards so he might straddle it in front of the other flyer. "He couldn't possibly have survived that long in the water, eh?" Reaching out, he touched the other pilot on the knee. "Are you all right Percival?"

The Fox looked up and nodded. He then turned to Commander Fleming and asked, "May I speak with Flight Lieutenant Corn privately, sir? I promise that after I do so, I will sit down and fully answer any of your questions."

The Sheltie looked at the Stag, who nodded. "Of course. Perhaps I'll go and have a cuppa… back in fifteen, will that be enough time?"

"Yes, sir."

"You're sure you don't wish to be checked into the infirmary for the night? We could do this in the morning. You're looking a bit off. I hadn't noticed it before… probably due to the lighting."

"Morning will be too late, sir."

Fleming rose from his chair which made a wood on wood scraping sound as it pushed back. "He's all yours Arch… make the best of it. If things are not straight when I get back, I'll have to deal with it on a harder level."

"We'll be fine, sir," the Stag replied, not exactly believing it was so. He'd known Marrek only briefly before the fellow went missing. Why it was so important that the Fox speak specifically with him bothered the pilot quite a bit.

When the screen door to the shack closed the Stag turned to the other flyer and asked him softly, "I think you know that Fleming is right chuffed with you. What's this all about and be up front with it… we haven't the time to lark about."

"Percival Marrek is dead, sir, I am his cousin Peter… Seaman First Class of the German E-boat S 32."

For a moment, Archie could say nothing at all. Finally, he managed, "Please continue. I will not interrupt you until the tale is told."

"My family immigrated to Germany when I was but ten years old. Until that time, we lived in Somerset, England. A few years before the war I enlisted in the navy just to get away from my father's fishing boat; only to be placed upon another boat and another and another, until I ended on the S 32. The war broke out and we are expected to do our duty, just the same as you and Percival. Her Captain is a good person and he does his duty as is expected of him."

There was a noise at the door and then a brief exchange of words. The person meaning to come in left without entering. During that time, the sailor stopped talking and simply watched the entrance. Archie tapped him on the knee and nodded that it was all right.

"We have rescued many British airmen as well as German as we cruise up and down the channel," he said, continuing. "My one wish, however, was to escape the Germans and come home. I found myself wishing that I was once again just a simple fisherman like my father."

The Stag nodded his understanding.

"Last week," Peter told him, "A Spitfire ditched near us. We saw him smoking badly and held our fire. When he splashed in, we pulled alongside and Captain Stoik ordered 'swimmers away'. I was one of those swimmers and was shocked as we pulled poor Percy from his cockpit. He was in a bad way, but awake. Of course I recognized him immediately and spoke with him in English. He recognized me too and I think that is what kept him alive for a while longer. He said he was glad to see me." There was a ghost of a smile on the sailor's face as he mentioned this.

"As soon as we had him on board, 32 was away at full throttle and we were again watching the skies though it was very overcast. I got Percy below, stripped him of his clothing, and dressed his wounds. He was quite awake and very talkative about what had happened to him. At that time I fully expected he would make it." The sailor hesitated for a moment. "He made me promise that I would seek you out and tell you."

"Tell me what?" Archie asked, forgetting that he had said he wouldn't speak until the story was done.

"He said he had help finding us."

"Help?"

"Yes… a radio call and then another aircraft. The pilot told him to follow and that when he saw a boat below, he was to ditch."

"Why didn't he use his parachute?"

"I don't know… except that perhaps he couldn't. He did follow, and he did ditch, and we did pull him out before his aircraft sunk."

"Who was the other pilot then?"

"Percy said it was another Fox, sir… someone named Terrance."

"Impossible!" the Stag exploded, rising from his chair. He was about to call the Fox in front of him a liar and storm from the office; turning him over to the guards. Posing as a British pilot and using his uniform was the act of a spy. Except for what the Fox told him next he would have done exactly that. The fellow's words stopped him cold.

"Percy said… he made me promise that I tell you of this if he could not, sir. I am to tell you that this other Fox, Terrance, was a vixen. She told him to remember her telling him this as it would be very important that it should be told to you."

Archie sat heavily back to the chair and stared at the sailor. Finally he told him, "You will take that information to the grave with you, is that understood? No one is to hear this again."

Peter nodded.

"What happened next?" the pilot asked him.

"After Percy died, we buried him at sea, but I saved his clothing. It was his plan. He said we looked enough alike that I could get back home in his place. I could then break the news to his parents in a more personal manner, giving them his greetings and love. When we were off the English coast and making an attack run on a freighter I jumped off of the fantail in the dark knowing they could not come back for me. I changed in the water, inflated his life vest and swam for shore."

"What is it you wish from me?" the Stag asked him.

"Percy told me I would have to earn my way back into the good graces of the English people. I understand that and agreed. I can tell you where the E-boat base is located and from which direction to attack, but I will only do so if you promise to spare E-32. It is easy to identify as the Captain had the decking above the bridge painted sky blue. He told me once that his old fishing boat was painted like this and he liked the color. The other boats are captained by good Nazi's and are painted regulation deck gray. He is a good person, sir, as are the rest of the crew."

"Why would you do this?" the Flight Lieutenant asked softly, still on the borderline of disbelief.

"England is my country, sir. I was not given a choice when my family left. Germany was once good… but something happened and that goodness has changed."

Rising from his seat, the pilot simply said, "I'll see what I can do."

Sir Ian was quick to act upon the information offered up by their new prisoner. Command was quickly called and informed that they had sensitive information that could not be passed along over the tellie. With their closeness to Headquarters, Wing Commander Stewart Falstaff was there in less than half an hour. An hour before dawn, 92 Squadron had six aircraft fitted out each with a 500 pound bomb and their pilot's assembled in the briefing room. On the wall was a large map and what photo reconnaissance pictures Wing was able to scrounge; which was not much.

"As you know," Commander Fleming told the pilots, "Jerry's e-boats have been bedeviling the shipping lanes on a regular basis. The timing of this information is incredibly opportune and comes to us directly from a source intimate with their operations. It has been confirmed as pukka gen by Flight Lieutenant Corn. Your route over will be straight in and straight back at Angel's five. When you see the coast, you will drop down to sea level. Coming in you will pop up and over the ridge line and drop immediately down into the harbor. This is to be done in the hopes that the sound of your approach will be negated and the attack will be a total surprise. Drop your bombs, strafe any targets of opportunity and then get the hell out again." He paused to look at his pilots. "Lieutenant Corn will be Flight Leader. Archie… do you have anything to add?"

The Stag rose. His flying helmet was on, and his oxygen mask dangled to one side as it did on all the pilots. He caught sight of Henry Babcock looking no worse the wear for his drinking. The Bull Dog smiled and winked at him.

"Last night," he told them, "It was confirmed that Percival Marrck has been killed in action. Because of this we now have the information that we have. This mission will be for him. One additional piece of information that I expect everyone to abide by; if there is an e-boat in port that has the decking above the bridge area painted sky blue, that boat is to be spared. This was an agreement made in the process of gaining the information we are acting upon. Are there any questions?"

There were none.

"To your aircraft then," Commander Fleming instructed, "And God speed. Go and make them hurt."

On their way out the door, Wing Commander Falstaff stopped Archie and then nodded to Fleming that he wished them to be alone. The

Sheltie followed his pilots out of the room without a word.

"I am told that Percival's cousin was able to give you confirmation that this information was good, but that you could not tell Captain Fleming the source of this confirmation."

"It was Terrance again, sir."

"Terrance? Again? Terrance is dead Lieutenant."

The pilot quickly told the story of how he found his way back to base in zero/zero weather, and then followed with the story Peter had related to him. "Terrance specifically passed on that I was to be told he was a she."

The old Bulldog smiled and grunted an acknowledgement. "At least," he finally said, "If the Squadron is to be haunted it is by a benevolent spirit. I was right then to let her fly for us. Best you be on your way Lieutenant."

During the attack there were three successful bomb strikes. Archie then led his flight out by flying down the valley of the fiord where the e-boats had been hidden. Inbound from the sea was one additional boat, back from its night of patrol. Flipping on his gun sight, the Stag lowered the nose of his aircraft in preparation of a strafing run but noted the sky blue decking even as the sailors scrambled to man their guns. Raising the nose of his aircraft, he climbed out of range, executing a single barrel roll as he did so. To the puzzlement of the boat's Captain, each of the following aircraft did the same.

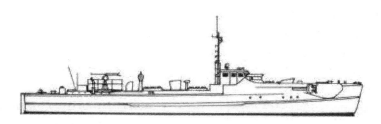

Coming back to Holy Ground, the flight found the sun well up in the sky. As the group circled their airfield, the Stag noted a plume of smoke rising from the fueling area. Upon landing, he pulled his canopy back, killed his engine, and called down to his ground crew asking them what happened.

"It's the bowser, sir," replied the Sergeant assigned as his crew chief. "Apparently the fellow operating it forgot to ground the lorry to the aircraft. The hose sparked and she went off." The grizzled veteran of the first war paused to spit on the ground. "Bollacks," he cursed, "Bloody waste of a good aircraft and fuel."

"Do you know who the operator was?" Archie asked as he lowered the cockpit's side door. "It was Timmons, sir," called up the Private who had just chalked the Spit.

Their eyes met and a shared understanding was immediately met. Neither said a word as it was understood things were to always be 'chin up, carry on, emotion does not win the battle'.

"Bloody hell," the pilot muttered as he climbed out of the cockpit. "What was that, sir?" the Sergeant asked.

"I said get her arms loaded and have her fueled up as fast as possible. We just poked a stick in the hornet's nest, so you can bet we'll be paid a return visit shortly."

Luck of the Irish

THEY SHALL NOT GROW OLD, AS WE THAT ARE LEFT GROW OLD, AGE SHALL NOT WEARY THEM, NOR THE YEARS CONDEMN, AT THE GOING DOWN OF THE SUN, AND IN THE MORNING,
WE WILL REMEMBER THEM

English Poet Laurence Binyon (1869-1943)

"I shoot to hit the machine, not the lad in it; at least I hold him no grudge, but I have to let him have it. See him first before he sees you, hit him when you fire as you might not have a second chance."
—RAF Wing Commander Brendan Eamon Fitzpatrick "Paddy" Finucane - Battle of Britain Ace

The Shamrock-Spit taxied in, bouncing up and down slightly as it did so. A Kiwi sprinted across the field. He was wearing the white canvass crosses of a ground marshaller and carried his paddles held high. This was not an aircraft stationed at Biggins Hill and the fellow had been caught snoozing by its arrival. With so many flights day after day, everyone was exhausted.

Napping was as routine as tea at every turn.

Though the event of visiting aircraft was not so uncommon, the large green shamrock painted on the side of this particular Spit marked it as very special. In the cockpit, oxygen mask dangling from his flying helmet, a grim faced Celtic Hound watched the fellow on the ground closely, following his directions to the letter.

"I need fuel, ammunition, and oxygen as swiftly as possible," he said into his microphone, after he'd cut the engine's fuel and the aircraft's brakes were set. "I need to get back to base as quickly as I can and if I can catch a few of the blighters on the way so much the better."

He switched off the ship's accumulator (*battery*) and checking his cockpit a last time finally rolled the canopy back just in time to hear Henry Badcock's bass voice shout out, "We don't let no beer boys (poor flyers) land here at Biggins, Paddy. Best you tuck your landing gear back up and take yourself over to Waterloo Station where you can catch a train ride back to where you come from."

The Hound unlatched the side door and let it fall with a bang. Standing, he stretched, sallied himself and then shouted back, "As I live and breathe, is it my old canary (*instructor*) Bad Ass Badcock? I hear they were actually going to rename the Tigermoth in your honor but with the consideration of the kite being female, the name they came up with was too vulgar to use."

There was laughter from the numerous ground crew that were present. They all knew and respected Henry Badcock and the jibe was a good one.

Patting the side of the fuselage over the large shamrock, the Wolf Hound queried, "What do you think of the old bus, Henry; she's a beauty, eh?"

"Looks just like mine minus the green blob of paint and all the iron crosses on her side," the Bulldog replied as he approached the wing's iron crosses on her side," the Bulldog replied as he approached the wing's front. "It's a pity the Old Sod (Ireland) is so adamant about maintaining neutrality. I understand they had a fit when you joined us. Who in blazes do they think Jerry will invade next if Old Blighty falls? It's all stepping stones to them says I."

"Perhaps they're hoping for the comeuppance of the British empire," the Hound offered. "Obviously not all of us share the feelings of our government."

"And thank God for that!" the former flight instructor told him. Standing straight, he saluted the other pilot. "And we thank you for that."

"Is that a royal 'we'?" Paddy asked, returning the salute with a wink.

"It's a 'just me' we," the Dog replied with a smile, "But I think everyone here would agree."

Next to Badcock stood another pilot, a tall Stag quietly listening to this exchange. Their eyes met and Paddy nodded to him. Both pilots standing near his wing's leading edge were in their flying gear. Both also looked extremely weary.

"We've done five sorts so far starting before the sun came up," the Stag told him. "Jerry's on the move it would seem and we hear the airfields are taking a real beating all round."

The fact that they had lost ten pilots went unmentioned as unlucky conversation. Hopefully most would have safely bailed out and would come home to fight again.

"Six here," the Irish Dog told them. "I think they have more aircraft than they have brains. Have you got any tea on the brew?"

Paddy's group had lost an even dozen though he was unaware of the exact number at this point. The thought of lost friends was pushed to the back of the mind all round as the job at hand was concentrated on. There would be a time for mourning later.

"We do," Henry told him. "Walk with us to the shack and I'll do the honors and pour out. We brew a good Sergeant-Major's (strong) tea here Paddy so I don't think you'll be disappointed."

After the Hound climbed out of the cockpit and jumped down from the wing, the Bulldog shook his paw warmly and made introductions.

"It's not often I have two former students with me at the same time," he said warmly. "Flight Lieutenant Archie Corn, I give you Flight

Lieutenant Paddy McCormick, and vice versa. I'd suggest you two pair off together cuz you're both blaz'n good, but that would leave me in the lurch. No offense meant Archie, but I've gotten rather used to ya being on my wing so there's no trad'n in what we got."

"Did he always talk this much?" Archie asked the Hound.

"Aye, as long as I knew him he did," Paddy replied.

"Would you prefer Patrick?" the Stag asked him, knowing how nick names might not actually be appreciated.

"About as much as I would Patricia," the Hound replied with a smile. "I was born Paddy and I'll die Paddy, thank you very much."

Henry held his arm out indicating they should proceed when the cry, "JERRY UP!" was yelled out by one of the ground engineers.

Automatically the pilots spun about and looked skyward. In the distance, six black dots were lining up on the airfield. Nowhere was there a single British fighter to stop them.

All three pilots looked to their aircraft. In a glance it was discerned that the ground crews had the Egham Spit done and ready while Henry's had been armed but not fueled. Paddy's, on the other paw, was now fueled but not armed.

"Oh hell!" Henry growled and then ran for his aircraft. As he did so the air raid siren began wailing.

Archie and Paddy, being of the same mind, were right on his heels. Reaching their respective aircraft, the three ungraciously leapt upon their wings from the front as the ground crews pulled the chalks and ran for cover. Only the aircraft fitters stayed to help the pilots mount up; their efforts blended with those of the pilots, flowing in a ballet of functional preparedness.

There was no time for the finer points of a refined preflight as taught during their months of schooling; now everything was by blind rote and done as quickly as possible.

Henry managed a belly flop that got him on top of the wing. Once there he momentarily looked as though he would slide down the other side until his fitter grabbed him by his flight suit and managed to hoist him up. "It won't do to be eating grass right now, sir," the fellow told him as he got the Bulldog stuffed into the cockpit.

"Thank you Charlie," the pilot told him, "Now jump for it, I've no time for the chute."

Reaching in, the fitter blatantly ignored the order and began hooking up the pilot's buckles. "Now what would my missus say if'n you was to have to leave your kite and had nothing on yer arse but bits of bum

90

paper? You live you can fly again and shoot some more of the bloody bastards down so I think I'll take my chances with Jerry's bombs."

As he spoke these words, he did what he said he would continued on with business. Henry, undeterred by the fellows fussing continued on with the business of starting the Spit's engine.

Rudder bias (*trim tab*) full right (*to compensate for the torque the engine*) – elevator trim one degree nose down – fuel cock on – brakes on – starter and booster coil buttons uncovered - magneto switches on – throttle half an inch open – engine primed – and all of this done in mere seconds.

"Contact!" the Bulldog yelled as he pushed both buttons in. There was a wine as the starter strained to overcome the compression of the engine and then with a cough and a black cloud of fuel rich smoke the machine came to life.

Pulling the stick full back to keep the aircraft's tail on the ground, Henry released his brakes and began to roll. "Run for it Charlie!" he yelled at the fitter and as he pulled his side access door closed. This time there was no argument. The fellow's well wishes were swept away by the prop blast and as he hit the ground the Spaniel dropped and rolled to cushion the impact. A second later, to the tune of the first bombs going off, he was running as fast as he could to the slit trenches as his charge pulled his canopy closed.

The bombs, beginning at the edge of the airfield, began walking forwards in quick succession. Advancing the throttle, Henry let his tail lift up as he began his take off. Out of the corners of his eyes, he found Archie on one side of him and Paddy on the other.

"I've got enough fuel to make one good circuit," he called over the radio, "I'll pull up high to draw any fighters off, you both split left and right. We'll join back up in a pincer. If any fighters follow me I'll pull them in over the ack ack."

"Wilco," the other two pilots called back just as the Bulldog hauled back on his stick and climbed almost straight up. This delighted the bombers as the bombardiers manning their forward firing machine guns opened fire. For the space of five heartbeats, the fighter was within close range and totally defenseless. Henry passed them by with no more separation than two hundred yards in a slow but steady climb to get above.

Archie, curling out and to the left, watched for fighters and was not disappointed as five of them dove on him. "Bandits at eleven 'o' clock," he called in warning.

"See'em," Henry replied, "Heading back down to the bombers."

"On my way," Paddy acknowledged, though there was not much he could do with his lack of ammunition.

The bombers were primary target. Ignoring the incoming fighters, the Stag continued his loop around which would bring him up and behind the JU-88's. He would not be able to prevent them from bombing the field but possibly he could knock a few of them out which would make for less that could pound them again in the future.

Henry was the first to draw blood. Reaching the apogee of his climb, he rolled over and dove full speed into the thick of the formation guns blazing. He strafed two in the passing and the second, his actual intended target, began to smoke. Stubbornly the pilot refused to leave the formation.

The bomber's pilot knew they were their own best protection. If he left this umbrella of defensive guns there would be no hope for survival.

"My kingdom for cannons!" the Bulldog called over the radio in frustration. "Two on your tail," Paddy called to him, "Dive down, I'm on'em."

Henry wisely followed the Hound's advice and dove. Paddy, undaunted by having no guns to shoot, crammed his Spitfire squarely between the two pursuing Messerschmitts. His maneuver happened so quickly, the German pilots didn't even have time to fire as they broke left and right to avoid a collision.

Archie, coming up from behind and under the bomber flight had his aircraft swept with machine gun fire from the combined tail gunners. Pushing his gun button, he returned the favor to his target in an eight to one ratio. The bomber's left wing broke off at the root spilling fuel and flames as it began tumbling. Two dots made it out of the cockpit and their parachutes blossomed a mere thousand feet above the ground. The Stag didn't even notice as he rolled left, saw one of the Messerschmitts that had avoided Paddy and was on him, ripping out burst after burst as the pilot evaded.

"The Schmitt's have turned back," Henry called out. "Gotta land... give'em hell lads!"

With the Stag's last burst the German fighter flamed into a ball of orange, its individual pieces blowing out and away. The Stag had no option but to fly straight through the debris. Something red splattered on his windscreen as other pieces of more solid debris bounced off of the Perspex. The Spitfire buffeted hard, shaking his body like a toy. Even as it did he was hauling back on the stick trying to gain altitude again; once more going after the bombers.

With the feeling of increased gravity, the sound of the straining engine flattened and the altimeter began winding upwards.

Above him, barely discernible through his canopy, he saw a trailing JU-88 with a Spitfire flying off of its wing. He could see that the bomber's right engine was shut down as it was yawing hard against a one sided thrust.

"Control," Paddy's voice calmly called over the radio, "Call down the flaming onions (*anti- aircraft fire*), I've got a bloke here that wishes to land and make amends. We'll need the body snatchers (*ambulance crews*) to be sure; his teeth are gone and the gunners bled out."

Ironically, upon landing, the wounded bomber fell victim to one of its own bomb craters and though a rescue was attempted, all but one of the crew was killed.

This picture and the details of the actual crash come from the web site of the Aircrew Remembrance Society; a site well worth visiting.

http://www.aircrewremembrancesociety.com/luft1939/rommel.html
Date: 20th September 1940

Unit: 1 Staffel/Fernaufklaerungsgruppe 123 Type: Junkers Ju 88A-1 Werke Nr. 0379 Code: 4U + EH
Location: St. Leonord, near Boulogne, France
Pilot: Leutnant Gerhard Rommel 69004/82 Injured (Born 08.04.1918 in Boeblingen.) Observer: Oberleutnant Gerd Hoffmann 69004/81 Injured (Born 04.05.1914 in Beuthen.) Radio/Op: Gefreiter Johann Adam 69004/80 Injured (Born 29.08.1918 in Haustadt / Saar.) Gunner: Unteroffizier Eduard Leuchs 54 Killed (Born 04.09.1914 in Buch / Ufr.)

REASON FOR LOSS:

Damaged by Spitfire of No. 41 Squadron (Bennions) during recce-mission (reconnaissance) to London, crash landed near to the Calais-St.Omer road, Pont de Briques. Eduard Leuchs passed away in Boulogne hospital on the 22.09.40 due to injuries sustained.

RAF Wing Commander Brendan Eamon Fitzpatrick "Paddy" Finucane

After attacking German shipping at Ostend and strafing three German airfields on July 15th, 1942, Finucane's wing regrouped to return to Hornchurch. As the group passed low-level over the beach at Pointe Du Touquet, Finucane's Spitfire was hit by machine gun fire that severely damaged his radiator. The engine overheated and quit, and the Spitfire was too low to allow Finucane to bail out. Losing altitude swiftly, Paddy was heard to say; "This is it, Chaps."

Witnesses reported that after a near perfect "splash" the Shamrock-Spit sank like a stone and despite all efforts; the pilot was never to be seen again

Night Flight

"It's so beautiful out tonight."

Her voice echoed in his head over and above the engine drone.

"The fires of London don't seem nearly as bad from way up here."

Archie looked to his right wing and found Terrance sitting upon its leading edge, her legs dangling over the side unaffected by the three hundred miles per hour slip stream. No matter how many times he saw her, the effect was the same; a chill began at his backbone and moved all the way up to his ears.

"I wish you wouldn't do that," he said into his oxygen mask.

"Do what?" she asked, looking over at him.

The edges of her dress fluttered slightly as if she were only in a light spring breeze. With no moon in the sky the vixen was difficult to see, so he banked the Egham Spitfire slightly putting her in front of the firelight coming from below. This made her more visible though the shadows playing over her figure and face caused a macabre ripple effect.

"You just show up like this," he near yelled at her. "You're dead Terrance. You were supposed to move on and into the light or some such thing; yet here you are still mucking about. There is an ugly war going on and you shouldn't be involved; all you'll get is more disappointment."

She stood and slowly walked down the wing, looking into the cockpit at him. The vixen smiled and he desperately wanted to roll the canopy back so she could squeeze in with him; but that was not possible at the speed he was flying.

"I get to be with you if only in a small way," she calmly told him, "So why would I be disappointed?" Her voice emanated from his headset now, sounding as it had when she was flying wing to him.

To this Archie had no reply so he righted his aircraft and scanned the sky looking for any tell tale signs of night bombers. As it was, the location of the Spit's exhaust stack was posing an ever present problem for his night vision. Even though the lads had painted it with a heavy lead based paint, the heat caused it to glow brightly enough that after looking in its direction and then looking back to the darkness you could see next to nothing.

"Egham Spit, Control, do you read?"

"Loud and clear," the pilot responded. "Is that you Chelsea? Who did you anger that you're working this ungodly hour?"

"No one, Egham, I volunteered. Status if you please?"

Terrance's paws pressed against the Perspex, now on the left side of the cockpit. "I think she likes you," her voice whispered through the radio.

There was dead spot full of static in his headset and then the carrier wave clicked on again. In the background he heard the laughter of females which was very odd given the severity of Control. "Say again Egham Spit? Someone down here obviously does not understand radio protocol."

"Angels Twelve just north of Holy Ground, speed three hundred, clear sky," Archie reported and then pulled his oxygen mask down so the microphone was away from his face. "Must you do that?" he asked the apparition.

"Do what?" she replied with an innocent smile.

"You know what I'm speaking of."

"Archie," she told him with emotion, "I so worry about you. We had one night together... that's all."

"One blessed night which I shall hold to my heart for all of eternity," he replied banking slightly to the right. As he did this he peered out on that side of the cockpit looking for the intruders who might be there. "To find love and to have it snatched away so very quickly is just wretchedly unfair. Now I have but the enemy to watch for and to repay in kind."

From down below he saw a line of tracers reaching up and towards him. "Control," he called quickly, pressing his oxygen mask back up so the microphone would be close, "I've got flaming onions looking for me, no other aircraft near. Climbing to Angels Two Five."

"Roger, Egham, calling them down." Almost as soon as the controller spoke, the antiaircraft fire stopped.

"They're not coming tonight love."

Archie looked back to his left but she was not there. Hearing a tapping he looked back to the right and her face was right next to his. She lightly kissed the Perspex.

"You're incorrigible," he told her with a smile.

"There; that's what I was waiting to see," she replied. "Now… have you ever seen what your aircraft looks like from the wingtip?"

"Certainly," he replied, "I do a complete walk-around before each flight just like you…" His voice failed him and she completed the thought.

"…used to."

Tapping the glass bubble, she made a pushing motion and it slid noiselessly back into its open position. Where the thunderous noise of the engine should have been, there was only the sound of a whispering wind. Archie looked forward and was quite able to see the blur of his propeller. Looking to his dimly lit instruments he saw the RPM's steady and all the other indicators were in the green.

"What are you doing Terrance?" he asked, turning back to her. "I can't just be leaving my senses at the drop of a hat like this. My aircraft will crash if I do not pay attention to it and most likely kill some poor family in their sleep."

"You are not leaving your senses," she told him. Holding out her paw she said, "Trust your wingman cadet. He's all you bloody well got when the bullets are flying and there's no one in your corner to sponge you down at the bell."

"Henry said that," the Stag quickly responded. "It was one of his mottos during flying school."

The vixen smiled and held her paw out to the pilot, her dress lightly flapping in the breeze. "Trust me then."

Reaching his paw out to her, their fingers intertwined and the Stag felt a peace he has not felt for what seemed an eternity. All the hatred and anger he'd built up left him as a demon will leave a rescued soul. In the blink of an eye, he found himself standing next to her on the wingtip of his aircraft. This was not something he would normally have done for fear of damaging the wing; not to mention it could never be done in flight. The splotchy green fuselage looked off without him sitting in the cockpit, but the Egham Spitfire continued on steady as ever.

"Have I died?" he asked without looking at her.

"To be sure you have come close several times," she told him, "But you are still very much alive."

The pilot looked all around the skies, feeling the moisture of the scant clouds as they passed through them. Breathing in, he smelled the smoke of London as it rose into the thin air through which they flew.

"Egham Spit, this is Control, over."

"She only wishes to hear your voice Archie," Terrance whispered to him. Squeezing his paw she leaned close. "Answer her."

"Egham, here," the Stag called back into the night sky.

"All is well?" Chelsea asked him.

"Never better," he responded honestly. "The sky is quite beautiful tonight. I should write a poem about it if I wasn't so damnably busy."

"I will hold you to that when you're back again. I shall make you a good tea."

"Radio protocol Chelsea my dear," he reminded her.

"I'm tired of the war Archie, and of all things such as radio protocol. If I could, I would go back to teaching school and living a sedentary life in the country. I would love to have a small cottage with a garden and a comfy kitchen where tea and toast would be a main stay of my existence."

"Everything in the green," he responded, "Time remaining on post approximately one hour."

"Roger Egham," she replied, making Archie wonder how much of this exchange had been said and how much of it had simply been imagined. Chelsea was as dedicated to the defense effort as any of them.

Terrance placed her face upon his chest. The noise of the wind faded, as the sound of loud snoring advanced. The wingtip was replaced by solid ground and the night sky by an aircraft's dark silhouette. Without question the Stag knew it was Henry's Spitfire. Batttle ready and wheels chocked it was standing by for the scramble. Here the Bulldog was fast asleep, fully geared up and ready to climb into the cockpit. Night sorties were done singly for safety. If you were the only aircraft in a given area then you were assured there were only viable targets all around you. Because of this, wingman followed leader who followed his wing for the entirety of the night.

Henry was therefore next up as soon as the Stag was on his way back. Take off was accomplished by lining up on a single shrouded light at the end of the runway just before advancing the throttle. At night with bombers about, it would be suicide to properly show the flare path. Getting airborne, then, was only just a little less risky than landing; whereby the long nose of a Spit was a definite disadvantage to finding the unlit ground.

"He smells terrible," Archie told the ghostly apparition as his nose found his friend's scent.

"When was the last time either of you properly bathed?"

"I can't remember," he answered honestly. "Last week maybe… the week before? There is never time and the ground crews are as worn out as we are. Death does not care if you smell bad." Thinking about the ground crews he told her with a chuckle, "We six'em and they fix'em. If it wasn't for that bunch we would've been out of the flying business long ago.

The scene blurred for a moment and then he found himself standing deep in the bowels of Control where the talkers all stood around the huge map board of England. Some of them were using long sticks to push aircraft markers around the board while others spoke quietly on radio headsets. Being night time there were not so many markers showing in the air, though there were enough. To the north he saw Blenheim markers for the aircraft that had actually been dedicated to a night fighting role. Twin engined and with a crew of three, they were not that much faster than the enemy bombers they sought to stop. They had been easy prey for the Messerschmitts during the day. For this reason they prowled the night sky, some fitted with the new radar devices which helped them find the enemy in the darkness.

As he watched, there was a series of radio calls, the last of which was not answered. Pointing to a particular marker, the talker, her face a mask of calm and collected thoughts, clenched her fist and then made a flat palm. The marker was removed from the board, though the enemy marker continued on and another of the Blenheims was vectored on an intersecting course. One particular Collie talker he noticed was working five different markers in the London area.

Though she spoke frequently into her radio gear and gave signals to those positioning the markers, her eyes continually went back to one particular aircraft.

'*She thinks of you...*' seemed to float in the air as the scene again blurred; changing into a smallish room within a French farm house that had been set up as an office. A Wolf sat at the single desk slowly composing a letter by the light of a flickering oil lamp. Archie recognized him as the same who had shot down his own wingman when that one was leveling out on Death's Run; aiming directly at him as he floated in his parachute.

Dear Fraulein Meyer,

I am so very sorry for your loss. Your son Günter was flying as my wingman when we were attacked by a group of ten enemy fighters. After giving a good account of himself and shooting down two of the enemy, he was lost over England...

...though his loss is hard, we must continue to trust in our leader's ability to guide us to that which is right and...

The Wolf stopped moving his pen. Closing his eyes, he sighed heavily at writing words he knew were not true. Terrance, letting go of Archie's paw, crossed to the German Commander and placed her fingers lightly upon his shoulder.

"Thank you," she said softly.

"Du bist willkommen (*You are welcome*)," he instantly replied in Wolf.

Realizing then that he was not alone, the officer opened his eyes, looking to his shoulder and the paw that was placed there. He then followed the arm up to the face and his jaw fell open.

"Fraulein, what are you doing here?"

She nodded in the Stag's direction and he turned upon his chair. The legs made a screeching sound on the wooden floor as they were dragged the few inches.

Archie, still dressed in his flying gear, oxygen mask hanging to one side, gazed upon the other pilot. His tiredness showed throughout his very being. Slowly... very slowly... he jerked to life. Remembering who he was, and who this was, and that their two countries were presently locked in a life or death struggle, he stood as straight as he could. Saluting, he said, "Flight Lieutenant Archie Corn, sir. I thank you for honorably serving your country and for saving my life; but I will still shoot you down if the opportunity presents itself."

Standing, the Wolf clicked his heels together and nodded his head slightly. "Oberst Dierk Locke," he replied, "You are welcome; und I would expect nothing less. You may expect the same from me."

The Wolf's eyes found his and there was an understanding that regardless of personal feelings, both pilots would represent their countries to the extent of giving their lives without hesitation... such was the fiber of the two.

The distant engine noise of the Egham Spitfire called as the scene before him faded. He sought her out in the night sky as a sailor will seek a lighthouse. Oddly, but not so oddly, he found he was now sitting upon a cloud gazing down upon the London fires. He found his aircraft's silhouette against the flames and smiled as it began a short series of lazy rolls. It was as if the machine was alive and knew he was watching.

"She looks like a toy from here," he muttered. Though he was alone, he knew he was not alone... that Terrance was the very cloud upon which he sat. Watching the Egham Spit he spoke only to hear himself speak the heartfelt words of reflection which mirrored exactly how he felt in the moment.

He was alone in the sky as he was always alone but for his aircraft.

The stars move in the heavens as
Her wings sweep round in a slow roll;
The fluid motion of unreality's reality.

Reveling in this corkscrew maneuver
Machine, pilot, and sky reach out
But find no solid anchor to grip.

No wane moon is seen to shine
And the sun, fast asleep long ago,
Leaves vacant the hearts of all three.

Earth is but a vain memory
Of lost love.

Life has become a battle of inconsistency;
Reflecting the insanity of our times.

Better to watch the stars move in a silent sky
Than to cry for their loss.

As her wings sweep round in this slow roll
The three embrace the only thing they have;
The fluid motion of unreality's reality.

At the finish of his poem, the Stag was once again within the cockpit of the Egham Spitfire. The drone of her engine now sounded more like the drone of bagpipes than the roar of an internal combustion engine.

Righting his aircraft, the pilot scanned the skies again for an enemy that was not there; and then smiled as soft arms enveloped him from behind.

"I love you," he muttered as he checked again his dimly lit instruments.

§

The Kiwi (ground crew personnel – flightless bird) played the dot of light from his torch up to the pilot's face. The light's reflective cone was turned backwards, a trick learned from the bomber crews who mainly flew during these hours. It allowed only a pinprick of light; enough to see by but not enough to disrupt his night vision.

"Did you say something, sir?" the Shetland Sheepdog called softly.

"Kill that light!" his Sergeant hissed from near the propeller. Though the Bull Terrier's voice was kept quiet it had an iron command instilled by two wars and the knowledge that a light at night, even a very dim light, could be seen for miles.

"Yes, Sergeant," the near pup replied as he clicked the light off.

"I catch you doing that again I'll kick your arse and then put you on kitchen duty for a week," the other dog threatened.

"But I thought I heard Lieutenant Corn say something; I was just looking to see."

"And did he?"

"He's asleep."

"Then leave him be. The pilots'r all clapped out these days. They get's no rest trying to save imbeciles like you from Jerry. Weren't for them we'd be hand to hand by now."

"You think so?"

"Know so. I seen the pictures of the barges parked all nice and orderly just 'cross the bleed'n channel wait'n to be filled up with Adolf's boys. It's a short ride from there to here and if we don't maintain the skies they can do it as they please; so you don't bother the Lieutenant none. You let him sleep. Control says Jerry's not com'n t'night. The order says 'stand down but stay ready'."

"Yes, sir."

"Sergeant, if you please, Percy. You know being called 'sir' gets me chuffed. Don't make me cross, eh?"

"Yes Sergeant."

There was a pause and then the Private asked, "Where do you think we go when we sleep?"

"To bed, I should hope. And why would you ask a blamed silly question like that?"

They both heard a giggle from the area of the cockpit that sounded distinctly female. They next heard a more masculine voice that, between snores, said, 'Stop that, I'm trying to fly the bloody airplane."

There was a moment of quiet and then Sergeant Quill told him, "To answer your silly question, I'm not really sure; but I'm thinking our Lieutenant has at least found somewhere pleasant to stay for a bit. Make sure you don't bring him away from there, eh? When he does wake up, tell'im the showers're fixed."

"But they was never broken," the Private replied.

"Just tell'im," Quill growled, and then disappeared again into the night.

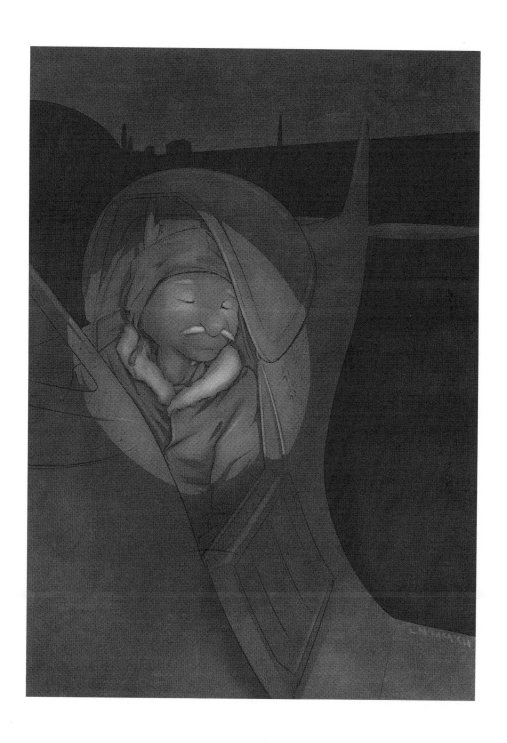

Conflict Over London

"The highest of distinctions is service to others." King George VI

§

Archie stood facing the wall as very hot water played over his head and body. He'd been surprised by the message the showers were repaired. Perhaps they'd been down from the bombing; he wasn't sure. Even so he was reluctant to leave his aircraft, claiming he was well rested and ready to fly. That reluctance lasted until his Squadron Commander handed him a strong cup of gunpowder (tea) and flatly told him, "You stink. Go have a wash and then sleep at least six hours. That's an order. If a scramble comes, you and Henry will stay in reserve."

It felt good to wash again, though the Stag expected to hear the alarm bell sound out at any moment. Even though he would not be allowed to scramble, he would fit out and stand by next to the Egham. An order was an order and he was so very tired. Closing his eyes he let the warmth envelope him as the soap rinsed off. In his mind he heard machinegun fire, radio chatter... and the silent screams of brave voices calling their final farewells.

"Looks like this is it lads... carry on..."

"Gone for a Burton... don't wait up..." "Alice... I love you..."

"See you around Archie... buy a round for me at the pub..."

"Ich bin fertig... Ich bin fertig..."

"I say, you look very tense, would you mind if I had a sit and we chatted a bit? I'm told I have a calming voice."

"Help yourself," the Stag replied, lifting his face to the shower head. "It's been a rough few weeks to be sure. Are you a pilot or a Kiwi?"

"I was a pilot... that is to say; now I'm in a.. ad.. admin I'm afraid. By the rules, I'm too old to d.. d.. do what you do. I'd gladly take a ride up, but my position is such that they probably wouldn't let me. I was Royal Navy during the Great War and then attached to the Royal Naval Air Service at Cranwell. When the Royal Air Force was formed up, I transferred over. The aircraft then were very much d.. di.. different, I'm afraid."

"I admire anyone who flew back then," Archie replied without opening his eyes. "Not even a radio and the airplanes were not much better than kites. Flying the Moth was fun enough but I can't imagine dogfighting in one."

"Yes, they were a bit flimsy I suppose, but you never realized that really because they were what you had to work with at that time. Mark my words; you wait and s.. se.. see what the aircraft are going to be like by the time the war is over."

The Stag sighed, "If I live that long." Taking a wash rag he ducked his head and cleaned off his antlers. "I've already seen improvements on the German fighters," he added from under the water.

"Have you now?"

"Yes… they've adapted to using drop tanks for extra fuel, but only an idiot would not have seen that coming. If an aircraft can carry a bomb, it can carry an extra fuel tank. Their pilots appear as raw as ours for the most part. Pity we haven't more time to train the youngsters."

"What would you do to improve the Spit?" the person asked. The tone of his voice earmarked true curiosity and not the sarcasm one might expect from an admin type.

"Heavier guns," the pilot replied promptly. "We rattle away with our 303 machine guns and sometimes it seems to do so little damage. The Messerschmitt has a 30 millimeter cannon in its nose and you should see the holes it will blow in a fuselage." Finishing his rinse off, he shut off the water and turned around. "What exactly do you do in admin?" he asked, blinking.

He was handed a towel and as he dried his face, his eyes covered and not seeing, he heard the other person tell him, "I'm the King."

§

Oberst Locke stood within the crowd at the Berlin Sports Palace listening to his country's leader. All commandants of import had been specially summoned for this event. Dierk, however, had also been ordered to the Luftwaffe chief's private headquarters afterwards for a special interview with 'Uncle Fatty'; which was the never to be uttered nickname for their commander-in-chief Reichmarschall Hermann Göring. There was then to be a tactical meeting attended by all of the high level commanders in which he was to be a 'special guest'.

To this point, Der Fuhrer had made his points punctuated by his usual pounding of fists on the podium and frequent pauses for applause spurred on by the party faithful. Only a fool would not join in on this exuberant ovation and the fighter pilot was keen enough to do so.

The odd little Wolf had worked himself into a real lather this time, incensed that the country they were bombing had the audacity to resist this powerful onslaught. Capitulation was expected and demanded but to this the English government had simply thumbed its nose. As Dierk watched and listened, the former army Corporal shrieked, "We will raze their cities to the ground. One of us will break, and it will not be National Socialist Germany."

Everyone stood and the statement was met with immediate and thunderous paw clapping.

The Staffel leader looked around the huge auditorium wondering at the stupefied looks of the other Wolfs and Dogs in attendance. As they continued to applaud, however, he found one other set of eyes doing the same; the eyes of an old Fox. For a moment those eyes met his, during which there was a small smile and a nod. For pleasantry's sake, Dierk nodded back to this person who was directly in charge of the intelligence gathering tool for their military, the Abwehr. Was it a good thing, he wondered, to be so recognized by Admiral Wilhelm Canaris.

As soon as the applause died the Fuhrer motioned for everyone to again sit and then further addressed the crowd. "In our fight with the English, it gives me great pleasure to introduce to you one of our very best fighter pilots. Though he has been invited and well deserves a place higher up in the Luftwaffe, he has humbly chosen to remain among the pilots, taking the battle to our enemy." The small Wolf paused to let the suspense build briefly and then called out, "Staffelkapitän Oberst Dierk Locke, would you come forward please."

The pilot was actually surprised by this. No one had so much as whispered to him that he was to meet face to face with his country's leader. Standing, he made his posture ramrod straight and then, making his way to the large center aisle, walked forward, stopping just short of the podium where he stood at attention.

Adolf Hitler looked down upon one of his top ranked aces and smiled. On airmen such as Locke the future of his country absolutely depended. The little Wolf was well aware of this and personally presenting the new Knight's Cross with Oak leaves in such a public forum would go a long way to maintaining his support of the German people… his propaganda ministry would make sure of it.

(Author's note: Knight's Cross of the Iron Cross with Oak Leaves [Ritterkreuz des Eisernen Kreuzes mit Eichenlaub] was introduced on 3 June 1940 to further distinguish those who had already received the Knight's Cross of the Iron Cross and who continued to show merit in combat bravery or military success.)

§

After their brief meeting in the shower, Archie received a smile and a wink and then The King excused himself to an impromptu tour of the airfield. This was to be a quick visit and work was not to be interrupted at his request. The enemy, he explained in his quiet manner, did not keep to a given time table. Not to be ready to meet this because of an unscheduled visit by the Sovereign would be most inexcusable. Waiting for him outside of the showers as an escort on the tour was Wing Commander Stewart Falstaff, his serious expression barely hiding his feelings at the conditions of both his aircraft and pilots. He stood at George's elbow every inch of the way during the visit. With them, though they remained very low key, was also a detail of body guards; ready to throw themselves in harm's way should it be required.

"So tell me Stewart," the King asked when they were finally walking back to the flight line. "What was the last encounter with our enemy?"

"First light, sir. The lads were up and flying in record time. I had sixty aircraft in the air and another fifty in ready reserve, engines warm. We flew them down to Hell's Corner (*the area of Kent in the south east of England where a majority of the fighting took place*) and trounced a mixed bag of Heinkels and Junkers. All told we had a good time of it, losing only six to their twenty. We also managed to get three of our pilots back alive. At that rate, however, I'll not have anything left soon. Those bombers that got through hit the area of Dover pretty heavily. They again concentrated on shipping and the seaports. Most of the other bombing raids have been aimed directly at the airfields. We've lost a good deal of men and equipment to that as well. The lads were then up again around ten hundred or so with no contact." He paused as he looked up at the sky. "As it is, we're expecting the call up at any moment. Jerry's got more aircrews and aircraft to use than he has the brains to use them; for that I'm grateful."

"Grateful is a good word, but I won't go so far as to say the enemy has no intelligence," George countered. "It's the leadership that's faulty. If I was to give it a word, I would say the fellow in charge has no patience. The war so far has been good to the Germans. They steamrolled the lesser nations and then mighty France simply gave in when their front door was pushed open. Obviously Hitler feels he can continue winning by keeping on with his school yard bully tactics. I believe that if we can hold him off, he'll lose interest and go somewhere there's no moat to stop his advance."

"I personally hope he goes to Blazes and stays there," Steward told his sovereign with a straight face, "But I'm quite sure he's again on the road to London."

"Perhaps we should be about our business then," the King told the Bulldog. "If Lieutenant Corn is ready, we will proceed. After that I'll get out of your hair and let you get back to winning the war. You did tell him didn't you?"

Falstaff glanced at the Lion standing next to him. Though he'd known the King for many years, a Lion was still a Lion and cause for some nervousness. "Well, sir," he replied with a slight smile, "Not exactly. I mean, I did tell his commander when we arrived but I am led to believe Commander Sheltie was immediately pulled away on urgent business in the hangers and forgot to inform the Lieutenant."

The King chuckled. "This should be interesting then. I rather like surprises, so long as they are good surprises."

§

Dierk sat in a high backed chair sipping a very good cup of coffee. He was presently in the ante room of Uncle Fatty's personal office within the Supreme Commander's opulent Berlin headquarters. After the surprise presentation of his medal by Der Fuhrer there'd been thunderous applause followed by countless 'Sieg Heils' and an immediate feeling of unreality. The community venue was so different than conditions on the front. He'd not expected a medal let alone that the leader of his country was going to present it to him under such public conditions. After Heir Hitler took his leave the pilot had been mobbed. He shook more paws than he had in his life time and was even pressed for autographs. A photographer magically appeared and over a hundred of the party faithful were allowed to have their picture taken with him. During this time he'd been served a number of Schnapps along with some of the best beer he'd ever had; thus the coffee.

The doors across the expansive room opened and a very large Wolf stood framed in the middle of them.

"Dierk!" he said expansively, "I am so pleased to see you."

"You are such a liar Hermann," the Staffel Commandant replied without rising. "You're a showman and you want something from me, otherwise I would be winging my way back to France by now. I'm sure you had a paw in the medal I was presented, did you not?"

The big Wolf laughed warmly. "You are the same Dierk I flew with back when we were battling the Brits over the trenches; but I see you forget that the person you are addressing is not the same person who flew back then. Do I get no respect?"

"Respect is earned, is it not?" Locke countered. "I seem to recall we were also flying against the Americans and that they had some pretty good aircraft. How long until we can expect this to happen again, eh? It is my understanding that history does repeat itself."

Goering waved a dismissive paw as he entered the room. "I can assure you the Americans will never enter the war. The most they will offer is to sell arms to our enemies. Their aircraft are no match for ours in any case and our U-boats now rule the oceans; what is sent will be disposed of before it can even reach England's shores."

The fighter pilot smiled. "I hope you're right." Holding up his cup, he said, "Your coffee is very good, may I take some back with me to France? The Poodles have no idea what good coffee is."

"Ha!" the Reichmarschall laughed. "I'm glad you at least approve of some small thing I've arranged. I had this sent in from the American territory of Hawaii. I will only say that I have some good connections, yes? I shall send you some. Would you like a strudel with your coffee? I have them made fresh every morning. My baker is the very best und he makes them very good."

"So I see," the fighter pilot replied nodding to the other Wolf's bulk with a wink, "They fit well upon you. As for me... I have a cockpit that is already tight." Setting his coffee cup down he stood and held his arms open, whereupon the larger Wolf came forward and gave him a bear hug.

"Come into my office now old friend," Goering whispered into his ear, "We have much to discuss."

§

Archie, feeling better for the wash and his having met the King so unexpectedly, stood in front of the Egham Spitfire. She was looking very good. Not having had to fly the night before he knew she was well rested as was the pilot, though he was a bit stiff for sleeping in her cockpit.

His fitter came up behind him and began fiddling with the straps of his parachute harness. The fellow was a Sheepdog with a face so full of fur you'd think he couldn't see. He also had a contagious smile and an equally contagious love of life. "It's a good day to be alive, sir," the sergeant told him as he fussed with the straps.

"Every day is a good day to be alive, Charles," Archie responded, "Let's hope we can again say the same tomorrow, eh?"

"Amen to that, sir. Did you hear we're supposed to have a bit of a ceremony then?"

"Not at all," the Stag replied, "What's it to be this time?"

"Not quite sure exactly, but word has it someone is to get a medal. I suppose it's all well and good to earn such a thing, but…"

"But?"

"It won't do us much good if the Nazi's goosestep their way onto our shores. That's why I'm here, you know. I'm too old to fly so I figured I'd help those that could as much as possible."

"Do you have family nearby?"

"Just my wife, sir. We sent the children off to the country. The eldest is looking after the other three. One less thing for me to worry about so's I can concentrate more on the job at hand… and there ya go, all ready to climb into the cockpit."

"Thank you."

"92 SQUADRON FALL IN…" the Duty Officer bellowed. "AS-SEMBLE PLEASE… FALLLLL INNNNNNN…."

When the pilots were grouped and at attention, they were quickly called to 'parade rest'. Wing Commander Falstaff with the King standing next to him, stood center on to the assembled pilots. Unfolding a piece of paper, he read the citation.

"There are times in this struggle to protect our country when we are left naked and exposed. These moments find us and we are embarrassed for our oversight… that is the best case scenario. The worst case scenario you are all only too well familiar with. A brief time ago we were in that worst case scenario when the 92 was back from mission and out of fuel with no top cover or reserve. A lone Spitfire returning from maintenance was the only aircraft in position to intervene. This would be the Egham Spitfire piloted by Flight Lieutenant Archie Corn."

He paused as he nodded to the pilot and then continued. "The intruders catching us in such a state were a Schwärme of Messerschmitt 109's and every one of them piloted by an ace. Lt. Corn did not hesitate, but dove straight in with no regard for his own safety. Passing the first two fighters, he over took the pair setting up on a strafing run placing himself in front of rear fighter and shooting down the lead. For these actions Flight Lieutenant Archie Corn is here by awarded the Distinguished Flying Cross."

As his fellows applauded, King George VI stepped forward and pinned the medal upon the Stags flight suit. "Well done Flight Lieutenant," he told him as his fingers worked the pin. "You have done your squadron proud."

At that very moment the alarm bell began ringing and the scramble was again on.

§

"You will like my latest orders Dierk," Goering said as he poured two glasses of Champaign. Passing one over to the squadron leader, he held his up and intoned a Heil Hitler as if saying a prayer and then clinked it upon the smaller Wolf's. "Und so… I thought to myself, I send my fighters over the channel to do fair fight, and the British turn tail and run. We cannot destroy them if they will not face us, no?"

"That's a fair assumption," Locke agreed as he sipped from his glass.

"I was reminded of my dear old Uncle," Goering continued, "Who taught me how to catch perch. He would always come back with baskets full of them. I asked him how he did this and the old Wolf told me, 'You must give the fish what it wants and then he will set himself upon your hook.' In Uncle's case, he tossed dough balls out into the water working the fish into a feeding frenzy. In my case, this morning I gave them bombers. It was a legitimate raid. We sunk many ships and damaged the harbors to a good point of destruction... but now... now my friend, I will be handing them a hook instead of a dough ball."

"What are you talking about Hermann?" Dierk asked, an icy feeling suddenly in the pit of his stomach.

"I gave them hundreds of fighters flying with the bombers and in bomber formation. They will take this bait and we will clear the skies of Spitfires and Hurricanes once and for all."

"Why was I not informed of this?" the Staffelkapitän asked, his jaw dropping open at the lunacy of this decision. "These are my men you are talking about. I need to be there for such an operation or they will..."

"What? You have a perfectly capable Staffelführer (*second in command*) to lead while you are away. If I had told you my plans then they would not have been secret und you would not have come for your medal ceremony."

"That's another thing, old friend," the fighter pilot spoke this with acid in his voice, "Why was I not told about this medal ceremony? You know damned well I do not like surprises."

Uncle Fatty smiled a Wolfish smile, not seeming to be affected at all. "Oh come now Dierk, the look on your face was worth it all by itself. Now then... I have cleared my schedule and we shall have a good lunch together with the other commanders I have called in. We are to have an important meeting to discuss tactics and such."

"I am sorry my Reichmarschall but I must go back to the front immediately. I am only a staffel commander and my men need me now more than ever. If we are lucky we will not have lost too many of them."

"A few lost to the greater good is hardly a bother now, is it?" With this statement, the fat Wolf watched the other Wolf closely. What he saw was exactly what he expected to see. Nodding, he accented to his underling's departure. "As you wish. You are right, your presence, though a pleasure, is not required. Fly safe; und kill as many Spitfires and Hurricanes in your travels as you can. I have promised Der Fuehrer we would control the skies above England and I intend to keep my word. The RAF must be destroyed und there is no room for any who would get in the way of this."

Placing his glass on the overly large desk, Staffelkapitän Locke came to attention and clicked his heels together, giving his old comrade a slight nod. "You can count on me Herr Reichmarschall. I will kill as many as come before my sights. Thank you for not taking offense to my departure."

"Think nothing of it Dierk; you are a true leader… I understand."

Once outside of the building the Luftwaffe officer found his car waiting for him. Getting in, he was whisked away; but once they were well out of sight of Goering's estate, it pulled to the curb. An old Fox, who had been patiently waiting in the shade of a street tree, got into the back with the fighter pilot. Dierk was about to protest but found himself fact to face with Admiral Wilhelm Canaris.

"You are a very brave Wolf," the intelligence Chief told him softly. "You are given a medal, held up as a national hero and yet you shun the attentions of your old squadron mate."

"I am a soldier," Dierk responded, nodding to the car's driver.

The Fox smiled and then turning to the German Shepherd behind the wheel. "You may proceed Otto. Take us to the airfield please."

Without a word the fellow pulled the car back out onto the road.

"It is but a short ride to where we need to go," the Admiral told the pilot, "So I shall be brief. If you wish to live, you will not take your aircraft back to France. I will arrange a ferry pilot for it… a fellow with Gestapo ties. His loss will not be a matter of concern."

"I don't understand," Dierk replied honestly.

"Then I will spell it out for you," Canaris told him kindly. "You issued an order to those in your command that went contrary to the whispered orders of the party; the one concerning flyers and parachutes. This was noticed, though I would not look to your men for the one who perhaps passed on this information. In this, you made a grievous mistake. The math was done and the party decided they could get more range, as you flyers might call it, out of a dead hero than out of a live one who does not support their cause."

Dierk again felt the icy barb in the pit of his stomach. "I see."

The Fox placed a paw on his and then whispered, "There was also a report forwarded to my office by an agent in the field of a British pilot who was in his parachute and saved from death by a German fighter pilot who shot down his own wingman. On the date mentioned, there was but one fighter in your unit listed as lost." The Fox paused just enough to let this sink in. "I am the only one who saw this report and it has already been destroyed."

"What do you want?" the Wolf asked.

The Fox smiled slyly. "So like a fighter pilot to be direct and to the point. I can appreciate that. I want nothing at all. Your men need you. Germany needs you. I only wish that you make it back to your duties alive. Your aircraft was placed into maintenance upon your arrival. I am sorry to report that it apparently fell off of the jacks during a routine landing gear check and was damaged. There is a bomber standing by to ferry out. I think you should request transport on it."

Turning again to the driver, Canaris told him, "Here is a good place Otto."

The car pulled over and the man in charge of military intelligence took his leave without another word spoken.

(Author's note: In the early evening of 15 Aug, German aircraft attacked Kenley airfield, but heavy fighter defense led to the bombers dropping their bombs as quickly as they could, resulting in the bombing of the smaller satellite field of Croydon by mistake.

Throughout this entire day, Göring and many of his top air force commanders were at a conference at his Berlin suburb estate of Karinhall. He had informed his aides that the conference was not to be interrupted for any reason. When he completed the conference at the end of the day, he was unpleasantly surprised to learn that on this day he had lost a total of 75 aircraft. This number was about 20% of the aircraft dispatched. The air crews who survived the day saw so much destruction among their own forces that some of them named the day "Black Thursday".)

§

92 Squadron took off in a roar of engines and quickly climbed. On the radio Archie heard Control vectoring in as many fighters as they could get their paws on. Radar had told of a huge formation coming across the channel. Altitude and position was called out, and some flights were held back by twenty minutes as reserve.

The resulting fight quickly progressed with aircraft facing aircraft; the Germans taking the worst of the beating. The following actual report might best sum up what happened.

Group Captain S.F.Vincent Station Commander Northolt 11 Group Sept 15th 1940

One of the Luftwaffe pilots who had to make a rather ungracious landing was the veteran Professor von Wedel. Like most of the Bf 109 pilots, they stayed with the Dorniers as long as possible, but the fuel situation forced them to leave early leaving the bombers in a very vulnerable position. On the return journey, his flight of Bf 109s were attacked by 605 Squadron Croydon, 1 RCAF Squadron Northolt and 229 Squadron Northolt all flying Hurricanes. It is believed that one of the Hurricanes of 1 RCAF Squadron followed von Wedel down. The veteran, not being able to out maneuver the Hurricane, was hit and his Bf 109 had lost its controls. He tried in vain to make a landing on Romney Marsh, but the controls did not respond, and he made a heavy wheels up landing at a farmhouse, destroying a shed in which a mother and daughter were sitting in a car awaiting the father who was about to take them out on a Sunday drive. Both mother and daughter were killed instantly. A local policeman arrived on the scene to find a battered and bruised von Wedel wandering around in an almost tearful state, and as he apologized to the policeman for what he had done, the constable simply asked " would you like a cup of tea sir?"

Smashing

(Told to the author by one of the Beefeaters at the Tower of London: "Oh yes, the tower did suffer bomb damage during the war which you can see in the brickwork over the Hospital Block; the color of the repair work bricking stands out. This was actually accidental. Adolf Hitler had standing orders for the Luftwaffe not to bomb the Tower as he had intentions of living here after he'd invaded England." Everything else was fair game.)

On the evening of August 24th, 1940 a German Bomber formation accidentally bombed some non-military targets in London. Winston Churchill immediately ordered reprisal attacks on non military German targets in Berlin. This prompted a furious response from Hitler, who ordered that a blitz campaign of bombing start immediately on London.

In reality, the German leader's anger gave the RAF a desperately needed reprieve. In this boxing match between the two air forces, the German Heavyweight Champion suddenly turned from pummeling his opponent to punching the referee; the British Peoples. They alone could have convinced their government to surrender. Being so punished, however, only strengthened their resolve to resist to the last.

In this, they turned and kept their eyes on the King, George VI, who from the beginning had remained their steadfast rock in a turbulent sea. Along with his family, he remained in Buckingham Palace where they continued with their duties as usual. During the conflict, a bomb dropped into the big quadrangle behind the east facade nearly killing him. During another raid the palace chapel was destroyed.

In total, Buckingham palace was bombed seven times.

George and his wife Elizabeth were devoted to each other and to their country. On Monday, September 23, 1940, he spoke to the people of his realm from the underground shelter at the palace in the midst of an air raid. In his speech, he praised the spirit of Londoners who continued to maintain their resolve to endure against the devastating enemy attacks.

The British people knew their king and queen could have fled to safety, but they stayed, sharing all the ordeals that their subjects endured. Their food and clothing were rationed and even though their home was Buckingham Palace, they spent many nights underground in the air raid shelter. When George found there was a dire shortage of parts for the Royal Army's anti-tank guns, he had a lathe brought into the palace and spent many hours at it helping to fill the shortage.

During this time, London families made brave but heartbreaking decisions to evacuate their children to places in the country where they might be protected from the bombings. The royal family, however, including the children, remained in residence maintaining solidarity with the common people and their suffering.

The Queen was once asked if she planned to send the children away from London to keep them safe.

Her reply:

"The children will not leave without me."
"I will not leave without the King."
"The King will never leave."

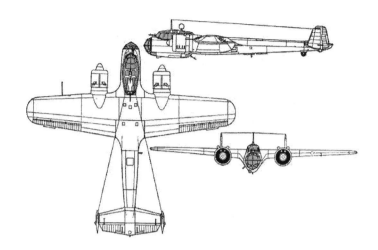

"Tally Ho!" Sergeant Timothy Buttran called over the radio. He then dove straight for the formation of three enemy bombers below him.

He did this alone. During the previous moments of 504 Squadron's heated attempt at the defense of London, he'd gotten separated from his vic of four Hurricanes; but this did not deter the young Fox… this was his country… his city… and he damned well meant to do something about it.

§

"Hey Otto!" called a smallish Doberman. Already suited up in his flight gear, he waved at his pilot as the Wolf came out of the briefing room with their bomb aimer. "Where are we going today, eh?"

Abel, a German Shepherd and the oldest among them, answered. "Where do you think we're going dummkopf? Command has given us but one target at the moment and it's a really big one. That makes my job of getting us there rather easy don't you think?" Since Abel was also their navigator he had to attend the briefing with the other navigators and pilots. He smiled at the youth and his excitement.

"London?"

Otto pointed a finger at his dorsal gunner and made a chirping sound with his lips. "Right on the numbers button head. They told us we don't need any stinking fighters since we're fast and maneuverable enough to out fly 'Tin Pot Tommy' and our gunners... that would be you and Günter... are the best."

(Author's note: German bombers would fly in 'kette' formations of three and four aircraft. They would then form up in three vics of nine total aircraft, called Staffeln. These, as viewed from a single location would appear straggled out and deceptively easy to defeat, which was not the case as the bombers were better able to support each other in this staggered guise.)

"Our kette has also been given the honor of a special target," added Abel, "We're to skip over the slums and drop a special hello on Buckingham palace."

Ludwig, called 'Luddy' by the entire crew, blinked. "That's not very nice," he replied earnestly.

"What's nice about bombing anyone?" Otto asked him. Reaching out the Wolf patted the leather flying helmet on the gunner's head. "It's called war Luddy. We try to kill them and they try to kill us. It is indeed stupid and not nice but what choice do you have when someone will not listen to reason. If the British decided to stop being so stubborn and surrender there'd be no need for this would there? They give us no choice but to show them we mean business; something I thought they learned at Dunkirk. Since they haven't figured it out yet the bosses have given us these bloody huge bombs with which to press the point home. Perhaps the Brits are just extremely thick headed like my dorsal, eh?"

"Besides," Abel added, taking the time to light a cigarette, "You don't think the British Royals are really home now do you? Big leaders like that don't stick around when trouble begins, they're considered too valuable. Imagine if we actually were able to kill them... what then? England would be a rudderless ship and their government would collapse; which would make things a lot easier for us, don't you think? Better we bomb the commoner and get them really pissed that their leaders have left them to rot."

The bomb aimer blew out smoke without removing the cig from between his lips taking the few moments he had for enjoyment, before having to climb aboard 'der Bleistift' (the pencil) where he dared not smoke for fear of blowing himself to heaven and back.

All three looked over to their aircraft, one of thirty stationed at this airfield. The ground staff was already standing by and calmly stood around chatting; waiting for the launch.

The Dornier 17 was a low level flier. It was also smaller than the other bombers being used to strike England but faster than most; almost as fast as a fighter and very maneuverable. The crew knew, however, that her time had passed. The war had changed slightly and now it carried too small of a bomb load and didn't have enough range. There was also the matter of its inability to climb up to the safety of high altitude in order to get away from the larger anti-aircraft guns. Nevertheless the crew loved their ship and would have no other. For months now they'd been together and had flown with great success in the earlier campaigns. All had been given leave to visit home and were treated like the returning heroes they were, complete with small parades in their home villages.

Now Death was their co-pilot and always there to watch with greedy eyes. All of them had been wounded to some extent, but it was never serious enough to get them more than a few days' rest. This adversity brought them closer together than if they were blood related. They were all good at what they did; and Otto was the best pilot in the squadron. His friends knew he would not let them down.

Today's payload consisted of two large bombs weighing 550 lbs each. The Dornier could carry four such bombs but the range was then so reduced that the trip to London and back would not have been possible. Günter had stayed with the aircraft to personally observe the loading process, making sure it was done right.

Though they took care not to show it, none of the four were all that enthusiastic about such a distant mission carrying only two bombs. A rack of 5 110 pound bombs would have been preferred but this far reduced the destructive force of the load.

"A bomb is a bomb," Otto told his crew the night before and then drained his beer glass. "They all do the same business in the end. They are supposed to remain inactive and safe until Abel drops them from the belly… but… that the safety pin is still in hardly makes much difference. If you're carrying a bunch of small ones and one goes off or if you're carrying just one really big bruiser and it goes off, you'll never know the difference; nor will you feel a thing."

"A bomb is a bomb," Luddy echoed with a smile and a swallow of beer, "They're all verdammt dangerous. I actually hate them."

"I hate them too," Abel chipped in, raising his glass, "But here is to the fellow who drops the bombs and gets them away from our persons, eh?"

"You slut… you are saluting yourself," Günter managed to mumble. He'd never been able to keep up with the drinking and his head was down on the table as he ostensibly tried to sleep. It was that or vomit and sleep was preferable. Like Luddy he was a Doberman but the others teased that he had a bit of Bulldog running in his veins because he was so stubborn sometimes.

"I have to praise myself," Abel countered, "None of you will do it for me, and if I might say so, every stick I drop hits the target." He swallowed what was left in his glass and then added, "Well… most of them do depending on the wind conditions."

He was referring to a mission they'd flown over Dunkirk where they were given a grouping of military tents to strike. Intelligence picked this to be a headquarters unit and it was given a high priority. Right in the middle of this grouping, however, was a tent with a white top bearing a red cross. Spotting this as he sighted, Abel chose to drop late hitting an equipment park instead. The miss was explained during their de-brief as adverse wind conditions. The rest of the crew had never countered this explanation; though it was occasionally joked about with a wink and a beer. Three of them laughed… one of them puked. The three, picking up their forth by the arms, changed tables and signaled for another round.

They joined Günter at the aircraft, finding him checking over a new device the end of which now stuck out by the tail of their aircraft. It was meant to be something of a surprise to any trailing fighters. Oil, nitrogen, and hydrogen cylinders had been fitted into the fuselage and attached to an external pipe fitted with a jet. When the unwitting attacker got close enough, the tail gunner was supposed to pull a lever and flames would shoot out the back, hopefully to toast both the pilot and his aircraft.

"So do you think you'll light Tommy's cigarette for him?" Abel called out to the ventral gunner. They'd all been briefed on the new weapon though skepticism was high.

"I shall roast his balls goot!" the big Doberman called back with a laugh. "Who knows for sure. If it was up to me I would have installed heavier machine guns… those I know would work, ja?"

"All of the aircraft have these things? Otto asked loudly, motioning to the other aircraft sitting ready for the mission.

Günter stood from his examination of the jet nozzle and walked to meet them. Wiping his paws on a rag he told his pilot, "Just the three in our kette. We have been chosen to try it out; something to do with the target we are to hit today. I'm guessing Buckingham?"

"Und you guessed correctly," the pilot told him, "So when we get back I will give you one of my cherished cigars."

"I don't smoke," the ventral gunner reminded him.

"I know… that's why I put up the prize, zo I shall smoke it for you. What exactly does this thing do?"

"It farts," Günter replied with a straight face.

Luddy laughed and Abel just managed to keep from doing the same.

"No, seriously," Otto told him, keeping an equally straight face, "What does it do?"

"Seriously, it's supposed to shoot flames at any following fighters… but all I've seen it do is fart out a stream of oil like a whale with dysentery. The dumm technician who installed it could only scratch his ass and shrug his shoulders. Or maybe he scratched his head… in any case he sits on his brains. Soooo… if a fighter get's too close, I pull a lever and whoosh."

"If it stinks like Abel's gas, it will peel his paint," Luddy offered with a smile. Günter and Otto were besides themselves with mirth; until Abel hiked one cheek up and ripped out some blue air.

"Don't you dare do that in the cockpit!" the pilot yelled at him.

The bomb aimer only smiled, but he did wink at Luddy.

§

Timothy slowly walked around his Hurricane, one paw on the fuselage his eyes alert for anything out of the ordinary. He noticed that not all the bullet holes of the day before had been properly patched. Considering that making his aircraft serviceable was a priority rush job, he found it in his heart to forgive the Kiwis this one time.

"So how does she fly?" a voice asked from behind him.

The Fox turned and smiled when he saw the Stag. "Archie! Right good to see you old fellow!" He extended his paw in warmth. "She's smashing. Not quite as quick as a Spitfire to be sure, but she's an extremely stable gun platform and a whole lot more fun to fly than the bombers they used to have us with. I've gotten three of the blighters so far... bing bang boffors."

Archie nodded to the holes in the aircraft. "Looks to me that they almost got you... bing bang boffors."

"It does happen," the Fox told him as they released from the shake, "You can't discount the gunners now, can you? What brings you to the 504? Certainly it can't be for the tea... we haven't had a decent cuppa since the Germans began bombing us."

"Fuel. Control had us stop here for convenience. Biggins has been bombed again and the runway's a shambles. It will take the engineers a bit to plow it all back into shape. In the mean time we couldn't stay in the air forever, so here we are. We'll be off again as soon as we're full up but in the mean time I saw TE-B sitting here and figured you'd be close by. You're still a Sergeant I see. I thought for sure you'd have been promoted to Pilot Officer by now; you've been with the RAF's Voluntary Reserve a long time now haven't you?"

"Since 1936," the Fox replied with a smile, "I turned it down, actually. You get promoted Arch and the next thing you know you're behind a desk having to stay pretty all day and no drinking with the lads at the pub. That's not the life for me." He leaned back against the fuselage of his ship. "And what about you? I've heard some interesting stories about a certain antlered pilot."

"The Stag smiled, "All lies and exaggerations I'm sure."

"I hear there's nine victories marks on your fuselage and a DFC personally awarded by the King?"

Archie's expression became distant for a moment, as if mention of the Iron Crosses painted on his fuselage had triggered something in his mind. Turning, he absently poked a finger into one of the bullet holes on the Hurricane. It was extremely large and obviously caused by a Messerschmitt cannon. "Funny they didn't patch this one since it's so big," he said. "I'm betting you'll hear a whistling noise when you fly."

An aircraft flew over and both pilots looked up. It did a wing waggle and they both waved, though it was doubtful the pilot was able to see them.

"It's a tough old world Arch," the Sergeant told him, understanding the other pilot's emotions of the moment. "I fly every day and never fully expect to land again... but I have so far managed to find my way home. You simply have to trust that she'll get you through it."

"She?" Archie asked, turning back to the Fox.

Timothy smiled a sly smile. "I was referring to your aircraft old boy. Might there be a femme fatale in your life we haven't heard about then?"

As they spoke, the squadron commander's orderly reached out through a window in their small field office (not more than a shed in actuality) and began pulling on the clapper rope of an old parsonage bell donated to this purpose. The bell had been found in a bombed out ruin and served as a reminder to the pilots of the 504 as to exactly why they were flying as they were.

"Time to go Arch," the Fox told him with a nod. "London needs her heroes once again, eh?"

Walking around to the other side of his Hurricane he mounted the wing. As he did so, his Fitter ran up and quickly climbed up behind him. The fellow fussed with and checked each parachute buckle even as the Fox swung his leg into the cockpit. On the ground, the Kiwi assigned to the aircraft stood ready to clear the prop and then pull the chocks when the pilot gave him the signal.

"Good hunting Timothy!" the Stag called loudly as he walked around the tail and stood so he could be seen. A multitude of engines all began starting up as he did this.

The Sergeant turned and, with a smile, flashed him a 'V' sign.

Archie flashed one back and then saluted. This done, he quickly made his way to where he'd left the Egham Spit and his own vic of four aircraft. The fuel bowser, he saw, was just driving off, indicating the Spitfires were again ready.

Without a doubt, they were sure to be airborne right behind the 504.

§

Otto monitored his instruments and watched the sky, enjoying the view which was incredible from within the greenhouse like cockpit. Since they were cruising at fourteen thousand feet, they all had their oxygen masks on. It was also times like this that he so appreciated his heavy flight jacket and gloves as the temperature became very cold at altitude.

"Crew report," he called over the intercom. Dorsal clear," Luddy responded.

Ventral clear," Günter repeated.

"Nose clear," Abel added. "It would seem the RAF is asleep Otto. Maybe we will be able to make our run, drop the eggs, and then fly away unmolested today."

"And maybe Winston Churchill will be inviting us for tea," the ventral gunner called back. "He might even allow us to land at one of their airfields and have us met by a chauffeured limousine, ya?"

"He would do that?" Luddy asked.

There was a burst of laughter on the intercom from the other three crew members. "If we're lucky, maybe he'll invite the King," Abel called from the nose. "Oh, wait, they won't be able to attend because we're going to bomb their palace to rubbish."

"That's not nice," Luddy called back to the bomb aimer.

"How many times do I have to explain it to you Luddy, you must not be so naiveté… it's what we do," the pilot called back to the youth. Turning for a moment, he looked at the gunner and gave him a wink.

"I know that, Otto… but I don't have to like it."

"Why exactly did you join the Luftwaffe?" Günter asked, looking out at the land passing below him. Spotting a familiar open area he asked permission to clear his gun.

"Wait until Luddy answers your question," the pilot told him, "I am interested in his answer."

"My father told me I should."

"A reasonable fellow," Abel responded, and then cursed his bombsite; a Lotfe A with a cracked lens. "Why did he tell you that?"

"He said if I joined the Wehrmacht (*army*) I would be sleeping in the mud, and crawling in the mud, and eating the mud… und I would probably die in the mud as well. I didn't want that. He said it was better to be cold at altitude and yet sleep in a warm bed every night."

"The food is better too," Abel added, giving his sight a thump on the side. "Hey Otto, I just farted, do you smell it?"

"I'm wearing an oxygen mask you moron."

"Oh yes… so am I."

"Please, Otto, may I clear my gun?" Günter pleaded.

"Why now?"

"Because that's a golf course down there! I hate golf… my grandfather made me carry his bag and he would strike me with his club if he made a bad shot."

"He didn't!" Luddy said, truly shocked.

"He did! I'll show you the scars when we get back. Look I can see them on the putting green! Please Otto it is now or not at all! I can really mess with their game if you let me."

"Fine… clear you gun, but don't hit them. We are not total barbarians."

128

"Ya," Abel called out merrily, "We are only Bavarians."

"Sing us a song Luddy," Otto called to the dorsal gunner, "I like Lili Marlene if you can remember the words. You have such a nice voice."

Günter ripped off a burst of five rounds while giggling like a madman, but since he did not push his talk button, no one heard him. On the ground the golfers all scattered.

And Luddy sang,

"Underneath the lantern,
By the barrack gate
Darling I remember
The way you used to wait
T'was there that you whispered
tenderly, That you loved me,
You'd always be,
My Lilli of the
Lamplight, My own
Lilli Marlene."

Twenty minutes later they were over London, fighting for their lives.

§

Timothy, having dove upon a group of bombers with his mates, had his aircraft raked by a diligent ventral gunner as he passed. Though his aircraft took several strikes they were all of a smaller caliber and from a single gun so no real damage happened. As he climbed away, he watched in horror as the missed flight dropped their payloads on the streets of London below. Cursing loudly he circled and climbed, trying to gain altitude so he could get the jump on the three lead bombers, which oddly had not yet dropped.

"FEINDLICHE JAGER AT ELEVEN 'O' CLOCK!" Luddy called out as he tracked the single fighter. It was still too far off to shoot at. Though it was every rookie's temptation, the Doberman was not a rookie. In his own right, he was an ace, having successfully defended his aircraft while downing five attackers; one Pole, three French, and one Brit over Dunkirk.

"Stay on this course," Abel instructed, "We will be at the target in thirty seconds."

"Red Two and Three, this is Red One," Otto called over the radio,

"Stay this course, we are thirty seconds out. Dog at eleven."

Two voices called a copy. Tracers began floating up from the bomber back and to the left. This bomber, Red Three, was in the staggered high position, while Red Two was staggered low.

"Dodgy bastard, aren't you?" Timothy muttered as he turned and began his dive at better than three hundred miles per hour. "Well run, run, as fast as you can, you can't hit me I'm the Gingerbread man."

Flipping his gun button off of safe he turned on his sight, figured his angles, and then pressed in on the bomber already firing at him.

"I can't see him Luddy," Günter called out, "Where is he?

"Closing on Three," the gunner replied as he opened fire, trying to help distract the single fighter. The dorsal gunner on Two opened up as well using the gun mounted on that side of the fuselage. With no turret that could spin and shoot in any direction, defending your aircraft sometimes appeared to be a crazed dance as the gunner leapt from one gun position to another. Sometimes the magazine fed gun to be used would be in a discharged condition and this took precious seconds to rectify.

The Fox gave the trailing bomber a long burst and it bellowed smoke from the port engine. The lithe Dornier began a turn to the left, flames licking out from the engine's cooling shroud.

Timothy banked right to pick up the next Dornier and took a spray of black oil on his windscreen. This clouded things a bit in his reflector gun sight but as soon as he had the image of the next bomber firmly in the reticule, he pressed the fire button again. Another burst and this bomber too sprouted smoke and flames.

"I'm hit, I'm hit," the pilot called out as he dove to the right. Two forms dropped from the back of the aircraft and parachutes blossomed.

Sergeant Buttran then banked hard left and gave back pressure to his stick to gain altitude. Short seconds after he pointed his nose down again to zero in on the lead bomber, angling in from high on the right rear quarter.

"Target in sight," Abel called over the intercom. The German Shepherd was totally oblivious to what was going on around him; such was his concentration. "Stay the course Otto; drop will be in ten seconds."

The young dorsal gunner squeezed the trigger of his machine gun and held it there. It was a gas operated MG with a tremendous rate of fire; but it had to be reloaded once the magazine was expended. That usually tended to occur at the most awkward of moments; which is exactly what happened.

As the Doberman's last few rounds flew towards the fighter Timothy pressed his own fire button and held it down, watching the bomber as it grew in his gun sight.

Amidst the hail of lead slamming into the aircraft's fuselage, Luddy took three .303 bullets to his chest and collapsed to the deck of the bomber dead. The self-sealing fuel tanks, however, kept them from blowing up.

Hurricane TE-B soaked up the bullets like a sponge but stopped firing as the wiring below the pilot's control stick was shredded. Her pilot didn't think in words. Images wrapped in emotions flowed cleanly through his mind. There was nothing to say, no screaming to be done, no battle cries meant to pass lips in blood curdling fashion; he simply reached a decision.

The Dornier's bomb bay doors cycled open. With this, the Fox adjusted his course just slightly and advanced the throttle to full while aiming his aircraft directly at the thin looking fuselage filling his gun sight.

"Five seconds..." Abel called over the intercom. "Four... three..."

Otto, hearing the hail like noise of bullets rattling through the fuselage behind him turned to find his dorsal gunner lying on the deck in a pool of blood. His mind registered that fact and also that Günter was struggling to climb out of his ventral position, his paw reaching towards the dead youth. The Dog's face, shadowed by a now dangling oxygen mask, wore an absolute expression of horror and sorrow.

There was a tremendous crash and the bomber's entire twin ruddered tail section parted company with the remainder of the fuselage; which then did a vicious front somersault. This cartwheeling freefall was so violent that both of the wings snapped off outboard of the engines.

Time stood still... and yet kept on.

Abel was thrown from his position at the bomb sight and pinned against the top of his bomb aiming compartment. For the long and terrifying moment that it took the bomber to fall from the sky he could do nothing but scream as he watched the ground approach through the glass nose. The bombs he would have dropped remained unarmed and did not explode when the earth was impacted.

Otto, who had been leaning out from his seat and looking back at his gunners, was ripped from the pilot's seat and smashed through the glass of the windshield. His parachute opened, but he never remembered pulling the release cord.

Günter struggled to get out of the wreckage all the way down to the earth but never managed to get the escape hatch open.

Timothy, finding his aircraft unresponsive to her controls tried without success to open his canopy. Grabbing his crash bar, he jammed it into the small space where the frames met and it rolled back slightly. Using everything he had, he tugged on the bar and the Perspex slid back just enough for him to squeeze out. Pulling the rip cord, he kicked his feet wildly as he watched the ground approach at breath taking speed. With a jerk his parachute opened, breaking his fall just twenty feet above the rooftops of the homes he'd been protecting. With a thump his backside hit the sloping roof of one of the houses and he slid down the tiles; falling off over the guttering and straight down into the garden below where he suffered a sprained ankle.

Dornier Do 17 Z-2 F1+FH Wk Nr.2361 of KG 76, in a spiraling decent, crashed into the forecourt of Victoria Station demolishing a small tobacconist's shop.

Hurricane TE-B, missing its right wing from the landing gear outboard, came straight down; impacting in the middle of the busy crossroads where Buckingham Palace Road meets Pimlico Road and Ebury Bridge. With close to a ton of metal in her nose (the Merlin engine) the kinetic energy behind the Hurricane was so tremendous it punched a large hole in the road into which the majority of the aircraft simply disappeared.

§

Archie stood naked in his small apartment, finally receiving twenty four solid hours off. He was alone and wished no companionship; having made this perfectly clear to his wingman who tended to dote upon him like a mother. The curtains were drawn tightly to keep any small amount of light from escaping per regulations. The night bombers were known to target but a single small light when it was seen from altitude.

Pouring himself three fingers of Scotch, he re-corked the bottle and then set the glass on the small table next to the couch.

Winding the crank on his gramophone, he set the needle to the record and listened to the notes of the music as the song began with a drum roll and a bugle call. These notes were followed by the entire contents of his glass.

Sitting on the couch, he watched the darkness wanting her to be with him. By the second stanza of the song, the scratchiness had left the words, and the voice became more and more like the voice he only wished he could hear again.

By the end of the song, the Stag was fast asleep... not noticing the ghostly figure that raised the record player's spindle, setting it upon the cradle. Bending, she kissed him on the cheek and then sat watching him as he slept. Not too long after the single candle guttered out and the room was left in darkness Archie was covered with a blanket and she was gone again.

§

In 1915, as a 22-year-old soldier fighting in the First World War, Hans Leip wrote his poem to express the anguish of separation from his sweetheart, a grocer's daughter named Lili. On sentry duty at night, he would always receive a friendly wave from a nurse going off duty; her name was Marleen. Thus the title of the poem was born.

In 1937, feeling that the darkness of another war was looming, Leip released his collection of poems, including 'The Song of a Young Sentry', under the title Die Hafenorgel ("The Little Organ by the Harbour"). It was his hope that those who had not lived through the First World War might be alerted to the pain and horror of wars fought in the name of "national pride".

Lili Marlene - Original version

Vor der Kaserne vor dem grossen Tor Stand eine Laterne, und stebt noch
davor, So wolln wir uns da wiedersehn
Bei der Laterne wolln wir stehn,
Wie einst Lili Marleen, wie einst Lili Marleen.

Unsre beide Schatten sahn wie einer aus.
Dass wir so lieb uns hatten, das sah man gleich daraus Un alle Leute solln es sehn,
Wenn wir bei der Laterne stehn,
Wie einst Lili Marleen, wie einst Lili Marleen.

Schon rief der Posten: Sie blasen Zapfenstreich Es kann drei Tage kosten!
Kam'rad, ich komm ja gleich.
Da sagten wir auf Wiedersehn. Wie gerne wollt ich mit dir gehn,
Mit dir Lili Marleen, mit dir Lili Marleen.

Deine Schritte kennt sie, deinen zieren Gang Alle Abend brennt sie, mich
vergass sie lanp Und sollte mir ein Leids geschehn,
Wer wird bei der Laterne stehn,
Mit dir Lili Marleen, mit dir Lili Marleen?

Aus dem stillen Raume, aus der Erde Grund Hebt mich wie im Traume
dein verliebter Mund. Wenn sich die spaeten Nebel drehn,
Werd' ich bei der Laterne stehn
Wie einst Lili Marleen, wie einst Lili Marleen

Lili Marlene - English version

Underneath the lantern by the barrack gate, Darling I remember the way
you used to wait; 'Twas there that you whispered tenderly,
That you lov'd me, you'd always be, My Lilli of the lamplight,
My own Lilli Marlene.

Time would come for roll call time for us to part Darling I'd carress you
and press you to my heart. And there 'neath that far off lantern light
I'd hold you tight we'd kiss goodnight, My Lillie of the lamplight,
My own Lilli Marlene.

Orders came for sailing somewhere over there,
All confined to barracks was more than I could bear; I knew you were
waiting in the street,
I heard your feet, but could not meet, My Lillie of the lamplight,
My own Lilli Marlene.

Resting in a billet just behind the line
Even tho' we're parted your lips are close to mine, You wait where that
lantern softly gleams
Your sweet face seems to haunt my dreams, My Lillie of the lamplight,
My own Lilli Marlene.

Author's notes pertaining to this story:

Post date: Friday November 4th, 2005 (RAF BBMF: http://www. raf.mod.uk/bbmf/) WWII Pilot Who Saved The Queen Honored Prevented German Bomber From Attacking Buckingham Palace

An RAF pilot who used his Hawker Hurricane fighter to ram a German bomber at the dawn of WWII, thus preventing it from launching an attack on the home of the British Monarchy, was honored recently for his valor -- 65 years after the event occurred.

Sergeant Ray Holmes was locked in a fierce chase with the Dornier airplane on a day in September 1940, during the Battle of Britain, as the German plane sped towards Buckingham Palace. Out of ammunition, and in a desperate attempt to bring the bomber down, Holmes used his Hurricane to ram the German aircraft, severing the bomber's tail.

The German plane spun out of control but missed the Palace, instead going down into Victoria Station, according to an Associated Press story. Amazingly, the bomber pilot survived. Holmes had to then bail out of his crippled fighter, as well, before it too went down.

In "Arty" Holmes' words: "There was no time to weigh up the situation. His aeroplane looked so flimsy, I didn't think of it as solid and substantial. I just went on and hit it for six. I thought my aircraft would cut right through it, not allowing for the fact that his plane was as strong as mine!"

In a ceremony Wednesday, Holmes' 504th Squadron, based at Cottesmore Air base in Rutland, England, received a sculpture of a Hawker Hurricane crafted from melted down pieces of the Rolls-Royce engine from Holmes' fighter. Although Holmes died last year at the age of 90, his widow Anne was on hand to accept his posthumous award.

§

A significant event took place on 15 September 1940, now known as 'Battle of Britain Day'. A famous casualty was Dornier Do 17 Z-2 F1+FH Wk Nr.2361 KG 76 flown by Robert Zehbe, part of which crashed into the forecourt of Victoria Station. In the same action Dornier Do 17

136

F1+FS, flown by Rudolf Heitsch, was found in a field near Shoreham. The Dornier was found to be fitted with a flamethrower, installed in the tail. Oil, nitrogen, and hydrogen cylinders were found in the fuselage, while the external pipe was fitted with a jet. Initially, it was concluded that it was a smoke producing device to feign damage. But it was discovered that it was a device that was triggered by one of the rear gunners to destroy a fighter pursuing the bomber from line astern. However, the lack of oxygen meant that the device failed to function, and only a continual spray of oil was emitted.

§

German aircraft from Norway would fly on missions to northern England ; because of the icy weather conditions, the barrels of their guns had a small dab of wax to protect them. As they crossed the coast, they would clear their guns by firing a few rounds at the golf courses. Golfers were urged to take cover.

British 'phlegm' was
never better illustrated
than during 1940; as
witnessed by this calm
notice.

RICHMOND GOLF CLUB

TEMPORARY RULES. 1940

1. Players are asked to collect Bomb and Shrapnel splinters to save these causing damage to the Mowing Machines.

2. In Competitions, during gunfire or while bombs are falling, players may take cover without penalty for ceasing play.

3. The positions of known delayed action bombs are marked by red flags at a reasonably, but not guaranteed, safe distance therefrom.

4. Shrapnel and/or bomb splinters on the Fairways, or in Bunkers within a club's length of a ball, may be moved without penalty, and no penalty shall be incurred if a ball is thereby caused to move accidentally.

5. A ball moved by enemy action may be replaced, or if lost or destroyed, a ball may be dropped not nearer the hole without penalty.

6. A ball lying in a crater may be lifted and dropped not nearer the hole, preserving the line to the hole, without penalty.

7. A player whose stroke is affected by the simultaneous explosion of a bomb may play another ball from the same place. Penalty one stroke.

When Pigs Fly

'Dogs look up to you, cats look down on you. Give me a pig! He looks you in the eye and treats you as an equal.'
Winston Churchill

Author's note: For those who will have a certain predisposition for the social status of Swines, you should understand that the use of a Pig for Maria Raskova's characterization was based solely upon Sir Winston Churchill's quote. I have more than a few friends who are Swine and admire them greatly. Using Maria's name for the ferry pilot of this story is meant as a dedication to her greatness. There are so many people, such as this great pilot, who helped change the world during the dark times of WWII; and history has all but passed them by.

Maria Raskova was a real person and a hero of the Russian people. Though it is doubtful that she ever flew for the ATA, she was the perfect fit for this story. In 1941 she organized 588th night bomber squadron composed entirely of women, from the mechanics to the navigators, pilots and officers. Using 95 MPH bi-planes, they were so effective that the Germans dubbed them the 'Night Witches' and placed a bounty on their heads.

Even at that, their male counterparts seldom recognized them as equals. You can find their story on-line.

The Air Transport Auxiliary (ATA) was the brainchild of a British Overseas Airways Corporation director, Gerald d'Erlanger. D'Erlanger approached the Air Ministry with proposals to form up a pool of civilian pilots to assist in the logistics of aircraft delivery. When Tops finally decided it was not viable to use combat seasoned RAF pilots to ferry aircraft, the idea was quickly adopted and the newly formed ferry organization was pressed into service.

Unlike the RAF, the ATA was not military but civilian. Because of this, they were much less restrictive in their recruitment policies, quickly snapping up pilots who were considered to be unsuitable for reasons of age or fitness. The Royal Air Force and the Fleet Air Arm therefore humorously referred to the organization as 'Ancient and Tattered Airmen'.

Being their main requirement was simply the ability to fly an aircraft, they had one-armed, one- legged, short-sighted, and one-eyed pilots. There were also pilots from neutral countries and, notably, women pilots

Representatives of 28 countries flew with the ATA

§

Wing Commander Stewart Falstaff stood before a mixed group of twenty pilots, all of whom were about to ferry much needed aircraft to the various squadrons around the country. He scowled without really meaning to. They were as varied a group as the old Bulldog had ever seen and mostly looked as though they would have no idea what an airplane was let alone how to fly one.

True to the ATA's recruitment policies, the pilots were largely foreigners and few questions asked except if they knew how to fly. There were five quite old Bulgarian Rabbits who'd flown during the Great War on the side of the Wolfs, but who now resided in England. There were three American Terriers, one a young female, one old enough to be her father, and one with a patch over his left eye. There were also six French Badgers, grouchy old females to be sure, four lithe Belgium Vixens pretty enough to make even the Commander smile (though he believed they should have been on the dance floor waving their skirts in the air), one Jamaican Colonial mixed breed female with a penchant for cigars, and one Russian Sow.

"First I would like to personally thank you all for coming to this party," he told them.

There were a few chuckles from the group, though the Badgers remained stone cold silent, a permanent looking scowl attached to their features. They reminded the Bulldog of his mother-in- law.

"I am going to skip the speeches this morning. So long as you know you have the British people's undying gratitude and the feel of a good paycheck in your pocket, we're good." Picking up a clipboard, he surveyed it to see what aircraft were to be ferried and where. His eyebrows went up when he saw the mix of no less than six different types. Besides bombers and transports, the list included one Hurricane and one Spitfire. These last two were actually the reason he was there.

To this point, the women were not allowed to touch these fighter aircraft. RAF command, holding to an old time 'males only' club attitude towards female flyers, forbad them to sit in these particular cockpits. They'd issued strict rules against allowing females the training to accomplish the mission and so had a valid reason to lean upon. The tried and true elbow to ribs humor went along with their reasoning. 'Why do you not allow a female pilot to fly inverted – because they'll have a crack up.'

Personally the old Bulldog thought this was rather funny and deep inside he would have loved to see one of the vixens with a 'crack up'; but he also had a personal experience with one particular female pilot flying his precious Spits and she was among the best flyers he'd had.

"As I read off your name, I will also direct you to the aircraft you have been assigned. Check in the Operations Shack for your destinations and be sure you watch them ring up Control with your flight plan. The reason I tell you to do this, and this information is for the new pilots, if you do not the chances you will be shot down by friendly fire increases tenfold. Archie (*anti-aircraft batteries*) can be a blind old bastard at times."

Going down the list, the group of pilots quickly grew smaller and smaller until there was but two of the females remaining; one of the Belgium vixens and the Russian sow; both were fair looking and both had proved to be capable flyers.

"You will follow me, please," Falstaff told them. "I have two very good pilots standing by to give you final instructions on the aircraft you are to ferry. They will then act as your escorts so you will not get lost." As they walked, the Wing Commander said, "Miss Vandenbosch, you will take the Hurricane and ferry to the Number 401 Canadians at RAF Northolt. Flight Lieutenant Henry Badcock will be your instructor and escort."

"Very good," the Fox acknowledged, her accent musical to the old Dog's ears. "We dance then."

"Miss Raskova," he informed the sow, "You will have the Spitfire to ferry and that goes to the RAF Number 310 Squadron in Duxford. Your escort will be Flight Lieutenant Archie Corn."

"Understood," she replied with a nod. Her accent, to the Wing Commander's ears, brought thoughts of bricks being laid.

Holding the door open for them, he allowed the ladies to move through first and then followed them out. Just down the small set of stairs and a bit to the right of the ready room two flyers waited for them. As the Wing Commander approached they snapped to attention.

"At ease," Falstaff growled and the pilots relaxed. This particular pair had been chosen for this mission because they were both very competent instructors and more specifically for the one because he secretly already knew firsthand the abilities of female flyers.

"Mr. Badcock," the Commander called out, using Henry's name rather than rank as the Dogs were old friends and even distantly related.

"Yes sir?"

"This is Miss Isabelle Vandenbosch," he said with a nod to the Fox. "She is to pilot the Hurricane for which you will be escort and instructor."

"Yes, sir," the Bulldog replied with a lecherous grin. The Vixen, for her part, smiled coyly back at him, flirting as much as she dared in front of the Wing Commander.

"Lieutenant Corn," the old Bulldog continued, turning his attention to the Stag.

"Yes sir?"

"Miss Maria Raskova will be your student today. She will pilot the Spitfire."

"Yes, sir."

"Gentlemen, and ladies, I have been instructed to push forward with this mission. For some odd reason the rest of our fighting fellows do not seem to think so highly of the abilities of women as pilots. I have personally taken one risk and put this to the test. I was shown the light, so to speak. For me, I would use both you ladies to fight this war in a dog fighter's heartbeat but I will take what I can get. If by ferrying fighter craft to the front lines you can free up some of my boys to take care of business then I will accept that as a small victory. One takes what one can get in life, eh?"

He paused to look at each of them so they were sure to know he was deadly serious.

"For the most part," he continued, speaking directly to Badcock and Corn, "Your students already know the aircraft she will fly. They have spent many hours with the Kiwis going over every detail but only from ground level and then by assisting in such things as engine ground runs and taxiing. Their only requirement is to be able to take off, fly straight and level, and then land again at their destination; nothing more. Am I clear on this?"

Both pilots responded with a 'Yes sir!'

"Ladies, do you understand?"

The pair responded seriously, 'Da' and 'Oui.'

"If you are attacked in route there will be no fighting back. The ferry aircraft lack armament in any case as they will be gunned up and sights set after arrival by the ordinance crews." Falstaff paused to let this sink in and then continued. "In this case, the plan is for the ferry aircraft to land immediately in whatever field is available. You will then abandon ship and run for your lives. I can repair or replace an aircraft shot up on the ground… I cannot replace a life lost. I can and do expect my fighter pilots to accept these risks; but you ladies are civilians and thus do not answer to such things." Turning his attention again to Henry and Archie, he told them, "The escort pilot is to turn tail and climb away."

"But, sir," the other Bulldog began to protest.

"No buts Henry," the Wing Commander replied. "Single plane combat against grouped enemy fighters is suicide at best. The Wolfs have the numbers on their side. If they lose one and we lose one, they have obtained a victory. It is imperative for the sake of England that the RAF make the Luftwaffe bleed buckets of blood. Casualties are a given and we understand that…" he paused and then sighed. "It's the shits," he muttered, "Let's just leave it at that shall we? This is all hush hush, mind you, so when you get to where you're going there will be no mention of these two lovely ladies. They will be met at the aircraft by my staff and whisked away to make their way back here via Lysander. You both can grab a cup of tea while your aircraft is serviced and then will make your way back here also for a debrief. I need not remind you to stay in close touch with Control."

"Are they familiar with the flight characteristics of the aircraft, sir?" Badcock asked, the instructor in him shining through.

Falstaff harrumphed just as a nearby aircraft started its engines. The similarities in the sounds were striking. "Ask them," he said gruffly, "I believe you will find they have voices and can talk. They are flesh and blood just like you."

"I'm sure Henry meant no disrespect, sir," Archie said softly. "This has all been rather sprung upon us; today we were to have a rest. That we are to be teacher and escort does complicate things a bit." Turning to the Swine standing next to him, he extended his paw. "My name is Archie Corn," he told her. "I am pleased to make your acquaintance. Do you speak English?"

"A little," she replied taking his paw in hers. Her grip was vice like and unexpected given her lithe figure. She smiled a smile that could have meant anything.

"Are you capable of flying a Spitfire?" he asked, disengaging from her hand shake in as gentlemanly a fashion as he could muster. He heard Henry choke back a laugh.

She snorted and the smile grew to her eyes. "I think we find out soon, Da? I learn to fly at Osoaviakhim. That was flying club for boys and girls in Russia back in 30's. We fly plane like your Tiger Moth and once a Yak 3."

"But a Spitfire is not a Tiger Moth," Henry interjected.

The sow looked at him and, as pretty as she was, her look was hard. "I fly Bristol Blenheim fine. I fly Arvo 'Anson fine. I fly Lysander fine. I fly Airspeed Oxford fine. I fly…"

"I say," Falstaff interrupted, "Where is Miss Vandenbosch?"

From the cockpit of the Hawker Hurricane next to them came a musically accented voice shouting to be heard above an aircraft taxiing past. "Are ewe going to talk all the day?"

"What about your walk-around?" Henry yelled at her through cupped paws.

"I dew ete 'alf an hour ago! Now move your arses we 'ave a war to win!"

§

"Control, this is Egham Spit departing Bristol and heading Northwest at Angels Ten, speed Two fifty, fuel topped. I am escort to ferry Spit Three Zero destination Duxford, over."

"Egham Spit," replied a female voice, "Proceed on your course. We have no reports of enemy activity in your area."

"Roger Wilco."

With that, Archie looked over at the other aircraft and gave Raskova a thumbs up. Other than his call to Control, they were to maintain radio silence during the brief flight. Communication if it was necessary was to be through the use of hand signals; though she too would monitor the radio. Unlike the Stag's Egham Spitfire, which was treated accordingly as a combat aircraft, the Pig's aircraft carried only half fuel which was more than enough to get her to RAF 310. This way, in case of a crash, precious gasoline would not be wasted.

'So far so good,' he'd thought as soon as they were airborne.

The ferry pilot's takeoff had been picture perfect and he was inwardly pleased she'd not used too much throttle thus keeping the engine torque to a manageable level. Vandenbosch, he noted, was a bit more right wing down than he would have liked, though the vixen corrected for this quickly. Within minutes all four aircraft were loosely formed up and climbing to ten thousand where they would stay for the duration of their flight. The ferry flight to 310, in and of itself, should last no more than forty five minutes.

Ten minutes out Henry waggled his wings and herded his pretty Fox more to the northwest where they would skirt around any major cities. This was intentional navigation and planned out in advance. In case of enemy fighters the girls would need a field to set down in and this would not be found within the parameters of a city.

Archie lagged back a little, letting the Egham Spit drop just behind so he could watch every aspect of the other pilot's flying abilities. So far, what he saw he approved of and would so write in his report. The other Spitfire was rock solid in its flight and as he came back up on her left side he noted the Russian ferry pilot had the good sense and ability of watching everything. With her oxygen mask on she appeared all business and every bit as male as any other pilot he'd flown with. She did not even give so much as a thumbs up as she scanned first her instruments and then the sky. He was surprised then when she pointed upwards and gave him the signal for enemy aircraft.

The Stag no more than glanced at where she'd pointed and his thumb was on the radio button as he called to her briskly, "Evasive action now!" Even at a distance, the yellow on the nose of the lead fighter was clearly visible, indicating it was flown by an ace.

Out of the corner of his eye, he saw Raskova do a wingover and head for the ground. Black smoke poured from the Spit's exhaust stacks indicating she'd pushed the throttle to full military power and richened the fuel mixture for low level flying. Every shred of his conscious then screamed in indignation as he followed orders and steered away from the incoming fighters; leaving his ward to her own fate.

It simply was not right.

§

144

Staffel Commandant Oberst Dierk Locke smiled slightly as he saw the two specs he knew were British fighters. Obviously they were on a training mission much as he was himself. He and his wingman, a rookie he'd taken on a 'fighting' run were far off the beaten path from where Luftwaffe Intelligence knew a wealth of British fighters would gladly do battle with them. Object lesson number one had been how to sneak in by staying just off the water until arriving over land. The radar's invisible eyes were easier to trick in this manner. Obtaining this goal, they had then climbed and begun their hunt. The second object lesson for his protégé this day was to learn how to act as a proper wingman.

New flyers to the staffel arrived with barely 30 hours in the seat of the aircraft their lives depended upon. Usually it was all they could do to maintain formation with their brethren and were thus almost as much threat as an untethered barrage balloon on a dark night.

Fuel, always being the limiting factor and not to be wasted, pressed these young Wolfs into situations they were not yet physically or mentally prepared for. As their commander it was his responsibility to lead them to the scent and then allow them to smell fresh blood ensuring that next time, when it really mattered, they would not be too squeamish to push the gun button.

As he watched the British fighters one aircraft dove for the ground while the other climbed away in the opposite direction from them. Obviously the instructing pilot had not been chosen for his bravery. This now gave him an opportunity to allow his rookie to experience an easy kill first hand. From the looks of things they would be in and out in a matter of minutes and then back across the channel quickly. Undoubtedly the alarm was being called out on the radio even as they began their attack and perhaps this would be lesson number three for the rookie; response is always secondary to the attack and thus always lagging in time... but you still had to pay attention to it.

No signal or call out was required as he pushed his throttle forward and dove. His trailing wing was required to follow and keep a sharp lookout for other fighters, thus protecting the lead's back. Rookie or not, it was what the Oberst expected and to not do as the Oberst expected was to be sent away to things best not thought about.

(author's note: Though this was not the case when flying with Oberst Locke, there were complaints among the German fighter pilots that the wingman approach to flying in battle was unfair to the pilots who ended always flying secondary wing to the leader; who was thus able to initially score all the kills. Decorations were highly sought and were

awarded after the following point totals had been reached:
Iron Cross 2nd Class 1
Iron Cross 1st Class 3
Honor Cup 10
German Cross in Gold 20
Knight's Cross 40

The Knight's Cross, which was worn on a ribbon around the neck even in combat, was recognized in the Jagdwaffe as a sign of a true Experte. Glory-hungry pilots were thus said to have a "neck rash", "itching neck" or "sore throat". This was a common disease in the Luftwaffe; sometimes even a fatal one - although not always to the one infected with it.

The Luftwaffe pilots and Wehrmacht personnel in general, wore all of their decorations in combat unlike their RAF adversaries.)

§

Archie followed his orders and climbed. In his head he kept hearing Wing Commander Falstaff's voice; 'If you are attacked in route there will be no fighting back. The escort pilot is to turn tail and climb away.'

This was countered by Henry's gruff voice marking a quote from the Stag's training days; 'You will hear many things and countless different opinions but I am here to tell you in no uncertain terms that a wingman cannot leave his partner's side under any circumstance! Fuk the overwhelming odds! Fuk the bloody count! Fuk the bloody medals! The other fellow's life is worth even sacrificing your own if need be; and if every pilot will think like this then there will be more of you buggers alive at the end of the day no matter what the cockup!'

Commander Falstaff's imaginary voice then made to counter this with a forceful command to obey or else and it pushed the Stag over the edge; inadvertently he pressed his radio button and screamed, "PISS OFF STEWART!"

"Say again," came Control's calm voice. "Who is this please? Use protocol and reply."

Winging his aircraft over, Archie pushed his throttle beyond full military and calmly replied, "Egham Spit here, Marsha. All is well, please pardon the static. See you for tea in forty."

"Copy Egham Spit, ETA Number 310 in forty."

"Might take a bit longer than that," he replied, lining up on the Locke's Tail End Charlie. The aircraft was just a spec at this point but growing quickly. "It's a good day for some lesson giving along with the ferry; I might take a bit longer."

"Copy Egham Spit, I'll pass it along."

§

Raskova did not do as she'd been ordered either. Dive to the deck, yes, that she did; but rather than look for a convenient landing spot she leveled out at tree top level and left the throttle full on as she began evasive maneuvers.

Flashing across a field of string beans the lithe sow nosed down to below the trees in a 'death be damned - catch me if you can' defiance of the Wolf chasing her. With the huge Merlin roaring for all it was worth her propeller came to within inches of the dirt. Vegetable tops shot far out to the side of her path as clouds of dust flew out behind making it look as if she were on fire. Coming to another line of trees she nosed up, passed over, and then went back down again instinctively kicking the rudder and jinking to the left, allowing the trees to mask her maneuver. Her Spitfire, missing almost a thousand pounds in guns, ammunition, and combat fuel load, made it nimble beyond belief.

§

Locke cursed. What he'd thought to be an easy target was becoming as difficult to catch as a fish with your bare paws. It could be done, but it took much patience.

Just topping the tree line, he stayed at that altitude hoping to close and drop down for a shot from behind. Try as he might, however, and as fast as his aircraft was, he could not close the distance enough to press his attack home. Where Raskova had jinked left, he'd anticipated a right turn and followed initially in that direction losing more distance as he performed an 'S' maneuver in order to find her again.

§

Archie came straight in at the trailing Messerschmitt flying a high angle interception course. He would have to catch this one fighter out before going after the lead aircraft or suffer the same fate of being shot down. The Wolf, committing the largest mistake rookies were guilty of, had his entire concentration on the chase playing out before him. He was blind to anything else and completely missed the Egham's approach until the last possible moment. In a panic he yanked back on his control stick as hard as he could. His fighter nosed up until he was hanging vertically from the prop and on the verge of a stall. This purely gut reaction did save his life. As the Stag gave his intended target a long burst he saw his tracers flash past just under the other aircraft's tail.

Banking away and to the left, he saw a huge dust cloud ripping along the countryside below, chased by the yellow nosed Wolf fighter. Now, forgetting about the wingman altogether he dove and steadied up on an interception course with Raskova's pursuer.

The rookie Wolf who'd come so close to dying, finally got his nose down and quickly found himself in a spin which he rode almost all the way to the earth before recovering. After that he turned tail and ran for the English Channel where he thoughtfully ditched his aircraft just off the coast of France in order to hide the evidence that he'd never even been hit.

§

Locke, his total concentration on the chase, pressed his gun button. Dual frequency vibrations shook the cockpit as he fired; the heavier being from his cannon and the lighter from his machine guns. The Spitfire in front of him pulled up a mere fifty feet to clear another line of trees and the tracers flashed under its tail.

The Spit had jinked left the last time this happened, so the Wolf anticipated seeing the same maneuver. Lifting his nose to clear the same trees, he tapped his rudder to follow the Spit's expected spasmodic maneuver.

§

Raskova felt the Messerschmitt's attempt to shoot her down. She knew he was there, having seen him in the mirror but that was only a glimpse as her total concentration was required for the type of flying she was doing. Now, with the hair on the back of her neck prickled up, she fought her instincts to climb out and seek altitude. Though she was not a trained fighter pilot, she was a Russian bearing the strains of Cossack blood from the history of her family. As the Cossacks ran with reckless abandon, she now flew her aircraft in the same way, making it bend to her will.

Reducing throttle just as she cleared the trees, the sow banked into a hard 360 degree right climbing turn, taking the Spit up to 300 feet as indicated by her altimeter. Once there she again applied power and found herself directly above and behind the yellow nosed aircraft. With no guns available she did the only offensive thing she could and pressed forward in an attempt to chew his tail off with the propeller.

Archie saw this and but for the hard reality of where he sat, would not have otherwise believed it possible. He was now positioned for a good firing solution but because the two aircraft were so close to each other he could not risk pressing the gun button.

"Cut power and pull back Raskova," he called to her calmly, "So I might clear my guns."

§

Not seeing the Spitfire when he cleared the tree line, Locke looked to his rear and felt the immediate ice water feeling of something bad about to happen. The aircraft he'd been chasing was now magically on his tail and at any moment he expected to be riddled by its machinegun fire. Pushing his throttle into 'emergency' he concentrated forward, beginning evasive maneuvers of his own. Black smoke and flames shot from the exhaust stacks. With this automatic over-boost and fuel enrichment the fighter pilot had approximately five minutes before his engine melted.

§

The Russian sow heard the radio call. Her brain took a second or two for translation and then her heart leaped as she realized her escort had not abandoned her. Pulling back to three quarter's power, she banked hard right and nosed upward out of the way.

§

Archie had the German dead to rights. His attack, though angled, was made at well under three hundred yards. As the yellow nosed Messerschmitt jinked and quivered in his gun sight his subconscious recognized the markings of the Wolf who had kept him from being butchered in his parachute. Just before pushing the gun button he moved his control yoke just enough that the barrage of lead riddled only the tail of the aircraft.

Locke, surprised at the fire coming from a completely different direction, banked hard right and climbed straight up, avoiding the same stall that had near killed his wingman. He then headed directly for the coast with half of his rudder missing and both elevators riddled with .303 holes. He would later be forced to take to his parachute off the coast of France when the aircraft finally became dangerously unmanageable. Oddly enough he was picked up by the same E-boat that had found his wingman.

The reunion was not a good one.

Giving up the chase, Archie climbed while executing a shallow bank to the left; looking to see where his Russian ferry pilot might be. He was surprised when he found her right off of his wingtip. She made a gesture to him indicating he should follow the wounded aircraft and finish him.

He, in turn, gave her the 'F' sign for fuel and then pointed upwards indicating they should resume their altitude and flight.

She nodded compliance and their flight continued on as if it had never been interrupted.

§

Upon arrival at RAF 310 the two Spitfires were marshaled over to the fueling area. Even as the engines were winding down the fueling bowser pulled up next to Archie's aircraft. Standing in the cockpit, the pilot waved to the Sergeant in charge.

"Fill'er up, if you please, and none of that vodka mix you chaps are so fond of, eh?" (*The 310 was a Czechoslovakian crewed wing.*)

As ordered, Raskova stayed in the cockpit, her oxygen mask hanging down, partially obscuring her face.

The Sergeant, a Czech national like the rest of the unit, laughed and waved. The two Kiwis that chocked their tires came around to the front of their respective aircraft and then the one called the other over to look at the propeller of Raskova's Spitfire. There was a spat of conversation and then the fueler joined them.

"What's amiss?" Archie called over to them.

"I think the ground come up to kiss this one, eh? There is green hovno (sh*t) all over the blades and belly."

"Must have happened before our time in the seat," the Stag replied calmly. "Our flight was a wonderfully calm walk in the park."

"Your gun tapes isss blown," the fueler pointed out with a smile. *(Cloth tape was applied over the machinegun ports to help maintain aerodynamic smoothness of the leading edge before a fight.)*

"Just a normal functional clearing for training purposes," the Stag replied with a stretch and a yawn.

A car pulled up and an officer stepped out. The three Kiwis snapped to attention, the senior of them saluting. This fellow, a Czech Brindle Dane, did not even return the salute. Instead, he barked a clear order in the unit's native tongue which sent the three fellows running back towards the maintenance shack. When they had gone, he came over to Archie's aircraft and stood by the leading edge of the wing. His face was a mask of disapproval.

Dismounting, Archie climbed down the wing pathway and then ducked under; coming up front to meet with him.

"How was your flight?" the Dog asked. His voice, with its clipped accent, emphasized its coldness.

"A veritable picnic," the pilot responded with his own coldness, "Ten thousand all the way and nothing but clear skies."

"So you say."

Looking at the other aircraft, and then checking the area to be sure they were alone, he waved to the ferry pilot, indicating she should join them. "Your orders have changed," he said as he did this.

"Why?" Archie asked.

"How the bloody hell should I know," the Czech retorted. "Probably to avoid any embarrassment at having one of our precious aircraft almost crashed during a simple ferry."

"What are you on about?"

The Dane looked at him, his blue eyes squinting slightly. "Women do not belong in the cockpit. I am your contact here, so yes I know... but that does not mean I approve."

"If the times were different," Archie told him softly, so Raskova would not hear as she approached, "I would take you out back of the hanger and beat the cabbage from your thick head. Do you even fly?"

"Three vics," the other officer replied smugly.

"I've got nine so piss off," the Stag shot back.

As the sow came to stand next to them, the Dane glanced at the side of the Egham Spitfire and, his lips moving, actually counted the iron crosses painted there. "I see," he muttered finally, "My apologies for being rude, sir. As I said, your orders have changed. There will be no pick up of the ATA pilot. She is to squeeze into your cockpit and you are to proceed forthwith directly back to Bristol."

"That's preposterous," Archie told him. "The only way we could do that is without parachutes."

"Perhaps so, but it is exactly what I was ordered to tell you. It's that or have her ferry your craft back and perhaps you can hitch a ride somehow." He motioned to the nearby shrubbery. "Have her remain out of sight while I get your ship fueled up. You may go and have tea if you wish, but not her."

"I'd rather choke on dirt than drink tea with the likes of you," the Stag replied. "Give me a whistle when she's ready and then pull the chocks and clear out. I'll handle the rest. When I break ground, you call and tell Control I'm on my way."

He then stalked off with Raskova in tow, heading back towards the nearby bushes where they could sit in the shade and rest for a few moments.

As the pilot watched the ground crew service his aircraft he heard a metal on metal sound of a cap being unscrewed. Feeling an elbow in his ribs, he turned to find the Russian holding out a flask to him.

"You are a good pilot," she told him. The seriousness of her expression calmed him and he smiled.

"Thank you," he told her, accepting the flask and taking a swallow. "And you are a bloody good pilot yourself. You really did chew vegetables with your propeller. That is just so incredible. I couldn't believe how close you were to the bastard... it must have scared the bloody hell out of him. If you'd only had guns."

"Didn't need guns... I was going to eat his tail," she replied calmly after taking a swallow of the vodka.

"You what?"

"I not say it right? Eat his tail... um..." She made a striking motion with her hand to fist. "Chop rudder off with propeller."

"Good Lord."

She offered him another swallow which he gratefully took, and then it was put away. "Best not have more," she told him with a strange smile, "Not want you feeling frisky with me sitting in your lap."

"Why are you here?" he asked, trying not to smile at her statement. He did indeed feel a warmth in his belly from the vodka and she was probably right.

"I learn to fly because I want to fly... top of my group even. When I go then to volunteer, recruiter for Voenno-Vozdushnye Sily (The Russian Air Force) did not want me. He said, 'Things might be bad but we are not so desperate that we put little girls like you up in the skies. Go home and help your mother.' So... I hear of ATA and come to England."

The Stag nodded his understanding. "It is indeed not a fair world we live in by any stretch of the imagination."

Thirty minutes later, sans parachutes, the pair was wheels up and heading back to Bristol.

§

Archie and Maria stood at attention in the Operations Ready Room for the airfield where they'd begun their day. Seated before them, and looking less than pleased, was Wing Commander Falstaff.

"So I'm to believe the ferry flight went without a hitch," the old Bulldog questioned, "And other than some additional training along the way you were Angels Ten the entire trip just as instructed?"

"Yes sir," the fighter pilot and the ferry pilot replied in the same voice.

"Good, I am glad to hear that." He hesitated and then asked, "And you returned in the same aircraft without parachutes; why was that exactly?"

Archie came forth truthfully about this and the Wing Commander's frown deepened. "I will resolve that issue and this will never happen again," he responded.

Shuffling some papers around on his desk, his finger tapped upon one of them. "Miss Raskova, you are dismissed and I thank you for your time and trouble. I believe there is a Dakota on the ramp generously provided to us by an overseas 'friend'. It is in need of a pilot as it will be moving up to Scotland for a time. You will have two passengers on board when you depart. Please see the duty Ops Officer for your orders and then begin your preparations. If you have a duffle I would suggest loading it."

Standing he offered his paw and they shook; her grip and his were both brisk and firm.

When she'd left, the Commander sat back down and gave Archie a very hard look. "The truth and I want it now."

"As the Yanks say, sir, it was a piece of cake," Archie replied calmly, "A walk in the park with a Sunday picnic thrown in. I wish all my flights were so…"

Falstaff held a finger up in the air, silencing the pilot. He then let the finger drift down to the paper in front of him where he read, "Green vegetable matter coating the leading edges of the propeller and underbelly of the aircraft."

"Certainly not mine, sir."

"Of course not yours, damn it! The ferry aircraft!"

"I wouldn't know anything about that, sir; must have been that way when we picked it up."

"And how do you explain what was heard over the radio… and I heard this myself mind you; 'Piss off Stewart?' " He punctuated the words dramatically.

Lieutenant Corn offered his most disarming smile. "I was practicing my singing, sir. It's a song for the Squadron's talent night at the pub."

The Commander cagily smiled in turn. "Sing it for me," he told the pilot.

Archie blushed and then giving it his best shot, sang, 'Piss off Stewart, I'll not lend you a pence - Your pounds're all buried - Leaving naught to fix your fence.' Pausing, he explained, "It's a parody of the Scotts and their thrifty ways, sir. Do you want to hear more?"

Falstaff opened his mouth to begin a shouting tirade when he was interrupted by gleeful laughter coming from behind a curtain. "I'm sure our friends the Scotts would love to hear that one Lieutenant Corn but I would not advise singing it in one of their pubs."

The curtain was swept back and Sir Winston Churchill stepped out. The old Bulldog had one of his ever present cigars clamped in his jaw, which he paused to light. "You spin a wonderful tale, son," he said between puffs, "But you are not a very good liar… and cheers to you for being so; just make sure you never to go into politics. Everything there is a lie but for the truth I speak… and you can only trust that so far."

He fixed the flyer with a gaze that was flint hard and Archie felt much as he had before his father after being caught out in a wrong doing.

Noting this discomfiture, the PM smiled. "Now tell us the truth and do not be afraid for the consequences. I gave Commander Falstaff the nod for Lieutenant Chrysanthemum and she did not let the British people down. She impressed me greatly when we interviewed. I would gladly do it again but we cannot continue to do such things in secret… we must break the mold of this males only club and never let it be built up again. To do that; I must know the facts."

"Could we sit please, sir?" Archie asked, his heart suddenly aching.

Sir Winston took the cigar from his mouth and pointed to a chair with it. He then took a seat next to the Wing Commander. Side by side as they were, the pair almost looked like brothers.

Over the course of an hour Archie told them everything. Beginning with his experiences of that day, he continued on to his history with

Lt. Terrance, including the stories he truly believed no one would ever believe; including how a Wolf flying a yellow nosed Messerschmitt saved his life.

Wing Commander Falstaff slid the report over in front of Archie and tapped it with a finger again. "And she really was flying that close to the ground?"

"Absolutely, sir. You should have seen the dust cloud. When she got the upper hand on the Wolf, she really was trying to butcher his tail with the prop."

"If we had a hundred more like her," Churchill added, "We would certainly turn the tables quickly enough."

At that moment a messenger knocked. Only after permission had been granted did he enter. Walking directly to the PM he quietly handed over a sheet of paper and then left again. Churchill gave it a brief look, smiled and gave it over to the Wing Commander who also smiled. Looking to Archie, the PM told him, "Good news and bad news, Lieutenant Corn. What you told us has been confirmed. One of our fishing boats reported that a yellow nosed German fighter crashed into the channel this afternoon right about the time you were to land. That was the good news. The bad news is the pilot took to his chute and was picked up by a German torpedo boat."

Archie felt a flood of relief, though he would have much preferred for a British vessel to have made the rescue.

"I think we can give you that one then," the PM said as he stood. "How many does that make now?"

"Ten, sir, but may I make a request?"

"Certainly."

"I'd like to share the victory with Maria. She certainly deserves it more than I do; I had guns to use where she was about to strangle him with her bare hands... so to speak."

"Done," the Bulldog growled with a chuckle. "And now, if you will honor me, I would like you to fly escort for that Dakota I spoke of. The Wing Commander and I are the passengers spoken of. We are scheduled to unofficially tour some of our airbases up that way and I think a few days rest in Scotland might do you some good." He winked at the Stag. "Not to mention that the Wing Commander here has arranged for a certain other pilot to be there to keep you company. Perhaps you could compare notes about flying or something."

Falstaff chuckled. "Or something," he echoed. "Just don't sing that bloody song while you're up there or we might find we've another front to fight right here at home."

The Americans

Advertisement in the New York Herald Tribune:

LONDON July 15 [1940]: The Royal Air Force is in the market for American flyers as well as American airplanes. Experienced airmen, preferably those with at least 250 flying hours would be welcomed by the RAF.

Author's note: The recruiter placing this advertisement was one of the most colorful mercenaries of the age: 59-year-old Colonel Charles Sweeney. Friend to Ernest Hemingway and several Latin American revolutionaries, he had placed notices for "opportunities" with European air forces at airfields and newspapers across the USA.

For his efforts, Sweeney was chased by the FBI, Nazi spies, and hounded out of the country by an American press eager to stay out of the war. The mindset of isolationism, more so than pacifism, was the reason for this. America had lost many of her sons coming to the rescue during The Great War (WWI) and as a whole nation, she was unwilling to do it again. Thus was born the 'America First' movement. This powerful interest group advocated the fact that America, just recovering from The Great Depression, had enough of her own problems to worry about, and the nation as a whole should tend to this first rather than the problems of the world.

One of the most famous advocates and spokesperson for this movement was none other than famed aviator Charles Lindberg. Lindberg had toured Germany before the war and the Germans liked him so much they not only showed him their latest and most secret aircraft, the Junkers JU 88, they let him fly a BF 109. Lindberg said of the fighter that he knew 'of no other pursuit plane which combines simplicity of construction with such excellent performance characteristics.'

He returned to America convinced that the Germans were so advanced over our nation's aircraft that we should not get involved in a war we could not win.

Yet, between June 1940 and December 1941, several hundred Americans volunteered to join the RAF. The best known were the fighter pilots, but many others served in Bomber Command as pilots, navigators and air gunners.

§

Archie and Henry were standing by their aircraft having a cuppa while waiting for the call up that would soon come from Control. They were talking softly together and keeping an eye on a strange little fellow wearing a straw hat and carrying a note pad. He'd been making his way down the flight line and not gaining much of a foothold among the pilots, as most simply ignored his presence all together. They'd been warned that to make conversation with him could be dangerous, as he would 'suck you in like quicksand' and have you spouting all sorts of nonsense which would then be published in his newspaper. 'Be discrete,' they'd been ordered by their executive officer when word was passed about the fellow. 'Be also cautious but; at all costs remain polite. We need America to like us.'

"Have you two ever flown with the Yanks?" Straw Hat asked as he came close. He was obviously American with a harsh accent to match. Ostentatiously, his newspaper publisher sent him over to cover the invasion of Britain – if it came to that.

Archie felt the hair on the back of his neck stand up. "Who exactly are you referring to, please?" he asked.

"The fellows assigned to Squadron 609," the correspondent offered. "I was hoping perhaps you'd met them. Why? Are there some here I'm not aware of?"

The Stag felt an immediate sense of relief. It was one thing to recall fond memories, but if he was put to questioning… "No," he replied, "Not met them and none here; though they would be welcome."

"Met them?" Henry said affably over top of his mug of tea, "I had to sign off on three of 'em when they volunteered. There were two tall fellows and one really really small chap. I can't recall their names at the moment but they did call the little fellow 'Shorty'."

"That would be Tobin, Mamedoff, and Keogh," Andras filled in as he walked over to join them. His oxygen mask dangled from where it was attached to his flight helmet. "Why? What's happened? They're all right aren't they?"

"We have a newspaper correspondent from…" Archie began to explain but stalled when he realized he didn't know anything about the fellow.

"The Sun Global," Straw Hat filled in for him, looking up slightly from scribbling in his notepad. Sticking out his paw to Archie, he said, "Albert Worthington, and you are?"

"Flight Lieutenant Archie Corn," the pilot replied with the shake, "And this is Flight Lieutenant Henry Badcock, and Pilot Officer Andras Dougherty."

The reporter was used to getting a cold shoulder from Britain's pilots, so the introduction was a bit of a surprise. America was still holding to its neutrality concerning the war, and since arriving in their country, he'd been an easy target for their desperate anger. "Pleased to meet you fellows," he responded, "Those are the gents in question, yes." Looking to Henry, he asked, "So I'm to assume you signed off on their flying abilities?"

Henry almost spit his tea out as his body tried to simultaneously laugh and swallow. When he had better control of himself, he managed to mumble something about the three barely being able to keep their wings straight and level.

"So they had no problems finessing the Spitfire into the air then," the fellow muttered to himself as he again scribbled on his note pad.

"I didn't say that," the former flight instructor barked.

Archie cleared his throat to get Henry's attention and then gave him a nod indicating calm was in order.

The reporter, an American Terrier, totally ignored the former instructor's comment and kept scribbling. "So what did you say then?"

"I said I signed off on them flying," the Bulldog told him in a calmer voice. "I was the chief instructor at Staverton, and Tops decided I should specifically be saddled with them when they came over from France want'n to join up. I even had to scrounge some cushions for the little chap to sit on just so he could see through the bloody gun sight."

"I heard Tobin got a 110 the other day," Andras spoke up, "And a shared kill on a DO over London. I say good show."

"How did you test their abilities?" the correspondent asked, nodding to the Corgi to confirm his statement while keeping an eye on Henry.

He had a good source of information now and he was not about to let it go. Nothing short of a scramble would keep him from dragging out the story now.

"Regardless of what they told me as to their actual flight hours," the Bulldog huffed, "They started out in a Tiger Moth. If they managed not to prang it do'n bumps and circuits, they got moved up to a Miles Master."

"That's a fighter?" the reporter asked, looking up suspiciously. "You moved them along that quickly?"

"Emergency fighter," Archie corrected. "It's fully aerobatic and quite a sweet flier; but only a fighter in case it's needed as it's much too slow. In fact, I believe the 613 actually has a few for squadron service; but it is really only an advanced trainer and service aircraft."

"With only one Vickers K all she's really good for is gunnery practice," Andras added helpfully. "I heard the American chap they call Red squirted his entire mag at a 110 first time out and never hit the bloody thing so I imagine he spent considerable time…"

"The emergency model has six guns," Archie interjected. Looking at the reporter, he told him, "It's a bit of a trick to hit the mark really. You have to lead him just enough and the tracer rounds don't always turn the trick. More often than not they alert the foe he's being fired upon. Experience counts for a lot in this." Looking back at Andras he added, "We have all been known to miss what we're shooting at."

"Is it true that all foreign applicants to the RAF have to submit to a short arm inspection?" Worthington asked next, moving on to something he'd heard and always been curious about.

"Well… it is part of the physical…" Henry began.

"With a full Wing Commander watching?" the reporter added quickly, one of his eyebrows moving up slightly with the question.

The color drained from Archie's face and for a second he thought he heard a very feminine giggle. "I… uh…"

"So tell me then," Henry fired up again, saving the Stag from swallowing his tongue. "Why all the interest in the Yanks, and why come over here instead of the 609 trying to dig up the dirt, eh? We wasn't born yesterday and they ain't the only ones to get a six on a Jerry aircraft. Archie here's got nine and a half, and young Andras four."

"And how many have you got?"

"Exactly none," the Bulldog told him with a wink, "But ask Archie there who he'd rather have as his wingman."

The reporter looked at the Stag who in turn nodded his head. "Exactly none other; Henry's the best. Did they really have to suffer a short arm inspection?"

"So I'm told. Of course I can't reveal my source," the Terrier replied with a smile. This one, his reporter's instincts told him, knew something.

"Careful there lad," Henry cautioned him, "Freedom of the press can easily be told off as a spy job, eh? That'll get you shot in a hurry at this time and place. Your country might be neutral but in case you haven't noticed there's a lot of Nazi spies and German sympathizers working your side of the street."

"So what's the word then," Andras asked, interrupting on purpose. "Are you Yanks going to pitch in like the lads in the 609, or will you let us die a slow and painful death at the paws of the Jackboots? I hear tell the American Ambassador… Joseph Kennedy I think his name is… was quite beside himself when the dozen came over and volunteered. I hear tell he actually ordered them home. If it wasn't for one of our friendlier MP's (Member of Parliament) they would have had to go too. Did they all come over as a group?"

"There are seven," the reporter told him. "Some came over when the Frenchies got run over and some came direct. Fiske was the first. He's quite the gentleman. We had a nice talk."

"I've met him too," the Corgi pilot claimed with a smile, "Back at the 32 Olympics. My father was a member of our Bobsled team. I was young, but I remember Fiske driving for the American team. He refused to go to Germany in 36. I suppose he had the good sense to see what was coming down the pike."

"Don't you mean 'Dogsled team'?" Archie teased, though he was surprised by this information. Andras had never mentioned it before. This caused a few chuckles and for a moment the Corgi was actually at a loss for words.

Looking directly at the reporter, Archie told him, "There were more Americans flying for us, but they claimed to be Canadian because of the neutrality laws. As I recall there were much more than a dozen in the group that came over from France. Some of them went over to Bomber Group. I believe those chaps are flying coastal patrols as pilots and navigators."

"Gunners too," Henry added, "and God bless'em for it. I can't say I could stand still and allow myself to be shot at the way those blokes do. It'd be like boxing without the footwork."

"You said 'were'?" the reporter asked Archie.

160

"I meant 'are,' but in some cases, I suppose 'were' is now appropriate. It was their wish to serve our country and King, and we shall ever remember that. As in most sports, the glory goes to one specialty or another and not so much to the chap who steadfastly holds up the middle, eh? "

"The fighter pilots're also in it for the thrill of fly'n the Spit, too," Henry added. "I know that for a fact. Fiske is actually quite adept at it, though I believe his group flies Hurricanes. He's got a cool head and doesn't press the risk button unless he has to. That's how you stay alive up there and make the enemy suffer for it. You play them like a fish letting them be the ones to do something stupid. That way they end up in your sights and not the other way around. He plays a good hand of Bridge too."

A whistle began to blow, and the pilot's all looked towards the Operations Shack.

"Time to get our marching orders," Henry muttered, tossing the remains of his tea on the ground. "I do hope the intel is good this time. It's bloody rotten when we all go up and end at the wrong address for the party."

"To tell the truth," Andras told the Bulldog, "I don't particularly like going up in three squadron strength. This 'Big Wing' formation experiment is just too unwieldy."

"We do tend to get in each other's way," Archie agreed. "I think groups of four up hunting is much better. At least then there is a reserve to catch the bombers on their way home as well."

"Never fear," Henry told the pair, "Tops'll soon see the light of this mistake. Come on; let's go hear the reports and then get on our way. I would guess from our visit today they're having us fly with the Yanks so that should carry the day, eh? What next... will they have us flying with the women, too?"

His conversation then trailed off into something about a certain Belgium vixen who did indeed know how to fly; and much more than that. (said with a wink and a chuckle)

Albert Worthington followed the trio to the Ready Room where the pilots were to receive their briefing. He'd been cleared for this and knew enough to be discrete in what he wrote. This would be reviewed by RAF Intelligence for content, in any case. before it could be wired back to the states.

While the squadron was gone, the Terrier toured the repair facilities on the field, taking his many notes. The maintenance being done to the damaged ships was nothing short of miraculous in most cases. He noted that everyone present constantly looked to the skies. If the enemy got through it was an immediate dash to the slit trenches. If the boys came back, it was then an immediate dash to the equipment they would need to refuel, rearm, and sometimes rescue. With a lot of luck the 'body snatchers' (ambulance team) would not be needed, but that was doubtful.

Within time, the fighters did come back again. One by one they landed and then taxied to a spot directed by the ground marshaller. As soon as a dismount was complete, the Kiwis placed a tow hook under the rear wheel and pulled the aircraft into a more concealed area.

As this was happening, the reporter was escorted back out to the line where he noted the damage done to aircraft that had previously been in good repair. When he came to Archie's ship, he found a hole in the wing large enough to stick his entire arm through, and its rudder looked as though it had been clawed by a demon. Passing around the back to get to the left side the newsman found half of the right elevator completely shot off.

"Henry chased that one off," the Stag told him as he unbuckled and stood in the cockpit.

"Did he get a kill?"

"Called it damaged. The old fellow is very honorable like that. He would never claim something he wasn't totally sure of."

"So your scores could be much higher than claimed, then?" The reporter scribbled this in his notebook.

"I suppose so," the Stag replied as he climbed down from the wing.

"Where is the old boy," the Terrier asked, "I'd dearly love to congratulate him and perhaps finish our conversation."

"You do what you must," the pilot told him as he came close, "But I would ask that you wait until tomorrow; perhaps at the pub after he's had a gallon or two."

"Why?"

Archie came to stand next to the Dog in the straw hat and said quietly, "Andras got his fifth victory today but right after he was sixed. His aircraft flamed. Henry is going to take that badly and you are an American after all. That might go hard for you. If we had your country's support, this entire battle may never have taken place. Andras was only nineteen years old."

"But I am here to support you," the reporter replied, "That's why I volunteered to come to England. You do have my sympathies."

"I'm sorry, sir, but sympathies do not win air battles; pilots and aircraft do. Henry and Andras butted heads when the old fellow first arrived, so they became special friends. Andras was full of himself and a bit of a hothead. Henry became his mentor and changed all of that. He would have bought the farm long ago except that Henry took him under his wing and taught him further; as he has the entire squadron. He's got a big heart, though he hides it well under that rough exterior he shows everyone."

"Look," the reporter told him, "I'll be totally honest with you; I'm hoping that what I write for my newspaper will help sway America's popular opinion. Trust me… I will be very liberal in your country's favor when laying on the words."

"You meant to say you are going to lie in our favor."

"Not lie, exactly, but certainly write in such a manner and with such emotion that it will sway the hearts of the most staunch 'keep your nose to your own business' sort of person."

"It's not the people you have to convince," the pilot replied acidly. His anger at losing a friend was finally taking charge of his patience. "It's the bloody politicians who make and enforce stupid laws that keep real and honest people like your seven Americans from freely giving of their services when and where they see the need. If it weren't for those few who have volunteered we would have been totally isolated with no hope of assistance at all. The fact that they're here at least tells us there are a few good people left where you come from. And so we wait and we watch while fighting for our very lives; praying that help will not come too late."

"I see," Worthington replied meekly.

The Stag sighed, "No… you don't. You're an American." He then turned his back and walked away.

Already, the ground crew was working on getting the damaged elevator off of the Egham Spit and a patch temporarily placed over the hole in her wing.

"How'd you fair, sir?" asked one of the Kiwis as Archie passed him.

"A 109 and half an 88," he replied without a smile. "Henry got the other half. Be sure it gets painted on his aircraft and do not take no for an answer. He earned it. I'll clear it with the commander."

§

The Sun Global – Sunday, August 3rd, 1940

163

Second Page found under 'WORLD AFFAIRS', bi-line Albert Worthington TODAY I CRIED FOR A MAN I DIDN'T KNOW

RAF pilot killed the same day he made ace.

Sometimes the story we read about adventure and glory is not all that it's cracked up to be. It is not a truth. It is not factual at all, and the main character is not always tall dark and handsome. There was a young fellow whom I met briefly yesterday, a reported hot head and arrogant person who, having met a mentor within the ranks of his squadron, became changed. The young fellow I met was sincere, honest, polite, and quite concerned for those with whom he served. Pilot Officer and Ace Andras Dougherty rose to the challenge of five victories but at a terrible cost. He was killed; and in the privacy of my hotel room, I cried for him. He was only nineteen years old and fighting to persevere in the protection of their very freedom… something all Americans are familiar with.

Andras Dougherty, red haired, laughing eyed, and with a natural curiosity for the things of life, wasn't the character in a story made up by some hack writer like the fellow pounding the keys in order to tell you of this event. He was a brash kid thrust into the world of grownups playing with their grownup play toys in a no holds barred game of conquest and destruction. He had to be brash just to make his way into the ranks of those he idolized; pilots such as Henry Badcock and Archie Corn. Through their leadership and camaraderie this young Corgi learned patience, cunning, and a quiet courage that so depicts the British people as a whole. Day after day the Germans come in the hopes of wearing these fellows down, and time after time these valiant Brits take to the air, repulsing every effort for what it is… unjust, violent, and illegal.

Their ground engineers, warmly known as Kiwis (flightless birds), are the best of the best; using what little they have to mend and patch and repair the ships that come back maimed and full of holes. I saw this with my own eyes. Archie Corn's aircraft had a hole in the wing large enough for me to pass my body through. By the following morning, when I had cried myself out, I saw in amazement there was no hole. Aluminum (to the Brits pronounced Al-oo-min'-e-um) is not wasted. Every little scrap is saved and sent back to be melted down for further use, along with every scrap of shot down German aircraft. Being cut off from the world, this small nation husbands everything it possibly can for the fight.

The one thing that is much harder to replace, however, is pilots like young Andras.

I was told that the day Andras shot down his first German bomber he knew he'd made a blunder. He admitted this to Henry Badcock sometime after they'd met, telling him, "I made a hell of a mistake with that one Henry; I went in too fast and had to slow down before I squirted him. It's a good thing his tail gunner was already done in."

It's hard to believe that the pilot's expression for shooting at another aircraft is 'squirting'. Perhaps this is a throwback to their childhood and the harmless toys with which they doused each other. I don't know this for sure but only speculate. I can tell you what I know for a fact; that these are a good bunch of fellows whose numbers fast dwindle.

Andras got a lot of Jerry planes after that first one. Some of his wing mates claim that in all he shot down at least twenty, but these pilots are the very stuff of honor and will never claim anything unless it can be positively confirmed. He was the youngest pilot in the squadron and he will be sorely missed. His smile and his good humored brashness were well known among his mates and they watched out for him as much as they could. I was shown a picture of 92 Squadron on a 'scramble order' dashing for their Spitters. All are wearing a deadly serious expression including this young chap... because that's just how it is.

You may have heard of some Americans who have already joined in the effort to turn back this German tide of aggression. I have met many of them and they all asked me the same question... 'When will the others come, Mr. Dougherty? They have to know how desperate things are.'

I lied and reassured them that indeed, everyone did know and they would be over soon enough, bringing with them the badly needed aircraft and supplies. You are not alone I told them and felt terrible in doing so.

The future of Britain at this moment in time does not look hopeful. Where the Tommy's repair their aircraft and do a good job of it, Adolf Hitler has all of Europe churning out new and better aircraft every day of every week. These are rushed to the front where they have ample pilots waiting to mount up.

From where I sit, and how I see it, the clock is ticking. Every day looks closer to the end. Even as I write this, the Germans are stockpiling barges with which to ferry their troops across the channel.

My young friend Andras did not die an easy death. As I understand it from the after action reports, he suffered a pilot's worst nightmare... stuck in the cockpit as your ship burns around you. He was a good fellow and not deserving of this. Though he was only nineteen he was a man who'd already lived a dozen lifetimes. 92 Squadron went up to meet what they thought were bombers and Andras was protecting one edge of their formation. It turned out there were no bombers this day. Seventy-five Me's were hovering at 30,000 waiting for them.

They came out of the sun and metal death was spit from the barrels of their guns.

The next day they went through Andras' locker. A Spitfire pilot get's $16 a week and he had near all of it tucked into an envelope addressed to his mother. That to me says a lot. He had expected his end and yet his thoughts were only of home.

Well, that's the story of a friend I knew for but a very short time.

You won't be hearing from me any longer, unless I am very lucky. I was always one to believe that you lead by example. Holding to this belief, with this article was included my resignation to The Sun Global. I won't be coming home any time soon as, unlike those subscribing to a particularly selfish 'America First' frame of mind, I see what must be done and have joined up with the RAF. It would seem that the time I spent joy riding in my little Piper Cub might actually now be put to good use. Flight Lieutenant Henry Badcock has even promised to personally teach me how to fly a Spitfire. No greater thrill can I imagine.

If I live past those first five most critical missions, Henry assures me I might actually have a 20/80 chance of seeing the end of the war. I am at peace with these odds.

To you Americans... you very true and caring Americans who I grew up being a part of, I will say this: If you saw your neighbor's house was afire would you stand idly by watching it burn; or would you rush to help douse the flames?

From where I sit writing this, I will tell you that I can see London burning my friends. I wish you well and will only add: 'Godspeed in getting your backsides over here.'

§

Henry Badcock was good to his word and with Archie Corn, taught Albert Worthington all they could teach him in their times between scrambles. He made five more than his first five critical missions scoring two and a half victories; a Messerschmitt 110, a Ju-88, and a shared victory with Henry Badcock on a Heinkel.

He was lost in heavy weather off of Dover on his eleventh mission. A fishing trawler reported hearing a crash and then finding the debris of a British aircraft. Among this and floating on the water like Moses' reed basket, was the former reporter's straw hat which he always carried with him for luck.

166

American volunteer pilots in the RAF, left to right:
Eugene 'Red' Tobin, Vernon 'Shorty' Keogh, Andrew 'Andy' Mamedoff,
Billy Fiske

Author's note: The sky can be a hard mistress even more so than enemy aircraft.

Billy Fiske *managed to land his Hurricane after suffering severe burns in a dogfight, but died from shock after his surgery. His aircraft blew up shortly after he was extracted from the cockpit by the ground crew.*

Eugene Quimby "Red" Tobin *encountered overwhelming odds on the first fighter sweep conducted by the British over the European continent. It was reported that he flew into a hillside.*

Vernon Charles "Shorty" Keogh *either suffered Cloud Disorientation or forgot to turn on his oxygen and crashed into the channel at high speed.*

Andrew B "Andy" Mamedoff *was lost in heavy weather when his squadron was sent north for further training.*

Uncle Billy's Batman

"Wake up, sir… you are needed!"

"What… yes… of course… is it a scramble?!" Flight Lieutenant Corn's eyes tried hard to open and focus but were resisting.

"No sir, not a scramble," the strange voice told him, "Lieutenant Badcock has stolen Commander Sheltie's motorbike and is running it up and down the airfield at full speed. If you don't get him to stop I'm afraid the Snowcaps might possibly shoot him for refusing to halt." (The Snowcaps were the RAF Military Police - *called this because of their white helmets.*)

"What?!"

Archie sat up on his cot and, blinking, looked at the Weasel standing next to him. "Who the devil are you?" he asked.

"I'm Uncle Billy's Batman."

"And where the bloody hell is…" he looked over to where Henry should be soundly snoring, "Oh… right… the motorbike."

From outside, there came the sound of a small engine revving to full throttle. It hit a crescendo and then seemed to fade a bit as it ran in a direction away from them.

"Has he been drinking?" Archie asked the strange fellow. "No, wait," he added after a moment's foggy thought, "We have to fly in the morning, and he'd never partake before that."

"Time is of the essence, sir," The Weasel told him. "I believe we should go now and puzzle things out later."

"Certainly," the Stag replied. Rising from where he sat he instructed, "Lead on."

Once outside they began to sprint along the flight line as if on some sort of strange call out. Archie, running in nothing more than his boxer shorts, noticed other people equally busy in the near darkness.

Mostly these were the Kiwi's trying to do maintenance upon the aircraft, but there were also the ever present sentries posted about watching for saboteurs. This was almost as much a threat as the Luftwaffe. A grenade tossed into a cockpit, or worse, into an ammunition supply, would be devastating. Most of those, he saw, were looking nervously in the direction of the motorbike's small red tail light. Two, however, wearing white helmets and MP armbands, began running a strange sort of footrace with him and the Weasel. Their intent, the Stag knew, did not come so much from concern for the pilot on the motorbike as it did for the parked aircraft which might possibly be damaged.

This footrace continued for a time with Henry, his nightshirt rippling in the night, always cutting around them and then racing off to the other end of the grass strip at full speed. His voice bellowed as he did this; as if he were a knight of the kingdom charging forth against some unknown enemy. No matter how much Archie called out, the errant Bulldog appeared oblivious. Finally, after a good half an hour of this frustrating chase, the motorbike swung in and stopped in front of their sleeping quarters, which was nothing much more than a tent set upon wooden decking on the ready line.

As the four drew closer, they could see the motorbike's small shrouded light shining dimly on the grass before the tent's entrance. Henry's stocky silhouette faced them. He was clearly not moving and the bike's small engine ominously putt putted away in idle.

"Control," Henry suddenly called out, "This is Bad Boy, over." There was a pause, and then he called again, "Control... do you read?"

The two Snowcaps, well in the lead of Archie and the strange little batman, stopped running and raised their rifles to the ready. Advancing cautiously at a now slower pace, they sighted in on the Bulldog's chest. Archie saw this and bellowed, "Belay that you idiots! Open your breaches; I've got this handled! We fly in the morning and I need this fellow as my wingman. He can't fly if you shoot him full of holes!"

The Stag, running up from behind, deliberately placed himself between the two MP's and his friend, keeping his back to them as he faced Henry directly.

"Spitfire Bad Boy, this is Control, over," he called urgently, "What is your malady?"

"I've taxied and I can't take off," the other pilot called back. His voice told of his apparent frustration. "The old girl has lost her legs and doesn't wish to go airborne for some reason. Have you any suggestions, over?"

In the near distance, someone yelled out, telling them to 'Shut the bloody hell up, I'm trying to sleep over here!'

Archie ignored the shouted imperative and continued walking towards his friend. "Did you remove the gust locks from your elevators, over?"

"Didn't see any on the walk-around, so I figured the Kiwis pulled 'em," the former flight instructor replied, still talking as if on the radio. "It's a possibility, I suppose."

"What kind of game are you playing at, old friend?" Archie muttered to himself as he slowly approached the motorbike.

"I do believe he's asleep, sir," whispered a voice to his right.

Glancing sideways, the Stag found Uncle Billy's Batman still by his side, helping block the Snowcap's aim. "I've seen it happen in the hospital wards," the Weasel told him, "But never on a motorbike."

"Would your charge be the same Uncle Billy as the 116's Squadron Commander?" Archie whispered to him.

"None other, sir. He calls me his 'luck', though personally I don't think I've ever won at a game of cards or dice. Good luck for him, perhaps, but not so good for me; he can be a real arse when he's a mind to be."

"Then why are you here and not there? If you were my 'luck,' I don't think I' let you wander about like this."

"I was won in a card game, sir; or rather my services were won by your Commander Sheltie. He wagered his motorbike, and being that he already has a batman, he allotted me to you and Lieutenant Badcock. Spades were called trump and he pretty much ran the deck. With his victory, I was sent straight out. Because of this, there was no forewarning, as you were sound asleep. I do hope they remember in the morning because they were both quite potted when the wager was set."

"So you were not so lucky, then?"

"I suppose it all depends how this turns out now, doesn't it?"

"And Henry?"

"He was asleep too, sir. I turned my back to straighten your uniforms, and he slipped out without so much as a giggle."

"What's that, Terrance?" Henry asked, turning to look at the motorbike's empty sidecar. The Stag's focus was immediately drawn to this. "Now how the bloody hell am I going to do that? You know good and well that raising the gear will put the old girl in the dirt."

Archie's senses immediately began waving a very large red flag. "Bad Boy, this is Control," he called to him, "Who are you speaking with, please?"

"Flight Lieutenant Terrance Chrysanthemum, if you please; or if you don't please, I suppose. He's flying my wing and just told me to raise my gear immediately… but I'm still on the ground…"

Before the Bulldog could even finish, the Stag had leapt forward and dragged his friend from the bikes saddle. Throwing him to the ground, he jumped on top of him and yelled, "EVERYONE DOWN!"

Everyone in the small group immediately dove to the ground with him. No sooner had they done so, an explosion ripped the night apart, lighting the area in a huge orange flash.

As they were showered with dirt, he heard Henry's voice bellow out, "Control… we've got us a bloody situation here."

§

Archie woke to find himself sitting in a small pasture full of small yellow flowers. The sky was clear with only wispy clouds slowly moving within the blueness. The air was pleasantly cool, and a breeze kissed his face even as he scanned the sky for aircraft.

A paw found his cheek from behind, and he recognized its touch immediately. "I suppose this means I've gone for a Burton, doesn't it?" he asked.

"The only Burton you shall have my love, is one pulled from a tap," Terrance told him, "Though I'm not sure it really tastes all that good. As I recall, the actual beer has a rather musty taste to it."

The vixen slowly came around and knelt in front of him. Dressed in her flight gear, the goggles full up on her forehead, she told him in a quiet voice, "We have just this moment, I'm afraid, but I will take what I can get." Her soft smile near melted his heart.

"If dying meant I could stay here with you, then I would gladly…"

The vixen placed a finger on his lips. "You must never say that, Archie."

"NEVER SAY THAT!" boomed Henry's voice, sounding a very long ways off. "YOU WILL NOT GO FOR A BURTON ON MY WATCH!"

Archie felt himself being shaken, and he could hear the sounds of the 'body snatchers' motoring up, their bell jingling.

There were other sounds too… aircraft engines being started and revved as the airfield came to life like a hornet's nest stoned from its place by an unwitting child. Commands were shouted as the fire brigade, arriving first, began working on the carnage. Fire hoses were dragged out, charged, and dutifully discharged, effectively extinguishing the small fire.

"I'm not gone," the Stag managed, his eyes still closed. "Stop shaking me Henry, you're making my brains rattle." When the shaking stopped, he spit dirt from his mouth and opened his eyes. "What happened?" he asked when he could. "Where's Uncle Billy's Batman?"

"Who?" the Bulldog asked.

"Uncle Billy's Batman," Archie replied and then paused to hawk and spit. "He's a Weasel… Commander Sheltie won him in a card game from Commander Billy of the 116. He told me so. You'd stolen the motorbike again, and we were chasing you around the field. He woke me up from a sound sleep, and we came out of the bungalow to talk some sense to you… but you were sleepwalking."

A star shell went off and the area was bathed in an eerie luminescence as the entire airfield came to the alert. The Stag found himself looking at a very worried friend who was quite awake and dressed in his flight gear exactly as Terrance had been. Looking down to his own body, he found that he too was dressed in a like fashion. The command 'HALT!' sounded out in the night, followed by gunshots.

"What's that?" the Stag asked, "What just happened, and where is Uncle Billy's Batman?"

"I'm guessing we had a saboteur sneak onto the field," Henry told him with a shake of his head. "T'was either that or Jerry had a dud thunk down on their last attack. We could have missed one during the clean up, and perhaps it decided now was the perfect time to go off. Though I prefer not to believe the boys could be that lax in their guard duties; I think more likely it was a grenade."

"That makes sense, I suppose," Archie agreed, but stopped talking as he heard another series of gunshots.

"Gor," he moaned, "You'd think Jerry'd already landed. I do hope they don't begin firing in our direction. Help me up now before they insist I take a ride in the 'meat wagon'."

The star shell fizzled out, and but for the dying embers of their sleeping quarters, the night became very dark.

Grabbing arms, Henry helped the Stag rise. As he did so, there was the noise of a motorbike, and Commander Sheltie arrived on scene. Dismounting, he strode to the two fliers. "We've had an intrusion, but they got the blighter. Is everything all right here?"

"Never better, sir," Henry reported cheerily, "Though I'm afraid our new sleeping quarters have been blasted to kindling. It's a miracle we weren't inside. I couldn't sleep and was gone to check the aircraft. Old Arch here apparently went sleep walking at exactly the right moment."

"I see," their Commander responded, a note of relief in his voice. Looking to the Stag, he questioned him directly, "Are you all right Lieutenant?"

"Yes, sir," Corn replied. "I do think, however, that if it hadn't been for Uncle Billy's Batman, I would've been done in right enough."

"Who's that?" Sheltie asked, and the Bulldog coughed loudly, trying to get the other Dog's attention.

"Someone he dreamed up, sir," he offered softly when Sheltie looked at him. He made a circled finger motion towards his head that suggested his friend might have suffered a concussion and was not yet quite right.

"It certainly was the oddest of dreams, sir," Archie added softly, "He was a Weasel and told me you won him in a card game; or rather you won his services."

There was a moment's silence as the Commander looked at the pair in the darkness. He then turned to his motorbike and called out, "Corporal Higgins, front and center, if you please."

There was a movement in the night as someone struggled to get out of the motorbike's sidecar, and then a smallish Airman came around to where they stood and dropped his kit to the ground. Coming to attention, he said, "Here, sir."

"Gentlemen," Commander Sheltie told them, "This is Corporal Richard Higgins. Corporal Higgins, this is Flight Lieutenant Corn," he said, motioning to the Stag, "And Flight Lieutenant Badcock. This is the pair I told you about. So long as you do not object taking care of both you'll have a home here at the 92." Looking back to the fliers, he told them, "I did indeed win the Corporal's services in a card game with Uncle Billy of the 116. You've both done more than your share so he is meant to lessen your burden a bit. I expect you will not abuse this privilege."

Archie cleared his throat. "Excuse me for asking, sir, but... are you presently potted?"

"I beg your pardon?"

"I believe, sir," Higgins interjected, "Lieutenant Corn was inquiring as to what you had for dinner; the one you had with Commander Billy, sir. They had potted meat, Lieutenant, but it was a very good dinner none the less; prepared by my own paw."

"You are Uncle Billy's luck, are you not?" Archie asked him.

The Weasel smiled, his pointy teeth shining in the darkness. "Indeed he did call me that, but it would seem he was not so lucky tonight; so I suppose that will disperse the myth."

The Sergeant in charge of the fire company came and reported to Sheltie that the fire was out and, for the time being, he was going to let his lads rest. They would come back with the sun and recheck the area. He did confirm that the damage was too small to have been an actual aerial bomb. With this in mind it was quickly ordered that guards would be doubled against further incursions.

"Now where were we?" the Commander asked them when he was done.

"We were talk'n of luck," Henry told him, "Of which I think old Archie here has had quite a good run of it."

"And a good thing too," Sheltie replied. "I do hope it continues because your four Spits are up with the sun. Go grab some tea and biscuits, and then come to the Ready Room. Control has already sent in the day's orders."

With that, he was back on his motorbike and motoring off to the 'ready shack'.

"You're sure your noggin's up for this?" Henry growled, placing his paw on the Stag's shoulder.

"What choice do I have?" The pilot asked in return.

"Give me a moment, sirs," Higgins told them, "And I'll have tea and toast for you. Five minutes more than that, and I'll have a hot meal you can wolf down before flying."

"Wolf?" Henry asked with a raised eyebrow. "Please don't tell me you're a punner."

"Not meant, sir, but it was a good one, wasn't it?" the Weasel chuckled. "Lieutenant Corn, I do hope my being here does not change your run of good luck. Shall I bring something for your head as well?"

The Stag extended his hand, and it was, in turn, firmly gripped by the Corporal. "Please do, my head is indeed pounding," the pilot told him, "Somehow, I don't think your presence will affect my luck, except to the better of course. Do you think you could manage some fried tomatoes with that breakfast we are to wolf down?"

"Certainly, sir."

With that, Uncle Billy's Batman was off at the double. Though it actually took fifteen minutes, he was quite good to his word.

John Bull(dog)

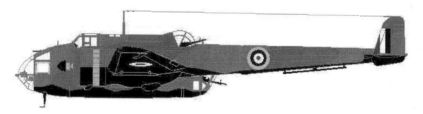

Sergeant John Hannah was the wireless operator/air gunner of an 83 Squadron Hampden bomber. He was awarded the Victoria Cross on 15 September 1940. During a bombing mission of landing barges gathered in the French port of Antwerp, his aircraft was hit by anti-aircraft fire and set ablaze. He stayed with his pilot and fought the fire, first with the two extinguishers and then with his hands, finally extinguishing the flames. This was done amidst leaking fuel tanks and machine gun ammunition that was cooking off in the flames and firing in every direction. His actions allowed the pilot to return their aircraft to base.

He is the youngest recipient of the VC for aerial operations.

(Note: The Victoria Cross is Great Britain's equivalent of the United States' Medal of Honor.)

§

Billy Braddock was feeling even more feisty than he usually did after a long day of video gaming. The Highland Hound was drunk and had caused enough noise in the pub that he was finally physically subdued and coldly tossed out into the street. It took five of them to do it; even though all of the five were old enough to be his grandfather and then some. At the time he'd felt proud of that. In a perverse way he felt he'd played the game on its hardest level and beaten the odds.

Before he was finally ejected, he'd faced each in his drunken anger. "You're not all so special! What're you here to celebrate... Battle of Britain Day? I'm a gamer so I've done all of that and more! I'm the best... the top Dog! All you are is old!"

He pointed his finger at one aged Bulldog who sat back in the corner watching. "You think you're pretty tough Old Bull? Bring it on and do your best cuz this here Hound ain't no fuk'n lightweight."

The Bulldog had laughed a hard derisive laugh and then given him a very odd look; one that said 'be careful what you wish for'.

That's exactly when Billy's lights went out. The pub's bar maid, having had enough of his bad manners, finally smashed a large beer pitcher over his head during his tussle with the five. It was thick glass and didn't break but easily turned the trick. With the impact the youngster's eyes rolled up into his head and his body slowly eased itself to the floor.

§

A massive paw gripped him by the collar and dragged him up off of the sidewalk. "Wake up Sunshine," a voice growled in his ear. "You had your fun so now it's time for you and me to go for a little ride."

"What? Where? Who?"

Billy attempted to get his feet under himself. He had a splitting headache and every word the voice spoke was punctuated by this pain.

"You're a reporter now?" it laughed harshly, "Just a moment ago you was the great drunken video game hero mak'n fun of those whose family lived what you only play at. You're ballsy, I'll give you that; but you're also very ignorant and disrespectful."

The large Dog pressed his face to that of the Hound and snorted. He looked just like the old fellow in the pub, only much, much younger. "My name is John Bulldog," he growled, "And I take care of mine what took care of me when the chips were down. You disgust me. I seen you thinking you're so fuk'n brave by railing on the old and worn down; then I had this thought that maybe you'd like to tag along for a night when the

176

ones your silly arsed games represent did their best in doing what had to be done. What say you to that, Billy Braddock? You gets to do your game for real, this time; and then you tell me how good you are."

For the first time, Billy noticed the heavy smell of smoke in the air and heard the jangling bell of a fire truck as it passed close by on its way to somewhere; presumably to whatever was on fire.

"Where am I?" he asked.

"Kent," the fellow replied, "The same place you started from." Releasing his collar, the Bulldog furthered, "It's now August 13th, 1940. Jerry's been pounding the area, and they're well armed with information and equipment. The bomber pilots all have pictures of their targets taken by Lufthansa on supposed 'weather over flights' during the years leading up to this moment. That makes it a tad hard to miss don't you think? When you know sump'ns com'n, you can plan like that." He paused to spit, his anger clearly showing through. "Their fighter pilots are also armed to the teeth and out to wreck what's left of our air force. Kent's just been bombed, and lucky you got away without a scratch." Grabbing the Dog's arm, he spun him about so he could see that the pub where they'd been drinking was gone. It had been hit by a five hundred pound bomb. What was left was merrily burning.

"Shouldn't we help?" the Hound finally asked half-heartedly.

"The pub owner and his family are dead," the Bulldog hissed at him, "There's nothing there to help with and the fire crews have bigger fires to worry about. This little one'll be left to go out by itself. If you'd bothered ask'n in between your beers, you would've been told their relatives rebuilt it in 1942."

Flash thoughts began going off like fireworks in Billy's mind. He saw a mother and her children gathered around the kitchen table for dinner. They were all there one moment and gone the next; buried under brick and rubble after a stick of bombs went off within their once peaceful neighborhood.

There was also a church holding evening services destroyed and a factory where engines were made obliterated.

In all, one hundred homes, two churches, five factories, and a school, were all damaged or destroyed; bombed into nothingness as the sun set and the night began.

"My God," the Hound managed.

"That's right," the other Dog replied, "My God; war really does hurt."

There was a moment as the Hound looked around himself. "I'm

dreaming aren't I?"

"No."

"It's a new 3D reality video game, then?"

"Not even close."

There was a distant explosion as a fire found a ruptured gas pipe. Billy cringed. "It's an on-line game then?" he finally managed.

"You're being treated to the real deal," the other Dog told him. "Remember these figures gamer, cuz every game – real or imaginary – begins with the numbers: 63,879 vehicles, 2,472 artillery pieces, 8000 Bren machineguns, 90,000 rifles, 76,097 tons of shells and ammunition."

The Hound blinked. "What's that; what we have to play with?"

"It's what we don't have to play with," John Bulldog told him and then spit upon the sidewalk again. "It was what the army left behind at Dunkirk. Operation Dynamo got the lads home, and God bless the small boat sailors that made it happen; but we lost enough of our supplies that Jerry knows we got next to nothing left to fight with. We also lost a good deal of our aircraft and experienced pilots try'n to defend a country whose government just up and threw in the towel." He paused, letting the information sink in and then told him, "The French had the biggest and best army and Jerry went through'em like a hot knife through butter. The only thing stop'n the German steamroller now is the channel and the RAF... which you are now a very minor part of."

Billy looked down and finally noticed the uniform he was wearing. "No," he said softly.

Whether this was meant as a 'no I won't do it' or 'no I don't believe this is happening', the Bulldog didn't bother to find out. Grabbing the Hound's arm he growled, "Let's go airman, time to mount up. You've got a real mission to fly. Every aircraft available has been ordered airborne to fight. You belong to Bomber Command now and we all have our jobs to do. Now march."

Billy was roughly pushed down the street.

"One of my aircraft," he was told from behind, "has diverted to West Malling in need of a gunner... that would be you, Mr. Gamer. I'll give you odds that yur gonna die today, so you best make peace with your maker; and that's just the way it is."

§

John Bulldog and his charge stood near the grass strip watching as an oddly shaped bomber landed in the twilight. It was ominously met by the 'body snatchers'. In the darkness of the night, one of the crew was taken away in their ambulance, and then the aircraft was quickly topped up with fuel.

As they approached, the pilot who was standing by the nose of the aircraft having a smoke, came to attention and saluted. Billy, still not sure exactly what was happening, was told to wait by the wingtip while the Bulldog continued forward.

"At ease," John told the pilot softly. "Air Commodore John Bulldog," he said extending a paw, "And you are?"

"Pilot Officer Conner, sir."

The Bulldog noted the other Dog's accent. "You're Canadian… thank you for serving. I was made aware of your radio message and got you a replacement for your gunner. The fellow is a bit raw but he should do." The Bulldog turned and looked back at a now flight mission equipped Billy Braddock standing a few feet away in the darkness. "Completely raw actually," he added, "But it keeps you from being completely empty in the back."

(*Author's note: Most all flight crews were very new to their posts – bomber pilots were only required 150 hours training flight time on their aircraft.*)

The pilot shot a glance at Billy and then whispered, "He's got no experience a'tall, sir? I mean, for God's sake, does he even know how to charge the guns?"

"I'll teach him personally," the Bulldog replied, "and quick. Your gunner is out of commission with the shits and heaves. That's why you declared and diverted to Manston. That leaves you a man short and you need to get airborne before Jerry comes back. Where does your mission go?"

"Antwerp. Intel came in that there's German barges gathered there. Eventually they'll be used in the invasion when it comes so we're to dart in, bomb the bastards and dart back out again. It feels good to be doing something other than 'gardening sorties' (*sewing anti-shipping mine fields*) for a change."

"Sounds simple enough." The Bulldog smiled, "You took a great risk landing with a hot bomb load; I admire you for that. Strike a blow for Old Blighty says I. God knows we've been too much on the defensive. We have to let Jerry know we're not gonna give in."

"Simple, hell…" the pilot growled, "We're most likely dead, and you know it. Between the flak and the fighters and these slow old crates…" he sighed, "The least we could hope for would be heavier guns to fight'em off with, sir."

"But you're going anyhow?" Billy asked from the near darkness. The pair turned to him, and he felt very small under their gaze.

"I'll take as many of the goose steppers with me as I can," the pilot told him casually. "My sons will grow up free if I have anything to say about it. You're obviously green and haven't seen what we've seen. They'll be wanting Canada next; just like they wanted France. Where do you think they'll go after taking Britain, eh? I'll tell you where, across the ocean snapping up everything they can grab. By God, I for one intend to make them pay dearly for their greed!"

The pilot frowned, giving this new fellow a thought. He was only a little older than Billy and carried himself straight backed with an apparent lack of fear. His disapproval was evident in the look.

"Very well, Commadore," he told the Bulldog, "If you think he'll complete us, I'll accept him, but for God's sake please make sure he knows not to shoot our tail off. You know the gun stops don't always work."

"My name is…" the Hound began, coming forward and extending his paw.

The pilot immediately rounded on him. "Did I ask you to report, airman?! Sir! The correct way to address me is 'sir,' you bleeding poor excuse for a mongrel! Who the hell gives a fig what your name is! You just guard my tail, and if we make it back alive, I'll ask your name the same time I bring you a beer at the pub."

§

Charging the twin machine guns mounted in the dorsal position was not as difficult as Billy imagined, though it was harder than simply pushing a button on his game controller. The linked ammunition was fed through a flexible rectangular feed line to the outside of each gun while the empty rounds fell down to a hole in the floor routed by a deflection apparatus fastened to the inboard side of the receivers. The gun position was not the glassed turret the Hound was used to playing with, but a simple open area protected from the slip stream by a clear Perspex fairing the back of which was open to the darkness of the night.

Bombers of this time did not have the huge engines produced in the later years of the war, so this arrangement was a weight saving method used by both sides. A powered turret, by itself, could weigh as much as a thousand pounds. The twin guns were gimbaled on a bar and Billy

180

could easily move them from side to side. Fixed metal stops kept the pair from moving into any area where they would do damage to the aircraft's twin tails, but the intention of the stop was only to alert the gunner. He got past them by lifting the barrels up to get them over, and many gunners took the risk of removing them altogether. The premise seemed easy enough to the Hound, though the sight he had to use was non-adjustable and primitive; nothing lit up or glowed or showed any evidense of an enemy hidden in the darkness of the night.

A paw tugged at the leg of his flight suit. The suit had been hastily procured at the West Malling fighter base and was a bit baggy; but warmth was its goal, not a fashionable fit. Turning with difficulty in the cramped confines of the crew compartment, the Hound looked forward at the radio operator. His bulky parachute pushed against the ship's bulkhead, and he made an angry face in his frustration. He was not used to such restrictions in his electronic world.

"You'll get used to that," the other Dog told him in a friendly manner, "There's not too much room in here. That's the reason she's called the 'flying suitcase'. The Hampden's a good ship though and our pilot's seasoned. My name's John, what's yours?"

"Billy."

Recognizing the accent, the radio operator smiled. "I'm from Glasgow; you?"

"The same; though my family moved to Kent in 2001. Da moved for the job and that left me to deal with the kids in school mak'n fun of m'accent. That dinna, set well I suppose; probably why I play th'games for so many hours. I kept to m'self pretty much."

The radio operator gave him a strange look.

"What?"

"Two thousand and one? What numb'r is that? Did ya make a mistake, or did my ears fool me a bit?"

From forward, the pilot yelled for his crew to hook into the intercom and then get buckled up for takeoff.

Thinking quickly, Billy replied, "Did I say that? Must be m'nerves… it's m'first mission. I meant thirty-one. How the hell do you move about in here? It's so cramped."

"Pretty much ya don't. So yur a virgin? I've got just over seventy hours now, so I'm a bit of an old timer I suppose. Never fear, the missions'r as bad as ever'thin you've heard and then some."

With a whining, splutter the port engine turned over and then coughed to life.

"Best ya buckle in," the radio operator advised as the starboard engine next came to life, "Take off can be a bit bumpy; especially with Jerry bombing the runways so regular."

§

As soon as the landing gear was tucked in, the order 'take stations' was given by the aircraft's pilot. Unbuckling, Billy moved to his guns and went through the charging procedures as had been briefly demonstrated by John Bulldog. During landings and take off, all guns were kept in an unloaded state against the prospect of a crash or hard landing. In such a case, a loaded weapon could discharge, possibly hitting the ground crew or other aircraft in the vicinity. For this very same reason it was rare that a bomber would land with an unused rack of bombs. With the safety pins all removed just before the mission, an inadvertent explosion by a jostled bomb would be absolutely deadly; better to dump your load in the channel.

John went to his radio and began tapping on the Morse key. Alternately listening and then tapping, again he soon had the short message un-coded. Pressing his 'talk' button, he told the crew, "Command says to proceed."

"Roger," the pilot called back, "We'll be flying over at ten thousand so we won't need oxygen." To Billy, he specifically said, "Dorsal… Wait for my command to test your guns. We don't do that over land if we can avoid it. Bullets cause lead rain, and we shant be killing our own by being stupid."

Pressing his own 'talk' button on the intercom, Billy gave a, 'roger, guns charged, safeties on,' and then moved them around on their mount getting the feel of aiming forty pounds of steel. He looked out at the stars which were very bright. With no moon, the starlight appeared magnified. In the distance, his peripheral vision caught a smudge eclipse of a small portion of the glittering brightness.

"BOGEY BACK THERE!" he cried out, forgetting to push the 'talk' button. Swinging his guns in that direction, he peered hard through the sight trying to find what he'd seen. A paw patted him on his thigh and he jumped. Glancing back he found the radio operator right next to him, his body squeezing up next to his. "WHAT'S A BOGEY?" he yelled to be heard.

"UNIDENTIFIED AIRCRAFT… I SAW IT BACK THERE HEADING THAT WAY!" he yelled back, pointing.

"Unknowns are called a 'foo fighters'," John told him by pressing his talk button, "Probably an inbound Jerry bomber. Hopefully, the lads from one of the fighter squadrons will pick him up. I need to report it. If you see a 'bandit' approaching from back here you press the button and report it and then you shoot, got that? They do have night fighters. It's important you tell our pilot so he can maneuver."

Pressing his 'talk' button, Billy responded, "Roger."

"I got that, John," Conner called back from the cockpit, not more than twelve feet in front of them.

The pair looked forward and in the soft glow of the instrument lights they could see the pilot flying their aircraft. Below him the navigator/bomb aimer had his sextant and charts out, plotting their position. He patted the pilot on the leg and gave him a thumbs up.

"Daniel says we're over the channel. Send your message on the inbound bomber, and then both of you clear your guns."

"WHAT'S HE MEAN CLEAR MY GUNS?" Billy asked without pressing his talk button, "I JUST LOADED THEM."

"HE MEANS TEST FIRE THEM. GIVE A BURST OF FIVE ROUNDS SO YOU KNOW THEY'RE PROPER READY, THEN SETTLE DOWN AND WATCH THE SKY SHARP LIKE."

John made his way to the radio and briefly tapped on the Morse key. When he was done, Billy aimed his guns out to the aircraft's left rear quarter and pressed his triggers. There was a spat of flame from the barrels and shell casings rained down through the ejection chutes to the hole in the floor. The heavy vibration coming to his paws startled him; it was nothing like his game controller. He'd never before fired a real weapon, and the feeling was exhilarating. His euphoria made him feel invulnerable. Let them come; he'd shoot every last one of them.

As the new gunner stood peering out into the blackness, he heard another machine gun fire a brief volley. Looking down, he found the radio operator now lower down and crouched just aft of his position. He was holding on to the single ventral gun's handles and quickly secured the weapon in readiness for use. As he watched the dark silhouette he heard John's voice on the intercom.

"Ventral gun ready," he reported.

Pressing the 'talk' button, Billy added, "Yeah, my guns're ready too."

"Would that be the dorsal mount?" the pilot inquired.

"Yes."

"Then report the dorsal guns are ready," Connor told him acidly,

"Where in hell did you train? You must report concisely what you mean gunner. There is no room on a mission for sloppy speech."

"Bomb Aimer's gun ready," Daniel reported from forward. There was a note of sympathy in his voice for the new comer.

"Good," Connor told him. "What's our ETA to target, please?"

"Forty minutes, sir."

"Very good. John, let me know of any inbound report messages from Squadron. We're about an hour behind them. I'd like to know their luck and any target information they can share. New fellow... you just keep your bloody eyes peeled and report properly if you see something."

"Yes sir."

Billy again stared out into the inky blackness of the night. Emotionally he was bruised from being dressed down by the pilot. This was not something he was used to. Pretty much, in his life, he was simply ignored. In turn he ignored the world. This sort of social interaction was new to him.

The depth of the sky and the amount of stars it contained amazed him. Living in the city and mainly staying indoors, he'd never noticed much more than the moon when it was full. The night air at altitude was also very cold.

He felt the paw on his thigh and looked back to find the other Hound near again. Moving his face close to Billy's ear, he yelled, "KEEP MOVING AS MUCH AS YOU CAN; IT'LL KEEP YOU AWAKE AND A BIT WARMER."

Billy gave him a thumbs up and a smile. The radio operator gave him a nod and a smile back. He then flicked on a small electric torch. The light, Billy noticed, was pin prick small, but it was enough for the radio operator to make the short distance back to his station without stumbling.

(Author's note: British bomber crews, flying mostly at night, would reverse the reflective cones in their flashlights so only a small hole was next to the bulb allowing just a pin prick of light to shine. In this way, the use of the light would not spoil their night vision. This information gleaned from watching a story on the sci-fi channel about a haunted bomber in a British museum – they reported seeing such a light moving about in the back of the fuselage, and an old RAF crew member wrote and told of the practice.)

Turning back to his open gun port, the gamer began watching out the back for enemy aircraft. Occasionally he would see a bluish flickering light which might have been an engine exhaust, but then again could have easily been a star... there were so many of them in the sky.

Having been lost in his thoughts, the new gunner must have certainly dozed because, with a jarring thump, his right machine gun came up and smashed him on the chin. For a moment, the Hound saw stars and they were not the stars in the sky.

"Bring her to six thousand," he heard in his headset, "And right eight degrees. Bomb dispersal is set for cluster."

The bomber took a distinct downward slant. and Billy had to hang on to the gun rail to steady himself. Looking down, he found the radio operator now crouched at his gun again, intently watching the sky below the aircraft. The flash of a searchlight coming to life briefly illuminated him through the glass, and the colors of his Mae West life preserver became a harsh yellow against the drab coloring of his flight suit. His parachute was firmly in its place across his backside and looked as though it might be a counterweight on a piece of machinery.

"Steady on now, sir," Daniel reported. "I can see the wharf, and it's packed solid with barges. I think we surprised'em good."

A series of 'krumps and thumps' shook the bomber as the German anti-aircraft batteries came to life.

Billy stole a look forward and found the pilot's silhouette sharply contrasted against the anti-aircraft fireworks show and searchlights illuminating the sky. The Dog hardly moved in his intense concentration on all things he needed to pay attention to in order to give the Bomb Aimer what he needed. In this brief glimpse, the Hound understood that the bomber was now flying straight and level which made them a sitting duck should they be found.

There was an explosion some three hundred feet below the aircraft. The vibration of it rattled through the aluminum skin. This was followed by another and another and another as more and more searchlights came to life seeking them out. Tracers now streaked into the sky all around them as smaller guns blindly groped the sky in the hopes of making a hit.

"Anything from behind?" the pilot calmly called over the intercom.

"Negative ventral," John called back.

Billy stole a glance out the back, doing his best to look over top of his guns. "Negative dorsal," he reported.

The bomber jiggled and then shook hard with a closer explosion. Then the bottom seemed to fall out of the floor as the aircraft lost altitude like a rock thrown into a well. The engine pitch hit a crescendo and then flattened out again as it struggled to climb back up to the height called out for by the Bomb Aimer. On the run in, he was actually in charge of the aircraft, not the pilot; though the latter was always at the controls. The wings rocked violently left and right as Pilot Officer Connor struggled to stay on course.

A search light speared them, seemingly hungry for their blood. Two more quickly followed and the flak began pounding the sky around them in deadly earnest. With a loud explosion, something blasted through the Perspex of the dorsal position's fairing. Billy felt pieces of it strike his face as something whistled past his ears. A warm trickle immediately began flowing down from the wound and he screamed in a purely survival reaction.

Below him, John ripped out a long burst with his machine gun, and at least one light winked out.

"Ten seconds to drop," Daniel's voice calmly called out. His total concentration was now on the target sight, his right fist clutching the 'pickle' switch that would release their bomb load.

"Nine... eight..." The aircraft shuddered heavily, momentarily interrupting his count. "Four... three... two... one... bombs dropped!"

With the loss of four thousand pounds, the aircraft lurched skyward just as it took a direct hit from a German 88 millimeter. The explosion was incredible, and a fire immediately started in the radio operator's area close behind where Billy stood. The pilot's canopy was simultaneously holed, and the sudden draft of wind blew the flames directly at the dorsal gunner. They engulfed him, scorching his face. He screamed and beat at the flames suddenly dancing upon his chest. His mind stuttered with the pain he was feeling, Getoutgetoutgetout...'

With an almost silent whistling sound, a fire extinguisher was played upon him. Its cold white cloud brought instant relief. Billy's eyes saw and his mind recorded as everything around him began to play out in the slow motion randomness of combat.

He could clearly see John now in the light of the flames turning from him with the fire extinguisher and spraying down the pilot who was also on fire. Connor had never left his position nor did he stop flying the aircraft. "Oxygen on, lads," he called over the intercom. "We're heading up to twelve thousand. I'll get you out over the channel where you can bail out, and may God watch over you."

His right paw played on the throttles, and he smoothly pushed them forward to their maximum. The engines now screamed in their struggle to climb.

In the wind, Billy could smell the leaking gasoline. It was raw, it was heady; it reminded him of when he was trying to siphon out a litre from the family car for his scooter and had taken a good mouthful. He retched, vomiting on the deck of the aircraft.

The flames then came back and were dancing around him. He swatted at them as they reached out to his flight suit, and he yelled again in his sudden panic.

"Right, then," called Daniel from the front of the aircraft, "We're over the channel. Best we jump now so we're still close to shore."

"Go!" the pilot commanded, and he needn't say it twice.

Looking back through the small cabin area of the Hampden, the bomb aimer saw John, his flight suit on fire, still battling the flames. The Radio operator was now using their second extinguisher. Behind John he saw the Dorsal Gunner dancing in the flames like a crazed puppet. With nothing to be done, the forward hatch was thrown open, and he quickly dropped out; fully expecting his crew to follow.

Billy looked wildly around not sure what to do. He felt the searing heat and saw the flames. Gut reation moved him towards the radio operator's area, and his foot went through the decking where the metal had melted, causing him to fall forward. The flames now reached the ammunition boxes of his guns, and the bullets began banging away like a string of firecrackers.

There was a whoosh of the fire extinguisher again, and then fresh cold air came up to greet him as John pulled open the aft hatch for him.

"JUMP FOR IT!" the Hound yelled. "TIS NOT YOUR TIME TO DIE! WE'LL MEET AGAIN ONE DAY! COUNT TO THREE BEFORE PULLING THE PARA CORD!"

Billy was so scared his bladder let go in the same moment he tumbled through the hole and into the darkness of the night. As the slip stream grabbed him, he banged his head on the underside of the fuselage... a parting reminder of the reality he was dealing with.

§

Extract from "The London Gazette" of 1st October, 1940 (Author's note: this article was found online. It is an actual verbatim.)

Sergeant John Hannah, No. 83 Squadron

On the night of 15th September, 1940, Sergeant Hannah was the wireless operator/air gunner in an aircraft engaged in a successful attack on an enemy barge concentration at Antwerp. It was then subjected to intense anti-aircraft fire and received a direct hit from a projectile of an explosive and incendiary nature, which apparently burst inside the bomb compartment.

A fire started which quickly enveloped the wireless operator's and rear gunner's cockpits, and as both the port and starboard petrol tanks had been pierced, there was grave risk of the fire spreading. Sergeant Hannah forced his way through to obtain two extinguishers and discovered that the rear gunner had had to leave the aircraft. He could have acted likewise, through the bottom escape hatch or forward through the navigator's hatch, but remained and fought the fire for ten minutes with the extinguishers, beating the flames with his log book when these were empty.

During this time thousands of rounds of ammunition exploded in all directions, and he was almost blinded by the intense heat and fumes, but had the presence of mind to obtain relief by turning on his oxygen supply. Air admitted through the large holes caused by the projectile made the bomb compartment an inferno, and all the aluminium sheet metal on the floor of this airman's cockpit was melted away, leaving only the cross bearers.

Working under these conditions, which caused burns to his face and eyes, Sergeant Hannah succeeded in extinguishing the fire. He then crawled forward, ascertained that the navigator had left the aircraft, and passed the latter's log and maps to the pilot. This airman displayed courage, coolness and devotion to duty of the highest order and by his action in remaining and successfully extinguishing the fire under conditions of the greatest danger and difficulty, enabled the pilot to bring the aircraft to its base."

§

A massive paw gripped Billy Braddock by the collar and physically shook him to wakefulness. "Wake up, Sunshine," a voice growled in his ear, "Did you have a fair ride?"

The young hound blinked and looked to the sky which was dark and twinkled with stars. "Where am I?" he asked.

"You're in Kent, outside the Hampden Pub," the person told him. The voice was familiar but different; now carrying a mark of age with it. "There was a power failure," it continued, "They broke out the candles, and it's got the aire of the old days; which is right comfortable, if you ask me. I was thinking of going home but seeing you here still lying on the sidewalk I figured it might be a good thing to see if you were still breathing."

The Highland Hound sat up and rubbed his head. "I seem to recall I was a bit of a jerk," he managed, "And then again, I seem to recall a whole lot more than that. What day is it?"

The old fellow harrumphed, hawked, and then spat. "'Tis still September 15th, Battle of Britain Day. I was gathered with those meant to remember... the children and grandchildren of the survivors. Aye, you were more than an arse and they was right angry with ya. If you're now wish'n to go back and apologize I'm sure it will not fall upon deaf ears."

The Hound nodded. "I think I'd like that," he admitted and then held his paw out for help up off of the cold sidewalk. It was gripped with a strength that belied the age shown upon the face he found smiling within the shadows of the dark night.

Upon rising, Billy felt something tugging at his shoulders. Turing, he saw yards of white silk draped out behind him and into the road.

"Stand at attention now, Airman," John Bulldog told him softly, "so I can help you shuck your parachute harness and flight suit. I don't think those inside the pub would understand all that much if you made your appearance dressed in such a manner."

Post Story Reality

Sergeant John Hannah, the youngest airman ever to be awarded the VC, went on to instructional duties but never really recovered his health. He was invalided out in 1942 and died soon after the war still in his twenties. He was survived by his wife and three young daughters.

In the churchyard at Scampton there grows a rose bush, 'The Hannah Rose', that was created in John's honour.

Pilot Officer C. A. Connor received the DFC (Distinguished Flying Cross). He was killed only a few weeks later.

Sergeant D.A.E. Hayhurst, navigator and bomb-aimer, received the DFM (Distinguished Flying Medal) for the part they played in the raid. He was listed as taken Prisoner of War in the October 3rd, 1940 issue of 'Flight' on page 283.

Of the actual Dorsal Gunner, the author could find no mention at all.

Sore Loser

"My name is Commandant Staffelkapitän Oberst Dierk Locke," the pilot said, rising from his table. "It is such a large tongue twisting title attached to such a small name and purpose. Please just call me Dierk. If one were to leave the tongue hanging out of their snout after pronouncing the whole of it, they would surely trip."

"But I like the way it sounds," the French Poodle told him with a giggle. She then tried to pronounce it but failed miserably.

The Wolf smiled at her efforts. Being French, she only came up to his chest but she was cute for a prostitute. Because of this, and because he was a male after all, though she'd come to his table uninvited, he did not raise a fuss. Also, unlike most Poodles, she'd let her fur grow long and unkempt. This highlighted her natural beauty, and she was quite beautiful.

"My great great great something grandfather fought with Napoleon," she told him during their first few moments together. "He died when his gun was overrun by the Germans. Things were different back then. That time, the French won, and then Germany became our fast ally. I wonder what ever happened to that peace. War is such a waste, is it not?"

"Unless you are the winner," he added. "What would you like to drink?"

"Something stronger than tea," she replied. "It is a wonderful night with a lover's moon, and I think that calls for wine."

"This is true, it is a wonderful night, and for a change, I am not required to fly in the morning, though I will review all the reports and see to the silliness that happened in my absence." He winked at her and smiled his best Wolfish smile.

Signaling the waiter the fighter pilot held up a large bank note, arranging for another bottle of wine, indicating it should be of a better vintage than what he'd been drinking. He and his might not be welcome in the 'City of Lights' but money was money after all. As he did this, her paw slipped over the one he'd left on the table. The Oberst did not move it nor was he in any way alarmed, though he had repeatedly warned his pilots of the dangers such an occurrence might pose.

'The French people do not care for us,' he'd told them bluntly, 'Because, if you haven't noticed, we have come here and taken their country away from them.'

To this, there was some chuckling.

'Zo… to keep from having a knife stuck between your ribs or your beautiful neck slit, you will not visit anywhere that is not on the safe list provided to us by command. You will also not go out in any less than groupings of five. Four of you will drink, if that is what you wish to do, and one of you will stay sober und so watch around for any trouble. Number five will always be armed and he will also carry a sergeant's whistle. If there are problems this whistle will be blown for all it is worth. The French do have a competent police force which is working in conjunction with our people but..." he raised an eyebrow. "Use your weapon only as a last resort. Is that understood?'

'Ja, Herr Oberst,' they'd all replied in one voice. He had then given the nod to his adjutant officer, and their liberty passes were distributed.

Derik, being the commanding officer, chose to ignore his own advice and went out alone.

"My name is Jeans," she told him, her accent making the words musical to his ears. Leaning forward, her breasts pushed out against her blouse which was discretely unbuttoned enough to allow them some 'breathing room'. "I am not actually from Paris," she whispered.

"Is that right," the Wolf remarked, smiling his best Wolfish smile. "And where is it that you might have been raised. I would certainly like to live there if all the fräuleins are as pretty as you."

The waiter arrived and served the wine, giving a great flourish to his actions in emphasis of the vintage. During this moment, the pair remained silent, both regarding the other as their bodies began emitting the natural lover's scents of attraction.

"I would be glad to show you the sights of the city," she told him when the fellow left. "Please excuse me for being forward; but time does not treat those such as us kindly."

Picking up his glass, he waited for her to do the same and then clinked them together. "Here is to time standing still," he told her gallantly. "I can understand and will agree that time will not treat me kindly. I am a pilot and when I fly, if my Messerschmitt does not crash all by itself for whatever mechanical problems that might occur, then a British pilot will certainly be the culprit to end my existence. They are a determined lot."

"Or Uncle Fatty will arrange your demise."

"I'm sorry?" the Wolf asked after spitting his wine back into the glass.

Leaning forward, she whispered with a smile, "It's all right, Dierk, the wine is not poisoned. It's actually quite good."

When the Wolf was able to speak again, he was about to say something caustic when she placed a finger over his lips. "I work for Admiral Canaris," Jeans whispered to him, "And I have very deep and reliable connections on both sides of the channel. The Luftwaffe is losing the war over England and word has been passed to me that Uncle Fatty is being a very sore loser. You are one of the many he seeks to blame for his losses."

"How could you say he is a loser?" Derik whispered back. "He is the Reichmarschall, he would not hold other's responsible…" even as he said this, the words stuck in his throat. "He stands at the right paw of Der Führer," the Wolf finally managed. "Your words are preposterous." Reaching into his tunic, he pulled out a Sergeant's whistle.

The Poodle placed a paw upon his. "If I wanted you dead, you would be dead. Blow that whistle, and we will both die. My people are watching and are prepared to take action. It has already been agreed that they will shoot me as well; so I am at as great a risk as yourself."

The Oberst blinked. Place him in the cockpit of his fighter and he would know exactly what to do, but here on the city streets of Paris he was truly out of his element. "I can understand why they would shoot me, though it would be stupid to do so," he told her softly, "But why would they shoot you?"

"Because my Georges is a very sore loser, too, and will take no chances. It was my idea to approach you. He was opposed; telling me that it would expose the organization; better to just leave you to your own. If I were captured, the Gestapo would be delighted to question me.

"Should this happen, a quick death would be preferred in any case." Leaning forward she kissed him on the lips. "Uncle Fatty is not doing well in the skies over England and your messages to him requesting such things as aircraft with more range are not sitting well. He is very angry with his old comrade. Your job is to shut up and kill more British pilots so he will look better in the eyes of Father Adolf… but you knew that."

"And so your message to me is from?"

"You have friend's in England, Derik… and you have friends in the Abwehr. You have but to ask and arrangements will be made to protect you. Your knowledge would be a valuable asset to Uncle Winston and you would be very much appreciated."

"I seem to have many uncles tonight," he replied, taking the time to sip his wine.

There was a soft whistle, and the Poodle smiled at him. "You are very handsome, and I am very tempted; but I must go now."

"And… if I decided to take advantage of your offer," he asked her, "How would I get in touch?"

"Come back here and wear that whistle around your neck openly. I will hear of it, and I will find you."

Giving him one more kiss, she rose from the table. Taking her leave she walked into the night and did not look back.

"Derik!" a voice called to him from a little bit too close. Turning to it, Locke saw his second in command walking towards him. This was surprising as he'd told no one where he was going.

"Hello, Johannes," he called back, "I am surprised to see you here. All is well with the children?"

"Most are drunk but no one was arrested, so I would say the night was successful. Who was this female just walking away… quite pretty for a Poodle."

"Pretty yes but a bit of a sore loser and no sense of humor. She wagered she could get me into bed tonight. I gave her a kiss, told her no, and kept a paw upon my wallet; so she left."

"A true pity," the other Wolf responded, "I would have gladly paid for her services." Picking up her unfinished glass of wine, he asked, "May I?"

"Help yourself," his commander told him, "And I shall even offer a toast." Lifting his glass, he said, "To Uncle Fatty… if they made a cockpit large enough to hold him, perhaps it would have the fuel capacity to stay in the air long enough that we could do something about the bloody Spitfires."

His adjunct laughed, clinked glasses with him, and then added, "If it were that large of an aircraft, most certainly the roar of its engine would sound like a thunderbolt as it passed."

The Fluidity of an Airwar

The opportunity to secure ourselves against defeat lies in our own hands, but the opportunity of defeating the enemy is provided by the enemy himself.

Sun Tzu

Never, never, never believe any war will be smooth and easy, or that anyone who embarks on the strange voyage can measure the tides and hurricanes he will encounter. The statesman who yields to war fever must realize that once the signal is given, he is no longer the master of policy but the slave of unforeseeable and uncontrollable events.

Sir Winston Churchill

Battle Report: Staffelkapitän Oberleutnant Paul Wolf

The Wolf sipped from a cup of ersatz coffee. It was horrible tasting but he needed something just to get his breathing back to normal. The debriefing officer knew this and allowed for it.

"There was not much for us to do," the pilot told him over top of the tin mug, "Pressure on us from the British fighters was intense. Unlike before, they were extremely organized this time and in sufficient numbers to be overwhelming. Does command have their heads up their rectums?"

"I will strike that last comment, Oberleutenant, but remember this report will be filed for intelligence gathering purposes."

"Good... leave it in, then because I most likely will not live through the day. Tell them in big bold letters to open their eyes! For what they ask, we need huge big bombers armed with cannons and fighter escort that can stay for more than ten minutes over target." It took the pilot a few minutes to bring his emotions under control before he continued with the task of remembering.

"We would be attacked by two to three squadrons of RAF fighters and then as soon as we beat off the engagement, another three squadrons were at altitude and ready to pounce. It was like we'd thrown rocks at a bee hive and knocked it down. We had no choice but to drop our bomb loads at random. I ordered this action hoping it would lighten the load and we could make as hasty a retreat as possible without any further damage to our aircraft."

The Oberleutenant had to pause again to compose himself. He'd just lost half the aircraft flying with him. These seasoned aircrews were all known to him by name. They were a tight knit group and being a very good leader, he'd taken the time to know each of them. They were his comrades. It was all too clear to him now that such a luxury would probably not be so afforded in the future. The basics accorded to battling in the air had now from the simple aggressions of Poland and France. He knew it first paw, and the Intelligence Officer sitting with him knew it from him, though past this point it was apparent that blind stupidity reigned supreme.

"After about ten minutes over London," he continued in a softer voice, "there was no longer any sort of formation to hold to. It became every bomber for itself as we were too distant to cover each other. My reckoning is that we were scattered over an area fifteen miles wide."

Though he struggled to hide the emotions he felt, it was obvious the Wolf was furious. "The pilots of the Hurricanes and Spitfires showed no mercy, Hans. It made no difference whether the bombers in what was left of my Staffel were crippled or not; they were not given the chance to land. I wish my report to reflect that it was plainly obvious that some of those shot down would never have made it back in any case."

Placing the tin cup on the camp desk, he asked to be dismissed. His aircraft was presently being rearmed and serviced for a second mission. He quietly explained that he wished to at least have a lunch before having to once again face this new aggression of the British pilots.

196

(Author's research note: On this fine day in September, South London was the worst affected by this raid, with Lewisham, Lambeth, Camberwell and some of the bridges across the River Thames all recording bomb damage. One high explosive bomb even fell within the grounds of Buckingham Palace causing slight structural damage to the building but putting a bigger hole in the lawns at the rear as it failed to explode. A power station in Beckenham was also hit.

The German bomber formations headed out towards the west, turning south near Weybridge. 609 Squadron Warmwell (Spitfires) chased them as they headed for the coast and took on 15 Dornier Do17s. A formation of Bf109s seeing, the desperate situation the bombers were in, joined in as did a few Bf110s.

Over Ewhurst in Surrey, 605 Squadron Croydon (Hurricanes) came in to assist. As the mêlée continued in fierce action over the town of Billingshurst they were joined by 1(RCAF) Squadron Northolt (Hurricanes) who took on the troublesome Bf109s. In the other direction, some eighty German bombers were trying to make good their escape towards the Thames Estuary. Fighter Command attacked in large numbers with squadrons attacking any of the escorts while others took on the merciless bombers.

The morning battle had been a disaster for the Luftwaffe. Many of the bombers crashed or blew up in mid-air. The remainder struggled for the safety of the French coast.

Because of the intensity and aggression shown by the pilots of Fighter Command, the bombers dropped most of their bombs randomly over a wide area. Damage was done, but not as much as was intended by the Luftwaffe commanders. The raid was doomed to failure the moment the first formations had crossed the Channel.

This time, everything had gone right for Fighter Command and 11 Group. Timing, position and height was all on the side of the RAF) [On 14 July 1936, 11 Group became the first RAF Fighter Command group formed, with the responsibility for the air defense of southern England, including London.]

Archie listened to the chatter on the radio as he sat on the ground in his cockpit waiting for the green flare. The ground accumulator was plugged into his aircraft so there was no risk of running down his aircraft's accumulator (battery). 92 Squadron was waiting in reserve and the pilots expected to be sent into the fray at any time. From where they sat, they could see the black puffy crumps of the anti-aircraft fire. Every now and again a rocket trail would streak skywards, ending in a small burst and a flash of white yellowish material as one of the rocket powered parachutes was sent up in advance of a low flying bomber. As crazy as the idea sounded, it actually had a telling effect on any aircraft that got tangled up in the parachute. It was also an economical weapon, as any parachute making it back to the ground was gathered up and repacked for another run.

A throat being cleared next to his left ear broke into his reverie and he turned to find Uncle Billie's Batman standing on his wing and holding out a mug of tea. "Lieutenant Badcock's regards, sir," the Weasel told him, "And he sent along a message that is just a bit vulgar. I'll repeat it if you wish, or I can clean it up just a bit."

Accepting the mug, he told the Corporal, "I'll take the clean version, if you please."

"He wishes to know if you would like to go to Madam Bella's this evening. He had news that they have a new group of girls over from Paris looking for work, and he plans to become familiar with each and every one of them personally."

Archie sipped his tea and smiled. "If anyone could do it, Henry could. He's got the stamina of a pup and the heart of a Royal Lion."

"And the horns of a Goat," the batman added softly. Looking to the sky and the clouds of flak to the south, he asked, "Do you ever get angry at the enemy, sir?"

Archie thought about this for a moment, and then told him, "Yes, I believe I do. I might not show it so much as some of the other fellows, but there are times… I lost someone very close to me recently and Wing Commander Falstaff told me I should go up and shoot down some Messerschmitts. His theory was that I would feel better for it."

"Did you, sir?"

"Not right then. Eventually I got over the pukes and stammers and got back into the air right enough. I had full intentions of doing exactly what he suggested. I even believe I took certain missions just to affect my own end I hurt so badly; but something happened to change my mind."

The radio crackled, and a burst of chatter spewed forth. The words, like bullets, flew right to the heart of the matter."

"Johnnie's gone for a six… twelve more of the blighters crossing the line… could use some help."

"Roger that; Blue 9 above and coming down. Tally Ho… beers later chum."

Archie sat a little further back in his seat, his back straightening as he looked to the skies; but the fighters were south of London and not visible.

"I had a similar instance, sir," Corporal Higgins said softly.

"You don't say?"

"It's true," the Weasel told him. "My family are all east enders, sir, and proud of it. I've lost ten relatives in the bombings so far. The closest was my younger brother. We never so much as even found a part of him to bury."

"I'm so sorry," the Stag replied at this given knowledge.

"It's all right, sir. As a batman I relished my permission to wear a side arm as I vowed to kill the first German air crewman I came across. As it happened, I had a change of heart and even saved the fellow's life when an old dowager Weasel made to stab him in the chest with a butcher knife."

"And why did you do that?" the pilot asked, feeling he's just stepped into a very private moment of another who had been hurt so badly.

The batman sighed. "He looked just like my brother; though I realized later there was absolutely no resemblance whatsoever. He was a Wolf, not a Weasel so the difference was quite obvious... but I did see my brother in him. Now you have to tell me your instance, sir."

"Control," came the call over the radio, "They've scattered and are dropping wherever. They're easy pick'n's, over. We could use some additional numbers."

"Stay together, lads," called a different voice, one Archie recognized as Group Commander Douglas Bader, "Co-ordinate your attacks and don't get off of him. Get as many as you possibly can! If Jerry loses an entire flight, think what message that would send."

"Now that would be a message," Archie agreed as further calls came in on the radio. Handing the cup back to Higgins, he winked at him. "I suspect we shall be taking off in the next few minutes."

Accepting the cup, the lithe Corporal asked in a serious voice, "What changed your mind, sir? About hating the enemy?"

The pilot looked at his batman, obviously trying to decide how much he could say.

"Nothing passes between me and the latrine, sir, except that which is supposed to," Higgins assured him, reading the look quite clearly.

"They're not all bad," the Stag told him. "They have a duty to do, just as we do, but not all of them are cutthroat murderers." Archie then told him of the incident where the German fighter pilot had shot down his own wingman when that one made to machine gun him in his parachute.

"I later returned the favor when I recognized his aircraft. He'd been trying to shoot down a ferry Spit and had the tables turned on him by a Russian sow flying for the ATA." He chuckled at the thought of what the expression on the fighter pilot's face must surely have looked like. "She was at least a thousand pounds light from less fuel and no armaments and by the time I got to her, she was trying to chew his tail off with her prop. I instructed her to pull back and I squirted him a good one. I had his cockpit square in my sights, but when I recognized his markings, I pulled back to his tail and chewed it up good. I was told later that he'd had to bail out over the channel."

He gave his batman a look that confirmed the seriousness of this information.

"And now you know something that was told only to Wing Commander Stewart Falstaff and Sir Winston Churchill, and even they were not told of my final actions. I could easily have followed and finished the job by the book, but chose to continue on with my escort mission."

"It was the proper decision, sir, I am sure of it. I speak some German, and the airman I rescued was nothing more than a farmer's son enamored with flying. He was but a gunner and now is but a prisoner. For him this terrible ordeal is over." Looking over to Flight Lieutenant Badcock's aircraft, he asked, "Is Henry aware of your story, sir?"

"No, I have not told him. The report was classified. He only knows I was shot down."

At that moment the Wing Commander's adjunct came out of the operations shack and fired a green flare high up into the air.

"Time to go, sir," the batman told his charge. "When you get back, I will have a hot meal ready and your clothing laid out so you can accompany Henry to Madam Bella's. If nothing else sir, the diversion will do you good. She would have wanted that for you."

The Stag, startled by the single word 'she,' hesitated in his engine start and looked to his wing; but the Corporal was gone. The engine roar of the Spit next to him brought him back to the present, and he continued in his job as he must.

On this flight, Henry bagged a 109, but Archie's leading edge gun tape remained unbroken.

A Different Kind of War

"All the business of war, and indeed all the business of life, is to endeavour to find out what you don't know from what you do."

Duke of Wellington

Unlike the previous war, there was now a common factor in the air forces of both sides; the radio. With this new tool fighting in the air had been revolutionized. No longer was the pilot alone in the sky relying on only hand signals to communicate with his comrades. Though long wave Morse code sets were still used in the larger aircraft, relatively short range 'voice' radio sets had come into service. These were heavily relied upon and mostly with little regard for who might be listening.

The British organization responsible for gathering radio intelligence was known as Y Service. Their job was to listen and report. Since everything about this air war was a relatively new experience, during the first three months of the war in Europe, the only messages paid notice to were in Morse code. As it goes, somewhere along the line someone mentioned the fact that ham radio operators were picking up voice messages which they could not understand on the 40 megacycle band using R/T (*Radio telegraphy*).

Y Service immediately procured a number of HAM radio units and almost straight away commenced to picking up German radio transmissions. The only problem was the overlooked fact that German pilots actually spoke the German language; and no one among them spoke or understood anything other than English. The story goes that, luckily, an anti-aircraft gun operator with the army stationed on Y Service's base did understand German. He was quickly transferred into the Royal Air Force.

Within the next few months, the RAF went on a priority recruiting campaign from within the Women's Auxiliary Air Service (WAAFs) in an effort to find personnel who not only understood German but also lived in Germany, as they would have a better understanding of the various dialects. By the beginning of the Battle of Britain, six or seven women with these qualities had been found and were pressed into the duties of Intelligence Operators. These WAAFs picked up on the R/T messages very quickly. They listened in on Luftwaffe pilots having conversations with each other, and soon it was realized that the German aircrews had absolutely no respect for secrecy. They would often mention the number of aircraft in their formation and sometimes even let their destination slip.

The Luftwaffe, on the other hand, was ill-served by its lack of military intelligence about the British defenses. Even when good information existed, it was ignored if it did not match conventional preconceptions.

As a result of pre-war intercepted radio transmissions the Germans realized early on that the RAF fighters were being controlled from ground facilities. On August 2nd to the 4th 1939, the Graf Zeppelin LZ130 conducted a *Spionagefahrt* ("espionage trip"). Loaded with high tech radio equipment, she listened in on RAF radio and RDF (*radar*) transmissions.

According to the memoirs of Commander Albert Sammt, *Mein Leben für den Zeppelin* (translation: "My Life For The Zeppelin"), he flew up Britain's east coast, stopping the engines at Aberdeen and pretending they had engine failure in order to investigate some strange antenna masts. They drifted freely westwards over land and saw for the first time the new Supermarine Spitfires which were photographed as they circled the airship.

During this trip it was correctly ascertained that British fighters were being command controlled from the ground. Although the Luftwaffe correctly interpreted these new ground control procedures; **they incorrectly assessed them as being rigid and ineffectual.**

Espionage through the use of actual spies did occur on both sides; though it was a very risky business for those who played the game.

§

The morning flight that day had stretched to no less than four flights happening one after the other; wherein Henry bagged a Messerschmitt 110 and shared a Junkers inbound for London with Archie. By the time they were done the Stag had only wished to fall into his cot and sleep; but there was his dress uniform all laid out along with a hot cup of tea on the small bed table.

"God bless Corporal Higgins!" Henry cried out when he saw this, "He remembered our date. We're heading to Madam Bella's Arch old lad and I will not hear a negative word about it. You need a night out."

Archie sighed. "I did promise."

The tea was drunk as they shed their flight gear and by the time they were back from the showers, Corporal Higgins was waiting for them with a hot dinner that smelled surprisingly good.

"How are things for your family Richard?" Archie asked as he eyed his plate. His stomach rumbled as he'd not eaten the entire day.

"They're holding up well, sir," the Weasel replied. "The rationing is hard but they make do as does all of England."

"Perhaps you could take this meal to them with my regards, eh?"

The Weasel looked at him and smiled. "I appreciate the thought, sir, but if I were to leave base with a package of food, it would look as though I were pilfering and I would be arrested forth with. It's even more drastic if you're caught with gasoline; you can be shot for that offense."

"I think it's a good idea," Henry chimed in, "You may take my dinner as well… especially since I intend to drink dinner at Madam Bella's. We'll walk you out and each will carry a package which you can take to the children for us. They've suffered enough; not right they should go to bed hungry as well."

The Corporal did not argue. Such a gift was from the heart and not to be turned down.

Getting to Madam Bella's was a bit of a walk. With the shortage of fuel cabs these days were as scarce as hen's teeth. Henry had jokingly made reference to pinching the Commander's motorbike again but the look Archie gave him clearly conveyed disapproval. That killed that idea, even if it was said in jest and caused no end to the Bulldog's muttering about someone in his company being no fun a' tall.

When they arrived, Henry was greeted like a favorite son by the bordello's proprietor. It was more than apparent that he was a favorite customer. Archie, because he was with Henry, was not questioned. In the business of illicit things, including girls, caution was always the rule and it was somewhat known that for a price one could obtain much from Madam Bella. She was a bit of a legend in her own right, having personally fought the Nazis in Poland before fleeing for her life. Though the house was well known for its offerings, it was also observed with a blind eye by the local constabulary; being that the madam took good care of the pilots from Biggins Hill. It was understood that these fellows were placing their lives on the line every day in the defense of Britain so every effort was made to make what little down time they had as sweet as possible.

After dinner and cocktails the fliers found themselves in good company; each of the girls being introduced by Madam Bella personally. The older Tatra Sheepdog had royalty running in her veins and this shone through just in the way she carried herself. Once her residency was established in England she, in turn, reached out to other refugees, helping where she could. The madam also established the means to continue helping by hiring girls to her hotel staff who were not too shy. As her staff's families became established the 'secret' income was not as much required so it was only normal the turnover rate was a bit high. This also worked to the madam's advantage as it kept the faces (and bodies) fresh.

Sitting on a very comfortable sofa, Archie spoke softly with Henry who sat opposite him on another couch. His mind truly was not on the girls who were a bit over friendly for his taste. Though their meal had been delicious, he'd hardly even touched the after dinner brandy. Nor had he smoked his cigar but rather tucked it into the pocket of his blouse. He knew Commander Sheltie liked cigars, and this would make a nice gift. He and Henry, thankfully, did not have to be back before noon the following day so they had ample time to enjoy themselves. The Commander had insisted, especially when he'd seen them all dressed up; so Archie was resolved in the allowance of his wingman's good time.

Henry was quickly claimed by a cute clipped French Poodle ear whisperer. Archie, though he was not really interested, was introduced to another French Poodle. Unlike her sister in arms, she was unshorn and very wild looking.

"My name is Jeans," she'd told him softly, holding her paw out.

Standing, the Stag took her paw and gently shook it. "I am pleased to make your acquaintance," he told her, "My name is Archie Corn, and I must offer my apologizes. Under the circumstances, my heart is not in the quest tonight."

"You're an old poop," Henry growled at him, "The least you can do is offer the lass a drink; she'll be much better company than me shortly."

"That would be very nice," the Poodle agreed with a shy smile. "I promise I won't bite."

"The brandy will be my treat," Madam Bella told them, "In honor of your victories today, I will even pour it from my very best reserve stock."

Looking at the girls, she told them in passable French, "They shot down two of the filthy German aircraft today so you treat these pilots very good. Do that, and you may keep the entire fee to your purses. If I could fly, I would be up there with them. What the bastards have done to my Poland sickens me."

"That's very nice of you," Archie began, though he didn't understand a word of the French. He'd intended declining the offer, but Jeans placed a paw on his shoulder and shook her head.

Leaning close, she whispered, "This is an honor she gives you, Mr. Pilot... do not say no. When the time comes, I will take you to my apartment, and you may sleep the night undisturbed on a feather mattress. I know this is what you need most. You do not need sex; you are exhausted. You may tell your friend whatever you wish in the morning. Perhaps then he will not pester you so much." She then, to Henry's delight, softly embraced the Stag who did not resist.

The evening became a whirlwind of enjoyment for the pilots then. Between the drinks and the unobtrusive female at his side, Archie was actually able to relax. Their conversation was kept light, though the topic inevitably swung around to Henry's favorite subject; the airplane they flew.

"And there we were," the Bulldog said loudly, "Flying around and around this silly gasbag like racers in a circuit event. I personally got so close I could see the Zep's Captain standing by the glass in the control cabin. I blew past at better than two hundred miles per hour and I bet it buffeted him really good. Can you imagine riding such a ship in the sky? He was actually standing in a control room as if he were on the bridge of a sea going luxury liner!"

"Wasn't that dangerous?" asked his French Poodle in feigned interest. She was cuddled up next to the Bulldog and it was obvious to Archie that she had but one thing in mind; and that was making her paycheck.

"Everything about flying is dangerous," the Bulldog laughed, "That's what makes it so wonderfully fun."

"Just like me?" the Poodle asked, giving him a kiss on the cheek.

"Just like you," the Flight Lieutenant agreed with a wink.

The Stag felt himself becoming nauseous with this feigned attention. "I didn't know you were there for that," he told his former instructor.

"There's much you don't know about me," the Bulldog replied in his humorous manner. "I've been at the business of flying since I was born; or so it feels." He winked. "The only reason they released me to fly with you, Archie old sport, was the fact I'd threatened to quit the RAF and go fly for the bloody Germans if they didn't."

"You didn't," squeaked his Poodle.

"He's just having us on," Archie replied for his friend. "What's the rest of the story Henry?"

"I was clocking some time in the Spit since I was to be teaching its use in the advanced classes," the former instructor replied. "She'd just come on line and we were all relatively new in the cockpit. While we were up flying this great bag of gas came floating down on us with the wind. The Captain reported he was having engine problems but Control wasn't buying that load of crap. They called out on the radio and sent us to rattle his windows a bit… and did we ever do that!"

He took a good swallow of brandy from his glass which had been served straight up with no soda. "My but that's good," he muttered.

Looking to his friend he told him, "I s'pect you were still just dreaming about flying at that time; weren't you Arch?"

"Actually, I was there," the Stag replied with a smile, "But on the ground with my family. We were on holiday and traveling by train to visit relatives in Aberdeen when we spotted the zeppelin. I find it so hard to believe they actually used those things to bomb London in the first war. My father knew of my interest in flying so he gave me his seat at the window."

"Well, I'll be," the Bulldog rumbled, "I had no idea. What a small world it is then."

The Poodle next to Henry chose that moment to whisper something in his ear, and the strangest smile crossed his face. "We shall have to speak of this again, Archie, but for now I believe I am going to retire for the evening. Don't wait up. I'll see you back at base in the morning."

"Be prompt," the Stag told him, "You know I don't like flying alone."

§

Archie woke, his nose twitching to the smell of frying eggs and coffee. He'd not slept this good in weeks and, in fact, had not even dreamed. That by itself was an indication of how exhausted he was. In the dim light of a single candle he checked his watch and noted it was still two hours before sunrise. He'd only just had five hours of sleep.

The bed jiggled and he found the wild looking French Poodle sitting on the edge of the mattress next to him. She carefully placed a mug of black coffee on the night stand and then leaned in and kissed him on the cheek.

"It is early yet, but we need to get you back to your squadron," she told him. "Your eggs are ready and placed between bread so you may eat on your way. I have a feeling it's going to be a very busy day for you."

"Why?" the Stag asked, suddenly very alert.

"It is just a, how you say, a gut feeling," she told him. "I did not hear the Germans bomb last night. When they do this, it is because they plan something big for the following morning."

"You speak as if you know them personally," Archie told her as he sat up in the bed. Reaching out, he picked up the mug of coffee gratefully. Smelling its aroma first as if it were a fine wine, he sampled it and sighed. Such common things were becoming harder to get the more the Germans bombed the shipping lanes and ports seeking to isolate the island nation.

"I know them well enough," she replied, "They took my country. They killed my brother who was a pilot in the French air force. They destroyed the village I grew up in. I mean to say… ummm… thee village… it no longer exists. It is gone."

"I'm so very sorry," he told her, meaning it. "I had no idea."

She blinked and nodded. "Most people do not look beyond the surface of others. Where we met… how we met… I am but zee pleasure girl, no?" The last part of what she told him was spoken with a very heavy French accent. "The Germans are ruthless," she continued in a near whisper. "They conquer and they dominate by killing everyone if there is any resistance at all."

"We will stop them here," he told her. "We have to stop them here. There is nowhere else for us to go."

"If you do not, then there will be no way to retake my France." She leaned forward and kissed him on the forehead. "May I tell you a secret?"

"Certainly," he replied, sipping his coffee. "I am often told that I am very good at keeping secrets."

"I do not make zee joke," she told him, "I will tell you something very sensitive. I will do this only if you promise above all else that you will not tell anyone where you heard it. This includes even your friend Henry, should he ever ask. "

Archie raised an eyebrow and smiled at her. "I am not a priest to whom you must confess," he replied in an attempt at a joke. She was but a refugee and a prostitute, albeit with a very good imagination. Her next comments, however, brought his landing gear firmly back to earth and even caused him a sudden chest pain as if his tail wheel had found a hole.

"Have you ever met Winston Churchill?" she asked him.

"I can't tell you."

She absently traced a finger along the scar on his shoulder which was still not completely healed. "Have you ever been saved by a German pilot?"

"I can't tell you."

She dipped a finger into his coffee cup and then sucked upon it as a child might. "His name is Staffelkapitän Oberst Dierk Locke. Have you ever flown with a woman?"

"Which woman?" he countered defensively, still trying to digest the fact that she knew of the parachute incident. Inadvertently he'd answered her question. When he realized this, he asked suspiciously, "Who are you?"

She smiled at him, displaying the image of sweetness and innocence. "I am the prostitute you paid to have sex with you."

"We never…"

She placed a finger on his lips and then followed it with a lingering kiss. "Of course we didn't," she told him when her kiss was done. "You are too much still in love. That much I know just as a woman."

Sitting back on the mattress, her demeanor changed and she said in a serious voice, "Now listen to me and then act upon that which you will suspect is the truth. The Boche at their field operational level understand that sometimes a low level raid can sneak past the RDF stations. When this happens the first warning the RAF has are their bombs exploding on the airfield. They mean to destroy you on the ground if they can."

She paused so this information would sink in. When she was sure he was paying serious attention, she continued.

"Particularly good in this low-level role is their Dornier 17. Sometimes, too, they will also use fighters with bombs though the fighter pilots resist this as an affront to who they are. They would rather hunt as Wolves. Both ways are fast, and with this surprise they are able to get away again since there are no aircraft in the air to catch them. They

208

will follow this mission with Messerschmitts conducting Freie Jagd (Free Hunts) to take out any who might have taken off to follow after the bombers."

"And this will happen today?"

"I don't know this for sure; but they did not bomb last night."

"I will have to hurry, then, as it's a bit of a walk," the stag told her. Swallowing the rest of his coffee straight down, he tossed off the covers.

The Poodle placed a paw on his arm. "Your batman waits downstairs with your commander's motorbike. Your friend Henry has already been delivered to his cot on your base."

He looked at her in amazement. "I owe you much," he told her.

"You owe me nothing," she replied. "We work to the same purpose, though we fight a different kind of war. We may meet again... perhaps if we do the night will be kinder to us both, and we might find the time to properly hold each other."

"I certainly hope we do," he told her.

Leaning in, she kissed him without reservation. When it was done, she told him, "You may leave any message you have for me at Madam Bella's. She is a good friend and hates the Germans very much."

"Does she know about you?"

"No... and you must not say anything to anyone. This has to be even more secret than the one you hold closest to your heart." She looked up into his eyes. "I do not really expect to live through to the war's end."

"Nor do I," he told her honestly. "I'd better go."

§

After Action Report

Commander Reginald Sheltie

At approximately 0540 Biggins Hill was attacked in force by German bombers at low altitude.

Flight Lieutenant Archie Corn, acting upon a hunch, convinced me to allow four of our fighters to take off before dawn and fly cover for the airfield. His argument convinced me of the probable attack – that since there had been no bombing the night before we should be ready for an attack with the morning's light.

These four aircraft met the enemy to the east of the airfield, flying head on into their formation. Twelve Dornier 17 aircraft were damaged

or shot down to one Spitfire lost. The pilot of that aircraft, Flight Lieu-
tenant Henry Badcock, collided with one of the bombers but was able
to parachute directly down to us at the airfield. He has suffered a bullet
through one calf.

> *Three kills have been awarded to Flight Lieutenant Badcock.*
> *One kill has been awarded to Flight Lieutenant Corn.*
> *Two kills have been awarded to Pilot Officers Smithe.*
> *Two kills have been awarded to Pilot Officer Weinstein.*

§

Wilhelm Canaris sat alone in his office. It was late at night and he was still reading over intelligence assessments. Some he disposed of with a laugh, wadding them up and tossing them into the waste can next to his desk. Others he would read several times and then carefully feed into the fireplace on the other side of his desk.

There was a soft knock on his door.

"Aufschreiben," he said without looking up.

An orderly moved through the door and, closing it behind himself, came to stand in front of the desk.

"What is it Manfred?" the old Fox asked, finally looking up from the document he was reading. "You're up late."

The Rat held out an envelope. "Wireless message, sir."

"How old?"

"Ten minutes."

The Admiral accepted the message and then said, "There is an expression I have heard that I am told Rats as a species hold close to their hearts; 'Wissen sie ihren platz aber wissen sie, dass sie besser sind.' (Know your place, but know you are better.) I rather like that as it says much. It is bold and speaks to a truth."

The Rat nodded without comment. His assignment to the Abwehr had not been an accident. The Admiral was obviously letting him know that he knew this and yet he had not been dismissed from the post. It gave him much to think about.

The Fox dismissed him and he left the room, quietly closing the door behind himself.

Opening the envelope, the Admiral smiled at the one word he read; 'Corn'.

Leafing through the pile of papers on his desk he found an after action report from that morning transmitted by Bomber Group 1/KG76.

'The formation was met head on east of the airfield by four Spitfires which passed through the formation without regard for their own safety. It is believed that the RAF pilots in desperation have adopted suicide tactics. One fighter collided with a bomber, and two others were shot down at a loss of only six bombers. The airfield was not reached but secondary targets were bombed to good effect.'

"Indeed," the Fox muttered, crumpling up the report and tossing it into the can.

The other paper, he carefully burned.

Fighters Fight

'Once committed to an attack, fly in at full speed. After scoring crippling or disabling hits I would clear myself and then repeat the process. I never pursued the enemy once they had eluded me. Better to break off and set up again for a new assault. I always began my attacks from full strength, if possible, my ideal flying height being 22,000 ft because at that altitude I could best utilize the performance of my aircraft. Combat flying is based on the slashing attack and rough maneuvering. In combat flying, fancy precision aerobatic work is really not of much use. Instead, it is the rough maneuver which succeeds.'

Colonel Erich 'Bubi' Hartmann, GAF, aka Karaya One, the World's leading ace, with 352 victories in W.W.II. Jagdgeschwader 52.

§

The RAF

Squadrons did not fly together as one unit; they were divided into two sections called 'Flights'. These were generally called A and B flights. Each Flight consisted of six aircraft divided into two sections of three aircraft.

To distinguish one Flight from another, each of these Flights was given a color code; such as red, blue, yellow or green.

Each Flight was given a Flight Leader and he would be known as number one, although during communications he would be known by his Flights color and the word 'leader'. The other two pilots/aircraft would then be known as one and two respectively. (example: Red 1 or Red 2.)

The standard fighter unit was the V shaped "vic". This involved one lead plane and two wingmen, with the wingmen flying very close to the sides and slightly behind the lead plane to form the V shape. Typically four vics would fly together one after another to form a squadron.

The problem with the vics were the formations were so tight that the wingmen had to constantly be watching the lead plane or risk running into them. This left only the lead plane to search the skies for enemy planes. After many complaints from the British pilots of the vics not being the optimal flying formation, RAF Fighter Command changed the squadron formation so the fourth vic would weave back and forth, theoretically giving them a better field of view. This resulted in the "weavers," as they were called, being picked off because the German fighters would attack them and get away before the rest of the squadron could leave formation and be ready for a counterattack.

The Germans called these vics *Idiotenreihen* (rows of idiots).

The Luftwaffe

For tactical operations, the Staffel was split into Schwarm (Sections of four aircraft) consisting of two pair, one pair being called a Rotte. The Schwarm formation consisted of a 'lead element' and a 'second element'. When viewing the formation from above, the positions of the planes resemble the tips of the four fingers of a human right hand (without the thumb), giving the formation its name 'Finger Four'.

The lead element is made up of the flight leader at the very front of the formation and one wingman to his rear left. The second element is made up of that element's leader and his wingman. The second element leader is to the right and rear of the flight leader, followed by the second element wingman to his right and rear.

Both the flight leader and element leader had offensive roles, in that they were the ones to open fire on enemy aircraft while the flight remains intact. Their wingmen play a defensive role. The flight wingman covers the rear of the second element, and the element wingman covers the rear of the lead element.

Four of these flights could be assembled to form a squadron formation consisting of two staggered lines of fighters, one in front of the other. Each flight was usually designated by a color (i.e. Red, Blue, Yellow, and Green).

§

The sky was blotched with clouds which arranged themselves in the haphazard style of a young child's attempt at sandbox castles. Some were squashed-looking with openings poked into them by God's fingers. Others rose to towering heights, blossoming out in mushroom-like coverings that came and went in various formations of imaginary armies on parade.

Ninety Two squadron received the order to scramble and had intercepted an inbound flight of Heinkels at Angels Twenty. The bombers, sixty of them, were escorted by no fewer than the same amount of Messerschmitt 109 fighters. These were positioned both close and further out for a better ability to hunt. This, however, did not deter Ninety Two's attack. Ignoring the fighter escort, the Spitfires dove straight in from the cover provided by the clouds, concentrating on the aircraft that would do the most harm to their countrymen.

On their first pass, two of the bombers blew up while another five began to smoke. Three of these left formation and turned back towards the coast of France, dumping their bomb loads over an empty countryside to lighten their load.

Yellow Leader Archie Corn, giving the 'tally ho' signal to his group, led them against a kette of four bombers right in the middle of the formation. Flashing through, two of the bombers dropped away, one in flames and the other with a disabled engine. Ignoring these two easy targets, the fighters quickly climbed again, looping up and over for a second run. As they reached the apogee of the loop they did an Immelmann, turning and rolling to invert their position after the loop's apogee to be upright during their second dive.

Red Leader Derik Locke, who's Schwarm was flying top cover, called 'Horrido!' and immediately nosed his group over to cut them off. Seeing the enemy first was an absolute must for success, and seeing him without being seen only made the job that much easier.

"Yellow Leader, Yellow Two," Sergeant Polis called, "Bandits at twelve 'o'clock." He was a Yorkie and just recently out of training. This was only his third mission. Yellow Three, also a Yorkie, was Pilot Officer Smithe. Smithe had been with the Ninety Two for a little over a month now and considered a blooded veteran.

"Roger," Archie responded. "Continue with the pass and then evasive; we'll dive away and recover northwards."

"Yellow Two copies."

214

"Yellow Three copies."

There was a spat of German on the frequency which was ignored as the fighters dove back through the bomber formation.

As they came through, three different tail gunners concentrated their fire on the Egham Spit, and she took several hits. No less than five bullets opened holes in the cockpit, spraying the Stag with metal shards. One such shard hit the flight lieutenant in the right arm, going deep enough to draw blood. This was ignored.

Placing the center bomber square in his gun sight, Archie pressed the fire button on his control column. His entire body felt the vibration of the eight machine guns as tracers floated towards the target in an almost random looking display. They made contact with the bomber's tail and pieces began breaking off. The ventral gunner stopped firing. In the split second it took for the guns to rake the length of the target a thousand thoughts ran through the fighter pilot's mind without his even realizing it. He mind was working in three dimensions and every alarm bell in his being was making a hellish racket. Glancing to his rear view mirror the Stag saw only black dots, but he could now feel the approach of the four German aircraft… they were closing; their speed better than four hundred miles per hour.

"Watch your back!" It was Terrance's voice in his ear.

"Henry's there," he responded, looking again forward. Tracers from the bomber formation were floating past him.

"No he's not," she reminded.

"Yellow Leader… Two… Three is smoking and I've got Jerry on my tail!"

Archie was about to yell 'bank hard' when there was an orange fireball to his right. He immediately rolled his aircraft to the left just as a steady stream of tracers passed through where he'd been. Throwing on full throttle, the pilot put both paws on the circular control stick and pointed the aircraft's nose straight down towards the ground in a spiraling dive.

Locke had the red dot of his Revi reflector gun sight square on the Spitfire when it rolled. As it did, he recognized the identifying letters painted on the side of the fuselage as the same one that had shot him up a few weeks earlier. "So.. again we dance," he muttered, automatically making to follow. Pressing the radio button on his control stick, he called, "Red Two return to escort. Professor; follow me."

"Folgen," came the terse reply from his wingman Professor Wilhelm Daecher. He'd already shot down Polis, choosing him as target when Locke centered up on the leader. The large Wolf was himself a veteran fighter ace, having a score of twenty victories. The fore portion of his aircraft from the propeller back, like that of Locke's, was painted solid yellow.

With the nose down and the throttle full on the ground now approached at an incredible speed. Time to impact from their altitude of almost four miles up was just over thirty seconds. With all fighters of this time having only manual flight controls a dogfight at over 400 miles per hour became more a test of pilot strength than tactical maneuvering.

"They follow," Terrance whispered in Archie's ear.

"Not now luv," he muttered, his eyes everywhere. As he spiraled down he briefly glanced at his engine instruments, all of which remained in the green. Looking in his mirror, he found the dots growing. He'd hoped the German's concerns would be with the bombers, but they'd smelled blood and he was now alone. The German pilots also had standing orders to kill as many British fighters as possible. The more done in, the less left to fly and the safer their bombers would be. England would then capitulate under the rain of bombs that would follow.

The Spitfire pilot, aware of how close the ground was coming began to pull out of his dive. The 'g' forces on his body began to multiply and the aircraft vibrated heavily as the wings strained to remain attached. Archie tightened his gut as much as he could; straining against the effects as his body attained a weight eight times normal. Now even the chore of moving the aircraft's controls required every bit of strength he had. The peripheral of his vision grayed out, and he felt his consciousness slipping away.

In his aircraft, Locke followed this maneuver. Having years of experience in the cockpit, the Wolf knew to additionally raise his legs and lean forward to shorten the distance his blood had to travel to his brain. This helped counteract the effects of the 'g' forces upon his body. At this point, his tactic was a simple one; follow and turn left or right inside the Spitfire's turn to make his shot. Doing this, he would shoot with 'deflection'; leading and firing at a point in front of his target. This would bring his bullets and the target together in the same place a few seconds later. His gun sight would be useless for this so the firing was done by gut judgment alone.

Archie, on the verge of unconsciousness, had few choices. The Spitfire was a known stallion of the air. If he turned to the left and inside what his attacker could do, he might be able to shake them enough to head for the coast and a possible friendly AA battery. If he turned to the right and the lead Wolf could not catch him, then his wingman, who was hanging back and waiting, would be in good position to cut him off.

Summoning all the strength he had, the Stag pushed his control stick to the left and hauled back on it; banking as hard as he could.

Locke didn't smile, nor did his brain feel any happiness in seeing the aircraft in front of him do what he'd hope would be done. Dropping his flaps to ten degrees, he began his following turn and heard/felt the aircraft's automatic slats bang open on the leading edge of each wing. This was the advantage of the 109 when compared to the Spitfire which had no slats and could only drop its flaps to a full forty degrees. Locke was now using all of his strength to control his fighter. Pressing his body against the side of the small cockpit for leverage, he forced the aircraft to his will. The thumb of his paw stood ready to press the two triggers, one for the synchronized machine guns and one for the cannon. Until the guns were armed in flight, these buttons remained collapsed against the control column. Now, they stood ready for the Wolf's gentle squeeze which did occur.

Archie sensed more than saw the other aircraft fire. Jerking the stick to the other side of the cockpit, he pulled it back to his gut, manhandling his Spitfire in an about face that drained the blood from his head. His vision, already grayed out at the peripherals, drained to blackness, and his ears stopped hearing. For a split second the darkness took him, and he saw Terrance dressed in flight gear, a determined look upon her face.

"Ich bin auf ihn," (I'm on him,) the professor called to Locke as he banked to follow. He was as obsessed as any other Luftwaffe pilot with increasing his score, and an opportunity such as this was never to be passed up.

As his vision and hearing returned, Archie suffered a few precious seconds of disorientation. He had to fight back a moment of panic. This was the trap where pilots were killed. Unconscious, they could not respond, and their aircraft made for an easy target. Eyes to the mirror, he did a snap roll to the left just as tracers flashed past.

Behind him, the Professor rolled in a like maneuver to follow and then blinked. He now saw two aircraft in his gun sight flying in a tight formation, one lagging slightly back from the other. "Dies ist ungerade," (*This is odd*) he spoke over the radio, not even meaning to. Lining up on the hind most aircraft, he again squeezed his triggers and watched as his tracers struck home with no apparent effect.

The two aircraft he followed now spilt in opposite directions. He immediately followed the one he'd been firing at, his vision graying again with the increased 'g' forces. When he came out of the turn and his vision again cleared, he found the aircraft had vanished like a specter.

The Wolf leader, cursing at his own bad luck and the other pilot's apparent skill, heard his wingman's call out that he was on the target. There was no need to respond. Their roles were now reversed of necessity. His mind immediately mapped out the turn he would do to continue around and come up behind. It was now his turn at watching closely for any approaching British fighters. Death seldom gave you an advance warning in this game; sharp eyes were as valuable as good marksmanship.

Archie, his course now reversed, found himself dead on to the yellow nosed Messerschmitt that had been trying to kill him. They were in a collision course with a closing speed of well over six hundred miles per hour. Gut reaction alone caused him to press his fire button as the aircraft passed each other with but little evasive maneuvering.

Derik, just about to radio his second, saw only the silhouette of the approaching Spitfire, yellow flashes illuminating its wings. Hanging on for life itself, he pushed the yoke forward just as three bullets found his windshield. The first missed his head by scant inches, the second nicked his right ear, and the third cut a groove in his right shoulder. Glass shards sprayed the entire cockpit, and if the Wolf had not been wearing goggles, he would have been blind. A split second later, his aircraft was buffeted as the Messerschmitt and the Spitfire passed belly to top.

Neither aircraft again turned, and neither looked back in their run for safe haven. Flight Lieutenant Corn fled to the safety of a temporary forward base close at hand, while Oberst Locke flew at a decreased speed back across the English Channel.

Professor Daecher, finding his commander in dire condition, circled him while scouting the skies for any other British fighters. When Locke assured him he was good to continue at his reduced speed, he climbed a few thousand feet higher and flew escort for the wounded pilot. The chase was over in any case as the Spitfire was now too far away to bother with; not to mention that their full on throttle escapades had depleted the precious fuel required to even follow the bombers.

Upon landing, but only after seeing Locke safely to the medical tent, he collared his maintenance chief and ordered his gun sight replaced. There was obviously something wrong with it, he explained, since he had never before seen a ghost aircraft during a dog fight.

Tactics and the Larger Picture

I would like to thank the 'Battle of Britain Commemorative Society' for their excellent web site where I have gained much insight to that which I wish to portray.

Fighter Command, as well as the Luftwaffe began looking into the reasons why very little progress was being made. The air war at this point seemed at a stalemate. Both sides called important meetings and conferences as they entered the next phase of the battle. Neither side, however, seemed willing to listen to those who were actually fighting the battles.

Air Chief Marshal Keith Park told a staff group conference that he'd become aware that many pilots were still chasing the 109 escorts, probably, he suspected, because of the thrill of high speed combat and inexperience. He went on to add. 'Now that the Luftwaffe is concentrating more on bombing missions it is imperative the bombers be regarded as priority targets.'

When the pilots heard of this order, that attacks be solely against the German bombers, they were far from happy. The tactic of selected squadrons attacking the escorts above while other squadrons attacked the bombers was working and was much easier to control because the combat would be broken into two different combat actions. If greater priority was given to the bombers, then;

a.　　they could be jumped upon by the escorts while concentrating on the bombers, and

b.   if all squadrons were to make attacks on the
      bombers as first priority, then the escorts would have
      to come down to the same altitude as the bombers
      making the task even more difficult, and

c.   if this method was to continue then the German
      bomber crews would demand even bigger escorts.

Flight Lieutenant Alan Deere 54 Squadron

The tremendous odds faced by the pilots of the 11 Group squadrons gave rise to criticism of Air Vice Marshal Park's tactics. I am in a position to comment at first hand on one aspect of these, and that was the policy of using selected Spitfire squadrons to draw off the enemy escort fighters, thus enabling the remaining squadrons, and this included the 12 Group Hurricanes, to concentrate more effectively on the bombers. Though this decision means a much tougher and unrewarding job for the Hornchurch Spitfire squadrons, I do not recall a single pilot saying other than he thought it an excellent idea. I strongly support this view, and on numerous occasions witnessed the rewards reaped when enemy bombers, shorn of the majority of their escort, were set upon by the defending Hurricanes which, excellent as they were, could not have coped so effectively without the intervention of the Spitfires.

On the German side of the battle, in a front line 'General Officer's briefing' on Luftwaffe tactics, Reichmarschall Hermann Göring sarcastically asked the commanders gathered before him what his pilots needed to win the battle.

Werner Mölders honestly replied that he would like the Bf 109 to be fitted with more powerful engines.

Adolf Galland, not wishing to let the Reichmarschall get away with his sarcasm, replied: "I should like an outfit of Spitfires for my squadron."

This left Göring speechless with rage as was intended.

Galland still preferred the Bf 109 for offensive sweeps, but he perceived the Spitfire to be a better defensive fighter, owing to its maneuverability.

§

Flight Lieutenant Henry Badcock limped into the pub where his friend Archie Corn had been given a room so he could rest. Archie, he found out from Control, had landed at RAF Rochford; one of the advanced fields closer to the coast. This was an old civil airport taken over by the RAF. Though the grass strip looked to be not much more than a farmer's pasture, it was more than enough for the Spitfires and Hurricanes needing a place to rest and repair. Lodging for the wounded pilots was mostly given by the local villagers, and their meals were served up at the pub.

"Oy," he called to the bar maid as he walked in. "Have you seen a good looking chap in a flight suit hanging about? He's rather tall and has a handsome rack of antlers on his head."

"Upstairs, third room on the right," the elderly Hedgehog replied. "I patched him up best I could. Learned the trade during the first war over in France where I was a Nightingale. He'll mend given time."

"Mend?" the Bulldog asked, alarm sounding in his voice, "Mend, hell... I need him to fly unless you're want'n to learn German."

She made a sour face suggesting she would be in hell before that happened and then told him, "Someth'in hit 'im in the arm. There was a bit 'o' blood but no real damage done. I probed the wound but didn't find anything. Mostly he's just exhausted. "Setting a glass on the counter with a soft thump, she filled it with whiskey. "This one's on me, luv, but the rest you have to pay for. I've still a business to run."

Henry thanked her, swallowed the whisky down, and then left three crowns on the bar all the same. If she'd patched up his friend, she deserved it... not to mention the whiskey was good.

"You shoot one of the bastards down for me and my Jimmy," she told him as she scooped the coins up.

"Roger Wilco," he told her with a wink. "What kind of bomber do you want me t' plug for ya?"

"One of those big gull winged bastards," she responded. "They bombed my cousin in London. I'd like to watch every last one of them burn."

"I'll see what I can do."

The Bulldog had to stop before the stairs and think about the climb. His ankle was swollen again and was throbbing thanks to the rigors of flying a Spitfire. Biggins Hill was hit again and he'd been arguing with Commander Sheltie about his physical abilities.

"I need to fly, sir," he'd explained. "Old Arch hasn't come back... if I'd been with him..."

The other Dog gave him a stern look. "It's not who is with you that makes the difference, Henry, it is the function of the team that wins battles, and I believe it was you who taught me that. Polis managed to land in a field, but his engine is a shambles. Smithe, unfortunately, went for a Burton. Archie made it to one of the advanced bases so he'll be camping out for a bit. Our field needs to be repaired before the flights can properly come back, so he was told to stay put. You'll just have to be patient; the wait will help you mend further. I need you well."

That was when the air raid siren began to wail for the third time that morning.

"The only plane left intact is mine," Sheltie told him, looking at the skies and making a spot decision. "It's down the flights. (*The area on an airfield where the aircraft were serviced between ops.*) Take it, and bloody well don't prang the undercarriage. I'll send Higgins to you and Arch. Call control after you're airborne and find out which base he's at. Go there and stay until called back. It was reported that he took some damage; do your best to cheer him up."

"YES SIR!" Henry yelled as he tried to run.

With a putting sound the Commander's motorbike pulled up next to the running Bulldog driven by Uncle Billy's Batman. With a bit of difficulty Henry managed to get into the sidecar, sitting sideways and leaving his feet out in the air.

"God save us all," Sheltie muttered as he watched this, "He's not only got my motorbike, but now he's got my airplane as well."

Ten minutes later Sheltie's Spitfire was climbing towards Angels Sixteen where the incoming bombers would be found. Three were called damaged after the lone Spit was done with them.

§

A large urn of flowers was delivered to the airfield hospital ward reserved for Luftwaffe officers. Each bed was surrounded by a sheet like cloth curtain, and the staff kept these closed for privacy as they hurried about their jobs. Officers were accorded privilege whereas the enlisted had only an open ward of some sixty beds. Wounded airmen were a dime a dozen during these times, and the medical staff were as tired as any of the fliers.

Finding the particular pilot she was looking for took the Poodle a few peeks into the various cubicles, but when she did find him she smiled and let herself in, careful to close the curtain behind herself.

223

"I asked for a bottle of wine, did you bring it?" asked the patient. The Wolf had a thick bandage wrapped around his right upper arm and one ear was encased in a soft plaster casing.

"No," she replied, setting the vase on the small table next to his bed, "But if I had known you so wanted one, I would have had someone inquire as to the vintage you preferred. If you wish, I can steal a bottle of schnapps from the doctor's quarters, but from what I see, they need it more than you do."

Locke looked up from the paperwork he was filling out and smiled. "Jeans, wasn't it? What on earth are you doing here?" Lowering his voice to a whisper, he asked, "Is it safe for you to do this?"

Leaning down she kissed him on the lips. "What do you think?"

"I think you are crazy."

She shrugged her shoulders. "I could say the same thing of you, no? You fly over a land that is not friendly and you have no way back should you be shot down… which I am told almost happened. The last time I believe you went for a swim?"

"It was a fluke; he got off a lucky shot."

"He being?"

The Wolf gave her a wry smile. "I would wager an Austrian mark that you already know."

"Actually I don't; so pay me," she laughed.

The curtain was swept back and a dark Dog in a leather trench coat stood looking at them. Two soldiers in black uniforms bearing shouldered machine pistols stood behind him at rigid attention.

"Am I come at a bad moment?" he asked softly, his accent Belgium sounding. His actions and demeanor bore no respect towards the persons he addressed.

"Merde," Jeans hissed and then followed it with another spat of French.

"Who are you?" the Dog asked her in the same language.

Jeans was about to reply in the invective when Locke's paw gripped her shoulder with enough strength that it caused her actual pain.

"She was to be my date, arranged for me by my brother pilots," he told the Dog in a very hard voice. "I may be wounded, but they, at least, understand I still have my needs. So yes… you have come at a bad time."

"You should tell your bed kitten to be more civil, or she might find herself placed in the Gestapo's 'protective custody,'" he replied, never raising his voice. Nothing in his demeanor changed to indicate he was intimidated in the slightest. "I won't take long Staffelkapitän Locke; my name is Kriminalkommissar Gundulf Faust of the Geheime Staatspolizei. (Secret State Police) I have a few questions for you concerning the death of Party member Leutnant Günter Meyer."

"He was a pilot. He died," Locke replied acidly. "Just like too many of the pilots under my authority that Command has deemed suitable to fly fighters. He was sent here before he was ready and was easily done in by the RAF. I wrote a report on it; I am sure you read it."

The Gestapo agent dug in a pocket of his coat and pulled out a pack of cigarettes. "Would you care for one?" he asked, holding them out to Locke.

"There is oxygen in use here," the Wolf replied, "I would not suggest it."

"Ah, so there is," the Dog replied, taking the time to light up. Exhaling smoke, he said, "Yes, I did read your report. You were on a training patrol with him as I understand it. I also understand you were not happy with him when he mentioned pilots in parachutes?"

The fact that the Dog had this information did not surprise Locke; although how he came about obtaining it did bother him. The fact that one had to fly while looking over their shoulders for two enemies only hampered the chore of command. "That is correct," he replied, not trying to hide a fact that was already obviously known.

"Und why would that be?"

"The pilots under my command are expected to do their duty to their country with honor. They are warriors, not butchers."

"I see." The Dog motioned to Jeans and said with a small smile, "I will go now so as not to interfere with your recovery Staffelkapitän Locke. Be sure to do her with honor, eh? Der Fuehrer needs you back in the air as quickly as possible, so if that helps…" He shrugged.

"I suppose he told you that personally?"

"We shall talk again of your report, Herr Locke," the Gestapo agent told him softly in response, "Until then…" He nodded and then deliberately closed the curtain with a flick of his wrists which caused a hissing sound of the curtain rings. He then left the room with the two soldiers hard upon his heels.

Leaning close, Jeans whispered in the Wolf's ear, "Talk to me only of love; in here there are too many ears."

§

Henry sat watching his friend sleep. As he sipped his whiskey, he reflected that Archie looked like crap. Their maintenance officer had been by earlier to tell them the Spitfires were ready. Since the airfield fell under regular attack, they were hidden close by but still able to roll out onto the field in short order.

The fighter pilots had the night to themselves while the Boulton Paul Defiants flew night sorties against the infrequent bombers braving the darkness. The poor old Defiants, being a two man aircraft and having no forward firing guns were not much more than candy for the Messerschmitts. Their crews, keenly aware of this, still continued to fly. With that fact in mind, they were at least relegated to the cover of night where they might possibly do some good. In the morning, with the rise of the sun, the Spitfires and Hurricanes would again be airborne and waiting for the bombers to come.

One more day... one more blood bath. One of the things about having a regular team in the air was that Archie and Henry had developed their own tricks; like not staying in the tightness required of 'vic' flying. It didn't matter who their third was because as soon as it was explained, the wisdom of what they did was understood and immediately accepted. The pity of it was that Tops would not listen to the experience of his pilots.

There was a soft knock on the door. Henry thought this was odd being that it was ten 'o' clock at night. "Doors open," he called out just loud enough to be heard, "Let yur'self in."

The door opened softly and framed a largish Elkhound wearing a long trench coat and an officer's Reme (dress cap). Just visible was his Royal Army uniform, the collar pins of which showed him to be a full Colonel. "I am looking for Flight Lieutenant Archie Corn," he announced, keeping his voice low.

"You found him," Henry replied without rising, "But I fear he is fast asleep. Being that we'll be up before the dawn, I would ask if you could postpone..."

"It's all right, Henry," the Stag said, interrupting his friend. "I've been awake for a while now."

"Bugger," the Bulldog muttered, "And you never said anything to me. I should be upset but lucky for you, I'm too stinking snockered to worry about it."

Archie slowly sat up in the bed and looked at the Dog. "You'll pardon me if I don't rise, sir, but my body is still a bit hammered. The bed is soft, and my bum hurts... so it's a bit more comfortable for me to just stay put."

"Quite all right," the Army Officer replied, "But may we speak alone, please?"

"Ahhh right… gotcha then," Henry muttered, "It's all hush hush.

I'll be moving downstairs then to the bar for a bit. Whatever it is I have no requirements to know about is probably for my own good and the good of my country and all of that. I understand this above all else, so I'll just check my curiosity at the hat rack next to the door."

"Cheers, Henry," the other pilot said, to his friend, "Don't drink too much, eh?"

"Last one for the night," he replied. Raising the glass he'd been working on he downed the contents. Pausing for a moment, he added, "I've been thinking about Andras lately, Archie, and that's a bad thing. It leads me to hate and then I tend to shoot the pilot rather than the machine."

"Does it matter that much which you shoot?" the Colonel asked.

"It does to me," Henry replied and then struggled to get out of his chair. Failing the attempt, he slumped back into it, muttered the word 'bugger' one more time, and then was solidly snoring.

"If you don't mind the noise," Archie offered, nodding at his friend, "This is probably the most secure place to have a chat." Looking to the strange officer, he added, "I am Flight Lieutenant Archie Corn, who might you be?"

"You may call me Colonial Blue," the Hound replied stepping through the door and closing it, "I'm with M.I.6."

"I see… so Wing Commander Falstaff sent you?"

"We spoke. I thought it would be best if I came to you straight away. These sort of things are best handled as soon as they are known." Motioning to the bed, he asked, "May I sit?"

Archie swung his feet down to the floor. Removing his coat, the officer took a seat on the vacated part of the bed.

"I met her rather randomly," Archie told him while rubbing his sore arm, "At Madam Bella's house of ill repute. It was Henry's glorious idea to go there." Looking to the officer, he asked, "Do you know about Terrance?"

Colonel Blue's face was mostly hidden in the dim lighting so his expression was unreadable. "I understand Terrance was an American volunteer and an excellent pilot. He will be missed, but not forgotten."

Archie smiled at the other fellow's deftness of craft. "Her name is Jeans," he said plainly, "And she gave me information on how and when Jerry was going bomb the airfield. She said, 'The Boche at their field operational level understand that sometimes a low level raid can sneak past the RDF stations.' That's not something an ordinary prostitute should know, is it?"

The Colonel took a note pad and pen out of his coat pocket. Squinting to see, he told the pilot, "Right then, let us start from the beginning."

"I don't want her hurt," the Stag told the other officer softly. "We got the upper paw that time and stopped a devastating raid because of what she told me. That's where Henry hurt his ankle."

"As I said," the Staghound told him again, his voice taking on a harder edge, "We shall start from the beginning and when I have all the information I can gather, we will wait and watch. This is a different game than what you play in the sky Archie... may I call you Archie?"

"I would prefer Flight Lieutenant if you don't mind, sir."

"It's a different game we play in M.I.6 than you play in the skies Flight Lieutenant. Someone like your Jeans is pretty much a small piece of a much larger puzzle; and yet possibly much larger than either of us could even hope to be. We will examine this puzzle piece, turning it every which way in the light while handling her quite delicately. Then we will reinsert it into the larger picture perhaps in a different position... such as within and under the protective umbrella of M.I.6. Being that she was so willing to get you in position to be waiting for Jerry, it could be that she has just handed us her calling card. If that is the case, she might be a tool that could possibly save millions of lives. I was a detective before the war and through experience understand that we will see much more than one might believe possible simply by putting the pieces together."

He hesitated seeming to weigh his decision and then said, "I will tell you something now so you will understand what I mean and it is not to be repeated to anyone; not even to the Wing Commander. Do you agree? "

Archie nodded his head.

"Very good. We know for a fact that Reichmarschall Göring does not believe the RDF stations are all that important. He has even ceased bombing them in lieu of other targets. Your Jeans has just told us that the pilots and their commanders are well aware of how important the installations are and apparently how to get around them. That is a huge piece to the puzzle that has just been put together thus far. It is obvious that Uncle Fatty is not listening to those who know."

"I see," the pilot responded. "He sounds a bit like Tops then."

228

Both of them shared in this statement with a chuckle and then continued the conversation until an hour before dawn. At this point they woke Henry and between the pair of them half carried half dragged him out to the airfield where their aircraft were waiting.

The Polish 303

"God defend me from my friends; from my enemies I can defend myself."

-- Proverb--

The No. 303 "Kościuszko" Polish Fighter Squadron was the highest scoring squadron during the Battle of Britain. It was formed in Britain as part of an agreement between the Polish Government in Exile and the United Kingdom.

As in all things there is dispute with the actual numbers and score placement. The British public followed the war in the same manner they would a sporting event. What I found recorded by historians actually sounded a bit like baseball statistics.

According to John Alcorn, 44 victories are positively verified, making No. 303 Squadron the fourth highest scoring squadron of the battle. It also had the highest kill-to-loss ratio; of 2.8:1. However, Mr. Alcorn was not able to attribute 30 aircraft shot down to any particular unit.

According to Jerzy Cynk and other Polish historians, the actual number of victories for No. 303 Squadron was about 55 to 60. According to Polish historian Jacek Kutzner the verified number of kills of 303 Squadron is around 58.8, which would still place it above all other squadrons regarding verified kills. Fractional victories come from shared kills.

The pilots of the 303, by their own tally, claimed one hundred twenty six 'Adolfs' shot down.

These particular fighter pilots fought with a viciousness not seen in their British counterparts. This was attributed to the fact that their country had been overrun by the Germans in an extreme display of cruelty and brutality. This included indiscriminant mass executions and the total devastation of Warsaw in retaliation for the country's continued resistance.

After researching their story, I was appalled at what two of my war time heroes allowed to happen at the end of the war; which was the giving over of certain countries to Soviet dominion. Poland was one of these countries and Stalin's treatment of her citizens was no less brutal than that of the Germans.

This capitulation of the allies to the Soviets even reared its ugly head at the London Victory parade of 1946. Since the No. 303 Squadron was the most effective Polish RAF squadron during the Second World War, some sources state that its pilots were invited to march in the parade; but the invitation was refused because no other Polish units were invited.

According to other sources, however, No. 303 Squadron was not invited in fear that this would upset Joseph Stalin and so they could not have refused the invitation that was not presented.

Either way… it was not right.

§

Three Hurricanes landed unexpectedly at the advanced base of RAF Rochford close to sundown. They were so badly shot up that the Kiwis present doubted they would ever be flyable again. Their pilots however, speaking a language none of the mechanics understood, made it clear through pidgin English and pantomime that they wished to be fueled, armed, and back in the air by the morning.

Henry standing a short distance away and next to his own aircraft, watched the arm waving and garbled words more in amusement than anything else. "OY!" he yelled, getting their attention. "Ludwik! Your mother's a German Shepherd!"

The Gończy Polski (Polish Hunting Dog) turned to the voice and grinned when he saw the Bulldog. "H'ry Badpenis!" he shouted back, "Your mother is French Kitty Cat!" Turning to his comrades, he spoke to them in Polish, pointing to Henry. His paw swept through the air imitating an airplane in flight and then it swept downwards, turning circles, obviously just barely pulling out in time to keep from hitting the ground. They all laughed, including Henry who realized which story it was that Ludwig was telling.

"JERRY UP!" someone shouted and all eyes looked upwards as the field's anti-aircraft guns began firing. 'Flaming onions' (40 millimeter tracer rounds) sprayed the sky in a pyrotechnic display of defensive might that seemed to have a hard time hitting anything. Where everyone else dove to the ground or ran to take cover, the Bulldog saw the three Polish pilots draw their side arms and begin firing at the lone strafing Messerschmitt. The attack took a scant twenty seconds from start to finish. The enemy pilot, apparently too rattled by everyone trying to kill him, didn't even hit anything. It would have been better if the anti-aircraft gunners were able to hit their mark but at least they managed to keep him at bay.

Getting up from the ground, the ex-instructor dusted himself off and calmly walked to meet the other pilots half way.

"Rzecz," the Hunting Dog yelled out.

"Friend," Henry responded, raising his right paw in the air in a good natured wave. "Dzień dobry dla ciebie (Hello to you) Prosze, o piwo proszę. (Please, a beer please.)" This exhausted the pilot's extent of the Polish language, but the other pilots still laughed.

"I buy for you," the pilot in the middle offered. He was an Ogar (Polish Hound). One of his sleeves was torn near the shoulder and there was blood dripping from his wrist.

"I think we need to get that looked at," Henry told him, grasping the paw.

Ludwig took his paw next and then the third pilot, who was a Chart Polski (Polish Greyhound).

"Is nothing," the Ogar responded. "Pour on Vodka… burn a bit but good for it. I am Witold," he told him, "You know Ludwig very good I think." Here, he made a slapping motion to the back of his other paw in imitation of a slap to the back of the head. "He was bad student, no?"

"He wasn't the worse I had," the ex-instructor responded with a wink, "As I recall there was a Czech fellow who was shoddier."

"This is Jan," Witold said next, motioning to the Greyhound.

That Dog nodded and held out his paw which Henry firmly shook.

"Archie and I got in a bit ago," the Brit told the three Poles. "We had no luck on the patrol but you can't expect to shoot them up every time you take off. How did you do?"

"Two each," Jan told him and then made flying motions with his paws complete with machine gun noises and little screams of anguish as the obvious German aircraft crashed.

"We had bad moments too," Ludwig told him with a wink, "But Kiwis fix, no?"

"Perhaps you would join us at the pub?" Henry invited with a chuckle. "They have good food there and the owner is a fair paw at the nursing so the pilot can be fixed as well. Perhaps she can pour on some of that vodka for you."

This was readily agreed to and as the pilots began to walk the distance, Corporal Higgins pulled up on Commander Sheltie's motorbike. Witold was quickly stuffed into the sidecar and rushed off to the pub so his arm could be looked at while the other three walked.

"Make sure you tell the old girl he's one of ours so she don't cut his throat!" Henry shouted at the batman's back as they drove away. This mistaken identity happened all too frequently after a bail out situation. It had now come to a point where all the Polish pilots carried small British flags and cards from Command stating they were indeed RAF.

§

Dierk sat at his desk, his ear still bandaged but otherwise looking his old self. All was paperwork for the past week. Since he was injured, the Staffel Commandant was forced to try and get as much done as he possibly could. He did make time to meet with the new pilots. He had four veterans arrive along with four rookies and immediately paired them up to fly training missions. There were orders for repair parts he had to sign as well as requests for entirely new aircraft to replace those that did not come back. So far he'd been lucky and his squadron's loss rate was much smaller than the others. There was also fuel, ammunition, ground crews, and mechanics, as well as all the lodgings and logistics that went with this; all of his responsibility to contend with.

The pilot had just uttered a curse and thrown the paperwork he'd been working on against the wall when there was a soft knock at his door.

"Hereinkommen!" he barked and immediately regretted his tone of voice when Professor Daecher stepped into the room looking quite dapper in his dress uniform.

"Here you are, Herr Oberst, und I see you are using a tried and true method for finishing paperwork." Bending, he picked up the scattered papers while continuing his happy banter. "I used to grade the papers of my students in a similar manner. I would throw them all into the air, and the paper that hit the floor first got an automatic passing grade."

"Und why would you do that?" Locke asked, his curiosity getting the better of him.

"Because facts are heavy, they weigh the paper down und it doesn't fly so well; much as a certain other thing I have observed which is: lies fly much better than truth. A bona fide person of education never stops asking questions, such as, why do those in charge always ignore the experience of those fighting their battles for them. I happen to be of the belief that if the Luftwaffe was in competent paws then the Wehrmacht would already be in England."

He stood and handed the papers back to his favorite wingman with a slight bow. "Bending like that makes the blood go to your head. It is good I am used to such things. I have missed flying with you Herr Oberst. When will you be released to duty?"

"Tomorrow," the Wolf answered, "Though I have no idea why they are making me wait. I have been ready for a week now."

"Perhaps they wish to be sure you can handle yourself in the cockpit again. You do need a fair amount of strength to do what we do." As he said this, the Wolf removed his hat and began looking about the room as if tracking a mosquito. "Perhaps what they are really waiting for in a statement from you."

"Statement? What kind of statement?"

"Oh I don't knowwwww… perhaps something like, 'I hate der Fuheur,' or 'I love the British,' that sort of thing. It usually plays well at a court martial."

He stopped and, smiling, pointed to the heating grate on the wall. "Just as I suspected, you have been leaving out your cheese again and it has attracted a listening Rat."

Turning, he said, "I propose we go out for the night. It will be my treat. Paris has a wonderful opera house. Listening to the sounds of Bellini belted out by an overweight Poodle might be painful, but it will do your bad ear good."

Locke picked up the pile of papers and tossed them further back upon his desk. "If you insist," he told his friend, "I will go; but only if I can buy you a proper meal afterwards?"

"Done," the other Wolf responded, "But you should know I am not a cheap date."

§

Archie looked up as his batman helped the wounded Witold into the pub. He'd been nursing a beer while waiting for Henry to arrive and this now was left on the table. "Richard? Who's this?"

"Flight Lieutenant Witold Nowak," the pilot told him, his voice sounding rough. "I need vodka, please."

"Archie rose from his table. "First we shall look at your arm and then the vodka; just in case you need surgery."

"I cannot kill Germans from hospital," the Dog barked. The bark turned into a cough and a moment later he was seated in a chair with his head between his legs to keep from passing out. In a moment he sat upright again and smiled. "You see... I am fine."

"All right then," the Stag replied as he carefully attempted to undo the top button of the pilot's flight suit, "I am glad you are fine but we really need to see what we have here under the suit. Then we shall know exactly how fine you are, eh?"

"Out of my way," the pub's owner told him as she pushed through carrying a metal pan containing her medical supplies, "You never remove clothing if there is a wound underneath, you cut it away carefully. What if his shirt is the only thing holding his guts in place, eh? And there you are trying to stuff the lot back in again."

Saying this, she took a large pair of shears out of the pan and snapped them at the Stag. "I've done circumcisions with these. You need fix'n up you come see me after I'm done here."

Archie, knowing the old Hedgehog's abilities, stepped back out of the way and watched her work. While she was at it, he attempted to engage the pilot in conversation to keep his mind off of the pain.

"I'm with the 92 and you?"

"303 Kościuszko," the Hound told him. There was then an intake of breath as the pub keeper carefully cut away the flight suit's material.

"I see it," she mumbled to herself. "Look at that, just under the skin and sticking out like a pimple head. Lucky for you the force of the bullet was for the most part spent."

"Not spent," the Hound told her, "Polish pilot's body like steel."

They all laughed at his bravado and then he grimaced as the old Hedgehog gripped his arm hard and dug in with just her fingers. A moment later and quite a few expression changes of both the pilot and the nurse, she held the bloody piece of metal out for everyone to see.

"Got it!" she told them. "Now we'll drink."

In short order, she had a fresh beer for Archie and Corporal Higgins along with a bottle of Vodka for Witold. As she finished up cleaning and stitching the Hound's wounds, Henry walked in with the other two pilots making loud noises about how hungry he was. Higgins quietly excused himself to the kitchen where he'd made himself very useful since being there.

"I say, Archie," the Bulldog greeted him, "Look what followed me home. Can I keep them?"

After dinner, the stout pilot plopped down behind the pub's piano and began playing a melody of songs that had everyone, including the pub's owner, singing along. During this the Sergeant Major in charge of the Kiwis came in and, over a beer, regretfully informed the Polish pilots that he could only manage to fix two of their aircraft by salvaging from the third. Henry stopped playing at this news and watched with a smile as the old Sergeant tried to bridge the language gap. When the fellow realized the three pilots were not quite understanding his words, he made airplane noises and then held up the first finger on his left paw with a thumbs up on with his right. He then did two fingers and a thumbs up. Then, holding up a third finger he shook his head sadly and gave a thumbs down.

"Kaput?" Jan asked.

"Kaput," he replied.

There was a spat of Polish cursing and then Henry laughed and began banging away on the piano again singing, "Kaput kaput kaput kaput and don't Jerry know we'll keep on a fight'n till old Adolf is kaput!"

§

Dierk and the Professor walked side by side down the street, their driver following slowly at a discrete distance. The opera had been exactly as Daecher said it would be; uplifting and refreshing like a cold drink of water to a thirsty soldier. Now it was the commander's turn to buy dinner but as yet they had not come across a bodega that appealed to them. Most had been filled with soldiers making the most of a night out; drinking beer by the gallon and singing the national songs they all loved.

The pilots, on the other paw, were in a more subdued mood.

"I understand you had a visitor at the hospital the other day," the learned Daecher told his commander.

"Which one?" Locke countered with a chuckle. "I had one who made me feel very good und another who made me feel very bad."

"Let us speak of the Rat sampling at your cheese," Wilhelm told him, taking a pipe from within his dress coat. As he packed it, he said, "I do not think he was so much after your tail as he was simply trying to instill the fear of being watched into the Gruppe. Did you know that when Napoleon's troops charged into battle they did so in the shadows of a portable guillotine that was brought along for the express purpose of ensuring their undying loyalty?"

"Noooo…"

"It's true. You do know that my field of study is history, do you not?"

"Und so... why are you here flying fighters instead of teaching in Berlin?"

The other Wolf, stopping to light his pipe, chuckled. "Because flying with you is so much more fun than grading papers. There are so few free thinkers these days. Most of those I had in my classes were sucked in by the officer corps as being a cut above the usual trench hound. Then, after I was given a little chat by the head of our local Brown Shirts, where he adamantly suggested I teach a rather perverted reflection of history, I left."

"Just like that?"

The other Wolf smiled a strange smile. "Well... I suppose in a roundabout way. I had a close friend in the navy whom I confided in and he suggested the Luftwaffe as a viable adventure; especially since I never was able to subscribe to the pack mentality of The Party. 'It would be much better for you,' he told me, 'to fly a single seat aircraft.' I saw the wisdom in this and my promotion was helped along."

"Und who might this naval officer be?" Dierk asked, taking a cigar out of his own coat pocket and lighting it.

The Professor smiled and then told him eagerly. "I was told you met him. Let us just say that he is a Fox. As a return favor I make a small report to him once in a while. Now tell der Professor young Dierk Locke, do you feel justified in what you do?"

"I am a soldier, as are you," the Staffelkapitän replied, "We each find our own justification in doing what we are ordered to do, yes?"

"You did not answer my question."

They stopped in front of another restaurant filled this time with soldiers all wearing black uniforms. They were holding up full beer steins which they noisily clinked together to a roar of voices toasting Der Fuehrer. It was rumored the smallish Wolf would be coming to tour Paris the following week, and the number of these black uniforms had swelled among the local population of soldiers.

One of the soldiers noticed them standing in the window and merrily waved in invitation. Both pilots waved back but declining the invitation with a shake of their heads, continuing their slow stroll down the sidewalk.

"You are familiar with the story of Publius Horatius Cocles or, as we were taught from childhood, 'Hero at the Bridge'?" Locke asked his friend.

"Of course," Daecher replied, sucking on his pipe. "I have taught about him frequently. In the last few years, it was one part of my study that I was encouraged by the University's administration to teach. 'Give of yourself and do not lose hope, though all around you, cowardice prevails.' It is a very fitting story for this war we are in, eh? Give of yourself," he pronounced, "und help Der Fuehrer conquer the world."

"Your sense of humor might get you in trouble old friend," Locke told him, glancing over his shoulder. All was quiet, and their car was following as it should.

"As it did you? We still have to discuss your visitor at the hospital."

"Which one?"

"Ah yes… the damsel or the dragon. Damsel first and then the dragon I think. I understand she is very pretty for a 'prostitute'. I hope you explained the Rat to her. If she means anything to you at all he will certainly hunt her down."

"Please allow me to finish my story first," Dierk replied in a serious voice, "und then we can speak of the damsel, eh? Cocles fought on regardless of all and prevented the army of Clusium from entering Rome by allowing his cowardly brethren time enough to destroy the bridge over which they would have crossed."

"And he lived," added the Professor, "which is the bonus part of the story."

"Perhaps I am like that fellow," Dierk told him, "I don't exactly see myself as being particularly brave but regardless of the cost, I intend to do my duty."

"But, my dear commander," Daecher countered playing the Devil's advocate, "Our army is the one advancing zo that would present us as the Clusiums; is that not correct?"

There was a huge blast and the sounds of shattered glass behind them. Instinctively ducking, both Wolfs spun to look behind themselves, finding the restaurant they'd just passed now nothing more than a fiery hole in the building. Their car, which had been sitting just in front of the blast was turned upon its side, the driver dead.

§

In the morning, Archie received word that Biggins Hill was once again cleared for action. He and Henry, along with Ludwig and Jan were to fly a patrol close to Hell's Corner and then head back to their respective fields.

Witold was the odd man out with his wound and no aircraft to fly. He stayed behind with Corporal Higgins who agreed to give the pilot a lift as far as Biggins, where he was required to turn over Commander Sheltie's motorbike.

The four were cruising south at angels twenty when Control called vectoring them on an interception course of eighty unknown aircraft coming in at angels fifteen.

"We shall meet them together," Archie called over the radio. "Priority is the bombers."

"Spitfires lag back," Ludwig countered, "Watch for fighters. Hurricanes go into bombers first."

"Tops' orders are for all fighters to concentrate on the bombers," Archie replied.

"Tops not flying here, eh?" Jan called. "We go in... keep Schmitts off us."

Archie looked to Henry who was flying close to his right wing. The Bulldog nodded to him.

"Roger Wilco," Archie replied to the Poles. "We will give you our best."

As the Hurricanes descended, heading straight in to meet the growing dots on the horizon, the Spitfires climbed and got above the escorting German fighters, of which there were four Schwarm (sixteen aircraft). Before these could dive to intercept the Hurricanes, Henry and Archie were on them so viciously the German pilots would later claim there were no less than ten Spitfires opposing them.

Jan and Withold got two Heinkel 111 bombers each. Archie and Henry each got a 109 and shared a Heinkel.

Word was sent back to the pub owner at RAF Rochford about the victory along with many thanks for her hospitality and care as soon as they landed.

This was followed by a personal note from Henry that they had done this one 'especially for you luv'.

Winston Churchill inspecting bomb damage in Battersea, South London, 10 September 1940.

Civil Defense
September 7th, 1940

Author's note: Living life in our day to day existence is to know and accept things as they are simply as a 'matter of fact'. You don't think about the details of your morning commute, you simply take your sippie cup out to the car, strap yourself in, and turn the key. Though they both accomplish the same function, your vehicle of choice now is totally different from the cars of the nineteen fifties. Back then there was nothing to strap in with, and you'd better not be drinking coffee because you had to manually shift the gears which kept your right hand and left foot pretty busy. There is no choice in this; it is life as we know it to be.

You accept 'what is' because we can only live within the times we are born.

It is only when we are able to look back at history, viewing huge blocks of time at a glance, that we are able to digest some of what happened. By doing this we will at least, perhaps, see and understand a series of intersecting events that 'alone' might have meant very little; but in a domino effect completely changed the outcome of what was to be.

Unfortunately, history loses the minute details of the everyday life that was lived. What we see has become two dimensional, presented for the most part, as factoids. The goal, therefore, of historical drama is to help the reader relive even a small part of what it was like to exist during the time represented.

§

To this point in the battle, it had been one nation's military forces against the other. If you will take an overview of all the aircraft used on both sides, it is easily understood that their functional design was based upon a 1930's concept of a war waged in Europe. Through the Battle of

France and Dunkirk, this worked well. Range and bomb load was governed by the size of the aircraft required to perform under rough field conditions.

A bomber, operating from an advanced battlefield airbase, would take off, fly no more than a hundred miles, hit its target, and then return to reload and repeat the process over again many times during the day.

Likewise, the fighters would take off, fly to where the battle was in a matter of minutes, engage, fight, and then return again. The ME 109 had a range (with a drop tank) of only 1000 kilometers with a flying time of perhaps one hour and twenty minutes. Ferry range on a Spitfire is listed as 1840 kilometers but was much shorter under combat conditions.

Multiple missions were expected and performed under these conditions. In this way, a constant attack on the enemy was possible while maintaining a smaller air force.

These facts are only so many numbers to us in the present. To the pilots living 'then,' these were critical details that were simply everyday life. Exhaustion prevailed on both sides.

When Britain was attacked, distance was pushed to the extended range for most of the German aircraft; but the Luftwaffe was still succeeding. The RAF was teetering on the brink of defeat under the onslaught against their airfields and support organizations.

One thing changed this.

The first German attack on London actually occurred by accident. On the night of August 24, 1940, Luftwaffe bombers aiming for military targets on the outskirts of London drifted off course and instead dropped their bombs on the center of London destroying several homes and killing civilians. Amidst the public outrage that followed, Prime Minister Winston Churchill, believing this had been a deliberate attack, ordered Berlin to be bombed the next evening.

Till now the war had been military to military in a tactical board game of one sided destruction. The mass cold blooded killings in Poland were only a foreshadowing of what Hitler's war machine was capable of in dealing with a civilian population. With the counter strike on Berlin came a very dark turn of events.

The following excerpts were taken from the historical files of the Battle of Britain Historical Society's web site. Look through the eyes of the people who wrote them.

Berlin Diary William L.Shirer 1940

Today the bombing is the one topic of conversation among Berliners. Its especially amusing therefore to see that Goebbels has permitted the local newspapers to publish only a six-line communiqué about it, to the effect that enemy planes flew over the capital, dropped a few incendiary bombs on two suburbs, and damaged one wooden hut in a garden. There is not a line about the explosive bombs which we all plainly heard. Nor is there a word about the three streets in Berlin which have been roped off all day today to prevent the curious from seeing what a bomb can do to a house. It will be interesting to watch the reaction of the Berliners to the efforts of the authorities to hush up the extent of the raid.

Hermann Göring September 7th 1940

This moment is a historic one. As a result of the provocative British attacks on Berlin on recent nights the Führer has decided to order a mighty blow to be struck in revenge against the British capital of the British Empire. I personally have assumed the leadership of this attack and today I have heard above me the roaring of the victorious German squadrons.

Squadron Leader A.V.R (Sandy) Johnstone, 602 Squadron, Sept 7th 1940.

All we could see was row upon row of German raiders, all heading for London. I have never seen so many aircraft in the air all at the same time. . . . The escorting fighters saw us at once and came down like a ton of bricks, when the squadron split up and the sky became a seething cauldron of aeroplanes, swooping and swerving in and out of the vapour trails and tracer smoke. A Hurricane on fire spun out of control ahead of me while, above to my right, a 110 flashed across my vision and disappeared into the fog of battle before I could draw a bead on it.

Everyone was shouting at once and the earphones became filled with a meaningless cacophony of jumbled noises. Everything became a maelstrom of jumbled impression — a Dornier spinning wildly with part of its port mainplane missing; black streaks of tracer ahead, when I instinctively put my arm up to shield my face; taking a breather when the haze absorbed me for a moment.

William 'Bill' Thompson Civil Defense Woolwich

We got the red alert, as was often the case when an impending raid was approaching from the Thames Estuary. But the usual practice was for the bomber formations to split up near the Isle of Sheppy and they then set course for the RAF aerodromes north and south of the Thames then we would revert back to a yellow. But in this case we was under a 'red' for longer than usual and messages started to come in that the bombers were seen coming up the Thames. Well, I went up and I have never seen anything like it. A thick blanket of black bombers, which must have been two miles wide, following the Thames.

Our station was almost at the road junction that now goes down to the Woolwich ferry, and we had an excellent view of what was going to happen. I think the first bombs were dropped just before the dock areas and the right side of the formation would pass right over us. We could do nothing but get back to our posts and pray like mad. The sound was deafening, the building shook and dust from walls and ceilings started to envelope our desks, we could do nothing while the raid was on, although a few phone calls came through, 'this street got it' and 'so- and-so building has got a direct hit. Then silence, slowly the phones died, lines had been cut, and we knew that once it was all over we would have to rely on messengers.

George Wilkins AFS Fireman London

"Saturday September 7th was sunny with a light westerly breeze. At 4pm, we on our Emergency Fireboat were ordered down to Tilbury. As we approached Tower Bridge we saw vast volumes of smoke on its eastward side rising white into the sunlight. We passed under Tower Bridge and soon were on the edge of an inferno. Everything was alight. Tugs and barges were flaming and sinking in the river. All the timber of Surrey Commercial Docks was blazing furiously.

The sun had disappeared and darkness was as of night. A strong wind was whipped up by the great fire heat which caused small flaming planks of wood to be blown about like matchsticks, and the river itself was as turbulent as a whipped-up small sea. Small crowds of people were here and there at the water's edge crying out for rescue. Warehouses and all sorts of buildings were burning on both sides of the river. Not until we were near Greenwich did we see the sun again and then only as a pale disc through the great ceiling of smoke. There I saw a gasometer alight. (A huge building like structure that stores natural gas.) To my surprise it did not explode but went as one great blue flame, like an enormous gas jet *lasting only a minute."*

§

Archie found himself lying flat on his stomach in the rubble that used to be the home of Corporal Higgins. It was hard to breath because of all the smoke and dust. It appeared that all of London was burning. He was maintaining a firm hold on Henry's ankles, who in turn was maintaining a firm hold on Corporal Higgin's ankles, who in turn was attempting to dig his young niece out the fallen brickwork. Next to the stag, though it was hardly visible in the dim light, was an unexploded five hundred pound bomb. 'Für Berlin!' he noted, had been painted onto its cold steel body.

Some four hours earlier they had been trying to prevent this from happening. They may as well have stood in the surf and tried to prevent the sea from crashing upon the shore.

"All aircraft, all aircraft, vector for London defense. Bandits west bound just crossing Broadstairs at angels twenty. Approximate strength three hundred, ETA fifteen minutes. Respond please."

"Yellow Leader here; Roger wilco (will comply)." Archie called back. To his squadron mates he called, "Sharp eyes lads, watch for the fighters but we go directly for the bombers."

"Yellow Leader, Yellow Two," Henry called to him, "I've got a bad feeling about this one. They never put that many bombers up to hit Holy Ground before and there hasn't been any reports of advanced hunters, over."

The Stag responded by clicking his mike button twice in acknowledgment. He felt it too.

Their patrol area presently had them just north of Cambridge so getting back put them over London at about the same moment as the bombers. This would give them half fuel, but as they were then flying just above their air base, combat range was hardly an issue.

Finding the bombers this day had been easy as their formation was so large it took on the appearance of a black malevolent storm cloud. Attacking them, however, was near impossible due to the extreme number of escort fighters; both Me 109's and 110's. The 109 could and did mix it up with the Spitfires but its time over target was severely limited. The twin engined 110, which was not so agile, was easier to defend against but if you were jumped by them and they had you on a diving attack it could still be very deadly.

This day the RAF's fighters were pounced upon as if they were a child's ball in a playground football match. The ensuing battle over London was massive. Those RAF pilots responding to the call out soon became frustrated past the breaking level. There was no turning the bombers' attack this time; the encroaching formation of aircraft was just too massive. The Junkers and Heinkels continued on undeterred just as if they were on rails.

Archie's group of six aircraft arrived as the Germans reached the outskirts of the city. Before they could attack, and even as they saw the black dots emerging from the bellies of the lead 'kette', they were jumped by twenty Germans fighters. Strategic flying quickly became totally forgotten on both sides as the dogfight ensued. Archie's two vics disintegrated as the struggle became every fighter for itself in just trying to stay alive. A 110 flashed in front of the Egham Spit, and the Stag touched his 'fire' button. His reflexes, however, lagged behind the event which caused a clear miss. In the same moment, a 109 latched onto his tail and he dove towards the smoke of London, manhandling his aircraft in left and right jinks and jerks as tracers filled the air around him. As he flew directly into the smoke rising from the many fires now raging below him, the German followed, staying on his tail. The chase went on for only two minutes but seemed to last an eternity, ending only with the onslaught of a Hurricane that seemed to materialize from nowhere.

The radios were alive with the life and death struggle in a jumble of warnings, commands, machine gun noise and screams.

"Watch your six…"

"Com'n round…"

"Climb up… climb up…"

"Bandits at eleven…

"Where the fuk are the archie units…

"Tell Rose…" [explosion]

A burning Hurricane flashed past the Stag's nose and plowed into a brick tenement some five thousand feet below. Archie, throttle full on, yanked back on his control column trying to gain altitude in order to attack the bombers that had somehow arrived right over his head. Feeling more than seeing a line of tracers flash past his wing, he yanked the control to the left in a violent maneuver that caused his vision to gray and his hearing to pan out.

A voice over the radio, sounding much as a tingling buzz , called to him. "Yellow leader, yellow leader, status if you please."

The Flight Lieutenant ignored the call out, being too busy to even think about it. The tracers followed him, and he snap rolled again and then pulled back hard on the yoke, bringing his Spit dangerously close to a stall as it slowly climbed straight up. Though the bombers were still too distant to attack, he began picking up defensive fire as they shot downhill at him. Two or three of their rounds pinged off of his canopy like hail. One bullet caused a crack.

"Get your bloody nose down!" Henry's voice commanded over the radio. For a brief, moment the Stag saw himself back in the front seat of a Gypsy Moth doing something stupid. Following the command, he passed the Messerschmitt 109 that was trying to follow him in this maneuver. This aircraft also pointing its nose towards the earth, exploded in a bright flash of orange as Henry Badcock streaked past, barely missing the wreckage.

"Much obliged," Archie called to his old instructor.

"Think nothing of it," the Bulldog responded from somewhere in the sky.

As the Egham Spit dove, the smoke from the now blazing wharfs enveloped it. When he emerged again, the bombers were done with their handy work and already turning tail for home.

"Yellow flight, yellow leader," Archie called over the radio, "Report."

Three of the six were still in the air but scattered. Rather than form up they individually returned to Biggins, which had not been hit at all.

§

"It's a terrible mess," the Civil Defense Warden kept muttering as they clawed their way through the rubble, "A terrible terrible mess. Old Winston should have seen this one coming. You don't punch a mad bugger in the nose and not expect a kick to the chops in return." When Henry and Archie showed up looking for their batman the fellow had initially been put off. "The whole of my neighborhood has been flattened," he near shouted at the pair, "and you want to be shown to a specific address?! There are no addresses any longer; it's all just rubble! Or didn't you bloody well notice?"

"I'm sorry, sir," Archie replied, "But we are very much aware. We were flying above you during the onslaught."

The Warden stopped to look at them as if waking from a bad dream. The pair were still in their flight suits complete with their helmets.

"What on earth are you doing here?" he asked them. "Get back aloft immediately and shoot more of the bastards down. We can't afford to lose you to an errant bomb. Shoo! Go away!"

"We're on rest," Henry told the fellow, who was a Weasel just like Higgins. It was the truth. As soon as they could, however, they stole the commander's motorbike and came looking for their batman who had not been at the field to greet them. "Our friend Corporal Richard Higgins is an East Ender, sir. During the bombardment we think he came home to help his family. We mean to find him and help if we can."

"My name is Higgins," the Warden told them. "You said his name was Robert?"

"No sir," Archie told him, "Richard. He has been assigned to Henry and myself as our batman. He is a superb fellow, and we mean to see him back with us in one piece."

An explosion occurred that shook the building. Plaster dust filtered down from the ceiling. All three of them looked to the glassless windows and the Warden muttered, "Late boomer. That's the real danger… you never know when one of them is going to go off and bury you in the debris." Nodding to a stack of styup pumps in the corner. he told them, "Grab one of those and fill the bucket with water… then follow me; Richard is my nephew. I'll show you where his family lives."

Born in the east end and having lived there his entire life, the Warden had to close his eyes and envision his surroundings as they were before the attack just to find his way. The smoke was so heavy at times that even taking a breath was painful. All along the way people were shouting out. Some looked for survivors while others yelled for help. Many of the buildings they passed were raging infernos throwing blast furnace heat at the trio. There was no hope for any caught within those.

The home guard Civil Defense units were now out in full strength, risking life and limb as willingly as the pilots did every time they went aloft. Some carried empty stretchers heading into the carnage, while others were half running, half stumbling back out again supporting their burdens. "Help here!" they would yell. "Help here… medic required!"

Piles of bodies lay about on the street corners; collected and stacked there in the haste of the rescue efforts. The living were first on their list of priorities while the dead needed no immediate assistance.

Archie noted that some of these bodies wore German flight gear. Whether the flight crews were alive or dead when found by the citizens of London was not asked nor volunteered; their tags were simply collected, and they were stacked aside from the others.

"It would have been about here," the Warden finally told them, trying to see through the pall of smoke. He had tears in his eyes, but his voice was firm. "I must be back to my post. Use your pumps to put out the little fires in your way when assisting. Use the water sparingly as I don't know when the water lorry will be down this way. If you find my nephew, tell him Uncle Walter said to keep a stiff upper lip and to kill as many of the blighters as he has a chance to lay his paws on. As for the two of you, you both owe me a fucking bomber. I want it blown up and not crash landed, am I perfectly clear on this? If it lands on me in the process, I can accept that knowing they won't be able to come back and do this again; so you shoot them down no matter what they're flying over."

"Yes, sir," both flyers responded with a salute. It was anger talking, and they knew this, but for now, they would make the promise, and if a bomber fell before their sites, they would in turn send a note describing its demise. It was small recompense for the fellow's efforts in saving their city not to mention the loss of his home and probably family members.

"Richard!" the pilots began yelling as they moved into the rubble that had once been a six story tenement. They looked and they dug. Occasionally they would find a body, and this they would move to the street corner as they'd seen others doing. Three hours into the mission, there was a faint response to their cries. Following the voice they snaked their way down into the rubble, finding their batman squatting by a hole in the dim light.

"This was my home," he told them in a matter of fact voice. The numbness of shock was about him, though he was still lucid. "Mum's dead. I found her and Auntie Pauline in what had been her bedroom. Auntie's husband is the CD Warden."

"Walter?" Archie asked him.

"That's right. How did you know?"

"He led us here," Henry said. "I'spect it's bad all round. We better not stay, Richard. Walter said to tell you 'Stiff upper lip'. If they are dead, there is nothing to do for them. I think it best if we let those better suited handle the excavation."

"My niece is in there, Mr. Badcock. She's alive and trapped in what was the kitchen. I can't leave her."

"Can we get her out?" Archie asked him.

"I think it may be possible. I can wiggle m'self in but getting out again would be near impossible."

"I'll follow you in and hold your ankles," Henry told him. "Archie can bring up our six and hold mine in turn. When you get her we'll act as a living rope and wiggle our way back out again."

"Thank you, sir, I appreciate that, but there is one more thing."

"Talk plainly, Corporal," the Stag told him, "Time is of the essence."

"There's a bloody big bomb lying just around the corner from this hole."

Henry laughed. "What a wonderful way to go," he told them. When it was apparent they thought he'd slipped a cog he added, "Nothing to feel, is there? Beats the bloody hell out of being burned alive in your cockpit; now don't it?"

Two hours later they were back outside the building, the shivering girl in her Uncle's arms and wrapped in a blanket given over by one of the ladies of the Women's Voluntary Service. The building was marked as having an unexploded bomb in it, and the area was cleared.

As the four were walking away, there was a tremendous blast and the rest of the building fell in upon itself.

Three hours after that, Archie and Henry were back sitting in their Spitfire cockpits. Their aircraft engines were still hot from having been flown in their absence by the members of Blue Flight. That mission had been uneventful as the Germans had not yet come back, and further flights were placed upon standby.

In short order, as the Kiwis hurriedly serviced and rearmed their charges, both pilots dropped off to sleep.

Two hours later, they were again starting engines.

We'll Meet Again

"We'll Meet Again" is a 1939 song made famous by British singer Vera Lynn. The song is one of the most famous songs of WWII and resonated with the soldiers going off to fight, their families, and their sweethearts. When asked about the Battle of Britain in an interview with the BBC, Dame Lynn said, "I heard it mostly. I was living in Barking which is just past the east end of London, and we heard so much activity overhead. I was driving around in my little Austin Ten with a canvas roof to theaters and various things. We were told that if we were out in the streets in the car, we were to get out and lay in the gutter which I didn't fancy doing." (This last remark was reference to the required actions of an air raid drill.)

When asked of Winston Churchill's speech about 'The Few', she said, "He was talking about a collection of very brave chaps and we are all grateful and thankful that we had them at the time. It's right and proper that we should remember them. They were a few but they did a fantastic big job."

We'll Meet Again

We'll meet again, Don't know where, Don't know when
But I know we'll meet again some sunny day

Keep smiling through, Just like you always do
Till the blue skies drive the dark clouds far away

So will you please say "Hello" To the folks that I know
Tell them I won't be long They'll be happy to know That as you saw me go
I was singing this song

We'll meet again, Don't know where, Don't know when
But I know we'll meet again some sunny day

Colonel Blue sat in a booth close to the piano player at Mama Bella's. A scotch and water sat before him, and he'd done a good job nursing it as the piano player banged out a non-stop melody of old favorites aimed directly at the hearts of the military types frequenting the establishment. Even at this early afternoon hour, the curtains were tightly drawn, and the lights were low. More than a few of the patrons present were stiff drunk and laying face down upon their tables.

Blue lit a cigarette and then swallowed down what was left in his glass before signaling for another. Upon arrival, he'd flashed ENSA credentials (Entertainments National Service Association) and made mention that he'd heard of a very talented young Poodle with the voice of an angel. An amount of money crossed Madam Bella's paw, and the girl was sent for, bearing in mind, and here the Madam winked, that she would need a moment to compose herself. This, of course, meant she was with a customer.

His drink arrived and was placed upon the table by a very pretty Poodle in a soft velvet dress which was not much more than a negligee.

"You wished to hear me sing?" she asked in a sultry voice.

"Indeed, I would," the Colonel told her, acting every bit the bashful gentleman recruiter. "That is, if it is not too much trouble? It's for the boys, you see. They need all the moral we can help them muster and if you sing half as good as I've been led to believe, you will be a true God-send."

Jeans looked up at Mama Bella, who signaled her to 'do as the fellow requested'. The old Polish Tatra was not in fear of losing a money maker such as Jeans since she would be well compensated by the government; not to mention a favor given is a favor owed. She also knew there were many, many more talented females where the Poodle had come from.

With a whisper to the piano player and a loose paw trailing over his shoulder, the young Poodle took her place at the old instrument. Letting her fingers play gently along the full range of the keys, she smiled and looked up to her surprise visitor. Pausing to frown slightly over the piano's lack of tune, she chose a song from memory and began to sing for him.

We'll meet again,
Don't know where,
Don't know when
But I know we'll meet again some sunny day

Gundulf Faust was seething under his calm demeanor. Taking a moment to settle his nerves, he lit a cigarette, inhaled deeply and then blew the smoke out into the air above his head. He'd driven all the way out to Geschwader 56 Jörke, Gruppe I, to take into custody one Ober-leutnant Wilhelm Daecher, only to be informed he'd missed the fighter pilot by a mere five minutes. This meant he would have to wait over an hour to make the arrest.

The Inspekteur der Sicherheitspolizei und des SD (local Gestapo Chief) had whispered to the Belgium Shepherd that Daecher was under suspicion of high treason and was to be brought in and 'closely' ques-tioned. In 1939, there had been a bomb attempt on Adolf Hitler's life, and it was thought that the former Professor might be able to shed some light on the incident.

The Dog knew better than to press for details. Ask too many open questions and you too would be suspected of something. That, in and of itself, would lead a person to the 'examination' room. Interrogation was Faust's specialty and the reason the Gestapo brought him in under their umbrella while his countrymen were being routinely lined up against a wall and shot. He looked forward to learning how deep 'der Professor's' treason went. The details he might uncover for his masters could bring him untold glory. It was for this that he did what he did, nothing more and nothing less. He was a realist. Staying alive in a world that was routinely killing itself took skill, courage, and the ability to please those in the up-per tier of control.

Keep smiling through,
Just like you always do
Till the blue skies drive the dark clouds far away

Archie advanced his throttle to half, and as the Egham Spit began to roll, pushed the yoke forward just enough that the tail left the ground. As her speed increased and the engine's torque was absorbed and con-trolled by the airflow over the wings, he further advanced the power lever to full take off. As soon as the aircraft broke ground, he brought the gear up and looked around to check that his flight was still with him.

"Yellow Four, Yellow Leader; I don't see you."

"Four here, my engine quit, sir."

Archie cursed under his breath but continued on.

So will you please say "Hello"

Locke watched his altimeter, leveling off at twenty five thousand feet. In the distance, England was a dark patch in a sky laced with lacy white cirrus clouds. "Stay close," he called over his radio. He did not give a call sign, deliberately keeping things simple. His pilot's knew his voice and for now that was enough. He had long suspected others were listening to the frequency on both sides. They were to rendezvous with a bomber group and had explicit orders to say close to them. He didn't like this as it confined his aircraft to a smaller area in which they could not dive into the attack. In this, they lost their effectiveness. True to his form, he kept his flight higher, in any case.

"Red Leader, Gänsemutter (Mother Goose)," his gruppe controller called on the radio.

'Gänsemutter' was a private alert code prearranged between himself and the officer in charge of communications. They came from the same village and, though following different careers, found themselves working together again. The Staffelkapitän was immediately on guard with this call.

"Sprechen," he called back.

"Message from Maintenance; they have questions about Der Professor's aircraft. A Mechaniker is standing by to take him to the hangar when he comes back. " The staffel had no hangar, so the implication was obvious; Maintenance – Gestapo, Mechaniker – Secret Police Agent.

"Copy," Daecher responded before Locke could even press his radio button. "Sheep at four o'clock," he continued, indicating the bombers they were to escort.

Following these visual directions, the Staffel Commander saw the bombers who were depending upon them for protection. In this flight, there would be over a hundred bombers and half again as many fighters. His Schwarm would maintain the upper rear area in order to dash in at the first sign of the RAF. They were now in good position.

Turning to look at his wingman who'd advanced to a position right off of his right wingtip, he saw Daecher touch the ear piece of his helmet and then salute him. Though they were wearing oxygen masks and goggles, he thought he could tell der Professor was smiling at him.

I was singing this song

Jeans winked at the officer watching her sing and smiled at him around the words of the song. Working for ENSA would have enormous benefits. She would be well taken care of and also have access to every British base on the island. The down side would be the inability to slide back and forth across the channel, but such was the life of a spy. Then again, she was not so stupid to not think that the Dog sitting and listening to her sing was not, himself, an agent. Time would tell; but for now time was on her side.

We'll meet again,
Don't know where,
Don't know when
But I know we'll meet again some sunny day

Archie heard Terrance singing again in his headset. This flight she was on to a newer song that had been sung for the squadron by Vera Lynn a few days earlier. She'd been well received and then they'd had to scramble right in the middle of her act.

"One of these days you'll rightly move on," he said into his oxygen mask.

"Perhaps," she responded, "But for now I am happy to wait."

"Yellow leader, Control."

"Yellow leader."

"Vector south. Incoming bandits London bound. Approximate strength one hundred."

"Roger wilco," Archie called back as he listened to the other squadrons being vectored onto the same formation. Today they would have numbers on their side; but still they were a much smaller number than the actual attacking force.

"Shall we each get one for Richard's Uncle?" Henry called to the Stag.

"Remember the hull numbers so we can add them to the note we shall send him," the flight leader added in agreement, "Sharp eyes now everyone."

Colonel Blue watched Jeans as she sang. Her breasts, unburdened by a brazier, swayed softly as her fingers drifted over the keys of the old baby grand piano. She winked at him and he allowed his heart to go out to her in an obvious manner; something she was accustomed to seeing in those who came to visit her.

There were perks to this job, both agents reflected; though one had always to be on their guard.

Keep smiling through,
Just like you always do
Till the blue skies drive the dark clouds far away

Faust stood in the operations tent watching the controlled chaos of the flight followers. He'd dismissed the two SS guards who'd come with him. After giving it some thought, and not caring for their puritanical attitude towards him, the Kriminalkommissar felt he would gain more notoriety for conducting a single handed arrest. There was only one pilot, after all.

Though he kept his features neutral, his eyes took in the entire scene before him as his mind's voice stayed cynical in its assessments. If it were up to him, the first thing he would have done was place the entire group in a large house where they could spread out. The dummkopfs had to know they needed to control the noise levels just so they could think; and also so they could be watched. Much live information would be coming in over the radios and why they did not have a trained intelligence operative present was beyond him. He also noted the officers present in the large tent were nothing more than flight crews out of rotation.

"May I help you?" asked a voice in his ear.

The Belgium turned to the voice and calmly looked at the person addressing him. "Und you are?"

"I am Oberst Schmidt," the Doberman told him. It was obvious he had deep German roots of which the Belgium could never claim. "I am the intelligence officer and as our units are about to enter enemy airspace, I must insist you leave this area."

"I think I would like to stay," Faust said softly, taking out a cigarette and lighting it. He did not offer one to the Colonel.

Guards were not required as everyone with the exception of three radio operators quickly came to the Oberst's assistance. Disarming the Gestapo agent they bodily picked him up and threw him out of the tent.

So will you please say "Hello"
To the folks that I know
Tell them I won't be long

Archie's group found the bombers easily enough. It was rather hard to hide in a near cloudless sky in broad daylight.

"Tallyho!" he called and pushed his throttle forward to full military.

They'll be happy to know
That as you saw me go
I was singing this song

"Derik," der Professor called over the radio. It was odd that he had not used a proper call sign, and the Wolf looked to his friend even though he was about to call, 'Horrido.'

"Give my regards to our navy friend," the Wolf radioed, "Auf Wiedersehen." With that said, he called the battle cry and nosed his aircraft over.

We'll meet again,
Don't know where,
Don't know when
But I know we'll meet again some sunny day

Yellow flight was totally blindsided by Red Flight's attack. Oberleutnant Wilhelm (Professor) Daecher never even fired his guns as he flew directly into Henry Badcock's Spitfire. The collision was tremendous and both aircraft became nothing but scattered wreckage dropping with the bombs that were falling on London.

Locke followed, screaming into his oxygen mask. Archie came into his gun sight and the dogfight was on.

Faust, leaning against the corner of a building, smoked a cigarette while watching a group of seagulls lazily gliding in the sky.

Jeans, finished singing, slowly rose from the piano's bench and crossed to Colonel Blue. Taking his paw, she led him out of Mama Bella's and up to her apartment.

Death

I visited war once.
I hoped to never visit it again.
Around me had been death and dying;
Most certainly it was a terrible sin.

Wishing n'ere another round
It then came to me on wings of flight
With guns and bombs a' pounding;
Intentions of preventing our fight.

How little they apparently knew us
And quite mistaken we'd been of them,
With a cry of 'In your arse Adolf!'
Brave England rose up once again.

—*An Old Guard soldier*

Little Napoleon MMXII

Corporal Higgins found the aid stations easily enough. Pretty much all he had to do was follow the ambulances as they made their way back and forth transporting the more seriously injured to hospital. Commander Sheltie's motorbike was well suited to getting around the rubble of the bombing, and there was a lot of it littering the roadways. Here and there, whole neighborhoods were blocked off with a Civil Defense officer stationed to warn of unexploded bombs. Occasionally one of these would decide to go off, making a further mess.

Archie, still dressed in his flight gear, sat in the side car with his fists clenched in anxiety. At every stop, he leapt out and immediately pressed for information on any downed fliers that might have been treated.

As soon as he'd landed, the Stag went straight to Commander Sheltie. Coming to full attention he saluted. "Henry's down over London, sir, permission to go and find him."

"Granted," the commander replied without looking up from his latest Intel report. "Take my transport. If he's alive, give him my regards and tell him to get his bloody arse back here and none of his shenanigans." Sensing something deeper than a bail out, he looked up and in a softer tone, asked, "Quickly, Arch, tell me what happened and then get going."

"A bloody hun flew right through him, sir."

"Right through him?"

"Yes sir, straight through as if he'd not even seen him."

"Were there any other such happenstance?"

"No, sir."

"Parachutes?"

"I was too busy to be sure, sir."

The commander nodded his head in understanding. "If he's dead, make arrangements to bring him back. If he's alive, get me a full report on his condition and what he might remember as an after action report. We'll have him sent up to Scotland to rehabilitate. I've got a flight now... you go and find Henry... that's an order."

"Thank you, sir."

§

Henry found himself sitting on a plain wooden chair in a white room. At least he thought it was a room as he could perceive no walls. He was dressed in his flight gear, and the stink of battle clung to him like a soiled pair of skivvies. In front of him and at a sociable distance (not too close, not too far) was another chair just like the one he was sitting upon.

"I don't suppose I could get a cuppa?" he asked out loud. His voice sounded normal enough, and that was at least a bit reassuring.

A paw came around from his side, and he was handed the requested cup of tea.

"Well, at least there's that," he responded, accepting the tin mug. Working to get his finger in the metal loop as quickly as he could against the heat emanating from the metal, he muttered, "I suppose this means I'm dead?"

Someone kissed him on the cheek. "Not dead," a very feminine voice whispered in his ear.

"I, on the other paw," said a very masculine voice, "did not survive our crash; but that was my intention, so I am not disappointed. At least I did not suffer."

Henry looked up from his mug of tea and found a German pilot now sitting on the chair opposite him. The Wolf was also dressed in his flight gear.

"I suppose that means I'm going to suffer?" the Bulldog asked him.

260

"Life is pain," the other pilot told him. "Perhaps that is why I was allowed to meet with you; perhaps it is also allowance for the mission I was a part of."

"Somehow I am not following this conversation," the British pilot told him frankly. "Under any other circumstance, I would be off of this bloody chair and trying to choke you to death, but as it is, I do not feel that would be appropriate; nor do I find I bear you any malice."

"Isn't it odd how death changes things?" the Wolf asked him.

"So I am dead, then?"

"As I understand it, you are somewhere in between. It could go either way." Saying this, the pilot groped his flight clothing until he found a particular lump. Smiling, he fished out a pack of cigarettes. Thumbing one up he leaned forward and offered it to his counterpart, explaining, "I deliberately crashed my aircraft into yours, und zo it would seem that is why I am allowed to speak with you. At this moment, frozen in time, we are quite close to each other, no?"

"You meant to kill me?" the Bulldog asked, accepting the cig.

"Not as an end… rather to kill myself."

"Why?" the Bulldog asked as he patted himself down looking for his lighter. Producing it, he held the flame out to the German before lighting his own. "The tea is good," he said as he did this, "You should ask for a cup; it might be a thirsty place where you're going."

Der Professor chuckled. "Where we are all going in the end, I am sure. I spent a lifetime studying such things, only to find out that I had it all wrong, in any case."

"I'll keep that in mind if I manage to pull out of this nose dive."

"It just happened… we are both still falling," the Wolf told him.

"So we are both still alive, then?"

"For the moment."

Henry swallowed down the last of his tea and set the cup on the floor. Drawing deeply on his cigarette, he exhaled a cloud of smoke and then asked, "What is it you want of me, then? Obviously there must be something, or this meeting would not be required."

"You are very astute for an Englander."

"I've been told that before. You're wasting what time we have… tell me."

"Der Fuehrer is not the leader the German people believed him to be," Daecher told him plainly.

"No shit," Henry muttered, taking another drag on his cigarette. He had no doubt that if and when he woke from this dream, there was going to be much pain involved.

"I saw this early on," Der Professor admitted. "In November of 1939, I was involved in a plot to blow him up."

"I remember that," the other pilot responded. "As I recall, old Adolf actually blamed the attempt upon the British and Prime Minister Chamberlain directly."

"He did, but those in charge of his security knew better and did not stop looking. I can assure you, they are relentless. I was warned they were waiting for me back at our base."

"And so you killed yourself?"

"Ya… Ich kenne zu viel. (*Yes… I know too much.*)"

"Knew too much," Henry corrected him. "What's your message and who do I give it to?"

Daecher got a very pained look on his face. He tried to speak and for a second he couldn't. "Find a Poodle named Jeans… tell her… tell her that 'Der Professor says Locke is the key'. Please also tell her I am dead."

Standing, the Wolf came to full attention and saluted his former foe in a military fashion… and then he was gone.

The Bulldog, continuing to sit upon his chair, shook his head. Taking another drag on his cigarette, he exhaled and then ground the butt under his boot. "Lock is the key," he muttered. "Now that bloody well explains a lot, doesn't it?"

Footsteps approached him from behind, but he didn't turn to see who it was. The legs that came into his view also wore flight gear. Looking up, he found himself in the presence of another British flyer.

"What?" Badcock asked this person, "He got two of us? He must have been one hell of a billiards player."

"I am Lieutenant Terrance Chrysanthemum," the other flyer told him. Taking her helmet off, she smiled, leaned down, and gave him a kiss on the cheek. "Thank you for taking such good care of Archie."

"You're female," he said softly in total surprise. "You and Archie… you were… that is to say, a couple?"

"You're exactly right," she replied, "You be sure to give him my love, please." Reaching down, she took a firm hold of the 'D' ring on his parachute and told him, "But that's a secret. Now brace yourself because this is going to hurt you like you've never been hurt in your life."

Henry's parachute blossomed, stopping his fall a scant five hundred feet above the ground. His scream of pain was nearly as loud as the falling bombs.

§

It had taken time to locate his wingman, but find him he had, along with a smattering of other pilots that had been shot down that day. All had been taken into the underground against the dangers of the bombing.

"Old Henry Badcock?" one of these pilots replied when asked. "Gor! Don't tell me they got Henry... the fellow was a rock. He kicked my arse good and proper during my training days, and right he was to do so."

"Mine, too," Archie told the fellow, "He was a tremendous instructor... is a tremendous instructor."

"It's all right, Lieutenant," the fellow replied at the hesitation, "I understand. We all understand."

"This here is the triage point," another of the pilots told him. He was sitting on the floor holding a bloody rag over his shoulder where a bullet had passed through. "They separate the fixable from the mortally wounded here; but I know for a fact that they give us pilots the benefit of the doubt."

Two medics arrived and helped the pilot to his feet.

"He's probably been moved to an operating theater and is undergoing surgery as we speak," the fellow told him, wincing as the medics checked his shoulder. "You might want to try further down the tube, though, just in case he got looked over in the fracas." With this, the pilot was escorted out, taken to the hospital to have his shoulder tended to. With luck, and some pain killers, he might be back in the fight a week from now.

Archie and Corporal Higgins, following his advice, looked further down the length of the underground station to the rows of dead and dying. These were being looked after by grim faced civilians who'd been drafted to the job, though they were all quite willing to help.

In the darkness, the Stag heard his name croaked, and his heart immediately sank. If Henry was here in this dark place, then it couldn't be good.

"Henry... is that you?" he called out.

"Over here, lad."

Finding his friend among the dead and mortally wounded, the Stag knelt in the dirt next to where the pilot had been summarily deposited. In the darkness, it was hard to tell exactly the extent of his injuries.

"Where does it hurt?" he asked softly, loosening the Bulldog's flight helmet and removing it from his head.

"All fucking over," the old pilot growled weakly. "I seem to have taken one heck of a knockabout. It must have been a bad'un because I even saw your girl."

"Try not to talk, Henry," Archie told him, "Conserve your energy. Higgins is here with me and we're going to get you out and to a hospital."

"I have things to tell you," the other pilot responded, "Just in case…" He shuddered a moment, his eyes closing tight and his tongue sticking out slightly to the side. When the shuddering stopped, he resumed just as if he'd never stopped. "Two things," he whispered, forcing Archie to come very close. Henry smelled of vomit and blood but the Stag pressed beyond this, placing his ear next to his friend's mouth. "First, Terrance says she loves you. You could have bloody well," he paused, wheezing heavily and then continued, "Bloody well told me he was a she. Second… I am to get a message to a certain poodle named Jeans. That's the name of your whore, isn't it?"

"Yes," Archie replied.

"It is very important you tell her Der Professor is dead. His final message was, 'Lock is the key'."

"What does it mean?"

"I haven't a bloody clue."

"He might not be in his right mind, sir," Higgins told Archie softly.

"Perhaps I'm not," Henry managed to chuckle, "but my hearing works just fine, Richard… it's just that the rest of me feels so very bad."

Two hours later, the Bulldog was sedated and resting in a proper hospital bed. The doctor who examined him found no broken bones and no obvious battle damage, though he would not rule out possible internal injury and a definite concussion. He would be kept flat on his back for at least a week and then sent for convalescence.

Corporal Higgins was left to attend to Henry's needs, should there be any, with orders to send word if his condition changed.

Archie then found himself knocking on Jean's door. He was so very tired. When she opened the door he was almost asleep on his feet. "Der Professor is dead," he muttered when he saw her. "He said to tell you, 'Lock is the key'."

Taking him by the paw, she led him to her bed. Getting him undressed, she then lay next to him as he softly snored thinking about what he'd told her. She was not so much surprised by the message as she was

264

hearing it from Flight Lieutenant Corn; Oberleutnant (Professor) Wilhelm Daecher was her brother.

Retribution

The effort of the Germans to secure daylight mastery of the air over England is, of course, the crux of the whole war. So far, it has failed conspicuously.....for him (Hitler) to try to invade this country without having secured mastery in the air would be a very hazardous undertaking.

Nevertheless, all his preparations for invasion on a great scale are steadily going forward. Several hundreds of self-propelled barges are moving down the coasts of Europe, from the German and Dutch harbours to the ports of northern France, from Dunkirk to Brest, and beyond Brest to the French harbours in the Bay of Biscay.

—Winston Churchill's broadcast September 11th 1940

Locke's aircraft had no more taxied to its place, the propeller slowly winding down, when Kriminalkommissar Faust detached himself from the corner of the building he'd been leaning on and boldly walked out onto the flight line. Standing off of the Messerschmitt's left wingtip, his hat cocked back at a jaunty angle, he kept his paws in his coat pockets and watched the pilot go through a quick post flight check. There was a line of bullet holes that walked over this wing, ending just before reaching the cockpit but the Dog was oblivious to this in pursuit of his master's praise. He stood waiting as one who had nothing to fear. The Gestapo had full authority over the rank and file of the military; or so he'd been informed.

There was a metal on metal sound as the fighter's canopy was unlocked and then tipped up and over to the other side. Pulling his goggles up to his forehead, Locke remembered this item was Der Professor's one regret of the aircraft he loved so much; that he could not slide back the glass and fly with the wind whistling around him.

The pilot yelled to the ground crewman (called 'Black Men' for their black work uniforms) who'd just chalked the aircraft, "Tell Günter the engine is running hot. I took a round or two in the left cooling system and had to shut it off."

"Yes, sir."

After this, he unbuckled and stood, taking time to stretch; ignoring the Gestapo agent and making him wait. The whole airfield was bustling and noisy as the aircrews brought back their damaged aircraft and wounded crews. Obviously those employed in the 'security' of the Reich were oblivious to such things.

"I am here for Oberleutnant Wilhelm Daecher," the Gestapo agent announced.

Locke, mustering all the self control he had left in his body, turned to the Dog and simply stared through him.

Faust, not to be out done, yelled to be heard over the many engines that were running. "Did you hear me Oberst Locke? Where is he?"

"He is dead," the Wolf replied coldly, deliberately forcing the Dog to keep his eyes on him. Taking the Lugar from his holster, he pulled back the action and let it snap home, chambering a round.

Faust reached for his own weapon and found the holster still empty from when he'd been evicted from the Operations Tent. Before he could turn and run, the 'Blackman' who'd come up to meet the Commandant's aircraft, struck him over the head with a wooden chock, knocking him senseless.

Locke, nodding to the fellow, unloaded his side arm and placed it back into his holster before dismounting. When he was on the ground and close, he said softly into the fellow's ear, "Take him to my quarters for now. Tie him up and gag him. Sit on him if need be to keep him quiet. I have to go and give an after action report, but when I am done, I will have some questions for this Dog. I will need two armorers you can trust with your life. Do you know any?"

"Dozens," the fellow responded with a smile.

Locke smiled back. "Just two, and absolute secrecy is a must, or we will have this fellow's brethren taking us all in for safe keeping. When you have this worthless piece of garbage secure, have the armorers move my aircraft to the range and set it up as if they were going to adjust the sights."

"Afterwards?" the Black Man asked.

"Leave that to me; but you needn't worry."

§

Archie's eyes opened in a semi-dark room. One small candle was lit and sitting on the dresser across from the bed. It took him several minutes to realize where he was.

"Jeans?" he called softly, but there was no answer.

Sitting up, he swung his legs over the edge. The floor felt cold under his feet. It was then he realized he was naked, though he didn't remember undressing. Searching his foggy memory, he remembered knocking on the Poodle's door but little else.

"I've got to get back to the field," he muttered to himself. "Right then... clothes first..."

Glancing at his watch, he squinted to make out what time it was. The hands indicated nine 'o' clock, but was it night time or the morning after? As if punctuating this thought, an aircraft flew over. The Stag recognized the sound as belonging to a Messerschmitt 110 flying at approximately three thousand feet. Shortly thereafter he heard the sound of another aircraft; this one undeniably British and in full chase.

"Bloody hell," he muttered, "It just won't stop."

Rising, he found his clothing neatly draped over a chair in the sitting room.

"Jeans... are you here?"

There was no answer, and the Stag suddenly felt very lonely. He shivered in his nakedness and then began to dress. No more than had he'd buttoned up the flight suit than the apartment's door opened and Jeans came in carrying a covered plate of food, the aroma of which made the pilot's stomach growl. She also carried a teapot, and the whole of her burden was placed upon her small dining table.

"I thought you would be in a hurry to leave again," the Poodle told him, "So I went to Mama Bella's kitchen and stole you some dinner."

"Dinner," he replied with a sigh. "I take it then it is the same day, only later?"

"Oui."

"Did we... ahhh... do anything?"

She smiled without turning to him. "You are a marvelous lover, I am sure... but no, we do nothing."

The pilot felt both relief and disappointment. "Jeans," he began, "If anything..."

Spinning, she cut him off. "Do not say that... ever! To do so is to curse yourself unlucky." Uncovering the plate she told him, "Come and eat now; and do so slowly. I will have a cup of tea with you, and then you can be off. Time makes no difference now. You could have slept the night away."

"But you brought me dinner," he countered, "So you were going to wake me?"

"Your batman stopped by," she lied, "He saw the motorbike and asked me to send you along when I was finished with you. He also said your Henry rests easily."

"Cheeky little fellow," the stag chuckled. "Bloody considerate of him to give me the time to finish, eh?"

She raised an eyebrow and smiled at him. "When you arrived here you tell me something in your tiredness… do you remember what it was?"

"Der Professor is dead," he told her as he sat at the table, "and that lock is the key."

"Do you have any idea what this could mean?" she asked softly.

"None whatsoever. Henry asked me to tell you. He said it was very important that I do so."

The Poodle nodded and then poured out the tea for them both. "I will leave with you," she told him. "You will go back to your airfield, and I will go and check upon your Henry. I think it would do him good to see a pretty face, no?"

"That's very considerate of you; especially at this time of night."

As he began to eat, Jeans asked, "Was she pretty?"

Archie picked up his tea cup and sipped, after which he told her plainly, "Yes, she was."

He felt a twinge of guilt at having reported her to Intelligence but it was a war and you could not be too careful for the country's sake.

As if reading his mind, she told him, "I have been approached by ENSA to sing for the troops. I am supposed to begin next week, so I will no longer be in London."

Archie raised an eyebrow over his teacup. "You don't say? That is wonderful news; it'll get you out of this hell hole. I honestly can see things getting much worse." As if it had been planned, a distant explosion punctuated his words.

Jeans, placing her teacup back to the table, reached over and placed both her paws upon his one. "I truly wish we were at a different place and at a different time, Flight Lieutenant Corn."

This one time, the spy really meant what she said.

§

The night was moonless and dark. Faust was securely tied to a stout wooden chair and gagged. Though he was blindfolded, he knew he was outside and in the open. His nose smelled exhaust fumes and burnt oil. In the distance, there were the sounds of aircraft engines starting, being run up, and then stopping again as the maintenance crews serviced their squadrons in preparation for the morrow's flights. The blindfold was roughly removed and his eyes found darkness. A second later, he knew exactly where he was because Locke leaned down and told him, adding a friendly pat to his shoulder.

"I believe you know who I am, Kriminalkommissar," the pilot said softly. "Not long ago, when I was wounded, you made a great point of coming into the hospital and showing me who was in charge, no? The French Poodles might call this 'krantz' but I rather think of it as blatant stupidity. Things change. Positions change. Power changes."

He paused to light a cigarette and felt the night around him. The air was cool, and the night was very dark. He reflected that if he were the British, he would be launching bombers about now.

"Do you remember the fellow you were asking me about? His name was Leutnant Günter Meyer, and he was a good Nazi. You might also remember you were enquiring as to what exactly had happened to him."

Locke took a deep drag from the cigarette, exhaled the smoke, and then, dropping it to the dirt, ground it under his highly polished boot. "I shot him down."

Faust made noises through his gag.

"You ask me why, zo I will tell you, though you know this is very dangerous information for me to tell you, no? But this is also a time for honesty, yes? You shall have your turn. He was about to shoot a pilot who had parachuted from his damaged aircraft… something encouraged by our leader, but also something strictly against my personal orders." Bending down, he came face to face with the Belgium. "I wish you to know that I am a Wolf of my word. I warned that if any of my pilots did this I would place them before a firing squad."

The Gestapo agent made no noise in reply.

"You have information I wish to know," the pilot continued. "The fact that I already know most of which I need gives me a great gift in latitude… zo… if you die, I do not care. If you live… well… that much is up to you. Unlike the office for which you work, my word is my honor. If I say I will let you live, then that is exactly what will happen… within reason, of course. Make some sort of noise if you understand this."

The Dog managed a soft grunting noise through his gag.

"Very good," Locke replied. "Here is the game then. You are sitting down range at our sighting area where the armorers range the guns on our fighter craft. Thus, no one at all will suspect anything. This is just one more function being attended to by our staffel. You are presently sitting in front of my aircraft und a thirty millimeter cannon, the target for which is directly behind you." The pilot hesitated just long enough for this to sink in. "Should you be struck by such a powerful round there, would be no identifying your body, which will then be buried alongside of those who have already died honorably for Germany. I honestly hate doing that to them, you being who you are, but it is expedient, and the dead do not talk, no? You are also not German, so you will not be missed so much. You certainly must have understood that when you volunteered for the job; which raises some questions about both your character und your intelligence."

The Gestapo agent's eyes swelled in the sockets as he tried to scream through his gag. As he did this, Locke, stepping back a few paces, told him, "You'll pardon me if I don't stand too close Kriminalkommissar, but the blood and brain splatter… I have my uniform to consider."

He then flashed an electric torch at the stretched canvas target behind his prisoner. From three hundred yards away there was a single bark of a large gun. The round was tracer and it streaked over the Dog's head missing him by a mere foot. The noise was like a whole hive of bees rocketing past.

Coming forward again, the fighter pilot said, " Zo! I will now remove your gag and you will talk."

As soon as he untied the muzzle, the Gestapo agent screamed, "YOU'RE MAD! YOU CAN'T DO THIS!"

The fighter pilot grabbed the Dog's snout with both paws forcing it closed. "I am mad!" he hissed. "Every day I take my little airplane und fly over to England just to kill people I don't know. Tell me what sane person would do this. I also watch those who fly with me die because the Oberkommando der Luftwaffe (*Comander in Chief of the Air Force*) is too stupid to remember from where he came. If he wasn't too fat to fit in the cockpit perhaps he could come and show us how it is done, eh? If he had guts enough to do this maybe I might just shoot him down too for being so fucking ignorant." He released the Dog's snout and stood straight again. "Und now my good friend has killed himself rather than come back to be arrested by you." He paused and the added softly, "I'm mad? I think not. Und now you will tell me what I wish to know or you too will 'have an accident'."

Faust's eyes grew even larger in the darkness. He'd never been on the receiving end of an interrogation before though he was well aware of how most ended.

The Wolf let him think about this for a moment, taking the time to light another cigarette which he then placed between Faust's lips in a friendly manner. Doing this, he gently patted the Gestapo agent on the cheek, making sure he had his full attention. "Now you will begin speaking which will keep this from becoming ugly."

"I don't know anything," Gundulf squeaked.

"Und how many good people you have questioned told you exactly the same thing?" the fighter pilot asked in a very cold and dangerous sounding voice. "Did you ever believe them and let them go; or did you continue the questioning simply because you enjoyed it?"

Walking backwards to a safe distance, he called out, "For your sake Kriminalkommissar I hope the armorers only tweaked the sight a little bit."

He then once more flashed the target with his torch.

§

Archie found Commander Sheltie in the showers and reported to him, giving him all the details on Henry.

"Well thank God he's still alive," the former farmer replied, "Too many of us are gone now Arch. It's getting down to where you and I are the only old timers left." Shutting off the tap he asked, "Do you fancy having a beer with me at the pub? They also serve a fairly good plate of fish and chips."

"I'm not scheduled to fly station cover tonight sir?"

"I've got some of the youngsters on that," the Dog replied, reaching for his towel. "After the pounding Jerry gave London today… my God that was bad, perhaps we'll have a small respite. I hope none of them prangs an aircraft trying to land. We're going to be needing them when they hit us again tomorrow."

Both pilot's paused for a moment. The now ever present smoke seemed to weigh on both their minds. There had always been bombs dropped on London but never this many and not always deliberately. All

273

thoughts of the bomber crews having even a shred of humanity were now gone.

"I suppose they feel it worked in Poland, so it will work here as well," Archie muttered. "I flew with some of the Polish pilots recently and they were quite adamant that they were here to kill Germans; not just shoot down their aircraft. Wouldn't you know Henry knew all of them."

"Of course he would," the Commander replied as he pulled on his trousers. "I think Henry knows everyone in the entire bloody country. Certainly he has a face equal to Churchill's for being remembered."

They both laughed, the tension broken for the moment.

"Do I have time for a shower?" the Stag asked him.

"By all means, old boy," Sheltie responded, sniffing slightly, "I'd say it was a must. You can even use the soap my wife sends. It's a woman's fragrance but I rather fancy it. She makes it herself."

§

Jeans found Corporal Higgins sitting next to his charge, sound asleep in the stiff wooden chair. He looked so young and innocent in his rumpled uniform. The old Bulldog lying in the bed next to him was quite pale and his breathing was a bit irregular. Moving to the other side of the bed, she placed the vase of flowers she'd brought on the small bedside table. Then, leaning over the fighter pilot, she gave him a kiss on the forehead.

Henry's eyes opened and he smiled a wan smile. "I'm not going to catch anything from that am I?"

"You're in the right place if you do," she responded, liking him regardless of the insult. "Archie told me where you were. Do you hurt?"

"I did," he managed, his words coming slowly, "But they shot me full of something and now I haven't a care in the world. You're a lovely thing, did you know that? I see now why old Arch favors you. Are you really a German spy?"

Her expression never changed as she glanced up to make sure Higgins was still asleep and that there was no one else close by. His question represented such a danger to her person. A secret told to just one person would spread like wildfire and if told to the wrong person; spies were hung.

The Bulldog giggled, his eyes closing momentarily. "You don't need to kill me... secrets safe... you helped us... owe you..."

Leaning close, she whispered to him, "I am not a spy in the way

274

you think, H'enry. I do not represent the Nazis. The person I work for knows our nations will eventually need to talk. I am to make contact and then wait. The help I give is thee open paw of peace. He does not believe England should be taken, nor do I. Tell me how to stop the German invasion."

The pilot slipped into snoring for a moment and then his eyes again opened. "You must convince 'Herr Wolf' (*this was purportedly Adolf Hitler's real nickname*) that he is absolutely buggered if he launches."

"I need specifics," she pressed, "Time is very short now."

Henry giggled again and then sighed. He suddenly looked so very much like his country's leader.

"Did you know your mutton head Adolf has only one ball?" he asked her. "He got the other blown off in the first war. The answer to your question is simple, mon Cherie; convince him that if he tries a channel crossing he'll lose the other one as well. We British control the air… it's that simple. Someone obviously has not told him that."

The Bulldog closed his eyes and began to quietly sing to the tune of the 'Colonel Bogey March'.

> *Hitler has only got one ball,*
> *Göring has two but very small,*
> *Himmler is somewhat sim'lar,*
> *But poor Goebbels has no balls at all.*

Card Shuffle

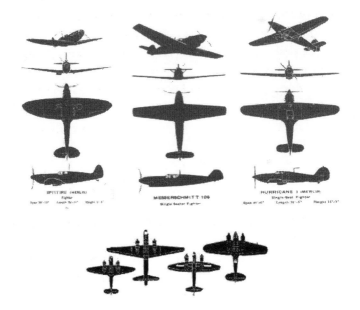

SPITFIRE (MERLIN)
Fighter
Span 36'-10"   Length 29'-11"   Height 9'-5"

MESSERSCHMITT 109
Single Seater Fighter

HURRICANE I (MERLIN)
Single-Seat Fighter
Span 40'-0"   Length 31'-5"   Height 13'-3"

September 4th, 1940

"It is a wonderful thing to see our nation at war, in its fully disciplined state. This is exactly what we are now experiencing at this time, as Mr Churchill is demonstrating to us the aerial night attacks which he has concocted. He is not doing this because these air raids might be particularly effective, but because his Air Force cannot fly over German territory in daylight. Whereas German aviators and German planes fly over English soil daily, there is hardly a single Englishman who comes across the North Sea in daytime…"

"…The people in England are asking, 'Why doesn't he come?', and I reply to them……'I am coming'".

Excerpts from the speech Adolf Hitler gave in Berlin while addressing an audience of women at the opening of the Winterhilfe at the Sportpalast.

During this speech, Herr Wolf informed his audience (primarily idolizing hysterical women) of the astounding success that the Luftwaffe was having over the Royal Air Force. He fed them largely inflated figures that indicated the Luftwaffe had actually shot down more RAF aircraft than the RAF possessed.

The truth concerning the confused state of 'command', however, can be summed up by the opinions recorded at an earlier meeting of the Supreme Commander and the two Commanders in charge of Luftflotte 2 and Luftflotte 3.

Feldmarschall Kesselring (Luftflotte 2) suggested that the time had come when the German Air Force should now make its attacks on London.

Reichmarschall Göring did not favor this, as he still believed he could crush the RAF.

Feldmarschall Sperle (Luftflotte 3), for his part, thought that caution should be implemented, as the British air force had more aircraft than the Luftwaffe had been led to believe.

During the whole of the Battle of Britain, Sperle's Luftflotte 3 and Kesselring's Luftflotte 2 fought side by side, constantly bombarding London by day and night.

§

As Adolf Hitler was whisked away from the Sportpalast, he smiled and made his small salute several times to those lining the street. These were his people; he was proud of them, but he was also afraid of them. In his honor and as a show of fearlessness, Berlin's streetlights were all lit. The Luftwaffe, however, had also been placed on high alert. An ominous threat was also floating in the air that if any British bombers flew over Germany this night there would be consequences.

When the big Mercedes limousine was clear of the crowds, the little Wolf sat further back in his seat with an appearance of relaxation. His brain, however, was racing as it always did after such an event. The crowd's chants were a heady brew, taking him higher than any drug available for his use.

Accompanying him, and the only other passenger in the back of the car, was his long time associate Rudolph Hess.

"Your speech was magnificent, Herr Wolf; every bit as good, if not better, as the very first time I heard you back in 1920," Hess told him.

"You say that, and I will believe you my friend, but only because I know you speak the truth for my benefit," the other Wolf responded. "I found my audience very uplifting, and that always adds to the fire of righteousness. How could you stand before such as that and not be proud of what Germany has done? If our forces were that exuberant we would now be standing on the western coast of England regarding the shores of Ireland."

"Ireland respects us; we would not have to invade them I think."

"Don't be so sure," the Wolf chuckled. "The Irish and the Scotts are related and the Scotts hate our guts."

"They hate everyone," Hess replied with a chuckle, "Including each other. They barely tolerate the English. Their's is a peace hammered out in Scottish blood and the undercurrents, if you look closely, are very dark. I think if things were right, they would support our cause."

"Meaning?" the other Wolf asked while looking out the window.

"Meaning that; if they were offered freedom from English tyranny, they would snap it up like you did Poland."

Hitler turned to him and smiled. "I have always liked the way you think, Rudolph. That would give us a pincer movement to squeeze the English like a walnut. Scotland from the north and Germany from the south…" He smacked one paw into the other. "It would be over just like that. I take it you have willing connections?" he asked.

"I am familiar with a certain sphere of influence." Hess replied with a minute smile.

"Time is the key in all things. It is the one thing that is constant. You cannot speed it up or slow it down, nor can you stop it; all you can do is plan against its unchanging existence. How much time would this take to organize?"

"I have things in place," the other Wolf replied softly. "I have the opportunity in my paws to give you what you wish politically and without occupation."

Hitler chuckled. "I'm sure you do my friend, but Hermann (Göring) has guaranteed me total dominance of the RAF. I had this talk with him just a few days ago. Once I have that, we will launch the invasion without hesitation. Any British ships that oppose us will be quickly sunk." When the other Wolf looked skeptical, he added, "I have no doubt this will be costly; but because of Dunkirk the English now lack the equipment to resist us effectively on dry land. Our blitzkrieg will continue, and things will be over very quickly."

"My way would mean peace, Adolf, not an attack. Without Scottish support, the English would be far too weak to resist effectively. They would have no choice but to surrender. I have friends…"

"Und I have enemies," Hitler interjected softly. "I do not have time to be very diplomatic. I have hinted strongly to the British government many times that I want a negotiated peace. I gave them Dunkirk," he said acidly. "I had the entire British army in the palm of my hand, and did I crush them? No! I allowed Göring to play with them like a cat with a mouse while waiting for them to capitulate."

"The mouse scurried to a hole, Adolf," Hess sighed. He was quite aware what that meant, as did the other Wolf. If the British forces had been captured at Dunkirk, England would be near naked against a German invasion. Their defense forces would have been so thin as to be almost non-existent.

Herr Wolf smiled at his friend. Removing his hat, he placed it upon the seat next to him. "I underestimated the British wherewithal, Rudolph. You have to admire them for what they did… it was very courageous."

"Our Luftwaffe did not stop it from happening."

"I doubt that anyone's Luftwaffe could have stopped such an undertaking," the Fuehrer admitted. "I am proud of our achievements, none the less. We again played the game and this time took the bully's (Churchill) toys away as was done to us after the first war. We are presently much stronger, are we not? Now the Englander hides upon his island. From the statistics I have read, even discounting by twenty percent for accidental exaggeration, we are winning. Having so very few fighters left to oppose our bombers, I think soon enough the people of England will tire of being beaten down every day and night. They will then force Churchill to capitulate and I shall appropriately imprison him and their imbecile King in the Tower of London; which I will then use as my headquarters."

"I only wish it was that easy," Hess replied softly.

"It worked in Poland," Hitler replied tersely. "After the pounding we gave Krakow, the Polish people totally gave up."

"Poland did not have the English Channel between them and our army. Nor were their aircraft equal to our own."

Herr Wolf did not get angry with this argument. Rudolph Hess was a long time supporter and friend; he relied upon his quiet opinions. After a moment's thought, the little Wolf said, "Pursue your peace talks and this thing concerning Scotland." He then smiled and added, "You might even learn how to play those abominable bagpipes if you think it would help... but act quickly; Sea Lion fast approaches."

§

Archie led his flight on a gentle northeastern turn back towards London. Control had a group of Dorniers flying in towards Whitstable and directed him to intercept. Though 92 Squadron was too late to keep the Germans from dropping their bombs, they did catch them out flat footed on the return trip with no fighter escort. It had been a duck shoot and ten of the twenty bombers were destroyed. Not one of the fighters under his command had been shot down, though there were plenty of bullet holes attesting to the tenacity of the German gunners.

As Flight Leader, the Stag had called 'Tally Ho,' and they'd come down from altitude at a good clip in a slash attack right through the bomber formation. Lining up on the lead most bomber, the Stag flipped his gun button from 'safe' to 'fire' and began peppering its fuselage some three hundred yards out. His speed was such that he closed the distance quickly and then overflew, a good many of his bullets striking the bomber. Streaking past, he hardly noticed the tracers ripping past his port wing so keen was his concentration on banking around for another go at the fellow.

After his second run, the bomber lost its tail and pitched nose over in a death spiral towards the beech below. It was followed by several of its mates along with many exuberant cheers of the rookie pilots. There was no joy in this for the Stag as he witnessed the pilot he'd just shot down bail out with a parachute malfunction. The small black dot plummeted towards the ocean and was finally lost to sight over the distance.

As he navigated his group homeward, his mind drifted though his eyes were everywhere. Colonial Blue had advised him to maintain his relationship with Jeans as if nothing were amiss, and he found himself growing more than fond of her. This caused no small amount of guilt for various reasons; but mostly because of the feelings he had for Terrance. Blue warned that she would be astute enough to recognize any small change in his attitude towards her. Yes she would be watched, but at a distance. There would also be a radio listening station set up across the street in case she tried to use that method for communications.

He thought he heard Terrance's voice whispering within the drone of his engine. She seemed to be less and less with him lately. Perhaps it had only been a simple case of traumatic pretend as an answer for all the strange things that had happened... and then again a lot had happened. He missed Henry, but there was nothing to do about that except be patient. Twice now, Sergeant Higgins informed him, the old Bulldog had been caught trying to sneak out of the hospital. Once he'd fallen down a flight of stairs, nothing broken thankfully, and once in the front yard he'd sat heavily upon the grass when he became dizzy. The doctor's report stated it would be another few weeks before he was able to climb back into the cockpit. 'Bloody hell!' the Bulldog's voice echoed in the darkness of his thoughts, 'Jerry will have landed by then and overrun the airfield!'

"Yellow leader," Control called to him.

"Go ahead, Control," Archie replied as he looked to his left and right, checking his new pilots. They'd handled themselves well today and he knew at least three had just become blooded. It was getting so they were lucky to have five hours in a Spitfire cockpit before being pressed into the ranks.

"In bound friendly, be kind and don't shoot him down, eh?"

"Control, we'll keep our eyes open."

"And bloody well you should," called a new voice.

"Henry?" the Stag asked, craning his neck to look back over his shoulder.

"None other! You don't think I'd stay 'number nine' (sick) for long, did you?"

"They discharged you from hospital?"

"Of course they didn't. I had to fight my way through the door just like they was Jerry trying to keep me out of the war."

"Tag along then, old fellow, but I'm afraid we're heading home."

"Shot your wad, did you?"

"Radio decorum, please," called Control. Archie recognized Chelsea's voice.

"Reference to the Royal Army's venerable old Brown Bess, my dear," Henry told her jovially, "They used to pack the ball in with wadding. I'm fully loaded, Arch, I'll watch the back end and fly cover while your group recovers."

"Much obliged," Archie told his friend with a big smile, "Form up... talk on the ground."

"Wilco," the old Bulldog replied.

§

Admiral Canaris sat alone in his large office in Berlin. The sun was setting, its light coming through the window in an orange fusion that played upon the wall. Sea Lion was fast approaching, and he was assembling a presentation of his intelligence assessment for der Fuehrer whom he had a meeting with upon his arrival back in Berlin. What he was aware of did not set well. The Royal Navy was still strong and poised to sweep down the channel should a crossing be attempted. This would not have been as much a problem if the Luftwaffe did hold air superiority. With as many bombers as they could put in the air at short notice, the big ships would not last long. The Stukas (shortened from Sturzkampfflugzeug, "dive bomber") were especially good at anti-shipping strikes if left unmolested by fighters.

He carefully examined a photograph with a magnifying glass. It showed the remnants of the small boat flotilla which was used so brilliantly during Dunkirk. They were purposely spread out and carefully camouflaged all along the Thames. He had no doubt what this meant. If the Wehrmacht was to attempt a crossing in motorized barges, this fleet would instantly put forth to stop them mounting whatever weapons they could lay their paws on. Again, if the Luftwaffe held supreme in the air, this would hardly be a problem; but from what he'd heard and read this was far from the case no matter what Goring told Herr Wolf. In real terms, if Sea Lion were to be attempted without absolute air superiority established the Wehrmacht stood to lose over half of its army. Such a disaster would make Britain's Dunkirk look like a walk in the park.

There was a soft knock on his door.

"Aufschreiben," he said without looking up.

Manfred came to stand in front of his desk.

"What is it?" the old Fox asked, not looking up from the photograph he was scrutinizing.

The Rat held out a small pill shaped metal capsule. "Carrier pigeon, sir. It is from England."

Canaris did look up then. There were only a handful of successful spies that he had control of in England and carrier pigeons were an emergency fall back method of communication. Taking the proffered capsule, he examined the markings on it. "Thank you," the Fox finally told his orderly, "This is but one more piece to the puzzle, I think. Is it good, or is it bad? Certainly, we will put the information to use no matter what it represents." Looking squarely at the rat, he asked, "And what news from your brethren, Manfred?"

The Rat looked perplexed, as if he was not certain he should speak his mind or if he should remain mute. Hermann Wilhelm Göring had personally brought him into the ranks when he founded the Gestapo in 1933, and he'd been a faithful servant to the cause... but things change... masters change. It had to do with respect and an adherence to sanity. In the shadowy subculture of the Rat, allegiances were known to change, but loyalty to one's nation never varied. If the Luftwaffe's actions, spurred on by the leaders of his country, were ever paid back in kind, Germany would be in great danger.

The Admiral motioned to a chair next to his desk. "It is my understanding that this office is safe. My duty and my concerns are for the safety and well being of Germany. If you have an insight to share that might bear upon this I, would greatly appreciate hearing it."

"I was just listening to the BBC, Herr Canaris," the Rat told him. "They are playing a lovely rendition of Wagner's *Ritt der Walküren* (Ride of the Valkyries). I had a good chuckle when the radio announcer dedicated it to our bomber forces, whom he claimed are terrified of the RAF and with good reason; they have already shot down more than half of what we brought to France. May I tune your radio to it for you?"

"Certainly," the old Fox told him. This was confirmation to something he'd already suspected... the watcher was being watched.

When the radio was playing in a normal fashion, Manfred came over and sat in the chair Canaris had indicated. Leaning forward, he said very softly, "The fighter pilot known as Der Professor is dead. The battle report indicates he collided with a British fighter."

"I had not heard of this," the Fox replied, and then a little louder, "This is wonderful music, Manfred, thank you. We should always take a moment to appreciate such beauty, even if it is given to us by our enemies."

"Conjecture is this was deliberate since there was a Gestapo agent waiting at his airbase to arrest him," the Rat continued, "That agent has since disappeared. He was a Belgium, and it is suspected he fled to Switzerland. The search for him was not so intense being that he was not German."

The music grew in strength and volume.

"Why do you tell me this?"

The Rat shrugged his shoulders. "We Rats have a saying; 'Nichts ist, während es scheint, dennoch ist alles, während es scheint.'" (*Nothing is as it seems, yet everything is as it seems.*) Louder, he said, "Enjoy the music, Admiral. As your servant, I must also say I fear you work too hard. Would you like tea?"

"Your concern is noted, but it is something I must do. Thank you, yes please, tea would be most welcome."

When the Rat had left his office, the spy master opened the little capsule and removed the small rolled up piece of paper. Using his magnifying glass, he quickly deciphered the code. The message read, "Contact established. RAF still viable. Der Professor is dead. Locke is the key."

Thinking about this, Admiral Canaris' mind made a cold assessment of numbers, and he began leafing through a pile of top secret documents lying in a basket on his desk. Sea Lion was slated for the seventeenth of September. Coming to the paper he sought, he found the Luftwaffe's orders for the fifteenth and frowned. Every bomber that could be mustered was slated to pound England. It was only too obvious Uncle Fatty had promised something he could not deliver, and he had no qualms about throwing away the lives of those under his command for the greater glory of himself.

'So be it,' he decided. If Der Fuehrer would not listen to anyone but Göring, then perhaps the numbers the Reichmarschall would have to report should reflect the true strength of the RAF. He might not be a player in this strange and deadly card game of world leaders; but he could certainly shuffle the deck to advantage one side or the other.

§

Derik sat at the same table where he'd met Jeans that first time. His police whistle, the lanyard around his neck, was carefully tucked into his tunic pocket. After his first glass of wine, he nonchalantly removed it and let it hang down his front as if in readiness to be used. After a time, when nothing happened, a feeling of disappointment crept through his body. Sighing, he refilled his wine glass. It wasn't that he truly wished to defect to England; he just suddenly had a need to see the strange Poodle again. He wished to be held.

With the information he gained from his interrogation of Faust, the fighter pilot's mind swirled with all that had happened so far. Germany was still first in his heart… and yet… after sitting and digesting the information he'd gained, he understood that his country was being taken in a direction directly opposed to its people's wishes. He also now knew that atrocities were being committed that he was hardly aware of.

Seeing the war from the air was not quite the same as seeing all that had happened from the ground. In the air, things were more imper-sonal; targets were bombed and aircraft shot down. Wake up, fly, come home, repeat. No… not home; just come back and then repeat.

For the most part it, was mind numbingly simple. Within this sim-plicity, however, the targets being selected for destruction were not even military. A few here and there could always be attributed to the fates of modern warfare; but wonton destruction…

"There you are, Derik," called a voice.

The pilot looked up to find his second in command approaching. He lifted his glass to the other Wolf and smiled. "Hello, Johannes," he called back, "I am surprised to see you here. All is well with the chil-dren?"

The greeting was old and familiar, reflective more upon the young and very green replacement pilots the Luftwaffe was providing the active units with.

"They are tucked in for the night, and I was almost there myself," he replied as he pulled out a chair and sat. "Then orders were delivered and I felt it best if I personally sought you out."

Reaching into his tunic, he took out a folded piece of paper and passed it over to his commander who accepted it but not before pouring his comrade a glass of wine.

"At first, I could not find you," Johannes explained, ac-cepting the glass, "Und I worried. Then I remembered the Poodle I saw you with that one night and thought to look here."

"You are very insightful."

"Not insightful," he laughed, clinking Derik's glass, "Just a romantic at heart. She was very pretty. I thank you for the compliment, however; though I only seek to do my duty."

Opening the envelope, Locke frowned. "These orders are secret. It would seem I am summoned once again to Berlin and no one is to know." He looked up at his second and sighed. "Are you a someone?"

Before Johannes could reply, Derik held up a finger in caution.

"Be careful how you answer, or I may have to shoot you."

Call

"Germany calling, Germany calling, Germany calling, here in the Reichssender at Hamburg; station Bremen and station DXB on the thirty-one meter band. You are about to hear our news in English."
—William Joyce – Lord Haw Haw

Archie and Henry's reunion was loudly applauded by their squadron mates, though they were quick to disperse as their aircraft were readied. The pair's reputation as a team was well established and Henry was looked up to by just about everyone who'd ever met him. Tough as nails and not one to back down over anything he felt strongly about, he was also kind in the way he treated others.

As they hugged and pounded each other on the back, the old Bulldog winced as pain flowed through his body which was far from healed. Looking at the Stag, he told him, "We need to talk and we need to talk now."

"We can't go far," Archie replied. "Jerry will be back at any moment. The fighters have been relentless in trying to call us out for a duel, and still we are only allowed to primarily engage the bombers."

"If they lose a fighter," the Bulldog reminded, echoing Air Chief Marshal Sir Keith Park, "it means nothing. If we lose a fighter, it means everything. If we are to stop the bombers, we have to be there to do so." The Bulldog glanced over at the Kiwis who were fueling and rearming Commander Sheltie's aircraft as if he distrusted their work. "In that, I

286

am in agreement with the old fellow, though I might take difference with some other of his other policies. The Germans are doing their best to rid the skies of us because, if they can, they will have a free paw at the total destruction of London, and lickety-split they'd be across the channel with no way for us to stop them."

He pointed to an area behind the aircraft. "So long as we're away from any other ears we'll be fine. I'd prefer to speak over a frosty mug but tea will do."

There was a clearing of a voice behind them and, as if by magic, Corporal Higgins was there with two mugs of steaming hot 'gunpowder'.

"Thank you, my boy," Henry told him as he accepted this. "The family is well?"

"Those of us who are left, sir," the corporal replied. "The children have been sent north to the countryside while the rest of us keep on."

"Thank goodness for that much. It's a terrible thing being done to the English peoples. We need to stop the buggers."

"Yes, sir, of course we do."

Henry sipped at his tea and then added, "You have been a God send during this terrible time, Higgins."

"Thank you, sir. Shall I make dinner for you both tonight?"

"I think we'll eat at Madam Bellas," the old Dog told him with a wink. "That's the one part of my body I've not had the opportunity to flight check since escaping the clutches of our fine medical staff at hospital. It's one thing to grab the old stick and wiggle your flight controls around on the ground but certainly another to test them out while you're airborne."

"You're not going to injure yourself again, are you, Henry?" the Stag asked him.

The Bulldog, having just taken another sip of his tea, had to spit it out, and all three of them were giggling like children.

As soon as Higgins left them, with instructions to leave word at Madam Bella's of their planned arrival, the Bulldog took the Stag in tow, and they walked to an area behind the flight line where they could chat privately.

"Archie, considering my recent, shall we say enlightenment; there are some things I need you to level with me about," the older fighter pilot began.

The Stag kept his face poker neutral. "Such as?"

"That intelligence chap... I don't trust him, nor do I like him."

"Colonel Blue?"

"If that's really his name, yes. He can't be very good because I stayed in the room with you during your debrief and heard every last word... well... almost every last word; I was snoring pretty damned loud."

Archie frowned. "You were drunk, Henry."

The Bulldog smiled over the rim of his tin cup, raising it slightly in salute. "So I was; but that did not stop me from listening. Has he done anything about your whore?"

"She's not a whore," the Stag replied, anger flashing across his face for just a second.

His friend regarded him with a raised eyebrow, his look speaking volumes.

"She might be many things, Henry," the Stag told him softly, softening his feelings towards what he knew to be a truth, "but she is not that."

"You do realize that by turning her over to MI6 you alerted the authorities to a threat and that the elimination of said threat by both sides is the usual method of taking care of things."

"Did you come back to make me feel worse than I already do?"

"No," the Bulldog told him with a very serious look. "I dragged myself back to see if we could prevent a German invasion of Old Blighty. While in the hospital, I had time to consider things and I think your girl (he deliberately did not again call her a whore) is the key. She came to see me and actually asked how the invasion could be stopped. God knows I was not totally myself with whatever it was they'd injected me; but I gave her some advice, and I think it's time to see if she did anything with it. I am not one to call out to The Almighty and expect a reply but I do feel there was more to my crash and burn dream than a mind trying to deal with death and destruction. I remembered every last little detail, including the part about Terrance, which was dead on; no pun intended."

"You heard me tell Colonial Blue about her," Archie told him.

"You're right, of course... but in the dream she said to tell you of her love. I was there... it was real... and your girl knows something we desperately need to know, too."

"JERRY UP!" someone yelled out.

There was the sound of engines starting, and both pilots were running back to their aircraft; tin mugs dropped to the ground, and their conversation, for the moment, broken off.

§

Jeans sat alone at a table in the dining room with Mama Bella listening to the big RCA radio the old Pole kept there for the entertainment of her customers. Being early afternoon, the dining room was yet empty. This made what she was doing easier, as there were no drunken distractions to contend with.

Though she'd worked both sides of the channel, the Poodle most recently had been placed outside of London at the behest of the same 'Uncle' that had Oberleutnant Daecher join the Luftwaffe. Her instructions were not to so much spy upon the English as it was to make a contact within who could put her in touch with those in charge of the British government. Because of this she'd met Archie Corn, given him good information as a peace offering and his instincts had done the rest. Admiral Canaris was wise in understanding that during a time of war, there was always a requirement to occasionally speak with the enemy. Those who worked directly for the head of the Abwehr all had one thing in common; they loved their country first. Her brother had been like that; and she had always followed his example.

So far she'd been disappointed. The officer who approached her made no effort at contact. Apparently he was mostly interested in sex, though he did sign her on to sing for the troops. Obviously, he wished her to show herself for who she was and then turn her with the threat of execution or perhaps simply feed her false information. This was the game of spy craft; at which he was not very good.

Information and how it was acquired was almost as important as its final use. Her brother's death, as an example, made her sad but the way the information came to her was a total mystery. Nothing like this had ever happened to her before. It was for that reason she'd taken the opportunity of visiting Henry at the hospital. Though he was obviously under some sort of sedation, his words struck true and she'd immediately sent them on by pigeon which she'd kept hidden among those in Madam Bella's rooftop coop. Now it was a matter of waiting for instructions.

Coming into the dining room, she'd poured herself a scotch being sure to leave the correct amount for her drink in the till. Trust was everything and Mama Bella's trust was absolutely required, though it was like playing with fire. If the old Tatra Dog ever had so much as an inkling of why the Poodle were truly working in the bordello there was no doubt her throat would be cut and her body disposed of in the bombed out ruins of the east end.

Next, she'd tuned the big RCA radio to the 'Reichs-Rundfunk-Gesellschaft (RRG)' German State Radio. Though Germany was the enemy, she'd explained to Mama Bella once, they still played a superior quality of music.

With a flourish, the orchestra finished and the station's announcer made his post performance explanation of what had been played. There was a pause, and then the English voice of William Joyce came to them over the speakers.

"Germany calling, Germany calling, Germany calling, here in the Reichssender at Hamburg; station Bremen and station DXB on the thirty-one meter band. You are about to hear our news in English."

The old Pole reached out to shut the radio off, but Jeans asked her to 'please' leave it on. "We both know the news they give us from either side is a lie," she explained to the aging Madam, "So if you believe the opposite of both and then add them together, you'll at least see a small part of the truth. I am very worried the Germans will invade, and things will go badly for us."

"The only truth I wish to hear is the death of Germany," the Madam told her softly. "May they receive exactly what they handed out to my Poland. If they do invade, I will take my largest kitchen knife and kill the first of them I can get close to."

When Jeans made no response, the old Tatra Sheepdog mistook the Poodle's concentration as a silent question about why she felt the way she did. "My entire family was dragged from our estate by the German Wehrmacht and shot dead in the courtyard. They gave no reason… they just did it. I was fortunate not to have been found and so buried each of them myself after the bastards moved on."

On the radio, the announcer was saying, *"Mr. Churchill in his pride filled stubbornness continues to allow the British people to suffer an unnecessary loss of life. Reports from Germany's victorious Luftwaffe indicate that the RAF is all but done in as evidenced by the daily unopposed bombings of London."*

'Unopposed bombings of London' was Jeans notification that an incoming message was now being posted to her through the context of the news broadcast.

"That's a lie," Madam Bella hooted. "I watch from the roof and the British fighters give them hell every chance they get."

"The RAF does not have such a luxury in this air war. Fifteen British bombers were shot down last night attempting to reach the coast of France in an apparent attempt to thwart the upcoming invasion which Herr Hitler has assured us will happen. Numbers do not lie and fifteen

was half of what was launched. This is a pittance compared to the hundreds of bombers the Luftwaffe strikes London with every day and every night. The English people should call Mr. Churchill and demand he step down. In other news..."

"Did you hear me Jeans?"

Jeans blinked. Fifteen was a date. It was now the thirteenth of September.

"Yes Ma'am, you watch them from the roof. Isn't that forbidden?"

"Who cares."

(*half of what was launched... which is a pittance compared to the hundreds of bombers the Luftwaffe...*)

On September 15th, twice as many bombers as usual would be striking at London. This was what she'd been waiting for. It was to be Göring's knockout blow to the RAF; the invasion would happen after this.

"I'm sorry, Madam, I'm afraid I was caught in a daydream," she replied, looking over to her patron, "What did you say?"

The old Polish Sheepdog, however, was now occupied with a Corporal whom Jeans recognized as Archie and Henry's batman.

After he left, Madam Bella came back to her and smiled a large money smile. "Your presence has been requested for a late dinner and the entire night already paid for handsomely, inclusive of a bottle of my best scotch. You are so very good for my business... I shall see that an extra allowance is placed into your account."

Jeans simply smiled back, allowing the old girl to believe that which she obviously believed.

§

Wing Commander Stewart Falstaff was sound asleep when he heard the telephone bell jangle. It did so just once; and then his paw was picking it up. "What is it?" he asked groggily.

There was a moment's explanation over the phone and then the old Bulldog asked, "Are you drunk? Who put you through to this number, Henry? In the morning, I shall have their balls for breakfast."

A different voice came onto the phone, one that Falstaff well remembered as a Stag and a very good flyer. "Lieutenant Terrance Chrysanthemum requests an urgent meeting with you, sir," it told him. "He wishes to know if we might come to your residence post haste."

The Wing Commander sat up in his bed, the sleep suddenly gone from his mind. "Come immediately; I shall prepare the tea."

Meetings

September 14th...

    Wing Commander Stewart Falstaff, dressed only in his house coat, stood in the doorway of his blacked out residence. Raising his left wrist, he attempted to see the time on his watch but was thwarted by the absence of any moon. Somewhere in the darkness and at a great distance, he heard the sound of an airplane. His ears told him it was one of his own, and the realization was at least reassuring; considering that not too long before there'd been the drone of bombers and a cluster of explosions.

    "This bloody well better be worth it," he muttered just as he heard the muted sound of a motorbike. When it came close, he proceeded down the walkway to the road and greeted the three riders. Driving was Henry Badcock. Riding on the saddle behind him was a French Poodle dressed in black slacks, a black top, and an aviator's leather jacket. In the sidecar, his antlers marking the silhouette as none other, was Archie Corn.

    "The water's on the boil," Falstaff told them quietly. In the hush of the very early morning fog it, almost sounded as if he were giving them a spy's pass code.

    "Much obliged to you, sir," Henry replied. "And what kind of tea will we be having?"

    "You'll have whatever I bloody well give you and then be on your way back to Holy Ground," the other Bulldog replied in a grumble. "And who might this be with you?"

    "My name is Jeans," the Poodle replied. Climbing off of the

bike's saddle, she extended a paw. "We have common goals, Monsieur Falstaff."

"I'm sure we do," he told her, taking the offered paw in his, "But I will withhold judgment until I fully understand the nature of your trade. Information and its validity is a tricky business best left to those who understand such things; I am but an old soldier."

Turning to the Stag, who'd finally gotten himself out of the small-ish sidecar, he said, "Good to see you again, Flight Lieutenant, have you seen our mutual friend lately?"

"I haven't, sir, but Henry has. Such as it is, this is what led us to disturb your sleep."

"I see. Please come in then."

Leading them to the kitchen, the Wing Commander double checked to see that the windows were properly blacked out more as a security precaution than regulation. He then took the time to fix and pour the tea before taking out a large pad of paper which he tossed down upon the table. On it, he wrote each of their names, and then his questioning began.

"Before we get to the 'why' we are here, I have to swear all of you to secrecy. What transpires in this room stays in this room unless I personally give the allowance," he told them. "This includes the persons who might or might not be foreign nationals working for the other side. I shall remind everyone present, inclusive of myself, that the penalty for spying is death by hanging. This will include the offense of aiding and abetting a spy. Do you three all so swear?"

There was a solemn tone in the three voices as they so swore in agreement.

Lifting his teacup, the Wing Commander said, "To the King."

All three of his guests responded equally.

"Now then, I already know the story of Lieutenant Chrysanthemum intimately," Looking at Archie, he nodded and the Stag nodded back. "So everyone will know, it was I who signed off on Terrance's being a fighter pilot. Though he was an American, I still believe the choice was a good one. That being said, Henry, it's your turn. Tell me what you know of the Lieutenant."

"I met her, sir."

Falstaff raised an eyebrow at the word 'her' and made a notation under Henry's name on his pad. "You did not join the squadron until after his demise," he replied calmly, "You could not have known 'him'."

"It was when I was crashed into, sir, by the Nazi… and let's just

294

say it straight; Terrance was female."

"Wilhelm was not a Nazi," Jeans interjected softly.

"He was bloody well flying a Messerschmitt," the Bulldog huffed at her. "Last I heard we don't make those here."

Jeans looked as though she was about to say something in retort and then glanced to Archie. "Terrance was female... your female?"

The Stag nodded but said nothing.

"Who is this Wilhelm to you, young lady?" Falstaff asked, interrupting.

"He was my brother."

"I see... I am sorry for your loss." The old Bulldog would gladly have danced a jig at news of a German being killed in the skies above London, but presently he was wise enough to stay objective and neutral in his feelings.

"He was a right gentleman in my dream," Henry told her as if trying to make up for his previous comment. "We shared a cigarette together."

"In your dream?" the Wing Commander asked gruffly. The insinuation of psychosis through head trauma was now out in the open.

"It was more than a dream, sir," the flier said quickly, "I remember every second as if it had been burned into my skull with a purpose; which I now believe it was. Look at me Stewart... just days later and not a scratch on me where I was sure considered a goner. When Archie found me I was lying among the corpses in one of the tube shelters. Perhaps you don't believe in Divine Providence, but I've certainly lived it."

"And Chrysanthemum was there?"

"Yes, sir... she warned me I was going to hurt badly and then pulled my D ring. I have no other explanation as to how I might have survived but for that. My aircraft was rammed at better than three hundred miles per mile. There was nothing left to it at all."

"And what did this German pilot tell you in your dream?" Archie asked.

Badcock became very serious. "He told me he was part of a larger plot to get rid of Hitler. He'd word they were waiting to arrest him when he got back to France, so he had to kill himself cuz he knew too much."

Falstaff wrote this on his pad and then muttered, "'Had word' insinuates it was over the radio. In that case, it would have been a coded message and if that is true it indicates he is not alone," muttered the Wing Commander. Looking up from his pad, he asked Jeans, "Why in hell didn't he just land and surrender then?"

"Would you have done so in the first war and given your aeroplane to the Germans?" Jeans asked softly. "Who do you trust in war? Certainly, there are German agents among your ranks, yes?"

Falstaff's eyes closed slightly in his regard of the Poodle. "And what makes you think I was in the last war aside from my obvious age?" he asked, avoiding the last part of her statement. That was something MI-5 was always working upon.

Jeans allowed herself a small smile. "For you to believe me, I must firmly establish who I am, therefore I will tell you. I work for the Abwehr and have been well versed in the RAF command structure. I was also told that you, in particular, have good connections all the way up to the Prime Minister."

"Smugness does not suit you, nor does it help your case," the Bulldog growled at her. "I must be convinced concerning the truth of your information which could also be nothing but lies designed to do us damage. Such things are all a part of war, are they not?"

"You were a part of 3 Naval Squadron which was formed at Dunkirk in late 1916. You were there from the beginning and stayed when it became 203 Squadron in the Royal Air Force in 1918. You had fourteen victories and you were shot down three times. You were awarded the Distinguished Flying Cross twice."

"All right, that's enough," Falstaff told her, seeming a bit embarrassed at this notoriety, "I'm still not that impressed. What was your mission here? Note I say 'was' as obviously you will not be allowed to return to it."

"My only mission," she told him, "Is to act as a communications tool between the British government and the one person within the German government who understands that even during war there is a need to talk. I was to make contact and give evidence of my desire to help, which I have done."

"That would be the raid we intercepted," Archie interjected. "You may recall they managed to avoid our radar and were about to attack Holy Ground. It also warned us that at least the German Command at the wing level is on to what our RDF can do and can't do."

"That was a bloody good save," Henry added.

"You had to bail out," Falstaff reminded him.

"Sure sure, but I got the bastard, didn't I?"

Archie lightly tapped the table to get their attention and then looked to Jeans. "Tell him," he instructed her.

"My brother's message to me was delivered through his discussion with Monsieur Badcock. I was told he was dead and that Locke was the key."

"That was a riddle I certainly didn't understand," Henry added, "Until tonight when Jeans explained it to me, sir. It was Locke as in L.O.C.K.E. the pilot and not lock as in door. It's the bloke's name."

Falstaff looked up from his pad. "Would that be the same Locke who flew in the first war?"

"Oui," Jeans replied.

"And the same chap that shot down his wingman to keep him from shooting me in my parachute," Archie told him.

"I've seen his aircraft many times," Henry told the Wing Commander. "He's a good pilot."

"An excellent pilot," the Stag added. "I've not seen better, present company excepted."

"I have heard him say the same of you," Jeans told the Stag with a slight smile.

"Focus," Falstaff growled at them.

When their attention was back upon him he instructed, "Jeans, tell me your message and how it came about; and then I shall decide how and to whom it needs delivering to."

When she had done this, Falstaff chuckled and looked directly at Henry. "Make him understand he will lose his only testicle if he attempts the crossing?" he asked. "I dare say, he'll lose more than that. He already lost a good chunk of his navy when he invaded Norway, and that's one weakness that has helped us greatly."

"The state of my condition at that moment would give me pause too," the Bulldog replied seriously. "Mind I was feeling no pain when she came for a visit. But… the fact that we know the Luftwaffe is going to pull out all the stops tomorrow… today is the fourteenth isn't, it?"

There was a chorus of affirmation from around the table.

"Very well then, I will suggest that we do the same and hit them with everything we can get into the air. We hit them so hard they can't possibly hide the numbers with their propaganda machine. Think of it, sir, if they don't come what have we lost but a day's fuel and a lot of patience."

Falstaff looked to Archie and the Stag nodded. "Bader's thoughts on the 'big wing' might finally be of use, sir."

Next he looked to Jeans. "Do you have any more details other than they're going to hit us hard on the fifteenth?"

She shook her head.

Placing his pencil on the table, the Wing Commander sat back in his chair, taking the time to sip at his tea while considering all that he'd been told.

"Very well," he finally said, "I want each of you to go back to exactly what you were doing. Not a word to anyone. All they need to know is that the three of you had one hell of a good night together. Understand from here forward that what you have done you have done for England. If credit is given for anything, it will be given to others who might not exactly deserve it.

The three nodded in agreement and understanding.

Using his tea cup as a pointer, the Wing Commander furthered, "Henry, you make sure to have whiskey on your breath when you get back to base. Archie, you do whatever it is you would do, and Jeans, you do the same. True or otherwise, mind you are all being watched and do nothing out of the ordinary."

"I do 'ave one request," Jeans told him in reply.

"And what would that be my dear?"

"After tomorrow, I wish for Lieutenant Corn to fly me back to France. If you have any message for me to carry, I will gladly do so."

"That you are alive and free should be message enough. Will you be back then?"

She gave him a small smile. "That remains to be seen."

§

When they'd gone and the Wing Commander came back into his residence, he paused by the door and sniffed the air. His pug nose caught the scent of aircraft and gunpowder.

"If you are here, Terrance," he said aloud, "Please know that England owes you such a debt of gratitude. If it were in my power, I would erect a statue in your honor and declare the day you died a national holiday. You also have my undying gratitude... no pun intended, mind you."

With that, he hurried to the bedroom where he woke his wife and asked her to help him get into his dress uniform. When she asked him why, he simply told her, "I must go and meet with Winnie."

§

September 14th... 0500L 10 Downing Street, London

Wing Commander Stewart Falstaff sat in the office of the Prime Minister waiting. He was one of the very few who had the privilege of immediate access to Winston Churchill. Where most would have been kept waiting in one of the many anterooms (and there to have a watchful but secret eye kept upon them), Stewart was let into the actual office while a messenger was sent for the PM. But for a service of tea and toast, he was left alone with his thoughts.

Presently there was the shuffling sound of slippered feet approaching the open door of the rear entrance. A moment after this, standing in the doorway, still clad in his pajamas and a robe, the country's leader growled, "What have you got Stew?" There was no doubt or annoyance in the question. If the Wing Commander was here at this hour then he had good reason.

Placing his tea cup back on its tray, the waiting Bulldog rose to his feet. For the hour of the morning, he looked as fresh as if about to go on parade whereas his counterpart looked face forward, much as the situation dictated… just woken from a sound sleep. During these times of crisis, Winston rarely left the city, choosing instead to stay in residence at 10 Downing Street; though he slept in a bunker against the chance of an accurate bombing.

"I have information," the Wing Commander announced quietly, "that the Luftwaffe intends to hit us with all they have tomorrow."

"Do you mean to say they've been holding back?" Churchill grumped, "Bloody cheeky of the bastards don't you think; offering a fair fight and then pulling their punches so you'll not think they're as strong as they are?"

Moving the rest of the way into the room, the PM closed the door. Stopping at the drink service he took two short glasses and half filled them both with whiskey. Handing one to the Wing Commander, he clinked it with his own and then went to sit at his desk which was mounded with papers and reports. "All of this," he said, indicating the pile, "and I've heard nothing that would indicate tomorrow would be any different than any other bloody day. They come, they bomb, they leave. Jerry's become as regular as the milk delivery fellow." Sipping his whiskey, he leaned back in his chair. "Tell me what you've heard."

The Wing Commander recounted all he'd been told very nearly word for word, inclusive of the parts concerning Henry's dream and Lieutenant Terrance. For his age, his memory was as sharp as ever and then some.

"What a lovely way of putting it," the Prime Minister chortled.

"Make the bastard understand he's going to lose his last testicle. I'll give Henry credit for his way with words. I wish I'd thought of it. Imagine the speech I could have made." Standing, he held up his glass and struck a pose of leadership. "Mr. Hitler," he said very seriously, "Should you choose to come ahead with your invasion, we shall stand upon the wide shores of our blessed island nation, and every mother's son among us will have their sights set upon your one remaining testicle. Rest asured... we will not miss."

"That would have stopped him cold I think," Stewart chuckled as the PM sat again. "You should also add the final part Henry told our spy; 'We British control the air... it's that simple.' I agree with his assessment that someone obviously has not told Herr Hitler this news. Apparently Miss Jeans got that message back to Germany. 'Our new friend' seems to understand its importance, and we apparently are to be given a chance at taking a kick at that lone dangling testicle. I'm not exactly sure why he's doing this, but there certainly does seem to be a difference of opinions concerning the feasibility of invasion among Hitler's commanders... not that they all wouldn't jump in a boat and paddle hard if he told them to do so." The Wing Commander paused for a moment and then added the inevitable. "It could also be a well-played trap, sir."

Churchill looked at him over his now empty glass. "I've told you before, Stewart, in my office you will not call me sir. We are friends on a mission, and the information you've just given me is not only invaluable, but heartening. I needn't remind you of the sensitivity of such intelligence."

"Of course not," Falstaff replied, understanding that this was something that had to be said.

"Hitler, as a leader," Churchill added, "is only concerned for his victories regardless of the price his people must pay. My guess would be that, because of this, the true cost has craftily been hidden from him. The Germans do seem to believe their own propaganda. After what Herr Wolf has accomplished in Europe, it's no wonder he wants to press on and add us to the pile. After that, I've no doubt he'll attack Russia. Stalin's no fool either. I'm sure he sees this regardless of whatever peace treaty he has with the Boche. On the plus side, if Hitler's own people are planning to kill him then it's only a matter of time before this war is bloody well over in any case. We've heard rumblings of this, but then again we've heard rumblings of the same concerning myself... however... this is the first solid proof, if indeed you can call it solid, that the possibility actually does exist."

"And then what?" the other Bulldog asked. "Do you think they'll give back all they took? And how can you pay for the lives lost? What explanation do you think they'll give? 'Oh look world... we agree with you and got rid of the crazy bastard who caused this cock up, so let's just all call it a day and go back to living, eh?'" He puffed out his cheeks, catching himself in the tirade and then said in a softer tone, "I highly doubt Hitler's cohorts would allow such a thing to happen."

Churchill actually laughed. "Of course it's not going to be that simple, but in any case we have the more eminent invasion to worry about do we not? Every intelligence report coming through this office to date has reported the same thing; Hitler has everything in place and the boats to do the job. We still have our fleet intact and on constant standby, but what good will they do after being attacked by the Stukas? Without constant air cover, the dive bombers will make mincemeat out of our battle group. That's not even to mention the u-boats and e-boats which will be thrown into the mix."

He thought for a moment while sipping at his whiskey.

"Observer Groups just yesterday claimed to have seen up to ten large enemy transport ships towing a number of barges from Calais to Cape Griz Nez. This was verified by Spitfires of the PRU (*Photographic Reconnaissance Unit*) flying over the Belgian and Dutch coasts. Bomber Command has done their best in hitting the barge installations. God love them for the courage they've shown; but their losses have been staggering. We can't keep the attacks up much longer and have anything left to hit them with if they do come. Intelligence now claims at least one third of the barges are submerged at their moorings; but what's not totally destroyed we can count on being raised. We could certainly use an edge." Looking at the other Bulldog, he asked, "What do we know of this Locke fellow?"

"All I know is what I told you," Falstaff replied. "He's one of their squadron commanders. Apparently, he's old school concerning honor. I flew against him in the first war, and he was good then. I'm told that has not changed with age."

"I'm interested to know why he is 'the key'," the Prime Minister replied. Pushing a button on his desk, the front door immediately opened, and a uniformed butler came in.

"Yes sir?"

"Get me Smithe," the old Bulldog growled at the fellow.

After only a moment an intelligence officer came into the room carrying a pile of papers. Though he'd been up most of the night, he looked completely rested, and his uniform was freshly pressed.

"I'm here, sir," he told the Prime Minister, "Are you ready for your morning updates?"

"No... tell me what you know about a fellow named Locke; he's a Jerry fighter pilot."

Without blinking an eye, the officer said, "That would be Staffel Commandant Staffelkapitän Oberst Dierk Locke, sir, of Jagdgeschwader 56 , Geschwader 56. His group is a constant thorn in our side. He flew in the last war and is an ace several times over. He is not considered 'the' top commander but certainly he is one of them. Not long ago, he was awarded another Iron Cross which was presented by Hitler himself.

Apparently there was much ado about this. Recent intel has him recalled to Berlin."

"Why was he recalled?"

"We don't know, sir."

"Find out what you can and be quick about it. I need to know."

Flipping through his papers, the officer told him, "There was one additional item that I brought in more for amusement that might actually add a little more to knowing the fellow, sir. A possible spy was captured by a farmer near Dover. The fellow in question was dressed in a British bomber crew's flight suit but didn't speak a lick of English. Upon interrogation he claimed to be a Belgium national trying to escape the German occupation. That explanation didn't hold water, of course. Upon a rather more intense interrogation, he confessed to being a Gestapo agent and that he was dropped via light aircraft in England by a fighter pilot named Locke. He claims he was sent to investigate a death plot against Hitler concerning one of the other pilots, but that fellow was killed before he could arrest him."

"Did we press for more information? I would think that a plot against our arch enemy would be something to investigate further wouldn't it?"

Smithe, finding the paper he sought, read through it quickly and frowned. "It would appear, sir, that this Gestapo agent was handed over to the Belgium government when they came for him. There are no notes as to how they were notified. They are here in London in exile."

"I know where they are," Churchill growled. "Tell them I want him back."

"I'm afraid that won't be possible, sir. He was apparently known to them and was immediately sent before a firing squad."

"Pity," Churchill growled, covering his disappointment. He rose and went again to the liquor service. "Another, Stewart?"

"No thank you. I have to go out and review the lads... let them know we care. Quite honestly, it's all I can do not to climb into the cockpit of a vacant Spitfire and join them. Then I have my other administrative duties to attend to."

"Thank you ,Smithe," the Prime Minister said as he filled his glass. "Do put a high import on that information concerning this fellow Locke. I will need it as soon as you get it so no matter what the meeting, please break in. I am especially keen to know who recalled him to Berlin."

"Yes, sir."

With that the intelligence officer left the room. Coming back to his desk, Winston pulled his chair out and sat back down.

"It would seem that our fellow Locke is a ballsy bastard," Falstaff told him.

"He's a Wolf, and a leader of other Wolfs," Falstaff told him. "He is old school and honorable. He is also sure enough of those under his command that he is not afraid of the Gestapo. That he did not just shoot the bastard or have him thrown into a propeller tells us, and mind you this is just speculation, he kept his word and let the fellow live."

The PM sipped at his whiskey and chuckled. "Be careful what you ask of the Devil, because he will always give it to you. What do you suppose would happen if Locke was taken out of the equation during a very large attack staged by the Luftwaffe?"

"Certainly, he has a very competent second in command," Falstaff replied, "Leadership would not be that much of a factor in the air..."

"But on the ground, during the planning stages, it would be," the Prime Minister told him, raising his glass slightly. "So Locke is the key, eh?"

"I'll see about shuffling the squadrons around a bit for better coverage," the Wing Commander commented with a determined look. Pouring himself some more tea, he asked, "What do we tell the others?"

"We don't tell them a bloody thing," Churchill replied gruffly. "We shall bugger on, business as usual; but this time, you have to give in and employ Bader's 'Big Wing'. If Jerry is pulling out all the bloody stops then so must we. Everything needs to happen just as it has every other day except this time we've been given the opening to kick Hitler square in the chops and then savor the moment when he bends over and vomits his guts out."

The Wing Commander smiled. "You have such a way with

words."

The Prime Minister laughed and then replied, "That's what comes from being the world's most famous orator."

§

September 14th… 0700L Berlin, Germany

Derik's driver dropped him off at the Haus Vaterland, a huge entertainment center in the heart of Berlin which housed numerous restaurants, dance halls, beer halls and a massive cinema. He'd been told he would be met inside but not by whom. Even at this early hour the center was packed to overflowing with all descriptions of military uniforms. Music loudly played from the dance halls as the 'Might of Germany' spent their last days before deployment trying to enjoy as much of life as was possible. Inside the complex there was every type of uniform imaginable. There was also the smell of food and of stale beer.   Those military types, who were sober enough to recognize an officer, quickly saluted and then carried on as the Luftwaffe ace passed by politely returning the salute.

"Oberst Locke," called a Rat dressed in civilian clothes. He did not offer to shake paws but instead held up a theater ticket. "The movie is 'Stagecoach' and stars a young American by the name of John Wayne. The Admiral is rather fond of American Westerns. I think he likes the way the good guys always wear a white hat. He says it makes knowing who is who much easier. You will find him in the top row waiting for you. At this time of the day it is quite private."

The flyer, presenting his ticket, was admitted to the theater where he took the time to purchase a bag of popcorn. Walking into the darkness of the movie's showing room, the Wolf stood for a moment allowing his eyes to adjust to the light and his nose to the various smells. The room, which was very large and in the style of an old opera venue, was occupied mostly by various military types who had been up all night and simply wanted a dark place to sleep off their many beers. The box seats, he noticed, were all unoccupied. In the flickering light of the projector he found just one person sitting way up in the last row of the balcony, directly under its window. This person didn't wave or in any way even seem interested in his presence, but was intently watching the moving images on the huge screen. Presently an old west stagecoach was being chased by a pack of Indians, the sounds of gunshots punctuating the non-verbal yelling that was so stereotypical of such movies. One fellow on the coach was valiantly firing at them from on top and behind the driver. Ironically it reminded him of the Luftwaffe's bombers over England. He munched at his popcorn for a moment and then began his climb to the last row where he moved in and sat down beside the old Fox.

"Look there," Canaris whispered to him, pointing at the screen. "The American Cavalry now rides to the rescue chasing away the Indians in the same manner you chase away the RAF."

Locke smiled in the darkness of the theater, the smell of the popcorn delighting his nose. Holding the bag open for his theater mate, he offered him some, and the offer was delightedly accepted.

"The only difference," he whispered back, "is that they arrived in time to keep the Indians from scalping the stagecoach crew. Why am I here?"

"In due time," Canaris whispered back. "Try to relax a bit. Enjoy the movie; we will take a walk after. There is much to discuss. Do tell me, though; the Gestapo agent you questioned, what did you do with him?"

"I kept my word and let him live."

"Wasn't that a dangerous thing to do?" the Fox whispered. He kept an eye on the Wolf in the darkness, watching for any tell tale facial expressions. He had not heard of any rumblings coming from the Gestapo other than the fellow was missing and presumed run off to Switzerland. "Wouldn't he run back to his headquarters and tell everything? He is Gestapo, after all, and they are not so good at keeping their word."

Locke looked at his new friend and smiled. "Ich bin nicht dummer der Herr Admiral. (I am not that stupid Herr Admiral.) I could have killed him, but I am a Wolf and live by the honor of my word. Without honor, what do you have left, eh? I dressed him in the clothes of a dead British airman and flew him to England in a Storch where I landed in a farmer's field and kicked him out. He thought the flight suit was from one of our bomber crews and was lead to believe that if he kept his mouth shut, he would sit out the war in a prisoner of war camp. I'm sure by now he understands the difference."

In the flickering light of the movie, the stagecoach was rescued and John Wayne, a pugnacious looking American Boxer, stood large as life among the horse soldiers milling about upon the backs of their mounts. The image was not lost on the old Fox; surely it was a reflection of the German ace sitting next to him as he stood among the fighter pilots under his command. The spymaster also knew that without his presence on the morrow his fighter gruppe would surely not do as well as they could have; which exactly fit into that which he needed.

"I wish to take Der Professor's place," Locke whispered when Canaris made no reply.

The head of the Abwehr placed a paw upon that of the fighter pilot and whispered, "We will speak of this later when you give me the details of my nephew's death."

§

The pair laughed as they walked near the Brandenburg Gate, comparing notes on the movie.

"Do you think the American cowboys were really like that?" Derik asked.

"I think that if you look back at the last war," Canaris replied, "you will see that they were exactly like that. They came into the fight with gusto and they had so much; where as we had so little. Our soldiers would actually raid their garbage dumps looking for discarded cans of food. It is something we should remember. If we do not end this war quickly they will be here again with their vast quantities of everything."

"I remember how they fought in the skies," the pilot agreed. "They were quite brazen." He thought for a moment and then added, "I see your point now. Yes, they are cowboys just like the ones I saw once in that Wild West show back in the late 20's. They do not have the discipline we Germans have; but they do have brass balls."

He stopped to light a cigarette, offering one to Canaris. The Fox politely declined.

"Back in 1931," Locke continued, "I actually met the American fellow who almost shot me down during the last war. He would have killed me, too, except that his single machine gun had jammed. He went on to win the pylon race that year. He was very tough and gutsy. His lady friend was equally so."

The Wolf looked around and found they were very alone. "So…I don't think you brought me here to watch an American movie. What am I to do?"

"I spoke at length with Herr Rudolph Hess," Canaris told him, "about our actual inability to invade England. I made it quite clear that, in my humble opinion, if we try a channel crossing we will lose over half of our army and perhaps as much as all of it. He agrees that the numbers being reported by the Luftwaffe are laughable." He held up a paw when the flyer appeared prepared to rally to the defense of his brothers. "Derik, I will tell you things now that cannot be repeated to anyone." He waited for the flyer's nod before continuing. "I know for a fact that Air Vice-Marshal Park has standing orders for his fighters to avoid fighter to fighter combat if they can. He has ordered our bombers to be their top priority. It is not that you are seeing less and less fighter aircraft because you have shot them all down. You are seeing less of them simply because they are remaining hidden and not rising to the bait of your fighter sweeps."

He let that sink in for a moment and then continued. "Tomorrow morning, I have arranged a very private interview for you with Herr Hitler. Over coffee you are to tell him exactly where the Luftwaffe stands in its subjugation of the RAF."

"That's it? No…" he made a motion with his paw as if gripping the air and strangling it.

"Absolutely not; and you must never ever mention that again. If and when the time comes for that I will personally notify you… no one else. Is that clear?"

"Ja, Herr Canaris."

"In case you are in doubt," the Fox told him, "you will find that the stories of Herr Wolf during the last war are true. He is very courageous. Several attempts on his life have already been made and he's survived them all. He's been imprisoned and even that only strengthened his resolve. He also has more body guards than you can count."

The Fox indicated they should continue walking.

"Somewhere along the way, our country caught fire for Herr Hitler, and he single handedly dragged us out of the pits of despair that occurred because we lost a war and became the distained country of the world. He led us back to the rediscovery of who we are as a people." Canaris nodded to a phalanx of soldiers practicing their marching. "Herr Wolf filled our national balloon with the hot air of pride and it has risen to heights that no one ever thought possible. Unfortunately for Germany, when the world finally tires of us, that balloon will be deflated once again, and an uncontrolled anger will wash over our country like a plague."

The Fox stopped walking and when Derik turned towards him he reached out and straightened the Wolf's tunic, brushing off some pretend hairs.

"Adolf Hitler might be a tad overzealous in his ambitions," the Fox said very softly, "But can you even imagine a Germany under the sudden leadership of Uncle Fatty? He is the next in line if something should happen to our leader." Looking directly into the flyer's eyes, he told him, "Change should have happened before we became embroiled in a war. It almost did more than a few times but Herr Wolf is far too lucky. Now things are too overly complicated to arrange a simple assassination. The leadership to replace the leadership is already in place against that possibility."

Taking the pilot's arm, he began them walking again. "Before real change can happen we will need to ensure the one who takes over is acceptable to the world as well as to the German people. He cannot be a Nazi… especially Göring, Himmler, or Goebbels. Germany, too, must reach a conditional peace with the world. That makes the passage even more difficult as you cannot cause so much death and destruction and then expect everyone to love you for it."

Locke chuckled. "That," he replied, "is an understatement."

"Russia looms on the horizon," Canaris continued without looking at him, "and if we do not yet have all of our resources dedicated to that single front we will surely have our asses handed to us."

There was a moment of silence, and then the Admiral smoothly moved into the pilot's instructions for the morrow.

"When you are delivered to Herr Wolf you will be asked to strip naked. Your side arm will remain with one of the guards and your clothing will be searched. You will then redress and wait. You will be watched for every second you are waiting. When you are with him, remain calm and simply answer his questions. Think of him as a fellow soldier and be a soldier in return."

"Göring is going to be very upset with me."

"Göring will be none the wiser," the old Fox told him, "I can assure you, Herr Hitler very much knows how to keep a secret. It is a long fall from grace and this is the second time Uncle Fatty will have disappointed our swastikaed god. I would not want to be him in a few days time."

§

September 14th… 0900L 92 Squadron at Biggins Hill

Commander Reginald Sheltie stood at the front of his group back to a blackboard upon which were drawn crude diagrams meant to resemble formations of aircraft. "I have just been informed by command that, beginning today we shall fly the entire squadron at the same time, and we are to do our best in supporting whichever other squadron is flying in our sector. Part two of this change of events is target priority. The bombers are still top of the list, but if there are fighters about you are free and clear to give them hell. This will only be in a way to buy time for whoever's shooting up the bombers. As always, Ground Control will give us our directions and you are to pay close attention to the radio. Stick to your radio protocols." Sheltie paused to look at his group and wondered which of them would not be back at the end of the day. "I do understand," he continued, "that many of you are new to our ranks and to you I extend my paw in friendship. My advice, however, is not quite so friendly. If you bung up one of my aircraft doing something stupid, I will personally see you digging latrines for the kiwis; am I clear on that?"

There was a chorus of 'yes sirs' from the group in front of him. Most were rookies; not much more than children right out of flight school with barely five hours in a Spit.

"When our time in the air is up, we are to land, re-arm, refuel and stand by. You will dismount, take a piss, get a cuppa, and then stay with your aircraft unless given the order to stand down. You may need to launch again as soon as you are ready."

There was the sound of a thump as Lieutenant Henry Badcock fell out of his chair sound asleep. Even after falling from height to the floor, his eyes never opened.

Archie nudged him with his foot, but still the Bulldog snored. Looking at his Commander, he shrugged his shoulders. "Jerry's been pretty regular the last few days, sir. They're not due until about 1500; what say we let him sleep? He's pretty done in."

"Church sermons and whisky the night before always put me to sleep, too," Sheltie responded not unkindly. "Aye then, drag him back to his bunk. What I have to say you've heard before. I'll be by your hut presently and give you a lay out since you're Yellow Flight Leader, but by God if the bell rings I'd better see him sprinting for his Spit or he'll be on aircraft washing detail for a week."

"Of course, sir."

With help, the Stag got his friend up on his shoulders and then managed to exit the room without hitting the other pilot's head on the door jamb as he left. Corporal Higgins was waiting outside the ready hut's entrance as if expecting such an occurrence. Archie's exit was made to a reverent quiet from the rest of the flyers.

As soon as they left, Sheltie said to those who remained, "If you lads fly half as good as that pair, you might just make it through the war alive. All right everyone, eyes front and let's go through the strategies again."

§

September 14th... 1200L Berlin, Germany

In Berlin, Adolf Hitler called a rush conference ordering all of his naval, air force and army commanders-in-chiefs to attend. After a sumptuous luncheon, Herr Wolf rose from his seat and all conversation stopped. "Warriors of the Third Reich," he addressed them, "At last, Operation Sealion is in full readiness. All of our barges are now in place and we have more held in reserve along the river banks," "If we plan now," he told them, "The invasion date can be set for one week from today; given that we need five days of good weather to achieve the desired results."

There was a robust applause from around the table though this was not news to them. The Generals in attendance were at least wise enough to hold their reservations to themselves.

"My friend Reichmarschall Göring assures me that the RAF is all but done in which is as it should be. Germany must make sure the Luftwaffe has complete air superiority over the Channel and over southern England for us to be successful. Herman," he said, nodding to the Wolf to his right, "I now give you the floor so you may make the announcement."

Göring stood, his body appearing to swell even larger than it was with the stature he'd been allowed sitting at the right paw of der Führer. "My fellow commanders of the greatest fighting force the world has ever seen," he told them, "Tomorrow the Luftwaffe will launch the greatest aerial attack the world has ever seen. Every single aircraft we have available will be launched in a knockout attack against the British. When what remains of the RAF comes up to meet us, if they dare..." he let this hang in the air in order to draw out a few chuckles, "They will be shot from the sky. With this, Operation Sealion will move forward on September seventeenth exactly as planned. Within mere weeks, I expect we shall meet again for a luncheon at Buckingham Palace."

§

Manfred Rat, on his morning walk, had noted the small chalk mark on the post box a few corners from Admiral Canaris' offices; though for all intents and purposes he saw nothing at all. Later that afternoon and at a prearranged time, he went to the radio listening room in the basement of the huge building where twenty agents of the Abwehr sat at short wave units. These agents were both listening and sending signals to and from all over the world. Here he took a seat at one of the units after sending its operator on an errand for the Admiral. At the exact moment the sweep second hand of the large wall clock came up to three 'o'clock (1500), he tuned the radio from the frequency it was on to one he knew by heart. The message he heard was very short and in a code that only he and his English counterpart knew.

"Who recalled Locke to Berlin?"

Dialing the unit to a different frequency, he waited a moment and then tapped out the coded number 'twenty two' which was the address of Admiral Canaris' office and the number his counterpart would recognize as the designation for that individual.

Not waiting for a confirmation he carefully dialed the frequency back again to its original position and continued listening in the headset. When the radio operator came back, he reported having heard nothing of consequence and turned the station back over to the youth.

It took exactly ten minutes for his information to be passed on to the Prime Minister of England.

§

September 14th, 1900L… Tirpitzufer 22 – the offices of Admiral Wilhelm Franz Canaris

"The launch date of Operation Sealion has at last been given as September 17th," Rudolph Hess told Admiral Canaris over tea, "Which again, if we want to be critical, should have been September 19th if, as der Führer estimated, it will take five days of preparation. Göring is such a moron, he can't even add five to seventeen. Adolf has given orders for a blitzkrieg aerial attack to be made in preparation for the invasion and again this was placed in the hands of fat Hermann. You would think Adolf would have learned by now that Göring is not the Wolf for the job."

"On the contrary," Canaris corrected the third highest Wolf in Germany's government, "Göring is ruthless, and this is exactly what our Adolf wants in a commander. The little fellow who once had his life spared by a lone British soldier has forgotten what it is like to be on the wrong end of the sights. His obsession with bombing London is not tactical and where we once had an advantage over the RAF, that advantage has now slipped away."

"What do you mean. 'slipped away'?"

"I'll show you the photos later if you wish, but what I have observed of the RAF is that they are hardly on death's doorstep. Their air-craft production has scarcely even been slowed. We shoot one down and they simply ferry another in to take its place. They've been rearming at an incredible rate, and new pilots to fly those new aircraft seem to be falling from the trees. The bombing of London has done nothing except to anger an otherwise peaceful people, so they have redoubled their efforts to strike at us in the only place they can... the skies." The old Fox placidly looked at the Wolf sitting in the garden with him and then said, "My pro-fessional estimate, old friend, is that if Operation Sealion moves ahead, we stand to lose the entire invasion force. Should that happen, France and our other captured territories might decide they can rid themselves of our depleted occupational forces."

For a moment, Hess' jaw dropped open. He then asked very softly, "Why has this information not been given to Herr Wolf?"

"It has." Canaris placed his teacup onto its saucer and then looked again at Hess. "You are the Deputy Führer are you not? You and I have somewhat the same job only on different ends of the spectrum. You believe in a negotiated peace with Britain. I believe in knowing as much as you can know for better preparation and execution of the tactical ele-ments. We both have presented our information and it is up to our Adolf to accept what we tell him... or not to accept what we tell him. I think that Herr Wolf has simply chosen to believe the inflated and erroneous numbers given over by Göring's offices of battle assessment. They are not so stupid in understanding that if their boss looks good, they will also look good. A blatant example of how we are going wrong is the British advanced warning system. What is the first premise of combat Rudolf? Is it not keeping your enemy blind to your movements?"

"Certainly, that is one of them, yes."

"Then why has 'Uncle Fatty' stopped bombing the British RDF sights?" He held up a finger. "Because he feels they are not that impor-tant. His battle commanders know better but they are prevented from acting and so the RAF is able to ambush our attacks, and we lose more aircraft and flight crews than we should."

"That is stupidity," Hess agreed, "Und so you have arranged for a stark and bitter truth to be revealed through Oberst Locke, yes?"

"That is what I am paid to do," the Fox admitted. "Though I am also paid to know exactly what else is going on in Herr Wolf's world. In-formation pertaining to those under him is always a welcome gift. In this way, he is able to correctly place his subordinates into jobs best suited for them. How are your flying lessons coming along?"

Hess blinked at this question but was otherwise nonplussed by it. He enjoyed flying and having the ability to go where he needed to go when he needed to go there, either officially or unofficially, was a great benefit.

"I am in the advanced stages of learning the BF 110. It is a very enjoyable aircraft to fly," he responded. "Now I will ask you a question. Do you believe there is still a chance for peace with England?"

The Fox nodded slightly. "Peace is not on the lips of our leader," he replied, "But behind the scenes the overture has never ceased playing. The messages sent through the Spanish Ministry and the Red Cross could have been well met; but in truth… that dark and very stark truth… I feel the unfettered bombing of London has dashed those hopes. Herr Wolf fought the British in the first war, and yet he seems to have learned nothing of their psyche. Winston Churchill has become the voice of the English people, and you can trust that what he says is what they all feel. As much pain and suffering as the Luftwaffe has caused them, I am surprised they are still taking prisoners and treating them well."

"There must be some hope," Hess responded; thinking of his plans for Scotland.

"There is," the Fox replied. "If Churchill can be removed politically, there would be a very strong chance at an armistice. If he is removed by force there will never be a peace until one or the other of our governments no longer exists."

"Very well," Hess nodded to the Fox. "I am grateful for the truth you have given me. 'Politically' is something I might be able to work on. Now then, where is the messenger of this truth we are to send to Herr Wolf? You have asked me to give him some training, and I think this is a good idea."

The Fox smiled. "I allowed Oberst Locke to nap upon his arrival here. He is utterly exhausted, though he would never admit to that. I then gave him a surprise in the form of a very sexy bath attendant so that he will be clean inside and out. He should be down shortly and we will have a late dinner so your tutelage can begin over food. You will play the part of Hitler, and so at the end, he will know how to properly act and respond. By doing this ,you will also have the full benefit of all that he is to pass on."

Hess held his stomach and burped softly. "I don't think I could eat another thing after the luncheon with Herr Wolf, but perhaps some coffee would be nice."

All

Winged craft
Cut through smoke filled heavens;
Running like children at Death's picnic
Playing a deadly game of tag.

Wolf and Dog
Dance among destructive sheep
Nipping at each other's heels and neck
While looking for the kill

Gray and green
Roundel and Cross
Death spirals down
Life lives with loss

Both sides gave their all.

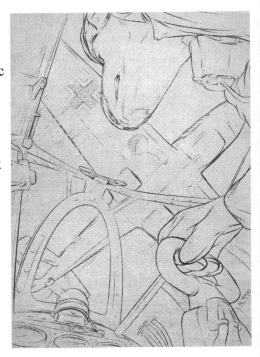

September 15th, 1940

Bearing ourselves humbly before God ... we await undismayed the impending assault ... be the ordeal sharp or long, or both, we shall seek no terms, we shall tolerate no parlay; we may show mercy – we shall ask for none.

Sir Winston Churchill - BBC Broadcast, London, July 14, 1940

0500 September 15th, 1940

In the predawn light, a Luftwaffe 'Blackman' was met by the pilot of a Dornier 17 bomber he was servicing. The mechanic snapped to attention and saluted, especially since this was the Wing Leader's aircraft. He was surprised when the pilot didn't return the salute but instead handed him a cup of coffee.

"Stop that, Heinrich," the Hauptmann told the fellow softly. "You're making me nervous; besides, it's still dark out and no one can see you but me. Is my aircraft ready?"

"Jawohl mein Heir," the mechanic replied, sipping at the black liquid. It was real coffee and not ersatz. "Today is the day? The English will surrender soon?"

"I hope so. I would like to finish this nasty business and go home.

We will be flying in at a high level today. It's cold and more work than normal, but the British seem to notice us less when we do so. How is the oxygen?"

"Full. The coffee is good, thank you. I have to be awake, sir, but shouldn't you still be sleeping?"

The pilot only laughed. "I have not slept all night, and so it goes with leadership, eh?" He paused to light a cigarette and then passed it to the Dog. After this, he lit one for himself. "What did you do before you joined up, Manfred?"

"I was a butcher, und my Bratwurst sausage was the best," the Blackman replied proudly.

The Wolf in the flight suit chuckled and replied, "I was a baker, und my Roggenbrot (rye bread) was the best, too. People came from miles around just to buy it. I think I miss that life."

***

Archie walked slowly around the Egham Spitfire's tail, softly talking to the machine as if it could understand him. The airfield was now crowded with fighters as another squadron had come in the previous night. Rumor was strong that 92 Squadron was about to fly off to Scotland for a well deserved, though ill afforded rest. The Stag knew better and was glad to see the preparations for what he knew was coming.

"Today's the day, old girl so I expect you to be at your best when things turn ugly. We shall have a very hard 'row to hoe' as the Americans like to say." He smiled at the thought of one particular American. "For the moment, we have the dawn patrol to fly just in case someone comes to the party early, eh? That should at least be a good warm up for the show."

"11 Group's meteorologists are predicting a good day for flying," a voice told him in the darkness, "But they didn't mention anything about farming."

Looking up, Archie found Terrance sitting in the cockpit. The dim moonlight passed through her form, creating a watery sort of image. She was leaning over the side of the raised up access door looking back at him, dressed in a flight suit and smiling as she always did.

"The forecast," she told him, "is for heavy cloud and rain periods overnight, which is expected to clear. The skies are supposed to be fine in most areas with a patchy cloud cover; no rain, but some spots might still catch an odd shower. By afternoon, this will clear and then give way to a fine and clear evening."

"Will I be with you this evening, my love?"

"I truly don't know."

"Who're you talking to?" Henry's voice growled in his ear. "Is she here?"

"Why aren't you having breakfast Henry?" the Stag asked his wingman without turning.

"I ate already. Corporal Higgins is bloody good to us. You should have eaten too. I don't know what I'd do without him. If we get through this cockup I might just offer him a job… if he was female I'd propose marriage!"

Even Henry heard Terrance's laughter and he smiled for it.

"I had a quick bowl of porridge so I could come out and prep the Egham," Archie explained, "It never hurts to have a heart to heart before going up. Terrance is sitting in the cockpit." The Stag told his friend this without turning. He didn't want to take his eyes from her visage knowing she would be gone when he turned back.

"Cheers, Terrance," the Bulldog said, nodding to the cockpit as he passed a tin cup of coffee over to his friend. "I'll take good care of him for you today, luv… and thank you again for pulling my 'D' ring."

"She says you're welcome and that you should have the kiwi's check the oil drain on your engine; the safety wire was not redone and it's loose."

"Bollocks! I'm on it… bloody mechs… how in the hell could they have missed something as simple as an oil cock?"

Archie, smiling at his partner's comment, forgot himself and glanced sidewise at the old Dog in the darkness. When he turned back Terrance was indeed gone.

***

Wing Commander Stewart Falstaff looked down upon the 'situation board' as he sipped the coffee one of the girls brought to him. Presently there were only two markers on the map. One marker represented an unknown German aircraft and the other a flight from 87 Squadron Exeter (Hurricanes) which had been scrambled to intercept. He'd been in the observation area all night napping on and off and smoking when he could take a break topside. Occasionally he would ask a question, but nothing too much out of the ordinary had yet been noticed.

The coffee had been presented to him in a standard RAF mug. When it was passed over, his mind momentarily slipped into his past and he'd seen a grizzled Sergeant passing up a well dented and steaming tin cup to him as he sat in the cockpit of an aircraft from the last war. In a very feminine voice, the Dog had said, "Perhaps they will take the day off, sir, and not come a'tall."

He'd blinked, and the Sergeant became one of the girls from Control, obviously on her own break but taking the time to see to his needs.

"I pray that is the case," he'd replied, "But they have not failed to disappoint us yet, have they?" He asked her name and then, lifting the cup, slightly thanked her; after which they both went back to their duties.

***

Oberst Dierk Locke's nose twitched as the scent of fresh coffee found his nose. He was in the most comfortable bed he'd ever slept in and his company the night before was, without a doubt, equal to the bed. Unfortunately, he'd spent most of the evening with Germany's Deputy Führer role playing what he would do the following morning during his meeting with the little Wolf who had so set the world on fire. And what was he to tell him? Obviously a straight forward attack using the truth was not the best option.

"You can't just blurt out, 'The Wolf you have chosen to lead the Luftwaffe is a fat moronic dummkopf!'"

Hess' explanation was simple and to the point. The Reich's number three then smiled to show he was serious but not so serious.

"I am not so crass to say something like that," Locke replied, "Even if it is the truth. Reichmarschall Göring apparently has fallen into the oldest trap known to the military; just because you were an adept warrior does not mean you are an adept leader of warriors. He has forgotten every dictum he lived by in the cockpit."

"Because it is not his neck directly upon the line," the other Wolf told him. "Death looking over your shoulder tends to sharpen your instincts. I am not here to dispute with you, Herr Oberst, I am here to coach you on what to say to Herr Wolf and how to say it. He is actually very sociable and will speak with you on an eye to eye basis. Approach him improperly, however, and his ears will fold over into deafness. Nor do we wish you to inadvertently say something which might inflame him… that is, of course, unless you wish to be placed before a firing squad for treason."

"I have only the welfare of Germany in the forefront of my mind," Dierk replied softly.

"Of course you do, Herr Fighter Pilot; but you must also remember that Herr Hitler is Germany."

Locke blinked and then said quite seriously, "Perhaps I should just go back to the front now and volunteer for a suicide mission."

"Isn't that what you already do on a daily basis?" Hess questioned. When the fighter pilot made no response the other Wolf nodded. "Now that we have that out of the way, stand and show me your best 'Heil Hitler'."

Now, as Dierk stirred to wakefulness, the smell of coffee made him long to be back at the front with his fellow pilots. Things were much simpler there.

His arm reached over looking for the female that had slept with him the night before but she was not there. His thoughts turned to the French Poodle he'd met but a few times; oddly, he missed her.

0600

There was no alert as of yet but the British crews were ready. Every aircraft of every squadron was armed and fueled. In close proximity to their mounts, the pilots slept or had a breakfast of gunpowder tea with eggs and toast, brought to them by the cooks. Henry, having overseen the correction to his oil drain, further saw to the positioning of their aircraft so all were faced into the wind. He then fell asleep in the cockpit of his Spitfire while Archie sat watching the lightening sky. The sun was not to be up for another forty minutes and across the airfield a peaceful quiet had descended like the calm before a storm. This was quickly disrupted by the klaxon calling them to take off … morning was now upon them.

***

Ten Blackmen tugged upon the tail of a Dornier, positioning it side by side to another for easier loading of the bombs which were lifted into place with a metallic click of the securing/release mechanism snapping into place. On one of the bombs was written in chalk 'eine Zigarre für Churchill'. Shortly behind, the ordinance crews were the fueling lorries which came down the line, carefully filing each aircraft to the last drop they could carry. The day before, the entire Luftwaffe had been given notice that this day was to be special; every crew should be prepared to service their aircraft as quickly as possible. To this end, whole trains of bomb carts were now positioned in readiness while overhead groups of fighters patrolled the area against the possibility of an enemy fighter or bomber trying to get through during this very delicate moment of preparation.

**

Winston Churchill was roused from a sound sleep at Ten Downing Street, which was his request of the previous day. Sitting on the bed, he sipped a cup of black tea as a simple plate of toast and eggs was presented to him. This he quickly ate and then gave instructions for his wife to be awakened.

"Tell the Missus to ready herself, as I wish to pay a surprise visit to Control. I'm the Top Dog in this flea circus, so I bloody well should at least see first paw how they handle things, eh?"

**

Sergeant Timothy York was taking a turnover report from the RDF operator just coming off duty, a Corporal by the name of Ben.

"Jerry was oddly quiet," Ben told him, "But you know as well as I they're usually up with the sun. I'd keep an ear open for the alarm, Timmy. They haven't been by to strafe lately, so I figure we're due. For m'self, I've taken to sleeping in the slit trench next to my tent."

"That's a good way to get your arse trampled," the Sergeant replied. "Me, I'd like to be on a machine gun when they come over. I probably wouldn't hit anything, but I'd feel much better for it."

His mate put a paw on his shoulder. "In here, Tim, you're far more deadly to them than by blowing off a few rounds in their direction. I've carefully considered it and figure we give the lads nineteen precious minutes to gain altitude and the upper paw. I'm surprised Jerry hasn't equally thought that one out yet."

The alarm sounded, and a second after they heard the thunder of a passing aircraft engine as a scattering of machine gun bullets passed through the building missing everything except the clock on the wall. This shattered and fell to the floor with a crash. Next came the sounds of the anti-aircraft guns blazing away at a Messerschmitt that was now long gone.

"Told you so," Ben intoned as they got up from the floor.

"You certainly did," the Sergeant replied. "The bastard caught us napping too from the sounds of it. Captain Sully's going to be right pissed about his clock. I wouldn't want to be that pilot if he ever gets his paws on him.

"System checks?" the Corporal asked.

"Double quick… if there's one, there's more we need to watch for. I'll report the attack."

***

Assistant Staffelkapitän Johannes Wolf laughed as he flew over the RDF installation with the dawn rising behind him. His spur of the moment trip was only meant to be a quick jaunt over the channel. He knew to do this at no more than thirty feet which would help keep him from being detected. Then it was pop up, make one pass, and then sweep inland looking for anything he felt should be shot up before heading back again.

He would not report his actions, so it would be as if nothing more had happened than a quick test flight. What he was doing was not by the regulations; but sometimes you had to be expressive just to get it out of your system. Lately the Staffel's orders had been mundane at best. 'Protect the bombers'… always it was 'protect the bombers'. If he'd wanted to fly bombers he would have volunteered to be a bomber pilot.

The Wolf was so euphoric at his sudden freedom that he hadn't even used his cannon when strafing. He could never have done this if Staffelkapitän Locke had been present. With him, it was everything by the book… or else.

***

Master Sergeant Rathbone of the Royal Observer Corp slowly climbed the ladder leading to the huge church tower five miles from the White Cliffs of Dover. At his age he felt lucky to be afforded such a view of the rising sun. Until the bloody Germans brought on the bombings his only thought for the church was his permanent exit through the side door to the cemetery. Duty again called, and he answered it the same as his comrades had. He might be old, but he still had very keen eyesight. Using the binoculars given over by the RAF, on a clear day he could tell a Dornier from a Junkers almost as far away as the French coast. Besides their eyesight his group of watchers also used their ears, boosting their hearing through a series of large cones all aimed towards the distant enemy and connected to the listener through rubber tubing. The running joke was their apparent ability to hear God's heart beat from their place in the church steeple; and so it was their call sign became 'God's Doctor'.

On the old Dog's oversized belt was a large thermos of tea which he would ritualistically share with the off coming spotters. They, in turn, did the same when coming on again. Though he wore a suit coat rather than a uniform, he still proudly wore his old service revolver. This was more out of habit than anything else. On his head, also out of habit, was a regulation 'Tommy Pot' helmet.

"Got someth'n," he heard Sergeant Whetherstone say just as his head cleared the trap door to the bell tower. The Beagle was their listener at the moment. "He's coming on low and headed right towards us! I heard gunfire… possibly from that post out on the cliffs."

His counterpart, Sergeant Cragg, jacked the bolt on their single Lee Enfield rifle. "E comes close enough'n I'm gonna give'im what for," the silver muzzled Lab growled.

Master Sergeant Rathbone, feeling the weight of his pistol on his hip, hurried to do the same.

***

"Confirmed," one of Control's talkers said loudly, "We have a single 109 inbound over Dover at angels one, flying inland. He just strafed the RDF station."

As Wing Commander Falstaff watched from above, a marker was placed on the board and moved to a spot on the map with a long stick. The Control Duty Officer glanced at the board and told the radio talker, "Coordinate 92 Squadron's Yellow flight."

"Yellow Leader, Yellow Leader, we have a single Messerschmitt inbound off of Dover flying at Angel's one."

***

"Roger, Control," Archie replied. "Yellow Two, did you copy that?" The Stag was leading a vic of six aircraft and didn't see the need to disrupt their advantage for just a single fighter.

"Right-o, I did," Henry replied.

"He's all yours if you can find him."

"Sorry to dash… Back in a flash," responded the Bulldog as he did a wing over. "Control, this is Yellow Two; can you direct me further, please?"

Locke took his time in the shower, enjoying the hot water for the simple pleasure it presented. For the final few minutes, however, he turned it completely cold; forcing himself to stand in its icy embrace. When he emerged from the bath, he found his uniform on a clothing tree looking even better than it had on the day he'd had it fitted. Manfred Rat stood next to it, hands behind his back. He neither smiled nor frowned.

Breakfast, too, had been set out on a table brought in for the occasion. After dressing the Wolf sat and opened his napkin. Placing it in his lap he took his spoon and cracked the soft boiled egg which was sitting upon its egg cup.

***

Rathbone emptied his pistol at the fighter as it streaked by to the accompanying bark of Sergeant Cragg's rifle. "I'll go two, maybe three good shots out of the six," he claimed, breaking the old Webley open and spilling its spent cartridges onto the flooring. "What about you Tommy?"

"Eh... posh... I don't know. I got off two rounds. I hope I hit the bastard. It'd serve him right. Call it in, John."

"Already done," Sergeant Percy, the forth member of their little group called out. "Control says 'Wing Commander's regards and thank you very much'."

***

Falstaff held back his intended humerous comment about crippled up old soldiers being given guns to tote about and gave the talker a thumbs up from his perch above the situation room; if he only had more like that bunch...

***

"Control, Yellow Two," Henry called out, "I see smoke in the distance. Tally Ho!"

***

Johannes had seen the church tower and thought it would be great fun to buzz the old buzzards he suspected would be there. England had watchers everywhere, or so the intelligence Dogs told them at almost every staff meeting. They barked a good song, but Herr Wolf's words sang an even truer song: 'A Wolf is not afraid… a Wolf is the ultimate warrior… Wolfs will rule the world as is their natural right!'

Johannes naturally assumed that would include the sky. He was surprised then, during a giggling outburst, when the canopy to his left shattered and the lead bullet, having spent its energy, stuck in the glass to his right just shy of punching all the way through.

A few minutes later, he was surprised again to find his engine temperature climbing past the safe arc on the gage. Without hesitation, he turned towards the coast and began to climb.

***

Manfred Rat stood behind Oberst Locke brushing his shoulders with a small whisk broom. "I understand Herr Hitler can be quite sociable if you tell him the things he wishes to hear," he said softly.

"So I've been led to understand," the fighter pilot replied. "Do you have any special insight you could share with me?"

"He likes officers who show no mercy," the Rat offered, "The more brutal they are, the better. The ones he keeps close would snap your neck without question and without so much as blinking. When you serve God, such is your nature."

Locke looked at the Rat in the mirror and growled very softly, "He is not God."

"And in that response… that arrogant push back of moral outrage," the rat replied also softly, "You will have been found out. My advice… my insight you asked for, would be the suggestion that you pretend you are a Rat and make sweet lips on Herr Wolf's butt cheeks. While you do this you might dare a quick sniff to find out what cheese he has been eating. He cannot see your eyes from that vantage point. He is very good at reading eyes but not so smart at understanding things military that are complex. He was a Corporal in the trenches and his thoughts are still there with his two stripes and what medals he won through daring and stupidity. His belief is that brutality wins wars. He will be resistant to believing otherwise."

Taking the Pilot's coat from the clothing tree, he held it out for the Wolf to slip into.

***

By the time Henry got his Spitfire into a shooting situation behind the Messerschmitt, the other aircraft had slowed considerably. Smoke was streaming from the engine and it was plain to the Bulldog that it would not remain airborne for long. Even at that it was obvious the pilot was trying desperately to gain altitude. With luck he might cross the channel and glide to a landing… but his luck had just run out.

Banking out and around, the Bulldog came up just off of the Wolf's wingtip. Getting the German's attention he made it clear he should land or else.

Johannes briefly waved and gave a thumb up that he understood. Tripping the emergency release, the Messerschmitt's cage like plexiglass canopy whipped away with the slipstream. Hauling back on his control stick Johannes next forced the aircraft straight up. Finally stalling with the diminished airspeed caused by the climb the aircraft laid over on its back just before going into a death spiral. At this point the fighter pilot simply unbuckled his restraints and dropped out with gravity. A moment later his parachute blossomed and Locke's second in command slowly drifted to the ground. Capture was inevitable; but the Wolf also fully expected to be liberated in only a matter of weeks.

"Control this is Yellow Two," Henry radioed.

"Go ahead Yellow Two."

"I didn't have to fire a shot, someone already got to'im. Scratch a 109 on the board and give credit where credit is due, eh? He's joined the cocoon club; Home Guard can pick him up."
"Roger Wilco."

0700

Yellow Flight returned to Holy Ground without incident, Henry arriving only moments before. The less fortunate Johannes was picked up by the local constabulary who gave him a cup of tea and then turned him over to the military.

Back slaps and paw shakes were exchanged in the bell tower of St. Mary's when Control called with the news… and then they quietly got back to the business of watching and listening.

***

Commander Falstaff hung up the phone after personally calling and congratulating Sergeants Rathbone, Percy, Cragg, and Whetherstone for downing the first aircraft of the day. "Britain is as proud of her old sons as she is of her young," he told them. "When we meet, and we shall, drinks will be on me."

***

Locke reported to the sumptuous foyer of Admiral Canaris' headquarters. Within moments, the old Fox was standing with him. Offering his paw, they held each other's grip.

"What you are doing this morning is saving the lives of thousands of our troops," the spy master told him. "It's not that the plan was a bad one; it is simply the fact that we do not truly control the skies. But for that I would have fully embraced the thought of having England join us. From what I have ascertained through our assets, the British have a 'Do or Die' attitude concerning the invasion. One report says they have fashioned cutters to mount on their training bi-planes for the purpose of cutting the parachutes of our airborne soldiers. Nor did all the small boats from the Dunkirk evacuation go away; only this time, they will be armed and ready to dash out against our barges."

"And the Royal Navy?"

"Poised to strike with enough air cover that we will not be able to stop them; damage, yes, stop, no. It will be a battle to make Jutland look like a walk in the park. The fish of the English Channel will grow fat from the many bodies."

"I will do my best," Locke told the Fox.

"That is all any of us can ask," Canaris replied. "Germany... our country... is grateful."

***

"What do you mean he's not back!" Jagdgeschwader 56's commanding officer screamed into the phone. He was at headquarters where all of the Geschwader leaders were to meet for their pre-mission briefing. It was bad enough that Locke had been recalled to Berlin but now his second in command was missing?

"He took his aircraft for a test flight, sir, as it had an engine change done last night. He was only supposed to be out for fifteen to thirty minutes; and that was an hour ago. I fear the worse has happened."

"Get your ass over here now!"

Eric Wolf ran from the operation's tent and climbed onto a motor-cycle that was parked outside. He was not the third in command by any stretch of the imagination. In fact, he had only twenty hours in the cockpit of a Messerschmitt, but he was doing as ordered.

***

Archie taxied in to be greeted by Commander Sheltie whose Spit-fire was parked next to where he'd been directed.

"I think the people of Egham have gotten their money's worth," the Dog called out to the Stag after the engine was shut down.

As his propeller slowly ceased spinning, the pilot looked to his commander and winked. "Just luck, sir."

"Bollocks! Luck has nothing to do with it; you're a damned fine flyer, Arch."

The Stag dropped the side door to the cockpit and climbed out. The ever watchful Higgins was already waiting for him behind the wing with a fresh cup of tea. Being a good batman, he'd also had one for Henry on his return. As soon the pilot had his feet on the ground and the pass off was made, the Corporal was hoofing it back to the mess tent to gather up something for them to eat.

"Did I hear Henry got one?" Archie asked as he sipped from the tin cup.

"He refused to claim it," Sheltie replied, "And if you check his leading edge gun tapes, as I did, you'll see he didn't fire a shot. That small victory goes to the watchers."

"Well jolly good for them."

***

"Well, jolly good for them," Churchill muttered when he got the note. He had a standing order that any good news be brought as soon as it was heard. "See to having a bottle of brandy and a box of cigars sent to them for me," he told the secretary who'd brought the note. The Bull-dog stood, pulling his braces up and over his shoulders. "Before you do that, however, please see to Mrs. Churchill and tell her the old man said

to shake a leg. I hate being late… especially when I am going to pay a surprise visit on someone who probably won't be surprised at all."

0800

From the outside Adolf Hitler's Chancellery had a stern authoritarian appearance. Locke was slowly driven up the Wilhelmsplatz and into the 'receiving' entry through great gates flanked by the bronze statues titled "Wehrmacht" and "Partei" ("Armed Forces" and "Party"). From there, his limousine motored into the Court of Honour. (Ehrenhof)

Black uniformed guards stationed at the gate came to attention and saluted the big Mercedes. To them he gave a small return salute. The pilot's guts churned, and he was suddenly afraid he would lose the single egg he'd eaten. Never had he felt this uneasy flying into combat. It was like he was embracing a python, and as he did so, it was subtly shifting its body to envelope him.

When the car stopped, another black uniformed guard came forward and opened the door for him. This Wolf, and Locke had noticed that each guard present was pure Wolf, clicked his heels together and saluted with an arms out 'Heil Hitler'.

"I have an appointment to see Herr Hitler," the pilot told the guard as he returned the salute in a smaller, more dignified fashion.

"Then you shall have to follow me," replied a very tenor sounding voice. The soldier holding the door seemed to stiffen even more than he was already. Following the voice, Dierk saw another very handsome Wolf in a resplendent black officer's uniform approaching him.

"I'm Reichfuher Heinrich Himmler," the fellow told him with a smile. "I heard you had an appointment this morning, so I thought I would come to greet you and personally see to Herr Wolf's security requirements pertaining to your visit. I mean this as an honor to you, Oberst Locke; you are quite the hero, and I had hoped to meet you… so… here we are, yes?"

***

Wing Commander Falstaff had just seated himself for breakfast when a messenger arrived from Control's floor. "Y section has informed us of a large amount of radio checks being performed by the Luftwaffe, sir."

Y section, being the radio eve's dropping section of the Royal

Observation Corp, gathered random clues early on; such as the warm up of radio sets just prior to launch. In this way they were able to arrive at a fairly accurate estimate of what was to come across the channel. By listening to the pilot's broadcast conversations, they were also sometimes even able to pick up on their intended targets.

"Right, then," he responded, "Bring the London squadrons to 'available'."

(Squadrons were maintained at their Sector Aerodromes in various "states of preparedness." The most relaxed state is "released," which meant the Squadron was not required to operate until a specified hour and that their personnel could be employed in routine maintenance, flight training and instruction, organized games, and, in some special permissible cases, the crews might leave the station. Next came "Available," where the Squadrons must prepare to be in the air within so many minutes of receiving the order. "Readiness" reduced this to a minimum and was the most advanced state used. Occasionally "Stand-by" would be ordered; meaning the pilots were required to be in the cockpit and at the ready with their aircraft pointed into the wind. To the front of each would be a spotter making sure things were clear to start the engine, while beside the aircraft would be the ground crewman in charge of pulling away the chocks and another who would disconnect the external battery cart. In this state, the moment the 'Scramble' alarm was sounded they were expected to take off within fifteen seconds.)

***

The armorer, a grizzled Sergeant who'd served in the first war, pounded on the side of Archie's aircraft to get his attention. "Any complaints, sir?" He held his machine gun charging tool in his left paw and had several loops of linked ammunition draped over his shoulder.

Archie looked over at the fellow from where he was sitting with his group of pilots. Per the usual, Henry was entertaining them with stories that educated, informed, and caused much laughter.

"None, Sergeant, thank you."

"Could you check my number six gun?" Henry called to the fellow. "It's been having a jamming problem lately, and God knows you need as many guns as you can get on Jerry cuz he's damned stubborn when it comes to dying."

The pilots laughed, though the Sergeant scowled. "Die'n's a serious business, sir; you can't expect Fritz to approach it all hap hazard like. You should have reported this yesterday. Taking it down now will be dicey for time. I do it, and I'll probably catch my tit in the wringer wif the Lieutenant."

"How long to change it out?" Henry inquired.

"Without checking the aim, ten minutes."

"Well," the Bulldog muttered, "Damned if I do and damned if I don't. What do you gents think I should do?" he asked the other pilots. As a group they were divided, each adding their pence to the pot. Holding up a paw, Henry looked to Archie. "What's your take on it, Arch?"

"Change it out," he replied. "You're a crack shot, Henry and can do with seven what most of us can't do with eight. A little bit off on the aim could even work to your advantage if you were off a bit with the other seven."

As the other's laughed good naturedly, Henry called to the Sergeant, "Change it out, please, good sir."

Just as he made the request, the standby bell began ringing.

"Well, Bollocks," Henry complained. "Time to mount up and then we sit and wait. Thank you, anyways, Sergeant… perhaps when we get back, eh?"

"Yes sir, I'll make a note on it."

***

Jeans could not pretend to be asleep any longer. Putting on a house robe, she went down to the dining room to see about a cup of tea. Madam Bella's home was outside of the city but only just. When things began she intended to climb up to the roof to watch.

0900

Sixty feet below ground, Stewart Falstaff was leaning over the railing of the observation room when an orderly came and told him the Prime Minister had just arrived and was waiting in his car.

"What?" the old Bulldog asked, "I had no notification there was supposed to be a visit. Bloody hell, I've my paws full and no time to give a proper tour."

"He said you would probably say this, sir, and asked me to assure you he would not get in the way. He also said that none of our people are supposed to do anything other than what their present duties require just because he's here. He has his wife and personal secretary with him and no one else."

"Well that's big of him, isn't it?" the commander growled, "Offer my apologies for not personally greeting them at the door and see him down to me, then," the Bulldog replied gruffly. "Bring tea and ask if they wish breakfast."

***

Commander Sheltie stood next to the operation's shack watching the sky. There were a few clouds, but as it stood there was more blue sky than white. This, he reflected, was both good and bad. It would be easier to spot the Germans; but the reverse was also true. They would not be able to sneak up upon the bombers, and the German fighters would see them coming and attempt interference.

Today he was Blue Leader, and his aircraft was a part of a vic of six. As in all the groupings, there were to be at least two seasoned pilots along with the newest to their ranks. Being a good leader, he reflected that it was wretchedly awful the way they were rushing the lads through training. Already this month, he'd lost three aircraft to simple bad landings. He also knew, however, there were not a lot of options. The German invasion had to be stopped… crashed aircraft could be repaired and pilots patched up both mentally and physically. They would be given a cup of tea and some aspirin along with the dictum, 'Fall off the horse, and you bloody well get right back on the saddle. Go fly!'

***

Dierk was escorted up the outside staircase of the enormous New Reich Chancellery by the Wolf in black. He'd heard the SS uniform was designed by a famous clothing designer to look especially sharp. He found the look quite so, though black was not his favorite color. Like the building whose steps he now ascended, it was meant as a statement. The Chancellery was commissioned in 1938 by Adolf Hitler and built in one single incredible year at a huge expense. Its entire existence was meant as a show piece to German prowess.

Their boots clicked on polished marble flooring as they entered a medium sized reception room from which double doors almost seventeen feet in height opened into a larger hall clad in mosaic. From this hall, they ascended several more steps, passing through a round room with a huge domed ceiling. Beyond this, the pilot saw before him a gallery 480 feet long. The only thing he'd seen before that equaled its size was a dirigible hangar.

"It is beautiful, is it not?" asked Himmler, stopping so they could admire the view. "I never tire seeing it."

"It's incredible," the fighter pilot managed in a near whisper, "All of this for just one Wolf?"

"Not for one Wolf," the black uniformed Reichführer told him, "But for all Wolfs. Ever since the last war we've been treated like the unwanted bastard child. With Herr Wolf came the time when we could show the world exactly who we were simply by putting our people back to work. If you do not demand respect, it will not be given, eh?" He motioned with his right arm expansively as if he were a tour guide. "We Germans built this wonderful building in one year... just one year. How many hundreds of years have the British been working on theirs, eh? Mind that Westminster will be bombed out of existence soon enough; but you of all people would know this."

"Soon enough," Dierk parroted softly, not believing his own words for a moment, "It certainly will be."

***

"KG KG KG Radiokontrolle (radio check)," Gruppenkommandeur Oberst Alois Lindmayr released the transmit button on his now warmed up radio set and listened for the 'click click' indicating he'd been heard. He had not added the III/76 with the KG because that was a giveaway. It was a given that radio broadcasts were listened to by the British. "A burglar does not knock on Eingangstür (the front door)," he warned his pilots in training, "So neither will you casually announce, 'Hey, Dog face, I am coming to bomb you now!'"

That always got laughter, but it was a point well taken.

"click... click..."

At the same time, he faintly heard another radio check as 20 miles to his north I/KG 76 also prepared.

***

Y section's Gretchen Wolf smiled as she jotted down what her ears told her; she knew this voice.

Early on in the war, England realized the importance of just listening. They also quickly understood that the right person was needed for the listening to truly gain an understanding of what was being spoken.

Required were people who understood the different dialects of the German language. Native born German females from all over the country were quickly recruited for the special 'Y' section set up to gather radio intelligence.

Gretchen was a perfect example. If she were a wagering person, she would have put money on the fact that she and Oberst Alois, (yes she even knew his name), had grown up geographically close to each other. To an English ear German was German was German, but to this she Wolf, the bomber commander's voice was like music from home.

She'd given this minute fact to her superior some weeks ago, and the voice was eventually attached to a unit. Intelligence was then able to give the unit's home base map coordinates.

"III/76 is warming up their radios," she reported to the duty officer.

This small piece of information was in turn relayed to the Y section coordinator within 11 Group's underground Operation's Room. The Control Duty officer then added this information to all the other pieces of the puzzle collected by the Royal Observation Corp's volunteers; some 50,000 men, women, and youths.

Making a decision to the validity of the information the officer spoke into his headset and a wooden marker was picked up and placed upon the map board in the location of where the bomber group was based by one of the map coordinator WAAFs of Control.

In reply, Falstaff changed several of the outlying squadron's status to 'Readiness' which required the ability of a five minute call out.

**

Eric Wolf came back from the Gruppe meeting full of excitement. In the absence of both their leaders, he was to lead not just a Schwarm, but the entire Gruppe. He'd arrived to the morning's mission meeting late and snuck into the back of the room just as his Gruppen name was called.

"PRESENT!" the young Wolf yelled out, coming to rigid attention. The rest of those in attendance laughed and there was a moment of embarrassment for the pilot. He'd never been to a planning meeting before so had no idea what to expect.

"I am glad you could make it," the Duty Operations Officer told him not unkindly. "Where is Oberst Locke?"

"Recalled to Berlin, sir."

"Pity. And Oberleutnant Johannes?"

"He took his aircraft up for a test flight and has not come back, sir."

"Also a pity," the officer told him with a frown. "Your Gruppe is to lead this morning. You will be flying close escort to KG 76. This morning's attack will primarily be a 'fighter' sweep, meaning you are to shoot down as many of the RAF fighters as have guts enough to meet us in the air. KG 76 is the bait, but we are not going to tell them that. JG 27 and JG 52 will fly in advance and JG 53 will fly top cover over the bombers. When the British try to avoid us in order to get to our bombers, as they always do, we will smash them between the hammers." The officer's instructions were met with good humored laughter and a few boisterous comments. That they might not come back was simply a fact these pilots lived with. Underneath the camaraderie they were warriors and would do what they must.

When the meeting was done, Eric raced back to his Gruppe to make preparations.

***

Status change came to 92 Squadron at Biggins Hill and was accepted quietly. Archie was already sitting under the wing of the Egham Spitfire trying his best to read a pocket novel; something supplied to the squadron by the local lady's chapter of ENSA (Entertainments National Service Association). Waiting was the hardest part. His mind was having a hard time grasping the written words of the simple straight forward story. The small book was an American western, and three times the pilot had now read how the bad guy, Black Bart, walked into the saloon and challenged the Sheriff. The parallel was almost uncanny, but this was something he didn't pick up on.

Climbing out from under the wing he checked on his five pilots. Henry was playing chess with Peter, while Jack, Robert, and Stanley (Polish descent but raised in England) were playing a three handed game of Euchre on a small folding table. Arrangements were already made with the ground crew to save the cards and table from the prop blast should Yellow Flight have to depart quickly. The aircraft, he noted once again, stood wingtip to wingtip, fueled, and armed. Checking the windsock, he was glad to see they were still pointed into the wind. Their ground crews likewise were occupied in waiting. He was reminded of a portrait he'd once viewed of His Majesty's Redcoats standing in a firing line watching the approaching enemy. They were patiently waiting for them to come within range. The Stag reflected that some things in war seemed never to change.

***

Stewart relented and climbed the stairs to greet the Prime Minister and his wife. It was more as a politeness to the Missus, he told his aid, that she should be properly greeted.

"Anything yet?" Winston growled as they shook paws.

"We've a possible attack, brewing so I've placed some of the squadrons on 'stand by'," the Commander replied. "Y Section overheard Jerry tuning the pipes of his organ, and RDF has two large groups now apparently forming up near the French coast. This, I think, is what we've been waiting for… that is; I think it is about to happen."

Unconsciously reaching into his coat pocket, Churchill came out with a very large cigar and stuck it in his mouth. Remembering the strict orders about smoking in the bunker, he fixed his sights on the Wing Commander and growled, "Go ahead and say it, I'm not allowed to smoke."

"I warned you," Stewart replied with an equally fixed look. "You will be deep underground, and the ventilation is simply not able to clear out the smoke. We have over two hundred people down there who we're depending upon to save our country. As much as they might also want to; no one smokes."

"Can I chew it?"

"I suppose you could. Would you require a spittoon or will a tea-cup do you?"

"You two will never get past the school yard, will you?" Mrs. Churchill chided. "Unless I'm mistaken, I believe we have an enemy to defeat? What would the WAAF girls think seeing the pair of you arguing over a silly cigar?"

Both Dogs looked at her and then chuckled.

"She's right, of course," Winston growled, "Bloody hell but she's always right."

***

The Reichsführer, touching Locke on the shoulder, nodded that they should continue down the hall. "Der Führer gave instructions that he would meet with you in his study," the Wolf told the pilot. He then led the pilot through the entrance doors and into enormous building, tak-

336

ing time to point out some of its lavish features. One thing Dierk noted, however, was the absence of people. Other than the occasional black uniformed guards seemingly sprinkled about for effect, there was not much more than a few scurrying pages wearing Hitlerjuggen (Hitler Youth) uniforms. When he asked about this, Himmler told him it was early as yet.

"More will be about later. It is a special day is it not? I presume this is why you are here; though your absence from the front must certainly have been felt."

***

Moving to the rail, Churchill took a moment to wave to the girls as they waited like the fighter pilots they directed. On the opposite wall was a board with lights on it and the names of the squadrons. "What's that?" he asked Falstaff.

"It's a tote board," the Wing Commander told him. "The current activities of No.11 Group's squadrons are all there and indicated by the lights. That way, we can tell at a glance what their status is."

The gigantic blackboard was divided into six columns with electric light bulbs for the six stations. Each of their squadrons had a sub-column of its own which was also divided by lateral lines. When a bulb was lit, it was indicative of the squadron's status. First were the three stages of readiness; 'Available' (twenty minute call out), 'Readiness' (five minute call out), and 'Standby' (two minute notice). Further, there was, 'taken off', 'enemy sighted', 'enemy engaged', and 'returning home'.

The Prime Minister carefully surveyed the Group Operations Room, which was like a small theatre some sixty feet across and two stories high. Below him was a large scale map table around which twenty highly trained males and females stood with their telephone assistants. On the left hand side was a glass box stage like area containing the five officers whose job it was to weigh and measure the information received from the Observation Corp as it came in. Radar being in its infancy, the eyes and ears of the Observer Corp were still the primary definitive for enemy identification.

On the right hand side was another glass box containing the Army officers who controlled the two hundred odd anti-aircraft batteries. At night, it was imperative to stop the batteries from firing over areas where the RAF night fighters were closing with the enemy.

As the Prime Minister watched, one of the telephone talkers received a radar report coming through that a number of enemy aircraft had

337

been detected building up in the vicinity of Dieppe, while another smaller formation had also been detected over the Channel just off the coast near Dover.

Falstaff informed the Prime Minister he was lucky because it looked as though he would witness the activities of the operations staff as they actually worked. He didn't even wink when he said this.

Tucking his unlit cigar back into his pocket Churchill replied that he would gladly just sit and watch. The other Bulldog nearly bit his own tongue trying to keep from responding.

1000

Dierk was surprised that he'd not been searched in any manner, though he was politely asked by an impeccably dressed guard to surrender his sidearm and dagger.

When this was done, Himmler nodded to him. "It was a pleasure meeting with you, Herr Locke. Perhaps we will meet again. If this is so I would enjoy the opportunity to dine with you."

"I would like that," the fighter pilot replied, surprised at the friendly attention of someone so high up in the Reich's ruling class.

Seeming to understand, the black uniformed Wolf told him, "Apparently, you are not aware that you are a national hero. They have dedicated an entire newsreel just to you, and our people have appropriately responded. Models of your Messerschmitt are now the toy stores' biggest seller."

"Let's hope then the British do not get lucky," he replied with a wink, "Every day they try their best to kill me."

***

"KG Alois, climbing out… spread out until we break cloud cover."

Gruppenkommandeur Oberst Alois Lindmayr released the button on his microphone and then listened. His group was well disciplined and would not respond over the airwaves.

"Copy," replied the duty Operations Officer.

The Oberst was an experienced combat veteran having won the Knight's Cross of the Iron Cross for the low level attacks he made in France. His Gruppen was hardly at full strength, however, and no matter how brave the Wolf and his aircrews were, he could field only nineteen

338

bombers of an original twenty nine; and these were in bad shape from their constant use.

At the same time, I/KG 76 would be taking off 20 miles to the north. This Gruppen could only field nine aircraft. The two groups were to rendezvous at Amiens and then proceeded to Cap Gris Nez to pick up their Bf 109 fighter escort.

Their first delay would happen after takeoff as the formation broke up in cloud and took 10 minutes to allow reforming. Two bombers failed to find the others and returned to base.

***

The wooden markers indicating the position of an enemy force near Dieppe were now pushed into a position near the centre of the Channel. Their strength was forty plus and Falstaff noticed that another marker had been placed slightly behind and to the left of the first marker. This also read forty plus but for both markers, there was no height reading. Another call went out to his station commanders and more squadrons were placed on 'Stand By' while still others came to 'Readiness'. Should the detected formation decide to abort or pose no further threat, these groups would receive the order to "Stand Down".

***

Dierk knocked softly on the massive oak doors. One of them swung open on silent hinges and he was greeted by a huge Wolf in a black uniform which was devoid of any medals or rank insignia. "Herr Hitler is expecting you," he said, clicking his heels together and giving a slight bow. His voice was surprisingly small for his size. "My name is Rochus und I will be with you the entire time. Before he arrives, I must ask you to submit to my search of your person Herr Locke. It is nothing personal and everyone having such a special interview as yours must allow this. I will also be standing behind you during the meeting but you needn't fear anything you say as I have been sworn to the highest level of secrecy."

The fighter pilot nodded. "Certainly; I understand fully."

Though the bodyguard looked a monster, he was surprisingly gentle in his search. He was also quite thorough. Satisfied, he motioned to the desk almost fifty feet from them. "You will wait there, please. Would you like tea?"

"That would be most agreeable."

As he walked, Locke automatically surveyed the room in the same way he would have the sky if flying. To his left was a huge marble topped table. This was partially covered with a cloth and there were several rolled up maps on one end. To his front was Herr Wolf's personal desk. On the Führer's side was a very large and comfortable looking black leather chair. This sat next to an equally large floor lamp which was set up as if for an evening's reading. On the 'guest's' side were two fabric covered chairs. Their backs were lower but they were also very comfortable looking.

When the sky warrior arrived at the desk he chose a chair and sat, keeping his back very straight.

1030

New formations were detected positioned between the towns of Calais and Boulogne. The markers on the map table now indicated that the enemy strength was 100 plus. Within moments another marker was placed just behind the first indicating 150 plus.

"Look at that," Falstaff mumbled to himself "It appears the Germans consider themselves on a picnic."

"What's that?" Churchill asked. The Prime Minister was standing at the Commander's elbow and so great was Falstaff's concentration he'd not even realized he was there.

"I said the formations appear in no great hurry as they're forming up very slowly. Apparently they don't consider what we have as all that much of a threat. This, Mr. Prime Minister, looks like the big one."

Eyes glued to the map, the old Bulldog ordered, "Get the Sector Station Controllers 'on the blower' and bring all squadrons to, 'Stand By.'"

Winston leaned close to his friend and said very softly, "There appear to be many aircraft coming in."

Without taking his eyes from the map board below him Falstaff answered in the same low tone "And we're ready for them. There will be someone there to meet them."

***

With the 'Stand By' order, Archie's group concluded their wait in an orderly and unperturbed manner. Archie tucked his 'pocket book' into a pocket on the leg of his flying suit while the card table was folded up and the cards put away. He then personally went to see each of his pilot's and wished them good luck and good hunting.

When he came back to his aircraft, Higgins was there to help get him into the cockpit personally though he had the fitter watching over his shoulder the entire time and fussing at him like an elderly grandmother.

***

Rochus came back with a tray of tea and sat it upon the desk in front of the pilot. "When Herr Hitler comes in, please do not jump up like a jack in the box to salute. He has requested that you forgo this ritual and simply shake paws as two gentlemen might when meeting for the first time. I am not sure exactly what you have been led to believe but in the closer more private meetings Herr Wolf is much like you and me."

"Thank you for explaining this," Dierk told the other Wolf.

"You are welcome, but it is nothing really. You are a national hero and I merely wish to side step any possible embarrassment caused by over enthusiasm or improper training. Some of what I have witnessed has been terribly... shall we say sickening?"

"Sickening... and how would that be?"

The body guard smiled. "A Wolf is not meant to sniff butt, no? From Dogs and such we can expect these things, but we are only Wolfs here... and Wolfs understand each other without all of the..."

"Butt sniffing?" Locke finished for him.

The bodyguard smiled. "Exactly. Do you take sugar in your tea?"

"I prefer it black please."

1100

An orderly passed a mug of strong gunpowder tea to Commander Falstaff. It was a little too hot, but he hardly noticed this as he continued staring at the map board. Watching the markers representing the large groups of German aircraft being moved along their route, he glanced at the tote board ordering 72 squadron and 92 squadron at Biggin Hill scrambled. Both flew Spitfires.

***

Eric Wolf watched to his left and right checking to see where the rest of the Gruppen was. In his haste to make a good impression he'd had his squadron take off a full ten minutes earlier than they should have; heading to Cap Gris Nez where they were to rendezvous with the Dorniers. He still, however, did not see the bombers. Even in his inexperience he readily grasped the Messerschmitt's problem of limited range. He could only give this situation a little more time and then they would have to turn back for fuel.

***

Archie was waiting patiently for the Kiwis to pull his prop through when the call came in. The mechanic in charge explained that he wished to pre-lubricate the engine a bit for starting. Point of fact; the Kiwis were simply trying to work off their nervousness. Every day had become like this. To them and the rest of the flight and ground crews it was just one more day of trying to thwart the Nazi war machine from coming to pay them a visit in person.

Within a minute and a half all the aircraft were airborne and climbing to altitude.

***

Alois tapped his starboard engine temp gauge hoping the higher than usual indication was a faulty instrument. These days the Geschwader had to field two Gruppen to do the work of just one. Most of the Dornier's, his own included, were in rough shape, having been worndown by intensive operations. Replacements were very slow in coming though the Reich's war machine was producing them as fast as possible.

Checking the skies around him he was also keenly aware they were down a further two aircraft. Those two had returned to base which was standard practice when becoming separated from the Gruppen. He would deal with their pilots when he got back. The two Gruppen, now at a count of only 25 bombers, rendezvoused at Amiens and headed towards Cap Gris Nez in search of their fighter escort. After the two met up they would head directly to their assigned target which was the Battersea rail lines next to Battersea Park on the Thames south bank. Though he'd heard the rumors that some in the upper command wanted the Luftwaffe to begin bombing civilian targets, he did not dwell upon this as he had more important things to think about. The idea of 'terror bombing' was meant to encourage the British people to force their government into negotiations; but so far Adolf Hitler had refused the idea and ordered only military targets be bombed, though they were in close proximity to the local populace.

"Tighten up, tighten up," he called over the radio. His growl was well known so he did not feel the need for the use of identifying words. He was a good commander and knew his bombers could not protect each other if they were too far apart. In the distance he finally saw the black dots that would be his protection. Eric Wolf's ears would surely have been burning if he'd heard the mutterings of this commander concerning his escorts.

***

Jeans watched Madam Bella climbing to the peak of the roof. The old Tatra Sheepdog clutched the knotted climbing rope with one paw and with the other she clutched a bottle of whiskey. "One of them floats down upon my house and I intend to bash him over the head with this bottle… and you do not interfere," she yelled upwards to the Poodle. "Have you seen anything yet?"

"No."

"Good… I want to watch them die."

***

"It is such a pleasure to see you again Oberst Locke."

Adolf Hitler, having quietly entered through the doorway directly behind the desk, smiled and offered his paw which Derik stood and accepted. The leaders grip was firm but not overpowering. Herr Wolf then motioned to the two chairs in front of the desk indicating they should sit.

"Rudolph told me the nature of your visit in advance," he informed the pilot. "Please don't hold that against him; he understands I don't appreciate surprises. He also mentioned he thoroughly coached you on your Sig Heil and claims it is the best he's seen; you will have to show me before you leave. Please also give my regards to Admiral Canaris when you see him again. I implicitly rely upon him to bring me the truth even if in the form of a messenger such as yourself. So far he has not disappointed me."

"I will be flying back to Paris as soon as we're done, Mein Heir," the pilot replied smoothly, "So I will not be seeing the Admiral again. In this I will be able to ferry a badly needed fighter back to my unit."

"Good. I agree that we need Wolfs of your caliber at the front as I am also keenly aware that we need fresh aircraft. Your presence must certainly be missed in the same way Uncle Fatty is missed here in Berlin. He's presently inspecting our Luftwaffe units in Belgium, so is quite unaware of your absence."

For a moment Derik was at a total loss for words and Hitler smiled, apparently achieving the surprise that he sought.

"I have knowledge of many things, Oberst Locke; one of which is how our Luftwaffe feels in general about the command decisions being made by the Wolf who leads them. I am hopeful that what you bring me is not simply this same dissatisfaction."

Dierk nodded, momentarily stunned by the apparent blunt honesty of his country's leader… but was he referring to himself or to Goring?

"No, Mein Heir, what I bring you goes much deeper," he finally replied. "I feel that Luftwaffe Intelligence has been giving you statistics not dealing in reality. It is only natural they would seek to please their masters so they grasp and present the wrong statistics. I am here to tell you that the RAF is far from devastated. I feel they are more like the boxer who allows you to tire yourself punishing his face bloody while saving the strength of his body for the moment your arms grow tired from the beating you've been giving him."

Hitler placed a paw on the pilot's arm and nodded. "I couldn't agree with you more," he said softly. He paused for a moment as the huge bodyguard served them tea. "To achieve our goals, however, it is important that we maintain the threat of invasion by continuing air attacks on military targets in the British capital." Sipping his tea, he smiled and said, "Thank you Rochus, this is very good."

Looking again at his guest, the smallish Wolf continued. "I have had several meetings concerning the tactics we now employ. Certain persons among my staff continue to push for straight attacks on civilian morale. They argue that the military and civilian industries are located too far apart to achieve a collapse of confidence by attacking only those and not the people directly. I do find truth in that argument. In actuality, that ego filled Dog Winston Churchill has forced what we are doing upon us by bombing Berlin. Retribution was called for but though I was pressed for strikes against residential areas in direct retaliation to what the British did to us I made sure to order that only military targets in London were to be attacked."

***

Finally making the rendezvous, Eric's gruppen spread out to give

344

close support. That meant flying 'with' the bombers which were much slower. To accomplish this the fighter pilots had to lower their flaps to maintain speed and distance. This requirement made the fighters sitting ducks when the enemy attacked from above. It took precious time to get the Messerschmitt back up to fighting speed; and when you were being dived upon this meant death. The one saving grace was the Britisher's avoidance of the fight in order to go after the bombers. As they streaked past the Messerschmitts would follow, picking them off from behind.

Flying with this increased drag also ate up precious fuel. All of the pilots were watching their gauges closely and none of them were smiling. To compound this malady the formation was also flying into a headwind.

"Look up Red One," called a voice over the radio, "We at least have friends."

The Dorniers with their escorts had finally been joined by the fighter aircraft of JG 53 who now flew top cover.

JG 27 and JG 52, sent out in advance of the main strike, flew in toward London at 16,000 ft.

The bomber formation crossed the coast at Folkestone at 11:36.

***

Falstaff watched the map board from his perch as if he were a god looking down upon the world; and indeed his eyes saw more than mere wooden markers. The buzz of voices in the room faded to his thoughts and became nothing more than the drone of a propeller.

***

Fighters from Lehrgeschwader 2 (Demonstration Wing 2) also formed a part of the escort now but their mission was two fold. Their orders were to fly in advance of the main force and drop 550 lb (250 kg) bombs. They would then resume their role as fighters, going after the RAF aircraft that might come up to meet them. Faster than the bombers, LG 2 took off as the bombers crossed the English coast. Even with bombs, the Bf 109s were expected to overhaul the bombers and attack London a few minutes before the main raids began.

***

One of the WAAFs, on the instructions of her telephone talker, took another wooden block and placed it upon the map board, pushing it into place with her stick.

"Here now, what's this?" Churchill asked at Falstaff's elbow.

"Apparently Jerry's seen fit to send a second wave. It could be a trap… let our boys tire themselves on the first group and then overwhelm them with the second," the Wing Commander explained. "Then again perhaps our friends are simply being daft and truly think we're down for the count." He thought about it, and then told the senior fighter controlling officer to his left, "Scramble the 229, 303, 253, 501, 17, and the 73. Have them sent straight in."

"Yes, sir."

As he was doing this, the old Bulldog leaned over the rail and yelled down, "Who's on radio with the 72 and 92?"

"I am, sir," one of the Collies called back to him.

"Tell the lads that the gloves are off. Everything is a fair target. Ignore the bombers and take on the high escort. They're to give'em hell."

There was a small cheer on the floor of the operations room and then it was right back to business as usual.

***

"Yellow Leader copies," Archie replied. "Yellow Leader to yellow flight, we are now released to engage the escorting fighters." There was an immediate chatter among the group and the other flights in the air.

They were now climbing through Angels Ten, and it was oxygen on, clear skies, and clear your guns. When they met, the Spitfires would be at their maximum altitude.

As the forces closed, around 120 Bf 109s and 25 Do 17s were now facing 245 Spitfires and Hurricanes.

***

At 1120 hours, the 504, 257, 603, and the 609 squadrons were scrambled with orders to attack the bombers directly as they saw them.

After observing the electric lights on the tote board the Prime Minister asked his old friend, "What have we left in reserve?"

Falstaff turned to the other Bulldog and told him, "That's it, that's the lot. We have no reserves."

§

Some of us would die within the next few days. That was inevitable. But you did not believe that it would be you. Death was always present, and we knew it for what it was. If we had to die, we would be alone, smashed to pieces, burnt alive, or drowned. Some strange, protecting veil kept the nightmare thought from our minds, as did the loss of our friends. Their disappearance struck us as less a solid blow than a dark shadow which chilled our hearts and passed on.

Squadron Leader Peter Townsend 85 Squadron RAF
(later Group Captain)

Archie's group pounced upon their Luftwaffe counterpart with a vengeance that was felt all the way down to Control. Once the command decision had been reached and acted upon, Stewart Falstaff had the radio connected directly to the loudspeaker system so all could listen as they continued in their duties of pushing the little wooden blocks about on the map board.

"Yellow Leader here," the Stag's voice was heard to say, "We're over Canterbury. 109's below at Angel's Twenty Three. Sun's behind us. Tally Ho!"

The radio quickly became a cacophony of banter as each fighter picked a target and descended with their claws out. Taken by complete surprise, no less than five German aircraft were hit on the first pass.

Turning to the officer by his side, Falstaff said, "It's time we test Mallory's Big Wing. The moment you see the Germans using the Thames Estuary as a navigation aid, order the scramble. That way 12 Group's RAF Duxford can meet them over Hornchurch."

The order was sent out at 11:20 and Duxford scrambled No's 19, 310, 302, 611 and 242. No. 242 Squadron Leader and Wing Commander Douglas Bader now led this assault with 56 fighters. They were airborne at 11:22.

(radio report) We're past, we're past... flamed one... I count three... Watch your back, they're following... [gun sounds... no voice]... Fuk I'm hit...

Archie's voice came clear over the airwaves, "Control, Yellow Leader, I see the bombers... looks like they're over Ashford."

(radio report) Bloody *XX** hun... I'm good... Get out of there Harry... Good... gave him a squirt... he's flamed...

"Yellow Leader, Control," called the calm voice of WAAF Lieutenant Chelsea Collie, "Can you make the bombers?"

"Negative Control, we're a bit busy at the moment. What part of Jerry not chewing on our tails has made the area between…" [gun fire sounding out in three short bursts] "Scratch one… you still there Henry?"

"Rock solid… nice shooting…" came the reply.

"They're blocking the way Control."

"Copy."

Falstaff's mind whirled with the aerial combat he was listening to. "Tell Nos. 253 and 501 Squadrons to head for Maidstone," he ordered. "If the bombers get through they'll catch them over London. Then tell the 603 to forget the bombers and attack the close escort directly." Turning to the Prime Minister, the old Bulldog gave a ghost of a smile. "We'll peel back the skin of the onion so we can get to the meat… engage the fighters and make them use up their fuel so they'll have to leave early from the party."

Churchill nodded but made no comment as he continued to watch and listen.

"Enemy below," came the call from 603's leader, "I count twenty five bombers inbound and that many or a bit more escort. Tally Ho!" With the report came the sound of his aircraft's engine revving as the pilot made a 'scream downhill.'

Each pilot of the 603, ignoring the bombers, was careful to pick out one of the escorts. The 109's, flying slow with their flaps out, seemed to be floating in the air just waiting for them. The radio chatter was both exciting and chilling as the war was listened to in a now firsthand nature by those in the control room.

"Indianer, Indianer, Indianer! Elf, O Uhr! (Indians, Indians,Indians! Eleven 'o' clock!)" came the warning cry over the radio from one of the bomber crews.

Even as tracers began drifting out from the Dornier's defensive gun positions Eric Wolf began the process of trimming up his aircraft and pushing the throttle forward. He wasn't as concerned with being hit as he was with losing a bomber. From experience and the stories brought back by his peers, he knew the RAF had been single minded in this aspect of the game; bombers first.

The young pilot didn't even have time to be surprised as his cockpit was riddled with over thirty .303 rounds. The 109 he'd been flying literally fell from of the sky.

Alois involuntarily ducked as a Spitfire rocketed past so close that it buffeted his aircraft. "Tighten up! Tighten up!" he yelled into his microphone, "Protect each other, not yourselves!" Even as he spoke the words, his tail gunner opened up with a burst that quickly drained the gun's magazine. Next to him, his bomb aimer more properly operated his gun in five round burst. The fellow was like a dancer, jumping from gun to gun as targets flashed all around them. Placing his aircraft on auto-pilot, Lindmayr grabbed the gun to his right and watched for a target. It wasn't long before he was squeezing the trigger.

Archie banked left, a Messerschmitt trying hard to follow. Its pilot, apparently new to the game, couldn't hold on to the turn. At the height of the 'G' forces, he flipped his aircraft over and headed for the coast, vacating the battle zone as fast as he could.

"Control, Yellow Leader," he called, "Enemy top cover leaving the area, shall we give chase?"

On the floor of Control a cheer went up though their work continued undisturbed. "Have them return to base," Falstaff ordered, knowing round two would be coming and probably in short order. "Then call Biggin Hill and tell them I want those aircraft refueled and rearmed in record time. Remind them there should be food, tea, and a shot of medicinal waiting for each of the pilots."

Oberst Lindmayr did a quick head count and was amazed to find all twenty five bombers still with him. He also felt the fur on the back of his neck stand up. This was not how the British fought. Suddenly they had backbone and were engaging the fighters in the same manner a child tired of being bullied will turn on his tormentor. A long burst from the gun next to him pulled his attention forward and he cursed as some twenty three Hurricanes of the 253 and 501 Squadrons arrived at the same altitude delivering a head-on attack. Alois' crews were experienced, however, and though the formation was buffeted with hits scored on both sides, they held their nerve and remained intact. JG 3 in turn attacked the Hurricanes dispatching two from the 501 Squadron.

Northolt's No.s 229 and 303 Squadrons were now also arriving and engaged JG 52 which had dropped their bombs and come back to aid their brethren. In a free for all dog fight the likes of which had never before been seen, aircraft contrails streamed all about the sky as each side attempted to dominate the other.

Amidst the fighter to fighter chaos, the bombers ploughed on taking some comfort that they'd apparently been totally forgotten in the clash. Reaching Lewisham the bomber commander was quick to also understand that his formation was now isolated and pulled his flight in even tighter. The Dornier's escorts, now embroiled in dogfights all over Kent were everywhere except flying cover. This lack of cover was further pressed home as the No. 605 managed to break away from the fight to deliver a twelve fighter attack scoring more hits on the Dorniers.

Still, Lindmayr's crews stubbornly held together and pressed on. One bomber, an engine smoking, lagged behind and was soon outside their defensive ring. This aircraft was set upon by four Hurricanes. Too far away for covering fire to be offered, the pilot set his aircraft on autopilot and ordered his crew to bail out. He would later die of wounds suffered at the hands of British civilians before the army could rescue him. One of these was reportedly an old Polish Sheepdog brandishing an empty whisky bottle.

"KG KG KG Approaching target," Alois radioed his group, "Bomb aimers make ready." Patting his own bomb aimer on the shoulder the Wolf nodded. The fellow abandoned the cockpit guns and quickly swung his body into the small glass enclosed cubicle of the nose where he turned on his bombsight and opened the bomb bay doors. The aircraft immediately slowed with this increase of drag, becoming even noisier than it was as the wind caught the exposed structure causing a heavy turbulence within the slipstream.

"Control, Big Wing Leader," Bader called in. "We're over London. Dorniers in sight. Tally Ho!"

"Left one degree," Alois heard in his headset and he pressed on the left rudder pedal ever so gently. "Hold… release in three, two, one… bombs dropped!"

For a full moment in time, as the 110 pound bombs dropped one at a time out of twenty four underbellies, there was no noise in the bomb commander's ears. The engines faded to nothing… the chatter of his crew on the intercom ceased… and all the Wolf heard was the soft whistle of the wind as it passed the dart like objects falling to the ground. There was no remorse or the consideration of death; there was only the thought that his mission had been accomplished.

Their target was hit.

The Battersea rail lines next to Battersea Park on the Thames south bank was struck; each Dornier's payload of twenty bombs carving a run 500 yards long and 25 yards wide. Some, however, fell on the high density civilian housing surrounding the train station.

This undisturbed salvo missed Clapham Junction but fell across the rail network tracks that connected it to Victoria Station north of the Thames and the main line heading northeast on the south side of the river. The damage done cut the tracks in Battersea at several places and a viaduct collapsed over a portion of the rails.

The raid's mission was counted successful by Luftwaffe Intelligence as rail traffic was halted. Four unexploded bombs further delayed repairs but the rail lines would only be out of action for three days.

With the closing of the bomb bay doors sound came back to KG 76's commander just as his cockpit was riddled by Douglas Bader's Spitfire. Miraculously he was not hit; but below in the bomb aiming compartment the bombardier screamed a silent scream as his intercom wiring was cut in the same moment his body was ripped apart by machinegun fire.

Within minutes, the Dornier formation was reduced to 15 aircraft and most of these were damaged. Six had been out rightly shot down while four were forced to leave the formation and attempt a run for home on their own, leaving a trail of smoke in their wake.

Ironically, the empty Dornier that had been abandoned earlier continued to fly on under its engaged auto-pilot. This attracted a swarm of fighters, none of which was successful in bringing the aircraft down. Eventually Ray Holmes of 504 Squadron rammed it with his fighter. This caused the tail to come off. In its death throes, the wings snapped off just outboard of the engines. During its spinning death, the gravitational forces caused the bombs to be released, which then hit or landed near to Buckingham Palace, damaging the building.

KG76, still doggedly hanging together, turned and fought their way back to the coast where they were met by a covering force of ME 109's. By this time, Falstaff had ordered all squadrons back to base in preparation for the next wave that was sure to come.

Now, almost as an afterthought, LG 2's attack was a complete wash. Flying in, the Messerschmitt pilots saw one rail station, released their bombs and then simply returned home. They saw only one British fighter, who reported the makeup of the formation.

With this report, they were not seen as a threat and so were ignored.

§

From the time that we had been over Maidstone until reaching the outskirts of London, we had been under extreme pressure. The British fighters had been with us since we had first crossed the English coast and had gathered in intensity all the time. Our escort had been doing a grand job with the Spitfires at keeping them away from us, and we thought that should things remain like this, then this bombing run would be made easy.

We saw the Hurricanes coming towards us and it seemed that the

whole of the RAF was there, we had never seen so many British fight-
ers coming at us at once. I saw a couple of our comrades go down, and
we got hit once but it did no great damage. All around us were dogfights
as the fighters went after each other, then as we were getting ready for
our approach to the target, we saw what must have been a hundred RAF
fighters coming at us. We thought that this must have been all the RAF
planes were up at once, but where were they coming from, as we had been
told that the RAF fighters were very close to extinction. We could not keep
our present course, we turned to starboard and done all that we could to
avoid the fighters and after a while I am sure we had lost our bearings, so
we just dropped our bombs and made our retreat.

Luftwaffe Do 17 Front Gunner Hans Zonderlind

Almost as soon as his crippled Dornier landed Gruppenkommandeur Lindmayr charged into Command and in a fashion entirely unlike
him began screaming at his Geschwaderkommodore, (*Geschwader commanding officer*).

"You said the British Dogs had only 50 fighters left to their entire
fucking air force and I've just lost half of my bombers!" he yelled, getting
right in the other Wolf's face. "There were hundreds of them! Hundreds!
We were hit by the Dogs flying in a unison I have never seen over England! We were sandbagged! Goring was sucked in! Duped! They totally
ignored us and went after the fighters until we were over the target and all
alone! Go and count the bullet holes in my fucking bomber, Manfred! My
bomb aimer is dead and my aircraft will never fly again! Better; call up
Fighter Command and ask them how many fucking fighters they lost!"

Oberst Manfred Bauer had never seen his friend this angry. The
Wolf's eyes were wild and the Commander nervously watched against the
possibility of Lindmayr reaching for his sidearm. "We told you exactly
what Herr Göring told us," he stuttered, "He said we had nothing to fear.
He said the RAF was all done. I had no idea this would happen. Intel
has reflected exactly what we were told." In a softer voice he advised his
friend; "Be careful what you say; you never know who is listening."

Lindmayr took a deep stuttering breath and closed his eyes,
slowly letting it out. Bauer looked to the other operational personnel present and signaled for one of them to bring a chair for the Gruppen Commander. When this was done, he chased everyone out of the room and
then pulled a chair up to sit beside his friend. Reaching back he opened
a drawer in his desk and removed a silver flask. This he uncorked and

passed to the bomber commander. "Did you hit your objective?" he asked softly, beginning the mission debrief he knew was so very important.

"Yes, we hit our stinking objective but what is the point? Twenty five light bombers are going to make a difference?" Alois blinked and then took a deep swallow of the schnapps. He forced himself to focus as he thought back to the mission. "The target was soundly hit. Until that time there were some attempted strikes upon us but our crews hung together defensively. I'd lost only one bomber up to that point. I'm telling you Manfred, the attacking fighters were initially more interested in our escorts." Reaching out, he gripped the other Oberst by the arm. "It was a trap! No sooner had we released and we were set upon by no less than seventy mixed fighters."

"Mixed?"

"Hurricanes and Spitfires. I have no idea where they all came from. It's a wonder they did not shoot all of us down. By rights they should have. You must get the second wave canceled or at least postponed until we figure out what the RAF has done. Perhaps send in only the fighters, but we cannot send in the bombers again."

Bauer gave a worried look towards the telephone. He would be expected to phone in a report to the Intelligence Directorate in quick order. Considering the 'feelings' of his superiors, he'd so far kept all of his reports as positive as possible. In many cases he'd reported many of his aircraft only as damaged when they were in fact kaput and only waiting for endgueltige vernichtung (final destruction of damaged aircraft).

"They are already taking off," he responded softly, "The best I can do is forewarn them of what they 'might' encounter. It is all part of the planned crushing of the RAF, Alois. You hit the railway linking London to the heavy industries of England's other industrial cities on the north and south-east of Britain. The second wave target is the dock areas of the Thames Estuary including the warehouses. This is meant to bring what is left of the RAF over one area where our fighters can have at them. Based upon the intelligence we were given I had to agree it was a good plan." He paused and then placing a paw on the knee of his fellow Oberst, said, "Give me the details und then go and tend to your crew. I need the facts if I am to report anything at all."

When they were done, and it was by far the highest mission loss Bauer had seen to date, he saw his friend to the office door and then came back to call in the report personally. It was not too late to at least postpone the second wave as the attack plan was perhaps altered in consideration of this new development. He would speak directly to the officer in charge and…

The phone rang.

Picking it up, he stiffened as the person on the other end asked specifically for him and then identified himself as Adolf Hitler.

"Yes Mein Führer," Bauer near stuttered. "How may I help you?"

"I want a report on the first wave of today's attack," the little Wolf told him calmly. "You will give me the absolute truth down to the last detail. I believe I need not remind you of the consequences of any omissions should they come to light?"

"Of course not Mein Heir."

"Very well then… how bad was it?"

The very fact that his country's leader had not asked how successful the raid had been indicated he most likely already knew.

"Six bombers of twenty five shot down with, I believe, another two crashing upon landing. I will still have to confer with maintenance but at least five more have been damaged beyond further flight until repaired. Of the remaining twelve, repairs are already underway, mein heir."

"I see," Hitler said. "This was not FLAK damage?"

"No mein Führer. The damage was done by the RAF."

"In what numbers?"

The Geschwaderkommodore paled knowing full well Uncle Fatty's wrath would be…

"No one is to know of this phone call Oberst Bauer," The voice on the telephone told him calmly as if reading his mind, "Do you understand? Not from me… not from you."

"Yes Mein Führer."

"When we are done you will make your reports the same as you always do, and then you will tend to your duties. Now; how many RAF fighters attacked us this morning?"

"Hundreds."

"Hundreds?"

There was a pause and the Geschwaderkommodore thought perhaps the connection had been cut. Then his country's leader asked,

"How many hundreds?"

§

Archie and Henry stood together drinking tea and munching on a sandwich that Higgins brought for them. The Batman, helping as best he could, also brought a plate full of extras for the rest of the pilots. They'd already given the intelligence officer their initial reports and when the fellow was done collecting what he could, he was off at the double to phone it into Command. As the pair watched, their aircraft were swarmed by the Kiwis fueling, arming, and patching the holes.

"We did bloody good, I think," Henry muttered around a mouthful of sandwich. "We didn't lose anyone of our group and it felt good to give the Hun fighters a hard time for a change. 'Take that and smoke it!' says I."

"I wonder how Bader's big wing worked out?" the Stag added.

"I would have loved just sitting on a roof top watching that one… imagine; entire squadrons of fighters with no interference as they hit the bloody bombers."

As he said this, one of the Kiwis produced a small can of black paint and a stencil, carefully adding another swastika to the side of the Egham Spitfire. The count was now up to 15.

"Here now," her pilot protested, "We've no time for painting silly emblems."

The fellow smiled at the Lieutenant and held his paint can up as if toasting him. "Always time for a body count, sir," he replied loudly over the noise of the service bowser fueling the Spit. "They got my pal Jarvis in a bombing raid last week. I would gladly paint on another dozen if you could manage it." With that he hopped off the wing and was gone off to the next fighter to help service up the oxygen.

"Leave it Arch," Henry advised him, "Just be careful not to smudge it as you're getting into the cockpit. I'm sure we'll be up again shortly. What time is it, anyhow?"

"Half past noon," Higgins offered. "And upon your return I shall have a special dinner whipped up for the pair of you."

"And what might that be Corporal?" the Stag asked.

"Well, sir, I did some trading here and abouts and came across a nicely aged bottle of whiskey."

"Good lad!" Henry exclaimed, merrily holding up his mug of tea in salute, "There will be some food too, I presume?"

"Kippers and beans, sir."

"That'll do just fine," the Bulldog told him, "though it'll bring on the farts to be sure."

"Has anyone seen Commander Sheltie?" Archie asked.

"He didn't come back, sir," Higgins told him in a quieter voice, "Perhaps he landed at an aux field."

"Or had to trust to his para, "Henry offered. "Good old cocoon club, eh? What would we do without our friends the silkworms?"

None of them wanted to even suggest their friend might have gone for a Burton... but yet... it was a possibility.

§

Damage estimates continued flowing into the command center, and all of them were quickly examined as the WAAF girls continued pushing the little wooden markers back in the direction of France. Some of these estimates were duplicate reports by different pilots shooting at the same aircraft, but even allowing for that the statistics were extremely good. When the reports were finalized, the RAF claimed to have shot down 81 aircraft. (Overall the attackers lost only six bombers and 12 Bf 109s, some 12.5% of their strength. The Dornier placed on autopilot and then abandoned was actually claimed nine times.)

Churchill was ecstatic and pounded Falstaff on the back after reading the final report which had been handed to him with a smile by the Commander who'd read it first. Stewart, being more of a realist and knowing air combat for what it was, understood the real number would be much lower, but he was quite happy all the same. This was something he absolutely was relying upon but in the reverse... what would the German pilots report of the British numbers? All the same it would be a huge shot in the arm for the RAF's moral. His own losses were always more of a concern and starkly more accurate. The final tally of aircraft down and this more easily accountable as true, showed Fighter Command losing a total of 13.

Noting the time and realizing the staff had not been able to change shift in the middle of an operation, Falstaff ordered food and beverage brought in.

"Good idea," Winston agreed, "And trust me I am craving a good cigar and a whiskey but damned if I will leave fearing I might miss something." His eyes went to the tote board where the lights showed all the squadrons out of service. "Have we not examined the procedures of readying our aircraft at a faster pace?" he asked.

"You can only go so fast," the other Bulldog assured him, "without having some sort of huge cockup. It's bad enough the Germans destroy our aircraft for us; we don't need to add to those numbers."

"But getting caught on the ground..."

"Is my biggest worry. You may have noticed the first wave had only a handful of bombers and a disproportionate number of fighters. My guess is they're banking on us being caught out and not able to get back into the air. That would mean the next wave will have the entirety of what they have left. If they manage that, and we cannot again get into the sky in force, we're buggered."

The Commander produced a flask and offered it to Churchill. The Prime Minister, suddenly looking grim again, accepted it gratefully. Taking a long sip he passed it back. Stewart, as much as he wanted to imbibe, did not partake; wishing to keep his wits as sharp as possible.

"I think I like the tactic of going after their fighters," he rumbled as he recapped the flask. "Regardless of anything else their bombers were left totally alone over London. That by itself is something to consider."

"It certainly must have struck the fear of God into the bomber pilots," Churchill agreed.

"When they saw all those fighters coming at them, you bet it did," Falstaff replied. He then pointed to the tote board as a cheer arose from the floor. "There we go… the first squadron just came back on line." Looking down at the map board he also saw new markers being placed over the coast line of France. "You can bet it's still going to be nip and tuck, especially with the 'big wing' being so distant." He pointed at the board. "Our friends are again forming up and you can bet this morning's raid will look like a walk in the park by comparison. I can imagine they are quite pissed that we haven't rolled over in submission." Turning to his aide he said, "Ring up the Twelve and ask them to assist again with their Big Wing. Have them call back as soon as they're at the ready."

"Wolfs," growled Churchill. "They're too hard headed for their own good. If any one of'em had bothered to stand up against pack rules we wouldn't be in this bloody mess."

Falstaff looked at him with just the barest of smiles. "As I recall – sir – you had one hell of a bloody fight just trying to change pacifist minds on our end of things. I believe I read a quote in the Times where you said, 'Peace is fine but war is better.'"

The Prime Minister chuckled. "Oh yes… I remember that one. It came with a damned fine caricature of me with devil's horns and extremely sharp teeth. I rather liked that image. The pacifists and their movement had a death grip on the minds of our people to be sure. Hearing them sing a different song now is certainly music to my ears; but if we do not stop this invasion all of that will be for naught and you can bet those same political types will quickly bend to kiss Nazi buttocks."

He turned and gazed again at the tote board. "It's a shame that our

American cousin's record still appears stuck in that same groove. Seeing us in dire straights, they're still singing the same song and refusing to assist."

"That'll last until they're given a good swift kick to the chops," the Commander replied flatly.

"Pity for that," Churchill agreed, "but I'm afraid you're right."

§

Jeans tucked Madam Bella into her sumptuous bed. The Tatra Sheepdog was pissed drunk and true to her word had attacked a downed German flyer after pushing her way through the crowd to get at him. She near beat him to death with the empty whiskey bottle. It took the Poodle and two soldiers to pull her off. Once home it required a good deal of effort with a washcloth just to get the blood off. The whole time the brothel owner never once stopped muttering the names of her dead relatives.

After this Jeans briefly saw to the establishment which was completely empty of clients. Then, flipping the 'closed' sign on the door window, she climbed back up to the roof to watch again. When she arrived back in Germany an eyewitness account would be expected.

§

After his meeting with der Führer, Locke was escorted out of the New Reich Chancellery by a lesser known side entrance. Checking his watch he found it to be just after eleven 'o' clock. The hour he'd spent with his nation's leader was quite social and yet passed in a blur of tea and conversation. His mind swirled with all that had happened in such a short time. Had he done the right thing? Would his interview make any difference at all? When the meeting concluded, true to his word, Hitler had the flyer perform his 'Heil Hitler'. He'd done it so perfectly, the little Wolf actually stood and applauded him, saying, 'Now I expect you to teach what you have learned to those under your authority, und after we invade England I will especially have them perform it for me during the victory celebrations at Buckingham Palace.'

A Mercedes limousine was waiting to pick him up and he noticed the driver was the same Wolf who worked for Admiral Canaris. Climbing into the back seat he found no one inside waiting for him; but his flight suit and equipment were all there.

Bending down the chauffer told him, "You are to change while I drive, Herr Oberst. You may leave your dress uniform on the seat. It will be taken care of and sent to you in France. I will have you to the airfield in thirty minutes where a new Messerschmitt waits for you. It has been painted with your colors and kills." Passing the pilot an envelope, he then closed the door to the car.

Dierk's mind was already automatically doing the math. The distance to his base was between 650 and 700 miles. There would be one stop for fuel with the midpoint field alerted and waiting for him, it would be an easy three hour trip. This brought him back to France at around 1530. That meant paperwork and then perhaps a quiet dinner with Johannes where his second could catch him up on the happenings occurring while he was gone.

Waiting until the car was moving and well away from the Chancellery, he opened the envelope. In it was a map of the French coastline with a circle around what looked like a farmer's field in Belgium. There was also a penciled in time of 2300 hours. Next to the time was the word Storch (Stork ligth aircraft) with a slash and then the name Jeans. With this were the instructions, 'Einzelnes licht an jedem ende des feldes.' (Single light at each end of the field.)

§

At 1415 the WAAFs of Control moved the first of their markers over the Kent coastline between Dungeness and Dover. This time the Luftwaffe flew combined formations of He111s, Do17s and Do215s at fifteen minute intervals. The Observer Corps estimated the count between 150 and 200 bombers. The fighters, flying as close escort and high altitude cover were the usual Bf110s and Bf109s. This number was estimated at approximately 400. In total a combined force of 600 plus aircraft were now headed north towards London on a front some thirty miles wide.

Churchill, when he and Commander Falstaff were given the word, uncharacteristically said nothing at all. Walking to the rail of the observation area, he stood looking at the tote board. His blank expression would have fit well at a card table.

After issuing the order to scramble, Falstaff also came to the rail where he once more looked down at the map board, marking the progress of the enemy aircraft. "I've given orders to take on the fighters first," he said softly. "That rather worked well this morning; run them out of fuel and then take on the bombers when they're naked in our sights."

"Naked," the Prime Minister harrumphed. "The vision of a German bomber pilot flying in nothing but his boxer shorts might be amusing but I would rather they simply be out of bombs and bullets."

§

"Jawohl, endlich ist das Tor für unsere Mannschaft gefallen"

"It is not necessary that whilst I live I live happily; but it is necessary that so long as I live I should live honourably."

(Immanuel Kant – German Philosopher 1724 –1804)

The call came in to scramble at 1410 hours. The roar of engines starting was almost instantaneous; all save one, which was the Egham Spitfire.

As the other aircraft of the squadron taxied out and quickly took to the air, Archie helplessly held his fingers on the starter switches. Though the prop turned through it arc right enough, there was not so much as a splutter from the engine. Finally his Crew Chief hopped up on the wing and pounded on the canopy to get his attention.

"You'll have to let off the starter so it can cool, sir," the aged Scottish Hound told him loudly. His accent clearly marked him as being from the north. "You seize it oop and that's another few precious h'oors gone just to change it oot."

Reluctantly the Stag complied. Pressing the 'push to talk' button on his yoke, he called to Henry. "Yellow Leader to Yellow two, over."

"Go ahead Yellow Leader."

Maintenance difficulties, you've got the lead."

"Roger Wilco, see you when we get back."

Flipping the radio switches off, the pilot released the catch on the canopy and slid it back. "How long to get it fixed?" he asked.

"Won't know until I open her oop, sir," the Sergeant replied. "If you want to take a cuppa at the operation's shack, y' can listen to developments on the radio. I'll send a runner just as soon as I know what we're up against."

"We just flew this morning."

"Perhaps the lass is jest tired, sir. It's been known ta 'appen."

"Or perhaps God is saving you for another go," chimed in one of the Kiwi's standing next to the aircraft.

The Sergeant gave the fellow a cross look and then to the pilot muttered, "That too is a possibility I s'pose."

§

Derik could hear the chatter on his radio as he flew. The afternoon raid was already well underway and here he was still fifteen minutes from his base. Having caught a good tail wind he was earlier than expected. His patience was now wearing very thin as the feel of combat reentered his psyche. By the time he arrived his fuel would be an issue but that could be remedied quickly enough. On landing he would be the only aircraft on the field. That meant the 'Blackmen' could get the fueling bowser to his aircraft without delay. He was also already armed so that too was one less thing to worry about. Ten minutes maximum and he would be airborne again and on his way to Britain, aiding in the recovery of any bombers needing assistance. His personal crew of two mechanics, Schultz and Peter, were the best and they already knew of his ETA. (author's note: every German fighter had two mechanics specifically assigned to it.) He would have a quick piss by the airplane, a swallow of coffee, and then be on his way. Upon his return he would then sit with Johannes and catch up on the Staffel status.

Though the pilot had only been gone for a few days it certainly felt more like a year. Getting his head back into the game of combat was not going to be so easy after all he'd recently had to endure. As far as the Wolf was concerned the Nazis could keep their politics. Politics muddied the water while its cronyism gave them inept leaders the likes of Uncle Fatty. Combat was more straight forward; give him a job to do and he would see it through no matter what.

A flash thought occurred of shooting down a Junkers tri-motor bearing Swastikas on its wings and fuselage. It was gone again before his next breath could even be taken. Indeed, for a moment he didn't breathe at all.

"Red Leader... Red Leader herauskristallisiert, dass sie?" ("Red Leader... Red Leader... is that you?")

"Ja," Derik responded scanning the sky and finding two aircraft less than a thousand feet above and behind him. This was very disturbing. Had he really been that oblivious? "Wie geht der Krieg?" (How goes the war?)

The Rotte (fighting pair) quickly dove and formed up off of the Staffelkapitän's right wing. The pilot in the other craft gave him a thumbs down. Derik recognized the aircraft's markings as belonging to his Gruppen though with its pilot wearing his oxygen mask he did not recognize the face. This was quickly remedied as the big German Shepherd undid the strap and dropped the mask just long enough for facial recognition. It was Emil, one of the more seasoned pilots under his command.

Putting his mask back in position, the other pilot radioed, "After this morning's mission, Eric and I were given airfield coverage as assignment since our aircraft were in better shape than the others. Once patched up the Gruppen was off to cover the bombers on their way home. So far the British have not ventured across the channel."

With a spiraling hand gesture, he indicated an aircraft going down and then held up four fingers. Flashing their hand sign for 'British', he began opening and closing his fist showing the numbers with his fingers... and the flashing went on and on and on.

Derik nodded his understanding. As he'd always suspected; intelligence on the RAF's numbers was very wrong. Over the radio he replied, "Continue your patrol, I will land, fuel, and go to also assist." He then called to his field. "Geschwader 56 Jörke... Red leader, do you copy?"

"Ja, Mei Herr," their radio operator replied.

"ETA fifteen minutes, I wish to be airborne again max schnell. Can you get a message to Johannes for me?"

There was a hesitation and then the operator came back on and told him, "I am sorry, sir, but Oberleutnant Johannes did not come back from a test flight this morning. I will alert the ground crew to your needs."

Derik cursed and slammed his fist against the canopy hard enough that he caused a crack in the plastic. He knew exactly what his second in command had done.

§

1450 hours

Even though most of the attacking bombers had been thrown off of their planned flight path, many of them managed to get through to the southern areas of London. If they thought most of Fighter Commands fighters were behind them and still engaged in combat over Kent and Surrey, they were in for a big surprise. Now, as in the morning session, they were met by 49 fighters of Bader's "Duxford Wing". Combined with a number of other squadrons that had followed the leading bombers and two other squadrons that had just joined the action, a total of some 150 more aircraft awaited them.

Archie sat at Commander Sheltie's desk in the operations shack. He was still in his flight suit and listening to the radio; picking out a voice here and there that he recognized.

The most poignant thing he heard among the chatter was one pilot's initial thoughts upon seeing the enemy formation before him. "Dive down lads and just keep your gun button pressed... there's so bloody many you can't miss!"

During the course of this chatter, a messenger came in looking for whoever was in charge. Seeing Archie behind the desk, he came to attention and saluted. He wasn't much more than a boy. "Beg'n your pardon, sir, but I have a message. Would you take it?"

"I suppose so... yes..."

Taking the proffered clipboard, he signed for the note and as the messenger ran off again, slowly opened the envelope.

It is with regret that notification is hereby given that the remains of Group Commander Reginald Sheltie have been identified still within his aircraft which was shot down during this morning's action.

Flight Lieutenant Archie Corn is hereby temporarily assigned Squadron Commander until permanent arrangements can be made.

The note was signed by a penguin Archie'd never heard of. *(Penguin - officers with no operational experience or haven't flown; from the fact that 'Penguins do not have wings'.)*

A moment later the air raid sirens began howling and at the same time, a private burst into the small shack. "Come quickly, sir, your engine is running and Sergeant Mac says Jerry could be here at any moment!"

At 1525 hours, the Egham Spitfire broke ground and was wheels up, beginning her climb.

§

"Control, this is Yellow Leader," Archie called, "I'm off late but better late than never; directions please."

"Yellow Leader, stand by."

"Arch, is that you?" Henry chimed in.

"Of course it is," the Stag replied, "The magnetos were both faulty. How did we do?"

"I think we did a blessed job busting ball," the Bulldog replied, his reference not lost on his friend. "The cloud cover has rolled in now and made it a bit more difficult for Jerry to find his target effectively.

We're low on everything and returning to base. Good hunting."

"Yellow Leader," Control called, "Head due south and keep an eye open for anything trying to get away."

"Thank you Chelsea, wilco, on my way."

§

"Red Anführer der Luft," (Red Leader Airborne) Derik called over the radio. His control group already knew his plans as he'd taken the time to call in upon landing. While on the phone he received a very quick briefing to which he simply replied, "Understood." His mission was not a free hunt but one of recovery. The bomber groups were being hit hard and it was imperative they cover the leg home as much as possible. They were still over there and from what was heard on the radio; being severely beaten up.

Not having to go all the way to London, the fighter pilot was less conservative with his speed. Oxygen mask in place, he climbed to altitude and headed straight across the channel. He was not concerned with the British RFD as they would not be giving a single aircraft consideration. In the back of his mind the thought occurred that this might make a good attack plan… hundreds of aircraft all coming from different places. This was immediately dismissed as foolish since there could be no solid defense. Other thoughts threatened to crowd his mind. All that had happened in the few short weeks came and went as he mentally pushed it aside; quickly slipping into the essence of flying and surviving.

As the Wolf crossed the White Cliffs of Dover, he began scanning the skies looking for aircraft.

§

Archie spotted the Dornier 17 flying almost directly east from its bombing run on London. In the distance it was no more than a dot in the sky but for the seasoned pilot identification was easy; especially considering the direction in which it was flying. Ducking into a cloud he increased his throttle to full power. Adjusting his course he kept an eye on the artificial horizon, the altimeter, the compass and his engine temperature. So far everything in the Egham Spitfire was ticking along exactly as it should. She sounded impatient for the conflict.

Cloud blindness now made it a waiting game almost exactly as was played out by Germany's U-boats in the Atlantic. The prey was

364

stalked under blind conditions with only an occasional peek at the target.

Especially since he was alone, the Stag maintained radio silence. There was no telling who might be listening.

§

"Indien, Indien, Indien! Elf 'O' Uhr! (Indian, Indian, Indian! Eleven 'o' clock!)" came the warning cry from the dorsal gunner as he tracked his target. He was also the ship's engineer, but during times of combat the gunner's position took priority. So far he'd seen only a glimpse of the Spitfire, but he was sure it was a Spit. "He follows."

The pilot, a veteran German Shepherd by the name of Rouse, did not panic. He'd just been one of the few to successfully make his bomb run and gotten away clean from the London debacle. His crew, showing exemplary bravery, stood by their guns giving measured bursts as they'd been taught to do. The only verbal outcry he'd heard on the intercom was when his bomb aimer's gun magazine ran out of ammunition at a critical moment. This was when he might have downed a Hurricane making a frontal assault. Luckily the fighter pilot's aim had also been off or they would all have perished. The aircraft passed so close that it severely buffeted the bomber. Collision was only averted by both pilot's moving their aircraft slightly in opposite directions at the last possible moment; the fighter up and the bomber down. Their closing speed had been dead on more than five hundred miles per hour and the passing was over in the blink of an eye. It would haunt the fighter pilot's dreams for months to come; this was his very first mission.

Pressing the radio transmit button Rouse calmly called out, "Achtung, achtung, achtung... Rouse One to any fighter aircraft in the vicinity of... " he looked out his window, "Dover. We are under attack and in need of assistance. Altitude fifteen thousand, speed two sixtyfive, direction one one zero."

There was a spat of static in his headphones and then he heard the words 'Zwei minuten.' (Two minutes). It wasn't much but it gave him hope. On the interphone he announced, "Help is coming be careful who you shoot at!"

Behind him and over the drone of his engines he heard the first stuttering sounds of machine gun fire.

§

Ducking out of the clouds, Archie found himself directly behind the Dornier with about a two thousand foot advantage in altitude. Flipping his gun button to 'fire' he pushed forward on his stick and made the downhill run. Angry sparks of tracers drifted up towards him as he calmly let the bomber fill his sights. When he felt he might actually reach out and touch the aircraft, he toggled a burst and then rolled to the right, streaking past in a full throated roar of engine and propeller. His mind recorded bits of debris flying from the right wing where he'd scored hits, but the small caliber of his guns and the self sealing fuel tanks of the bomber kept the damage minimal.

A single bullet cleanly passed through his Perspex, passing just over his head and through his shortened antlers. The pilot hardly noticed.

Derik was close enough to see the attack but too far away to do anything to prevent it. Diving in pursuit he automatically estimated an intersection point and aimed his aircraft at it. Activating his sight he flipped the gun switch off of 'safe'. Most of what he did was near the unconscious level. He didn't speak, he didn't think, he simply did. It was what made him so very effective in combat.

Archie banked hard left, coming around in a climb so he could make another pass at the bomber. Even at the all out speed of the fighter he could easily lose the larger aircraft if he didn't play his cards right. Maneuvers and climbs slowed any aircraft and Dorniers were known for their speed. Climbing also meant less distance covered laterally as well as the drastic reduction in speed from ascent. In more physical terms it was akin to a fully equipped soldier running uphill.

Tracers flashed past his aircraft just as he flew back into a cloud formation. He'd intended a straight on climb, but now reflex had him bank hard to the right. Ignoring his pursuer, he maintained a tight circle while continuing the climb that would bring him back around to where he could return the favor should he find the other fighter. The tone of his engine changed as the propeller dug into the air trying to keep the Spit from its approaching stall.

Derik, not even taking the time to curse his bad luck, banked away and climbed as steeply as he could. The 109's slots clunked open as he too narrowly skirted a stall. Instinct told him to stay on the fringes of the cloud his enemy had disappeared in. If he was to find the Spitfire he had to have eyes on visibility.

"Do you see him?" he called over the radio.

"Nein," Rouse replied. In the distance France's safety called to the bomber pilot in a siren's song as he and his crew anxiously swept the skies with their eyes. If attacked the pilot was ready to instantly take evasive action.

Inside the cloud Archie again changed course as he had a second thought about going after the Messerschmitt. How better to hurt his enemy than by downing what he sought to protect? In one respect this was ironic. Where the British pilot sought to protect his country, the bomber now represented Germany. By attacking it perhaps the other fighter pilot would understand that they could never win; the British people would never give up. 'Death Before Submission' was more than a simple motto.

With these words floating in his unconscious, the Dornier again became his primary target. In simpler terms; it would be much better if he could keep one less bomber from coming back and attacking his country again. Pressing his radio button he called out, "Control, Ninety Two Yellow Leader, I have a Dornier homeward bound… Tally Ho." Under his breath he muttered, "Better late than never."

He was surprised when Commander Falstaff's voice came back to him. "I'll give you a bottle of brandy if you give me a smoking hole Archie. Good hunting."

In Control, Winston Churchill stood next to the Commander. Both listened to the radio, wishing it was him in the cockpit of the fighter. To physically strike a blow in the name of his country would have been such a satisfying feeling. To risk their lives doing this the pair would have made willing payment to the Devil's piper in allowance for the dance.

Flattening out his turn the Stag brought the Egham Spit to a course aiming him towards France as he continued his climb inside the cloud. For a moment the aircraft popped out long enough to mark his prey as half a mile's distance and a thousand feet above. The cloud covered him again and he began a mental count, his mind already having calculated his closing speed and distance.

"I saw him!" the ventral gunner called out, "Seven 'o' clock, but he's back in the cloud again."

"Behind us and low," Rouse called out on the radio.

"Copy," Derik responded, quickly reversing his course to follow the bomber. He was in a perfect position to pounce, but if he was to be effective he would have to get closer.

On the ground, Master Sergeant Rathbone of the Royal Observer Corp pointed to the sky and the aerial ballet playing out above them. "Up there, boys," he told his fellow observers, "Looks like one of ours is chase'n two of theirs."

"I'll call it in," he heard Sergeant Whetherstone reply.

"Nay Percy, don't bother... they're outbound. Let's not clog the lines." To the sky he yelled, "Come on'n nail the bastard laddie!"

Sergeant Cragg joined the shout with a loud 'HOOZA!' as all three watched the duel play out almost a mile and a half above their heads.

The Egham Spit shot out of its cloud cover directly even with the bomber. To the bomber crew it appeared as if it had the uncanny ability of seeing through such conditions. The attack was flat out and straight in. Archie, keeping his eye and sights on the target, gave it three bursts. The long and middle distance attempts missed, but closer in the aft fuselage was riddled. The Stag distinctly saw pieces of the left rudder blow completely off as he passed. The Egham Spit was in turn hit five times, but as with his own guns the small caliber rounds of the bomber's defenses merely punched holes in the aluminum of his fuselage.

Seconds later there was a very uncomfortable vibration in his stick as a single cannon shell passed through his right elevator. Luck remained on his side as it was a non-explosive round; though it punched a large hole in the flight control. Fighting gut reaction Archie glanced in his rearview mirror and then rolled left into a spiraling dive leaving his throttle full on.

Derik, close behind, followed. The spray from his guns went wild, painting empty sky with their florescent trails.

Using the speed of his dive, Archie pulled back on his stick while adjusting to kill the roll. He couldn't afford to lose too much altitude or the bomber would get away. As his vision grayed under the 'G' forces placed upon his body, he found refuge in a cloud where he again climbed.

On board the Dornier, Rouse's crew cheered as they watched the chase, thinking the Englander had fled. This died in their throats as the Egham Spit appeared in an open space below them only to disappear again. Their enemy was followed an eye blink later by the yellow nosed fighter trying to protect them.

"We saw him," Rouse radioed. "You are close behind."

He heard a double click response of affirmation in his headset.

Dierk was now blind within the cloud. He had no idea how high it went or in which direction. The risk was huge with the possibility of crashing headlong into his adversary as he searched. The Britisher could be most anywhere... or nowhere at all if he'd decided to leave the area. His gut told him that would not be the case with this one. The pilot was a stubborn one or he would never have made the second pass. Glancing at his fuel gauge his mind estimated time remaining and then looked to his

ammunition counter where he also noted he had perhaps half of his allot-ment left. Moving his throttle into emergency over boost he gave up the tail on chase and climbed back out into the open; again seeking a position above and behind the Dornier.

Archie clutched the circular grip of his stick with both gloved paws as he equally muscled his aircraft through another high 'G' ma-neuver, hoping it would bring him once again into a good firing solution on the bomber. His fuel was good, but this was hardly a concern. If he ran low he could land anywhere below and still be recovered with little problem. Ammunition was certainly more of a worry as his counter told him he was down to one hundred rounds per gun from the original issue of three hundred and fifty. Pushing his throttle 'through the gate' and into the area of +12 boost emergency power, his engine fairly screamed with new power and he saw the needle of his vertical speed indicator move upwards dramatically.

"Indien, Indien, Indien!" the dorsal gunner yelled as he aimed his weapon. "Nine 'o' clock tail on, just out of the cloud! Cowboy is further out and in the clear," he added, referring to the yellow nosed Messer-schmitt now bearing in but still too far behind to prevent the attack.

"Do you see der Indien?" Rouse called over the radio.

"Ja," came the fighter pilot's terse reply. Locke was furious that he'd again missed stopping the attack. As with the Spitfire's first pass he could now only calculate a convergence and fly towards it; pressing his engine once again into over boost.

Archie's sense of where things were sharpened to a level he'd never before experienced. He saw the bomber and the gunner now firing at him. He knew the sky around him and its clouds. He also knew exactly where Locke was.

It was time to end this.

Bringing his throttle back to prevent his engine overheating, he lined up on the Dornier with an exact knowledge of what he was going to do. Unconsciously he pressed his radio's transmit button and began to softly voice the song he'd made up seemingly so very long ago. "Piss off Stewart, I'll not lend you a pence - Your pounds're all buried - Leaving naught to fix your fence."

In Control Steward Falstaff looked squarely at Sir Winston Churchill, his eyebrows going up in surprise. The Prime Minister smiled,winked, and then growled; "Now there's one calm professional. Perhaps we should look into publishing this particular song Stew. It seems to work quite well for our Flight Lieutenant."

On the completion of the ditty, they heard three distinct short burst of machine gun fire.

The Dornier's right engine flamed. Rouse immediately pulled the fire handle which shut off the fuel and feathered the prop. Next he fired off the engine's CO2 extinguisher. All the while the sounds of his crew returning fire surrounded him, filling his world in a cacophony of battle and the smell of cordite.

Dierk saw all of this and cursed, again feeling helpless against the onslaught of this one aircraft. Switching his gun sight back on his mind estimated a convergent course that would take him within firing distance of the escaping Spitfire.

This time, however, the Wolf was very wrong.

As soon as he'd done his damage, Archie pulled the Egham Spitfire into a hard right bank, not letting up until he was head on flying at the other fighter.

Closing speed for the pair was better than five hundred miles per hour… eight point three miles per minute… 0.139 miles per second… seven seconds to impact.

At the five count both pilots pressed their gun buttons and held them down. At the last possible moment the Messerschmitt went slightly high and the Spitfire slightly low causing a sever buffeting as one passed the other. Locke banked hard left and headed for cloud. Corn did the same but to the right.

Both disappeared in the blink of an eye.

Rouse, his paws full trying to keep his aircraft heading towards France called to his crew; securing all but the dorsal gun position so they could watch for any signs of fire on the wings. They were now out over open water and losing altitude but he was confident they would make it home; barring the stoppage of his remaining engine.

§

Archie's eyes swept his cockpit instruments. His compass said he was now flying due north. His altimeter's glass lens was cracked, but the indicator still appeared to be functioning and showed an even ten thousand feet. His artificial horizon also showed straight and level.

He was about to call Control when the cloud thinned and he found himself apparently flying in formation with the very pilot who'd just tried to kill him. The other aircraft had a streak of black smoke trailing from its exhaust stack indicating an impending engine failure.

Oddly the Stag felt no sense of panic and did not attempt to bank away. The German was peering at his indicators and had not yet looked up. This changed in a second with little surprise registering in the Wolf's eyes.

Both pilots removed their oxygen masks in the same movement. Archie made the hand signal for 'out of ammunition'.

Dierk made the hand signal for 'low on fuel'… and then saluted.

The British pilot returned the salute and then both aircraft banked away from each other.

"Control, Yellow Leader," Archie called on the radio.

"Go ahead," Falstaff replied.

"One Dornier damaged… Ammunition nil… returning to Holy Ground. Sorry sir, no smoking holes."

"Copy that. The Prime Minister sends his regards and we both extend a 'well done'. Drinks on me tonight in any case… you were all magnificent."

"For all of us," the Stag responded, "Thank you, sir."

The airwaves then went silent and the drone of the Egham's engine filled his thoughts as he put in enough rudder to come around to a homeward course. His aircraft sounded pleased and the pilot was reminded of a cat's purring.

"The clouds come and go," he heard in his headset. Her voice was like a soothing medicine to his pounding heart. "Just like two aircraft from different worlds. I am very proud of you Archie."

Her words came with his glance at the ammunition counter. It showed each gun having twenty rounds left. Looking to his right he found Terrance formed up on his wing tip.

He smiled and his heart indeed hurt at seeing her vision. "From the same world love; just different governments building them," he told her without pressing his 'talk' button. There was no need. He knew she could hear him just as he could hear her. "I thought I would never see you again. Is it now over?"

She shook her head sadly. The clouds came back again and she was gone.

§

Commander Falstaff stood outside the entrance to Control next to the Prime Minister. Mrs. Churchill was already in their limousine with his secretary, patiently waiting for her husband. The pair was alone for the moment in the cool dusk of early evening.

"What do you think Stew?" the old Bulldog asked the other. For all intents and purposes they truly looked related. "Did we make Herr Wolf understand he would lose his one remaining testicle if he attempts a channel crossing?"

Falstaff chuckled and produced his flask. He'd thoughtfully had it refilled since its last use. Passing it over, he said, "If we didn't, then the bastard is totally deranged and will get what he deserves."

Churchill raised the flask slightly and said simply, "England will never surrender."

Falstaff, accepting it back, lifted it in a similar fashion and agreed, "England will never surrender."

"Do me a favor Stew," the Prime Minister instructed, "Let us finish the day on a positive note. Ring up Bomber Command and have them launch everything possible. Tell them I wish them to bomb the snot out of every Jerry barge they can get their sights on." Accepting the flask back again he raised it slightly and intoned, "In this way we will say, 'Thank you very much for the day Mr. Hitler, and here is a little dessert for your enjoyment'."

He passed the flask back to the Commander after taking a good swallow. He, in turn, lifted it and said, "Never, never, never, give up."

Sir Winston smiled. "I like that… may I use it?"

"Certainly sir."

"Don't call me sir."

"Yes sir."

The pair shared a quiet laugh then. Their work was far from done and both understood this.

The times were something to be lived through.

Rest was for the afterlife.

"Never, never, never give up."
—Sir Winston Churchill

§

"The war continued of course."

Group Commander (retired) Henry Badcock regarded his museum tour group through the eyes of someone who had been there. He suddenly felt very tired. Trying to explain the war to people who had not lived through it was becoming more and more difficult.

"Though September 15th was the turning point in the Battle of Britain, things were hardly over," he continued. "Girding our loins and counseling each other to patience, we continued the fight, resolving to lay down our lives for the sake of England if that's what we had to do. Many of the lads I flew with did exactly that and now they are little more than a footnote in a history book."

"I would fly for England," said the little Fox girl who'd so touched the old Bulldog's heart during the tour.

"So long as I am alive," he said, reaching to touch her nose, "you are exactly the England of which I speak and I would willingly be your wingman."

Straightening again, he looked back to the adults of the group and told them, "We had a great leader in those dark dark times. His name was Sir Winston Churchill. The writers of history will paint him however they wish depending on what they desire to prove… but I am here to tell you he stood shoulder to shoulder with us and led this country by never looking at the back of another's head."

Stepping up to the small stage in front of the group he told them, "Just for a moment I would like you to pretend that I am that great fellow as I recite for you a portion of the speech he made on the BBC radio, July 14th, 1940. I'm told I do a rather good imitation."

Touching a switch on the wall, the lights dimmed but for a spotlight that illuminated the old time microphone next to the podium which the retired pilot stepped forward to stand behind. Placing a pair of reading glasses upon his pug like face, he held up a well worn piece of paper and began to read aloud.

"And now it has come to us to stand alone in the breach and face the worst that the tyrant's might and enmity can do. Bearing ourselves humbly before God, but conscious that we serve an unfolding purpose, we are ready to defend our native land against the invasion by which it is threatened. We are fighting by ourselves alone; but we are not fighting for ourselves alone. Here in this strong City of Refuge which enshrines the title-deeds of human progress and is of deep consequence to Christian civilization; here, girt about by the seas and oceans where the Navy reigns; shielded from above by the prowess and devotion of our airmen-we await undismayed the impending assault. Perhaps it will come tonight. Perhaps it will come next week. Perhaps it will never come. We must show ourselves equally capable of meeting a sudden violent shock or-what is perhaps a harder test-a prolonged vigil. But be the ordeal sharp or long, or both, we shall seek no terms, we shall tolerate no parley; we may show mercy-we shall ask for none."

When he was finished, there was a hush and he held a paw up to keep it so.

"As a pilot… one who flew Spitfires during that time… I would like to now read you a poem about that proud aircraft which was written by my dear friend Flight Lieutenant Archie Corn. It's called simply 'Airplane' and is dedicated to his Egham Spitfire. I should explain that as a means to raising money for the purchase of these aircraft, a community that could raise the sum of 5,000 pounds would have a Spitfire named after it; and so Egham did, God Bless them. By today's standards, this would equal to around half a million pounds."

Clearing his throat, he began his recitation with great feeling and depth.

Airplane

"Not alive, as in living and breathing,
Not a creature of mental instability,
She rises from the ground as a thoroughbred
To the sole purpose of her breeding;
Meant to jump high up within the thinness
Of the atmosphere
And I am awed."

"This beautiful creature abides my presence
Huddled within her cockpit amidst
Lumens of exactitude and indication.
Like a tumorous lump benign in my existence,
She understands the requirement for my touch."

"How much longer until she will be free
To live among the clouds with the ghosts of her ancestors?"

"As we fly together, I dream for her
Knowing that in the end, when she is worn out,
Much as her pilot she will be laid to rest,
Never to fly again."

"We will be but ghosts of what went before then,
Remembered for a generation or two
Until even that is taken by oblivion."

"And yet we both shall ever hear the music of children's voices
Pretending they can fly"

When he was finished there was not a dry eye in the tour group.

"What happened to your friend?" the little girl asked for everyone.

Henry smiled at her, but it was a sad smile. "He was killed in action my dear."

"But his airplane is here."

"He was flying another on that day. The Egham Spit was later relegated to training duties and after the war I found her in the scrap heap. I brought her here and you can see the wonderful job the Kiwis did restoring her. I still fly her every now and again."

After the tour was completed, Henry came back into the museum feeling very tired. Finding the museums afternoon maintenance attendant, he told him, "Do me a favor Johnnie, I removed the wax figure of Archie Corn to Commander Sheltie's motorbike sidecar during that last tour."

"Right, sir, move him back again I will."

"No, no," the Bulldog replied, passing over a folded hundred pound note, "Leave him where he is. I want you to take the Egham Spit out to the tarmac and fuel her up just like in the old days. While I am still able I would like to spend a bit of quality time with her."

Johnnie gratefully accepted the bill, tucking it away in his pocket. His rent was due and he was a bit short. "You'll be all right, sir?"

"Of course I will. I'm just feeling a need to revisit the past for a bit. I'll have the cook make me a good breakfast in the morning."

"Just like in the old days, sir?"

Henry clapped the fellow on the shoulder and smiled his very best 'meet the enemy head on' smile. "Just like in the old days Johnnie."

Gone for Burton

In commercial flying, they say the really good pilots don't have any stories; there's nothing to tell but the boredom of safe take offs and even safer landings. To this, I would grumble something which might, or might not, include the words 'cow poop'. Obviously, the captain I've been tasked to fly with is not a very good one since he hasn't shut up since we made altitude. I can't wait for our approach to roll around so he has to be quiet by law. God help me, but I got stuck with a merry old Royal Bull Dog, and from the sounds of his accent, a Bristol lad at that. Somehow, I can't picture his bulbous frame in the seat of a fighter, but that's what he claims he was; a Spitfire pilot. Pure guff, says I!

"Excuse me, sir, but you said you flew a Buford Blueberry? Was that a transport or one of those huge gliders?"

I shouldn't have goaded him, I suppose, but I was pretty well fed up with his fanciful war stories. These were modern times, and this was a modern aircraft with about as much zip as a rail car with wings.

"You best watch your mouth, pup," he shouted at me, turning bright red. His pushed in looking face actually wore a snarl, and for a bare moment, I thought perhaps he might strike me. Apparently, cargo transports and gliders were quite the insult to the fighter types. "Know your place, you wet behind the ears diapered little snot. Close your ears and open your mouth is all yur good for, apparently ya egotistical little brass balled shit head! I flew Spitfires; the best damned aircraft in the war, bar none, and sod anyone who says different!"

Apparently I'd touched a raw nerve with a 2000 volt magneto wire. I should have kept my yap closed, but being a Corgi, I just had to

378

have the last word. "Really? I've always heard the Messerschmitt 109 E Type could fly rings around the Spitfire. Statistics don't lie, Captain. As I recall, the Wolf engineers had it balls on, and the performance data collected during the war clearly showed the superiority."

Giving me the most disapproving look I'd ever seen, the old bastard flips the autopilot off and tells me to take the wheel so he can go have a squirt. "Keep your oxygen mask on while I'm gone," he instructs me, as if I didn't know to do that. "It's for safety, though I suddenly find the cockpit stinking of unpolished brass green."

When he got back he was sipping a coffee. "None for me thank you very much," and he didn't speak another word except for what was required.

I had no idea silence could be so cold.

§

We landed in Stonenpassen right on schedule. The old boy personally took us in, and I will admit, the landing was glass smooth. The wheels didn't so much as squeal when we touched down and there we were on the ground taxing in. The crew had a three day required rest here. I was rather looking forward to sitting next to the hotel's pool by day and maybe do a little clubbing with the stewardess' at night. We had three onboard and I knew at least two of them were good for it. If only things had been that easy… if only…

Rest?

What's rest when you have a war to fight?

§

A small Fox with very large ears turns from the airport terminal's window where she's been watching a silver tube with wings taxiing to the gate. There's a large clock on the wall behind her which is slowly turning backwards and her demeanor is of one who has a secret. She holds a cigarette in her right paw, the smoke curling up around her head.

"In every occupation," she says in a dead pan expression of seriousness, "there is the fledgling and there is the seasoned veteran. Nowhere is this more poignant than in the cockpit of an aircraft. George Corgi, hatchling flyer of the first degree and wearing his bright new wings on the front of a crisp new uniform has found himself serving as First Officer to one Captain Henry Badcock. He has made the mistake of forgetting the very first rule of aviation; respect experience. The veteran is still alive so he obviously did something right."

"Though he has three days off in a city that lived through the last war, it is doubtful First Officer Corgi will find any rest. Inadvertently, and through an ego never before tarnished by the requirements of war, he has crossed the line that separates his everyday reality from The Fur Side."

§

OK, so I screwed up.

Yes this was my first 'for real' commercial flight with the big boys. Yes I had an inside connection that got me on board with the company and placed into training so I could sit right seat on milk runs like Stonenpassen. It's all about building your hours so someday you'll get to pinch the Stewardess' bottom while going for a squirt.

As it is, Stonenpassen had been so bombed out during the war that almost the entire city is newly built. That meant the airport had the latest and greatest of everything; including top notch air traffic controllers. I was warned well in advance by my peers not to joke with them over the radio and to 'never ever' crack wise about incoming bombers. That advice was understandable and I held to the warning; but at this point I desperately wanted to get my paws on the crew scheduler who'd let old Spitfire Badcock muscle his way in to take the flight as captain. He should have warned me off on that one too!

Badcock, still grumping as if I'd stolen his favorite toy, left me with the post flight check and close up of the aircraft. He then took off with the stewardess' in tow; all of them Collies and not a bad looking one among them. Apparently, they knew more about his reputation than I did and were quite taken with the pug nosed old bastard. Perhaps I deserved it for being cheeky. This wasn't the first time I'd had my tail handed to me for flapping my gums. What could I do but chalk it off as another lesson learned the hard way. I would have to catch up with them later. It was an easy guess I'd also have a long hike to the hotel as the crew bus would come only once. No bother really; a Corgi's legs are short but they're stout. I figured after such a long flight the tramp would be good for me.

Striking out on my own, duffle in paw, I padded along until I'd built up a pretty good thirst. I was in luck as Stonenpassen was renowned for two things. One was their beer gardens, which were among the best in the world, and the other was the little known fact they were home to the largest porcelain toilet bowl factory in the world. I suppose there is true irony in this. If you look at it with humor, you'll see they have you at both ends of the spectrum.

Spying one of the gardens, my eye was drawn to the sign above the door which bore the likeness of an old Wolf fighter aircraft.

'So be it', I remember thinking to myself, 'And the fates have spoken.'

As in most bars the lights were low and the air cool with more than a hint of stale beer; perfect for dodging the day and unwinding. In my uniform I stood out from the locals like a brass nickel in a pocketful of silver. I was used to this actually and rather enjoyed the notoriety it gave me. What's the expression; 'Women love a fellow in uniform'? Making my way to a quiet booth I threw my duffel in first, sat, and then signaled for some service. The place was pretty incredible actually. Pictures of all sorts of Wolf aircraft from the war hung on the walls. Some bore the autographs of the pilots standing next to them and still others hung with individual medals below them; obviously awarded to someone who no longer had a use for them.

The waitress, an older yet quite pretty poodle, paused to light my cigarette before taking my order. She was wearing a name tag that said 'Jeans' and I noticed the lighter had a strange emblem on it; a heart shaped falcon. Inside of the bird's outline was a spider impaled upon a fencing sword. It didn't take me long to notice the barkeep watching me as he dried a huge stein. He wore an eye patch and one side of his neck, the side with the patch, was bare of fur as if it had been touched by fire.

"Did you fly?" I called over to him.

"Ja… Messerschmitt 109s," was his only reply. He then filled the stein and handed it to the barmaid for delivery.

How unfair the world was, I reflected as I gazed upon the fellow. Here he was most certainly almost killed and his only reward was to linger among his memories in this bar while His Royal Arse Henry Badcock was allowed to lord it over my cockpit.

After that I drank in silence until I was ready to leave. Surprisingly, there was a car waiting for me outside. The uniformed driver stood quietly curbside wearing a very old style uniform. He was also holding up a small sign with my name on it. Perhaps, I reasoned, Badcock felt guilty about how badly he'd treated me and sent this fellow to bring me to the hotel.

Too many Stonenpassen beers had gone down the old hatch while I looked at the pictures on the bar's walls; I was too tired to ask any questions. As the driver opened the door for me, I simply threw my bag in and then climbed into the back after it; where I promptly dozed off.

§

"Wake up!"

The shout was right in my ear and my eyes popped opened. At the best of times my nervous system seemed to have a buffer zone that kept me from jerking and jumping during times of shock. 'Nerves of steel,' my mum would say. 'Stupid id'jut child,' my Da would reply. Of course when the bucket of water hit me I was up and swinging. This was followed by the coarse laughter of at least five Wolfs. Damnation but I would know that accent anywhere. Stranger still; I understood every last word they spoke.

"Look there Fritzi, Herr Brass Balls comes up like a real fighter, ja?"

"Ja, Howler, mitt der vasser com'n zee fists of…"

Fritzi never finished whatever he'd been about to say because my right paw connected. It flattened his nose with a satisfying thud. Next my foot swept the feet out from under the one holding the bucket and he went to the floor with a jarring thump. Picking up the wooden chair at the table next to me I was about smash it over his head when there was a shouted command.

'STILLGESTANDEN!'

Where everyone that could immediately snapped to rigid attention, I was left holding a chair over my head, blinking at what my mind was finally recording. The five individuals who apparently anticipated some fun at my expense were all wearing the same black and gray uniform. Gold eagles decorated their collars and each bore an arm patch of a spider impaled on a fencing sword inside of an almost heart shaped outline of a falcon.

"Was geht hier vor? [What goes on here?]" asked a very civil sounding voice edged in ice.

"Ve are dancing, Herr Commandant," the one named Howler replied a little too calmly. Had we not been interrupted, I am sure I would have bashed his brains out, so I was just a little bit stunned that he would make an excuse for me. There was a mumbled chorus of agreements.

"Und vat exactly is this dance called?" the Wolf asked, looking directly at me. His uniform was exactly like all of the others except his collar was done up tight around his neck and he wore a short tricolor ribbon culminating in what I recognized as the Wolf's Knight's Cross with Oak Leaves and Swords… only a few notches below their highest decoration of the war.

"Die Messing Farren [The Brass Bullocks]," I muttered, not being able to come up with anything better. My mouth tasted like mud and even I could smell the vomit on my breath.

"You flew well yesterday, Lieutenant," the Commandant replied, his face poker straight serious, "But that is no excuse for you to drink yourself to stupidity. What if we had to scramble?" He left that hang in the air for everyone's benefit, and then, when the timing was perfect, furthered, "If this happens again, I will have you and your mess mates digging latrines for the mechanics, am I clear? You all have a responsibility to each other… it is how you will survive. Fly alone… die alone… zo… like a good Staffel, you will be punished together, no?"

In the distance there was an explosion but no one seemed to notice. As for me; there were only the eyes of the Wolf through which he willed me to abeyance. "Jahohl, Mein Herr," I replied softly, setting the chair slowly to the floor.

"At ease," the Wolf gently commanded and the room loosened up considerably. To me he said, "Sit in the chair, Herr B. B. before you fall over."

As bad as I felt, I didn't question the order. Yes this was as odd as it could get. Yes, upon regarding myself, I found I too was wearing a black and gray uniform. Some things, I also noticed, are able to be changed and some things are not. Though I wore the uniform, I still had the build and coloring of a Corgi, perhaps a third less large than any of the Wolfs in the room. If this was meant as a practical joke, it was well planned out and executed. Pity I felt too ill to have a good laugh over it.

"Yesterday," the Commandant began, "Our Royal friends doggedly tried once again to force us to submission."

There was a group chuckling at this comment. I looked up at our apparent leader from where I sat with my head almost between my legs. He looked vaguely familiar, as though I'd seen him before somewhere… but my brain was not yet banging away on all of its cylinders.

"I vould like to zay that we showed well for ourselves, having shot down three Spitfires to the loss of only one Messerschmitt; but the loss of a pilot or any aircraft is a matter of somber reality. It is true they left with tails between their legs; but we lost Jeffry."

There was a quiet pause as the Wolf began to slowly pace among his pilots.

"As you all know," he finally continued, "I claimed but one Spit-ire, while Herr B.B. shot down the other two."

To my amazement, everyone applauded loudly. Looking up, I found the Commandant smiling at me and leading the applause. For some reason I felt I should stand, which I did, nodded to him and then sat again before I fell over. Coming to me, he reached into his breast pocket and pulled out a handful of grass. Holding it out to me, he said softly, "Eat this and go puke behind the barracks, you will feel better."

I took it from him gratefully after which he told the room, "They were here yesterday and that means they most assuredly will be back tomorrow to extract their revenge; but this time we will be waiting for them. Beginning at dawn, we will sally two aircraft at a time to cover the field. Conserve your fuel as much as possible. You will have drop tanks and fly to half of the internal tank. When you get to this point you will buzz the field, where upon the next two will take off. When the Royals come in it will be at treetop level… a fast pass to strafe and bomb. Those flying cover will dive upon them which will scatter their formation and neutralize the attack's effectiveness. Those on the ground will then take off and fly to the attack. Engines will be started and idled every 30 minutes to keep them warm. Are there any questions?"

No one had any.

"Goot… Get your heads straight and report to your aircraft in one hour. Go over them with your mechanics and then ve will make flights of two. Watch for targets, hit and come back." Looking to me, he said, "Herr Brass Balls, you vill be my wing. Now go eat your grass und puke; best to get it over with." Placing a paw on my shoulder he told me, "I remember how it was with my first kill. You vill get past this."

§

As I walked towards my aircraft my mind was in a steep dive, its wings stuttering and on the brink of snapping off. If this was a dream it was the most detailed and realistic dream I'd ever had. I even had flashes of my old philosophy teacher grinning at me and asking, 'What is reality?' If he'd been real I would have punched him and darned if I didn't think he knew that too.

"Herr B.B.," my mechanic called to me as I approached. At least I assumed he was my mechanic. Apparently my nickname was the Royal expression: Brass Balls. "I have your aircraft ready for you, sir." He then snapped to attention as I walked around the craft.

On both sides of the hull, in extremely large painted letters, were back to back red B's

On the rudder I saw two freshly painted small vertical bars bearing British insignia and the word 'Spitfire'. As I finished my walk around, the mechanic saluted me. "It was Herr Oberst's orders, sir. He believes you deserve a special recognition symbol." The little Skunk smiled at me then and said in a lower voice, "Three more kills, sir, and you become an ace; then I can paint your aircraft's nose yellow."

The hairs on the back of my neck suddenly stood on end. I'm not sure if it was the idea that I'd actually killed someone or if it was the fact that I was falling into this dream hook line and sinker. I decided to test something. "Tell me... ahhh... how shall I address you old sport?"

The mechanic gave me a sidewise glance and a strange smile.

"What is it? What's wrong?"

"Nothing, Mein Heir... except... you sounded rather British for a moment. It was a good impersonation. I am Feldwebel (Sergeant) Aloysius Skunk, Mein Herr... but you knew that."

"Of course I did. And why do you not fly? I can see the love of it written on you clearly."

He looked down a bit, his eyes suddenly not meeting mine. "Because I am not a Wolf," he replied softly. "Thank you for reminding me, Mein Heir."

"And what am I?" I asked. Certainly my jaw must have dropped as he made his last statement.

"A Wolf, sir," he told me as if by rote. He then got this boyish smile and glanced up at me. "A Wolf with two kills und a very good flyer. I've watched you, sir... you are not ham fisted like the others in your group." Placing a paw on the aircraft, he said, "She flies for you, Mein Heir; as if you were her lover."

He was very earnest in what he was telling me. I looked at my paws and saw a Corgi's paws and yet there I was in a Luftwaffe uniform. Fishing a pack of smokes from my breast pocket, I motioned for the Sergeant to walk a distance away from the aircraft and then offered him one. Stuffing a paw into one pocket, I came out with a cigarette lighter emblazoned with the squadron's emblem; 'the spider on a stick' as I wanted to call it. Shaking a cig out for him, I took one myself and held the lighter for both of us.

When we'd inhaled and each let out a cloud of smoke, I mimicked flying through it with my paw, much to the Skunk's amusement. "So you would like to be a pilot then?" I asked him.

"Very much so," he responded. "Perhaps later in the war I will be given a chance, ja? Right now we need to win und to do that, you need a good mechanic; that would be me."

I nodded, and then, keeping an eye open for anyone's approach, I grilled him on the aircraft. I asked him what did he think, what did he know, how in heck you even raised and lowered the landing gear. The last thing I needed was the Commandant's name and then I felt I could fudge my way through almost anything.

"Aloysius, I'm afraid I drank too much last night and though my stomach feels better my head has swelled and I'm having a brain fart."

"Brain fart, sir?"

"Yes… brain fart… I, for the life of me, cannot think of Herr Oberst's name. Imagine my embarrassment should he call me on the radio and I didn't know how to respond."

The Skunk chuckled as if he'd been expecting this question.

"You find that funny?"

"No, sir," he responded, dropping the cigarette butt on the ground and grinding it under his heel, "But Herr Locke said that you were so drunk last night you would probably forget your own name this morning. He said nothing about his."

"How many kills does Herr Oberst have now?" I asked.

"Sixty five. I dare say there is no one his equal in the air."

"I dare say," I repeated, grinding my own cigarette under heel and letting the expression run away to nothing. Walking back to the aircraft, I inspected the name under the cockpit. It glared back at me in stark Wolf; Oberleutnant George Wolf.

"Fuck me," I muttered, and then from the other side of the aircraft I heard an engine roar to life followed by several others.

§

Locke was beyond good and his patience with a rookie was incredible. We flew west over a vast countryside of farmland. As we climbed to altitude I could see the channel ahead of us, though we did not venture out so far. Taking off in the Messerschmitt 109 was a bit of a trick. Damned if I didn't almost roll right over and barrel into the ground as soon as I was airborne. The torque the huge engine and propeller exerted was incredible.

"Too much throttle, Herr B.B.," I heard over my headset just as the roll began.

In a panic, I chopped power and almost nosed in while working the stick and rudder pedals like a madman to recover from the roll. Finally gaining control of the aircraft, I pointed her nose to the sky with a howl of happiness.

"Where is that fighter pilot from yesterday?" asked that same voice in a chuckle. "Climb to ten and continue east at two hundred. I'll catch up and take the lead. Stay on my tail and do not lose me."

"Ja," I responded calmly. The word felt strange but correct all in the same moment. My mouth was obviously speaking Wolf, but my brain was still thinking Canine. Yes, they had their similarities, but...

"The proper response would be 'jahohl', Oberleutnant, but then again I prefer calm and steady rather than exuberance when flying. In the air I am simply your lead and you are my wing man. Keep the radio chatter that simple. We are formal on the ground because the military dictates we must be. After the war, if we are both still alive, you may then address me by my first name of Dierk."

Pulling my throttle back and leaning out the fuel mixture with a mind to engine temperature, I watched the altimeter wind around and around, mindful that I still had a need to see everywhere around me. It was a chore to be sure, but one that I was finding enjoyable. Even with the bulbous drop tank mounted on it, the aircraft had such an incredible feeling of power. Touch the stick and she responded like a ballerina; so unlike the lead sled I was used to sitting right seat in; and so unlike the trainers I'd spent hours and hours flying. I soon became lost in just the sensation of it... the engine noise, the glint of sunlight off of the glass, the sound of the air rushing past, the sensuous feel of the stick in my paw...

With a jarring thump of disturbed air, a yellow nosed Messerschmitt over flew me in a dive that left bare feet between my propeller and his underbelly.

"Was that the stick or your penis in your paw Oberleutnant B. B.? I flew upside down above you just now trying to figure it out before diving. You are quite dead, by the way."

Before I could stop myself I'd pushed the throttle forward and was diving after the other fighter; or at least I thought I was. Within seconds, we'd both punched a hole in an errant cloud and when I came out on the other side he was nowhere to be seen.

"Are you behind me?" Locke asked calmly.

"No, " I replied, trying to keep my voice steady. I was pissed to be sure. If I'd known we would be playing silly games I would have...

"I have just killed you again," he said in that deadly calm voice. "You have now paid back the two kills from yesterday. Shall I have the stripes taken off of your rudder?"

"Jahohl!" I replied a little too strongly. Fucking bastard!

There was a chuckle over the radio set. "Did you just call me a 'fucking bastard'?" he asked in his deadpan voice. "I can assure you my family is quite pure in its breeding… all well documented; all Wolf."

I strained my neck looking for him, trying to remember if I'd actually spoken the words. Finally I found him by holding my thumb up to the sun, causing it to eclipse. "No, sir," I responded nosing the aircraft upwards. "I did not say that."

"Mind your engine temp and conserve your fuel Oberleutnant. Leave the throttle at full for too long and things begin to go badly."

Mentally cursing myself, I inched the throttle back to climb and away from full military power. I then jettisoned my drop tank to reduce drag. Even in the lead sled we had to watch that little bit. Easing off of the stick, I banked and began an easy spiral upwards to join my lead. Obviously climbing into a fight was not the optimum way to attack; score one for the teacher. This time, I kept my eyes bloody well on him, though he made no effort to evade me.

The rest of the patrol was pretty boring. Nothing was spotted and pretty much all was just practice staying on Locke's tail where I would range left and then right; always watching and looking for an enemy aircraft. I would be told later by my mess mates that this was indeed a rare day as none of them saw anything while in the air. If nothing else, they also told me, in cases like this when some of our own bombers were sighted they would be given a cautious fly by and if the crews were relatively new a mock dogfight might ensue so everyone could practice tracking with their guns.

Coming back, I was to land first as I'd taken off first and so gently ranged in having been given the 'all clear' flag when doing my fly by. Landing the Messerschmitt, I found, was not so easy. With the flaps and slots down it handled well enough at low speeds. In that there was no problem in maneuverability; but as soon as the wheels touched the earth I could sense things getting dicey. Let's just say the feeling was similar to riding a bicycle on ice. I had to fight to keep my body from tensing as the hair on the back of my neck stood on end. Where all the trainers I ever landed were gentle and would stay on a straight line 'paws off'; the Messerschmitt immediately began jinking left or right on its own due to the narrowness of the landing gear. I kept the tail in the air as long as possible so I could use the rudder to good effect and stayed off of the brakes. When the tail finally settled I then, very carefully, used the brakes to slow further. Being a tail dragger, I was also immensely aware that too much applied brake and the airplane's nose would flip down to burry itself in the dirt. Touch one side or the other too hard and you could also spin out in a ground loop collapsing the gear. Either accident had the same effect of putting you out of action.

Opening the canopy, I taxied to my ready spot, near blind from the nose up attitude and near choking on the exhaust fumes. This called for a lot of rudder and brake work as I occasionally slewed to the right to see what was ahead. My paws were sweating as I worked and I grumbled curses wondering if I would ever wake from this dream. Most likely I would be sitting in the booth at the beer garden with drool running down my chest.

Then I saw a red fare cross the field and people began running everywhere.

Before I could even contemplate what I was doing, I'd pulled my canopy closed again and pushed the throttle forward, rolling in the only direction available; straight ahead. At that point I had no idea who or what was directly in front of me. In twenty feet my tail was back up and I could see again. Unfortunately there was a hanger taking up the area I needed to go through in order to get airborne. Mechanics and Wolfs were running out of the building and more than a few were waving their arms at me.

There was nothing I could do at this point but pull back on the stick and pray. With the engine howling and the prop literally chewing through the air, I barely cleared roof. The wind sock mounted there was not so lucky as it was instantly shredded. Eat or be eaten, I thought as yellow material sprayed outwards. At that same moment a burst of tracer flew just over me at a diagonal.

I quickly found out that reality during the high stress moments of combat slows down considerably. You haven't time to think so much as react. That's why your training is so crucial; you need to react in the proper manner. In my case, you could say my training was a big fat nil, but at least… well… I can't take any credit; things just happened the way they happened.

Reality: if I had banked to either side, the up turned wing would have been riddled. As luck would have it I pushed down on the right rudder pedal as hard as I could and the craft's nose swung to the right just as the Royal Spitfire overflew me. "Bollocks!" I swore and mashed down on the firing button. There was a mechanical stutter and the aircraft shook as my two machine guns and single cannon hammered out in blind retribution for a well done sneak attack. Apparently my rounds found the fellow's fuel tanks as there was an enormous explosion. In the split second I had to see what happened I watched the unlucky bugger pin wheel into a large oak tree and burn. Instinctively I banked away keeping my throttle full on to avoid flying through any debris. Black smoke poured from my exhaust as the fuel injection system did its job to perfection pumping an overly rich mixture into the cylinders. I climbed then looking left, right, above, below, behind, over and over and over, until I saw a Spitfire at tree top level screaming in towards the airstrip. He had Locke full in his sights and though the ace was already attempting to climb back up I knew the Royal pilot had him cold.

Without even considering I could be killed, I rolled and began a power induced dive equally screaming with the howl of the engine as my gauges clearly red lined. Not even aiming I punched the fire button and tracers reached out at the Spitfire. My cannon was first to run out of ammunition, but the machine guns continued rattling as I overflew and then banked left as tight as I could to get back on his tail. My leading edge slots fell out indicating I was very close to stalling but I wasn't concerned with close. I had him… he was mine… he was… To my surprise, the fellow's landing gear popped down as he too banked to the left, trying to reverse his direction.

As a boy and listening to every story available about flying, the one thing I knew for certain was; '*Landing gear down in a combat situation is the same as an infantryman raising his arms and waving a white flag – surrender!*'

That was when I saw Locke bearing in from my right with a vengeance. "He has surrendered, Mein Herr!" I called over the radio. "He is my prisoner!"

All I heard in response was, 'Das ist mir furzegal! Er ist ein fucking bastard ohne Ehre. [*I don't give a fuck! He is a fucking bastard with no honor.*]

Obviously Herr Locke had forgotten his own admonition about getting angry. Leaving the throttle full on, I followed the Royal, stuffing my aircraft behind his, blocking my Commandant's shot.

"Royal Dog, Royal Dog," I called over the radio. "I accept your surrender, land immediately or be shot down."

Herr Locke followed my commands on the radio translating them to Dog. The thought that the Royal pilot might not understand Wolf hadn't even occurred to me.

There was a stream of expletives that colored the radio waves red and then the pilot's gruff voice said something about 'bloody Hades freezing over'.

"Your landing gear is down," I called out. "You cannot gain speed to escape."

Locke, now flying to my right, kicked left rudder and fired off a volley of tracers directly across the Spitfires path. He followed this with what I took as a translation of my words. Too low to bail out, the Spitfire dropped speed and his canopy rolled back. A paw came out into the slip stream and waved. We were dead on to the airfield, so landing would be in and simple. Seeing that my fuel warning light was on, I checked my fuel gage and saw we were not a moment too soon; I had only about ten minutes left in the air.

§

To say pandemonium broke out when we landed would be an understatement. No sooner had the Royal switched off his engine, he was surrounded by a multitude of pilots and mechanics. More than a few pistols were pointed at him as he climbed out of the cockpit seemingly oblivious to any of it. He had a scarf around his neck and a leather flying helmet with his goggles pulled well up onto his forehead. He was a Bulldog to be sure and as obstinate as they come.

"I want to speak to your Commander!" he bellowed at those gathered around his craft. "I did not surrender!"

My mechanic came forward and cordially relieved the fellow of his pistol. This he handed to me as I walked up, fresh out of my own aircraft. The crowd parted when they noticed my presence as if I was some sort of ancient deity and they were the ocean. Word spread quickly of what had transpired from those who'd witnessed the miracle of my clearing the hanger, the snapshot kill, and then the dive that had saved Herr Locke... but for all of this I was totally unaware except for the fellow who now stood before me.

Standing at attention, he saluted me, and says, "Flight Lieutenant Henry Badcock, 92 Squadron at your service, sir. There seems to have been a mistake, I did not surrender. I did not put my landing gear down... damnation they came down all on their own. You should have shot me down. I sure as shit would have punched your ticket."

For the life of me, I didn't understand a word he said, except for the name. It was Captain 'The Spitfire's The Best Aircraft Ever' Badcock; a much younger Badcock to be sure but it was him. Either my dream had just gotten better or it had become a true nightmare. Gor… if he ever even suspected I was flying for the Wolfs…

"Aloysius," I said to my mechanic, "What the devil is he saying?"

"I think he is complaining we did not offer him a beer upon landing," my mechanic replied with a smile. "He's doesn't know how lucky he is that no one has shot him yet."

"He claims he never put his gear down," one of the other pilots told me. I saw that it was the one we called Fritzi. I nodded my thanks to him for this information.

"There will be no shooting," I called out loud enough for everyone else to hear. Turning my attention to my mechanic, I then said, "Do me a favor Aloysius; be a good lad and check his landing gear handle. Tell me if it is up or down."

The little Skunk pushed past the surprised Bulldog and climbed up into the cockpit. "The handle is up, sir," he said loudly after a second's inspection, "Fuel is just over half."

"Sprecken zee Dog?" Badcock tried and everyone around him laughed.

"I speak Dog very well," Commandant Locke said as he approached. The men separated for him as they had for me and I suddenly found myself standing next to the tall Wolf. Returning the enemy flyer's salute, he nodded to me and said in Dog, "This is Oberleutnant Georg Wolf. You owe him your life because I was going to kill you." He quickly translated for everyone else present. There was a murmur amongst the troops.

"I think he was saying he never put his gear down, Mein Herr," I told Locke. "My Sergeant has confirmed his lever is in the up position."

"What a pity," the other pilot replied. His voice was like ice and I wasn't sure if he was angry with me or Badcock. Finally he said, "He's your responsibility, Herr B. B. Your actions today obviously lived up to your Staffel-Spitzname so I should not be too upset with you. You are a competent wingman and as it turns out saved my hairy ass when it needed saving."

He thought about this for a moment, or perhaps about something else… I can't be all that sure; but when he was done thinking he told me, "Get Herr Royal Dog cleaned up and bring him to the mess hall for dinner. He shall be out guest for at least the night and then we shall send him on to be processed as a prisoner of war."

Looking to Aloysius, who was still sitting in the Spitfire's cockpit, he told him, "Paint two more stripes on Herr B.B.'s rudder. We shall give him credit where credit is due."

As the Wolf calmly walked away, my back was pounded upon as I was loudly congratulated by the Staffel. As to poor old Badcock, he was left standing by his aircraft in total confusion. Walking up to him, I extended my paw. "Oberleutnant George Wolf," I said, introducing myself. "Beer, ja?"

To his credit, old Henry shook my paw, though I could see he was still very angry. "Lieutenant Henry Badcock," he replied, "Beer, nein… tea, ja."

§

All went well, considering the war time circumstances. We were all pilots and as pilots we held ourselves to a higher code than the 'ground pounders'; or so we thought. It was an illusion to be sure. Without a doubt, there was as much compassion and good intentions among the regulars as anywhere. In our case we simply had a cleaner more viable playing field called the sky. In some respects we viewed our side and their side much as opposing soccer teams. On the field anything went and then some. Any dirty trick you could dream up was perfectly acceptable. On the ground, however, we were all 'gentle creatures' full of polite manners and solicitudes. Only two rules had to be followed during such events. One must never insult another's wife and one must never ever insult another's aircraft.

Of course Flight Lieutenant Henry Badcock just had to go and break that rule.

"And I say the Spitfire is the best aircraft ever built," he told our group over dinner. As guest he was sitting on our commander's right and I was seated on the left. Herr Oberst Locke translated for him, his eyes watching each of us for our responses. "The Spitfire's done right well against the Messerschmitt, thank you very much. I mean; I don't know for the life of me how you chaps can stand to fly such an ugly little machine."

We had been served sausages, boiled potatoes, and sauerkraut for dinner, all to be washed down by gallons of good Stonenpassen beer. It was a special occasion for us and so the cook had pulled out all the stops. As soon as our Commandant translated the Royal's words, I felt a knot in my stomach and knew the fabulous dinner was a wasted effort.

"Herr Locke has sixty five kills," Fritz countered, sitting up very straight and nodding to Herr Oberst. "Many of them were Spitfires. Not to mention Herr B.B.'s fantastic shot which felled your brother pilot."

Locke seemed hesitant to translate this exactly, but he did, where upon Henry sallied forth with, "Gerwalt Lank was shot down just yesterday by a Spitfire. Squadron Leader Archie Corn got him right enough. He tried to turn inside the SL's Spit and got shot up pretty bad. He was lucky; bailed out and was captured by our ground troops."

This caused quite a stir. Lank was the Commandant of Staffel 32 and two hundred miles to our north. This was the first we'd heard about it. He was last known to have eighty kills. There was much discussion and then I had a thought. "Who is this Archie Corn?" I asked and Locke translated.

Henry pointed his fork at me and said, "That was the fellow you shot down yesterday. He insisted we split up to maximize the surprise. Bad decision that... if I had stayed on his tail I would have nailed you before you buggered him."

Henry's foul language had a telling effect on our Commandant. Yes it was true he was known to curse a mechanic's blue streak when provoked; but in fairness he always carried himself like the Alpha Wolf he was. I could see the tightness in the corner of his mouth. Since I was the one who captured the goat and brought him to the dinner table, I would most likely receive a very telling reprimand and penalty such as digging latrines.

After a few more beers, Howler bangs his paw on the table and curses the rounded lines of the Spitfire. "The airplane looks like a fat strudel stuffing baker's wife," he remarked.

Locke laughed hard and then translated.

Badcock countered with, "She's got the metal of a good stiff cock and has pushed it up the Messerschmitt's arse more than a few times. Now you want to talk about ugly, your aircraft has all the beauty of a proctor's idea of truth and all the elegance of a right angle."

It quickly went downhill from there to the point that Badcock stood, knocking over his beer and demanding that we prove the superiority of the Messerschmitt. "Put up or shut up; I'm calling your bluff. Show me your Wolf brass balls. I say we match our planes from take-off to twenty thousand feet... see who gets there first. Whichever does begins the dogfight. No shooting until you get there either; just like an Irish duel."

That one raised all of our eyebrows. When asked for an explanation Badcock gave us a contemptuous look as if we were all uneducated; we Wolfs, who match cut for cut in Schlager duels. Even my blood was boiling at this point.

"You fight with a cudgel and a top hat," he explained, his paws doing a lampoon of the fight. "First you have to knock off the other fellow's hat before you can hit him on the head. He knocks yours off'n he's free to beat you to death while you still have to knock his hat off before you can match him. So I say you have to get to twenty thousand before you can fire... keep the other fellow down and it's all yours."

"Bollocks," I muttered, tipping back my beer and missing the rest of what Badcock said.

Suddenly I found all eyes on me.

"What?"

"He asked where our brass balled Wolf was," Locke told me with a strange smile. "You brought him here, Herr B.B. Are you feeling up to his challenge?" There was a chorus of voices egging me on to accept.

Herr Locke leaned forward so only I could hear him and said coldly, "Und this time kill the uncouth bastard."

That pretty much settled it. When we were done I called for Aloysius and instructed him to have his mechanics fix the Spitfire. When he gave me a questioning look I told him, "It's a long story but I fly against the bastard in the morning."

"How exactly do you wish me to fix the aircraft, sir?" He asked very softly.

"I expect it to be rightly and properly fixed, Sergeant. What kind of person would I be if I did not win this contest on my own merit?"

"Jahohl, Mein Heir," he said with a smile and a salute. "As you say, it will be so."

§

The following morning I stood with Badcock towards the rear of our aircraft watching the sun come up. Their silhouettes in this early light were remarkably different. The Spitfire's lines were smooth and rounded, whereas the Messerschmitt's were lean and sharp. Where the Royal's underbelly was clean, the Wolf's was marred with an egg shaped fuel tank which was a necessity for gaining any reasonable amount of time in the air. With a mere seventy six gallon internal capacity you learned early on to nurse every last ounce when it was possible.

Taking out a pack of cigarettes, I thumbed one up for Badcock and one up for myself. He accepted it in a quiet humble sort of way, so very unlike the Bulldog of the night before.

"I know you don't sprecken Dog," he says to me, "But before we begin I want to apologize for last night." He winked. "It got me a chance to fly the old Spitfire at least one last time."

I looked at him and no translation was needed. Without a doubt, the blustery exterior was nothing more than a cover for what was really underneath. I winked at him and smiled. "Is goot morning," I managed. "Fly goot... bail out wenn schlecht. [*when bad*]"

We both came up with lighters in the same instant, flicking them and holding them out for the other. Closing mine with a metallic click, I leaned forward and let him light me up. He then lit his own and we both took deep drags, letting out a cloud of smoke.

Thumbing my lighter over in my paw, I saw it had the squadron's emblem engraved on one side and the back to back letters B.B. on the other. Motioning for him to follow, I led the way to the side of my Messerschmitt. Pointing to the back to back B's on its hull, I next pointed to the same initials on the lighter and then to my chest. "Herr Brass Balls," I told him and smiled. "Es ist mir, du dumme alte Bastard." [*It's me you silly old Bastard.*]

With that I pressed the lighter into his palm, pointing to myself and then to him. He smiled in return and pressed his own lighter into my palm. I looked at it and saw that it too had his squadron emblem on it. On the reverse side were the initials H. B.

"It's me you silly young fool," he says in perfectly accented Wolf. "Good luck, and may God protect you, because I will shoot you down if I get a clear shot."

I looked at him for a second and then chuckled. "You're a cagey old fellow," I told him softly and then shook his paw firmly. "I am glad to have met you and I am sorry for your fellow."

"Likewise," he told me, "And I am sorry too; but that is the nature of war. He'd have killed you just as quickly."

When the cigarettes were finished we walked to the front of the aircraft where all but two of our pilots were waiting. Nearby a pair of engines roared to life. A moment later two of our fighters taxied out for takeoff.

Herr Locke pointed at them and said in Dog, "If you try to run

Herr Badcock, they will shoot you down. The rules are exactly as you stated them to be. When I give the signal you will both take off and climb to twenty thousand feet. You cannot fire until you obtain altitude.

If you shoot Herr B.B. down, you will be allowed to fly back across the channel unmolested by this Staffel. I cannot vouch for any of the others so for that you will be on your own.

Badcock executed a perfect Royal salute, "Sir!"

Locke motioned that I should walk with him for a moment.

"I will be on the radio at all times," he told me softly. "I think perhaps I was rash in taking this wager. We have a perfectly good captured aircraft to play with; we should use it to our advantage."

"We cannot back out now sir," I told him.

"Why not?"

"Honor, Mein Herr."

"Of course," he responded, "How could I have forgotten? Is there anything you wish me to hold for you?"

Reaching into my pocket I pulled out the lighter Badcock had given me along with my cigarettes and identification papers. These I handed over without comment. It was simply something we did for each other. In this case Herr Locke was more of a father figure than a Commandant.

"Goot," he said accepting them. "I vill give them back when you land. Do nothing stupid, ja?"

Ja, Mein Herr," I responded. To say I had mixed feelings was an understatement. I now knew the pilot I was to try and kill; he was no longer just an enemy machine in the sky. Turning back to my fighter I climbed onto the wing and into the cockpit.

§

The engine noise from both aircraft was strikingly different. The Messerschmitt 109 had a much throatier sound than the Spitfire and its starting procedure was quite different. Whereas the Spit started on her own using an electrical starter, my aircraft had a centrifugal device that was hand cranked up to speed by my mechanics. We were given a moment in allowance for warm up and then Herr Locke held up his flare pistol and made a circular motion with it. As it was, we were exactly wingtip to wingtip and at the ready. Badcock cranked his canopy closed and I pulled mine down, finding the close confines of the small cockpit both familiar and comfortable.

Over the radio I heard someone ask if we were ready. Henry was immediate with a gruff, 'Ready.' I responded in kind and a moment later a green flare illuminated over the runway. With the signal, our engines advanced. My tail came up as it had the day before in twenty feet. I was clearly airborne first and ahead by two body lengths at the end of the runway. The morning was glorious. The sun was just coming up on the horizon so that the countryside was still shrouded in shadow. I didn't opt for max climb power but left the engine at full take off for as long as I dared, keeping an eye on the engine temp as well as the Spitfire flying behind me.

Climbing through 8,000 feet I went on oxygen, securing the mask to my snout with one paw. Turning in my seat, I vaguely saw the Spitfire behind and below by a good thousand feet. The one thing the Messerschmitt did not have was good visibility.

Remembering to be cautious I checked the fuel mixture and engine temp again. When I reached altitude I clicked the clock's stop watch function and saw it had taken me exactly seven minutes from take off to twenty thousand feet. It was a wonderful feeling but presently I didn't have time for wonderful feelings. Pushing the radio button I called out my altitude, jettisoned my drop tank, and then banked around to begin my attack. The sun coming up in the east, I noted without even thinking, was neither a hindrance nor a help. I could see Badcock just below me as I was sure he could see me. He must have been furious that I'd beaten his wonderful Spitfire to altitude. Keeping the power on I dove even as I turned on the reflective sights. Lining up on him I thumbed the safety off. It would be a straight on shot so I didn't even have to adjust for tracking. It couldn't get much easier.

With my burst, the Royal Bull Dog broke right and then came back left again in an exaggerated 'S' maneuver to throw off my aim. I streaked past and now it was my turn to curse as I lost valuable altitude recovering from my dive. I heard him call out twenty thousand as I pulled out and began climbing again. Our positions were now reversed.

My engine howled in protest as I kept the power on. At altitude the Messerschmitt's fuel injection worked much better that the Spitfire's carburetor but now I was low Dog in the pile and for the moment I'd lost him in a small cloud. As I approached, he punched back out again banking well over and coming at me from broadside. I imitated the turn, pulling bodily on the stick for all I was worth. Unlike the lead sled I was used to, there was no hydraulic boost on any of the aircraft's controls. Strictly speaking, it was the pilot's muscle and the machines mechanical heart melded together; the one being an exact extension of the other. As in the battles of armored knights, guts and intelligence were not enough... you needed true strength to win a dogfight.

The maneuver was a mistake and I knew it from the beginning. The Spitfire's pleasingly rounded wings had much less load on them than the Messerschmitt's and Badcock easily turned inside of me. The moment I saw his tracers I dove with full military power on and dropped like a brick. Even at that I caught at least five rounds through the wings.

My fighter's engine had no problem with the inverted G force maneuver. Henry's Spitfire, on the other paw, burped and stuttered momentarily, its fuel floating upwards in the carburetor as he tried to follow. This allowed me a greater lead in the dive which most likely saved my life.

The airspeed indicator climbed into the red; well over four hundred and twenty knots indicated airspeed. My controls stiffened to the point of non-responsiveness and compression recovery became primary to my mind. I was now riding a shooting star and did not wish to be a crater in the ground; which would happen if the wings ripped off. Chopping the power I began pumping the rudder and ailerons to slow myself down. The altimeter was winding down like an out of control clock and it was now I noted my fuel was down past half. As I saw this the fuel warning light blinked on indicating I had only twenty minutes left. Getting back on an approach to the airfield was now mandatory but I pushed the thought away so long as Badcock was above me.

When my speed was down to three hundred I ripped my oxygen mask off and rolled to the right, flying into a convenient cloud. My altitude was now at just under ten thousand and I continued in a tight turn doing three full circles before coming back to my original course and going back to full power. If I was lucky, and if Badcock had followed in the dive, this would put him directly in front of me and most likely high tailing it to the coast. He was half full when we started and this was far more than enough for a quick dogfight and escape; which would have been on the forefront of his thoughts. In doing this, my mind had already figured in the possibility of landing at the Staffel next up the coast to refuel. It was something I had to do... it was honor... it was expected by my Commandant... it was...

"Herr B.B.," called our ground controller, "Return to base. Flight oversight; return to base."

I saw him not more than a mile ahead, throttle obviously pulled slightly back from his safe power limit for economy. Just as I'd expected he was heading dead on to the coast. True to the agreement of the wager, the pilot had fought and fought well so this was allowed and the two covering fighters were no longer there.

I pushed my throttle to Emergency Power, determined to catch him. He would not be looking back and it was a dead on run with no gun deflection or windage to figure into the mix. Having nothing else to worry about, I simply hung on, riding my aircraft like a horse at full gallop.

"Herr B.B.," Locke's voice called over the radio, "Break off and return to base."

I did not respond. Something inside me was incensed at missing the retreating Spitfire. A voice inside my head told me I was Wolf! It then spit out an entire series of words that I did not understand... words with a Wolf accent. A different voice inside my head was also calling to me, saying, 'Let it go Corgi Dog... let it go!'

My indicated airspeed pressed at three eighty and froze there while my engine temperature rose to well over the red line. I smelled heat and exhaust fumes and pulled my oxygen mask back on. Badcock's Spitfire grew in my gun sights from a small dot to something where I could now make out the details.

"Herr B.B. return to base! This is an order!" demanded Locke. When I did not respond, he shouted, "YOU WILL RETURN NOW! RETURN..."

Flames sprouted from under my engine cowl and smoke swept into the cockpit. I would have been blinded but for my goggles. Pulling the canopy's jettison handle on the right, I felt the wind sweep in, pulling at my harness in an attempt to pluck me from the cockpit. Three more seconds and I would fire and then chop power... two... one...

Strange and terrible things happen when an engine seizes full on. This dramatic stoppage of force, coupled with the incredible torque of the huge spinning propeller literally tore off the front of my fighter. This ripping action, in turn, flipped what remained of the fuselage end over end over end; streaming flames from the ruptured fuel line. I did not cry out. I did not howl. There was no time to do anything... except die.

§

I woke in the booth at the beer garden. The place was empty except for me and the barkeep. The only light that was on was a single overhead incandescent bulb inside a tin hood.

"I was wondering when you would wake," he called to me from behind the bar. "I think you drink too much, ja?"

"Sure," I managed. My mouth tasted like something dead and my eyes felt as if they had sand in them. "What time is it?"

"It is three thirty of the A.M. First Officer Corgi. Perhaps you go home now, eh?"

"Where is home?" I asked stupidly.

"I have asked that same question many times," the Wolf responded as he came around the bar. Sitting down across from me, he reached into his pocket and pulled out some grass. "Eat this," he told me, "And go puke. You will feel better. When you come back I give you a large glass of tomato juice so you have something in your gut, ja?"

When I looked skeptical, he shrugged his shoulders. "Wolfs do it, Dogs do it... it is a time honored tradition because it works. Go ahead, I vill fetch the drink."

What can I say? The toilet stunk like all toilets in beer gardens stink but he was right; when I finished, I did feel better. Washing my face in cold water, I looked at myself in the mirror. Besides being one huge body ache, my uniform shirt looked like I'd slept in it and my eyes were bright red.

Making my way back into the bar, I went to the booth and sat across from the strange Wolf. The tomato juice was sitting on the table waiting for me. Drinking it straight down, I extended a paw and said, "My names George Corgi, what's yours?"

He shook my paw warmly. "The war is over, you may call me Dierk."

"I was four years old when the war ended," I told him. "It lasted six." I don't know why this seemed important, but it did.

"Ja," he said quietly, digging a pack of cigs and a lighter out of his breast pocket. "I know this."

Shaking one out of the pack for me, he next thumbed the lighter open and lit me up when I was ready. As I breathed in a grateful lungful of the rich tobacco, he snapped the lighter closed again and then placed it on the table top. Taking a small leather folder out of his pocket, he placed it with the lighter and slid them both over to me.

"You asked me to hold these for you. I am pleased to now return them."

"I must have been some drunk," I muttered, picking them up and sliding them into my pants pocket, "Because I sure don't remember doing so."

The one eyed Wolf laughed a strange laugh. "How do you Royals say... you were really Spitfire?"

"Pissed," I corrected with a smile.

"Amazing that one word can carry so many translations, my young friend."

There was a car horn outside the door and I turned to look, my attention temporarily diverted.

"That would be your ride," he told me, rising from the booth and picking up my duffle. "You are to have a goot life, ja? That is an order."

"Jahohl, Mein Heir," I replied automatically; not even realizing I had done so.

§

When I got to the hotel, the sun was just coming up. I was actually met in the lobby by Captain Badcock. He was down trying to have his breakfast but at such an early hour no kitchen staff had yet arrived. Seeing me walk in, he motioned me over.

"Where the bloody hell have you been?" he asked acidly.

"You left me to walk," I explained. "I stopped at a beer garden and apparently had too much to drink. It happens sometimes."

"For three days?" he asked.

I blinked, his statement hitting me like a fighter's slash attack. "I was… three days?"

"We leave this afternoon," he told me with an absolute look of disapproval.

"If you vill follow me, Mein Herr," the desk clerk told him, coming back to the desk, "I can give you coffee, but the cook vill not be in for another hour."

"Fine," he says, turning to her. "Please make it for two as my First officer has finally decided to show up and I am sure he needs it."

When we were seated, old Henry takes out his pack and thumbs up a cigarette. Not bothering to offer me one, he placed it between his lips and then found my outstretched paw thumbing a lighter to flame. He leaned forward to take advantage and then spotted the emblem on its side. Two things happened: he turned quite pale and then blowing out the flame he snatched it away from me.

"Where did you get this?" he asked in a near whisper.

"The barkeep at the beer garden gave it to me," I told him. "He said I'd given it to him to hold for me." Fishing into my pocket I pulled out the small leather wallet. "He gave me this too, come to think of it. He had just one eye and looked like he'd been burned. He said he'd flown Messerschmitts during the war."

Together we opened the wallet and found ourselves looking at the picture of a young pilot standing in the cockpit of a German fighter. The view was down the nose of the aircraft and the Wolf was quite handsome. On the other side was an official looking identification paper stating the fellow's name to be, Oberleutnant Georg Wolf.

Henry reached into his pocket and took out his own lighter. placing it on the table and pushing it over to me. "Does this mean anything to you?" he asked.

I picked it up and examined it closely. On one side was the outline of a strange looking falcon. Inside the outline was a spider impaled on a fencing sword. Turning it over, I saw the back to back B's.

A cold chill swept through my body. At that moment, as I looked up and met the eyes of my old adversary, the desk clerk brought us coffee.

Seeing my reaction was answer enough for the old Bull Dog. "Tell me everything you remember," he said plainly, "and do not leave out a bloody fucking thing."

By the time I was done breakfast had come and gone. There was a quiet moment and then Badcock said, "I never told anyone that story… not even command. I was far too embarrassed at having let my Spitfire be captured. That and if I'd told them Archie and I had split up they would have had my balls for breakfast. My report was accurate through the raid on the airfield; and then I told them I had engine problems and set down in a field. That night a farmer helped me fix a fuel line that'd come loose. I looked for Herr Locke after the war but the best I could do was, 'Missing in Action'. I did manage to find Archie's grave."

"Did you… well… did you leave him there?" At this point I was feeling true guilt. Perhaps I asked because I just didn't know what else to say. "I understood that the Wolf's were very good about things like that."

"I brought him home. They'd buried him in a French cemetery and it was nice enough but I arranged transport and had him interned back in England next to Flight Lieutenant Terrance Chrysanthemum."

"Why'd you do that?" I asked

Pushing back in his chair, he told me bruskly, "I had my reasons. Now take me to the beer garden."

Actually, I was more than happy to do so as I desperately wanted some answers of my own. When we got there, however, the only thing we found was a bombed out ruin.

Above the door and still hanging from one mount, was the beer garden sign that had attracted me on my walk. The picture of the fighter was still on it but it was full of bullet holes; probably from the invading allied army. The tail of the aircraft had seen flames and for a moment I felt them washing over me again.

Before I could stop myself, I was leaning over what had once been a window puking my guts out. When I was done, I found Captain Badcock standing close with a fistful of grass. He wore a sad expression.

"I'm afraid they've all gone for a Burton, son. It's called 'war' and it isn't pleasant. Go ahead," he told me holding the grass out, "Eat it and puke again, it'll settle your stomach. Wolfs do it, Dogs do it… it's tradition because it works. It'll help you get past knowing it's not a game… that you've killed another living breathing being. My final count was fifteen and don't think I don't reflect upon that."

All that I'd experienced flowed over me then like an ocean. When I finally could speak, I asked him simply, "Why?"

The old boy just shrugged his shoulders. "I don't know," he replied. "It was just something we had to do. Kill or be killed, eh?"

§

As the camera pulls away showing the two uniformed figures in front of the bombed out ruins, the small Fox's voice is again heard:

"First Officer George Corgi has discovered the madness surrounding an age old question that has perplexed those pressed to be warriors for as long as there has been war upon the face of the planet. Where there is more than one Alfa there can be no rest and so all the games ever played in youth are bundled up and burned as sacrifice to the highest game of all; to win is to live, to lose is to die."

"Kill or be killed is but an excuse exhorted by those who would have you fight for a cause that might or might not be so very honorable; turning a vibrant and living world into a vast cemetery."

"That this excuse is false does not matter. To remember that it is false is important."

"The moment we forget this, the moment we cease to be haunted by its remembrance, then we become the grave-

404

diggers; something to dwell on and something to remember, not only in the Twilight Zone but wherever men walk God's earth."

—Rod Serling – 'Deaths-head Revisited' – November 10th, 1961

The End

Hitler knows that he will have to break us in this island or lose the war. If we can stand up to him, all Europe may be free and life of the world may move forward into broad, sunlit uplands. But if we fall, then the whole world, including the United States, including all that we have known and cared for, will sink into the abyss of a new Dark Age made more sinister, and perhaps more protracted, by the lights of perverted science.

Let us therefore brace ourselves to our duties, and so bear ourselves that, if the British Empire and its Commonwealth lasts for a thousand years, men will still say,

"This was their finest hour!"

—Sir Winston Leonard Spencer Churchill (1874-1965)

Obituary:

Group Commander Henry Badcock was the archetypal dashing fighter pilot. During WWII he shot down at least 15 enemy aircraft; escaped from enemy occupied France with the aid of the French Resistance; and was three times awarded the DFC – one of only 47 pilots in the Second World War to be so honored. He also became, in the latter days of the war, the third pilot to shoot down a German jet, becoming a part of the select group of pilots to fly the RAF's first jet fighter, the Meteor, in combat.

Henry Harold Badcock was born in Bristol on February 3, 1910. Flying ran in the family blood: his father being a Royal Air Force instructor who had served as a pilot in the First World War, during which time he met his wife Maria, a Royal Flying Corps driver.

Henry joined the RAF in September 1930 and as his father before him, became a flight instructor. Shortly after the onset of the war, he was assigned to No. 99 squadron at Biggin Hill and was instrumental in the defense of London during the Battle of Britain.

Following the outbreak of the Second World War 92 Squadron reformed on 10 October 1939 at RAF Tangmere. Initially it flew Bristol Blenheims but in early 1940 it became operational on the Supermarine Spitfire, various marks of which it flew for the rest of the War. 92 Squadron first saw action over the Dunkirk evacuation beaches. During the Battle of Britain 92 Squadron flew from RAF Biggin Hill. The Squadron was the first into action on September 15, 1940 now known as Battle of Britain Day. Under the aggressive leadership of Commander Reginald Sheltie, and later Commander Archie Corn the wing flew to engage the Luftwaffe all through the war.

Badcock achieved his first success on August 15th 1940 when he was awarded ½ of a JU88, the other half being given to then Flight Lieutenant Archie Corn.

After the war Badcock became a Captain for the British Overseas Airways Corporation, maintaining this position until his retirement from flying in 1970. He then became Assistant Curator and later Curator of the Battle of Britain Museum at Biggin Hill just outside of London.

Group Commander Badcock had no surviving relatives. At his willed request there will be a small service at the Biggin Hill Chapel after which he will be laid to rest at the Biggin Hill Cemetery next to war time friends Archie Corn and Terrance Chrysanthemum.

§

I read this for possibly the hundredth time as I sat in the anteroom of the Museum Curator's office. I hadn't learned of the old boy's demise until late and was not able to be present at the service which I'd heard was even attended by the Queen. Staying true to his request her attendance went unannounced and the ceremony was kept simple. For that I was gratified.

I'd had the obituary laminated and mounted to be posted upon the wall of the museum's office somewhere. I felt Henry deserved at least that much recognition. The post had already been taken over by the Assistant Curator who was less known to me but I'd received a summons from his office and so here I sat waiting, though it didn't appear the fellow was even in.

After the Stonenpassen affair, as Henry and I came to call it, we became more than just good friends. He became a mentor to me and taught me a great deal about flying. He even introduced me to my wife, who was a brand new stewardess at the time. 'She's the one for you,' the old boy whispered in my ear; and darned if he hadn't been right.

In these later years, with my promotions within the company causing a great deal of travel, I suppose I was less of a friend than I should have been. Henry was the first to tell me; 'Life leads and we follow.' It's a poor excuse, I know, but there you have it.

"Mr. Corgie?"

I looked up from my reverie to find a lovely young Corgie Dog dressed in the W.A.A.F. uniform of the Battle of Britain era. For all intents and purposes she could have been the daughter I never had.

"That would be me," I said. Placing the obituary on the seat next to me I stood and took her extended paw. "Please… call me George."

"Did you know that Welsh folklore says the Corgi Dog is the preferred mount of fairy warriors?"

"I had no idea," I replied to this strange greeting, "but if I ever find one sitting upon my shoulder I'll be sure to let you know; complete with pictures."

She laughed and her voice was musical. "I'm glad you came," she told me. "I wasn't sure you would."

"I only wish I could have made the service. Henry was very special to me. So you summoned me and not Mr. Whatshisname?"

"He was special to all of us, sir. That is correct, I sent for you. This concerns your bequeathment. If you will follow me please."

Before I could ask anything, or even get her name for that matter, she'd turned upon her heel and headed out of the office to the museum proper. I had no choice but to follow and follow damned quickly as she didn't dally. Presently it was after hours and though the lights were on no one was there but us. "Could you tell me how he died?" I asked to her back.

"Exactly as he wished," she replied over her shoulder, "Flying."

This certainly threw me a double bounder and I was totally taken by surprise. "So you mean to say he was in an aircraft when he died?"

"That is correct," she replied, heading down the stairs to the hangar area.

"Whose airplane?"

"His airplane."

This perplexed me even more. Obviously she was not one to give out stories. "I wasn't aware that Henry even owned an airplane."

When we reached the bottom of the stairs I caught up in order to walk by her side. It suddenly felt that I was the wingman of this little formation. She was knock dead gorgeous to be sure and though the uniform was dated and a bit frumpy looking, if fit her like a glove. Somehow I don't think a modern dress would have suited her in any case.

"Most certainly he did," she replied. "In fact, most of the aircraft in this museum belonged to him. Henry Badcock made it his mission to preserve as many of the war time aircraft as he could. I think he knew they would all go away some day."

"Like him?" I asked, and felt bad that I did as soon as the words escaped my lips.
"Yes," she responded.

We were passing by a Messerschmitt 109 E model as this exchange happened. Here she stopped. "Would you like to take a closer look at Emil before we continue?"

Stonenpassen came back to me like it had happened yesterday and I remembered flying for the Wolfs even if it had been a dream... but what a hell of a dream. "May I?"

"Most certainly. You will find that it has been perfectly restored to the condition it was in the last time it flew for the Germans. The paint coloring and markings were Henry's personal choice. She is airworthy and exercised once a month to keep her so."

Everything came back to me as I slowly made my walk-around, beginning at the front and moving around the craft clockwise. Two back to back 'B's marked her sides, looking oddly out of place on a Luftwaffe bird. When I came to the pilot's side I stopped and looked at the titles written below the cockpit in black. Oberleutnant Georg Wolf was painted first as the pilot and under that Feldwebel Aloysius Skunk as crew chief

"It took Henry a great deal of time and much research on those two names," I heard from behind me, "But they are authentic, as is the aircraft's paint scheme."

"It's certainly not the same aircraft?" I asked, turning to her.

She smiled a delightful smile that was full of laughter, though she remained coolly British in her demeanor. "No," she replied. "That aircraft was gone long ago; a marvelous race that ended in tragedy. This one was recovered from a farm near Dover. It was repaired and used as a test platform so the allies would have a better grasp of what it was truly capable of. She was another of Henry's rescues, due to be scrapped by those who saw no further need for her existence."

Pointing to the name of the crew chief, I asked her, "Did Henry ever find out what happened to this fellow?"

Walking to a display case next to the aircraft, she nodded to it. "Come and see."

I did, and found several pictures, one of which had a very proud looking Skunk standing next to this very aircraft in the museum. There was a small plaque next to it telling how Oberleutenant Aloysius Skunk had survived the war after flying Zerstörer aircraft on both the Russian and Western fronts. After the war he married and opened a bakery which his family still runs.

"Well I'll be," I managed, "He actually got to fly after all."

"He received two decorations for bravery," my escort remarked. "It was indeed good to see him visiting with Henry and sharing stories." I looked at her, expecting an explanation of this but she offered none.

"Henry was found sitting in the cockpit of the Egham Spitfire," she told me instead. "The engine was still warm to the touch and the fuel tank was near empty."

"Well I'll be." It was the only thing I could think to say. She was right… it was the way old Henry would have wanted to go.

"Follow me please," she instructed and we were off again at a brisk pace, passing aircraft after aircraft of the era, including one Beechcraft Model 18, or "Twin Beech", as it is better known. Oddly enough it was in RAF colors and had a Chrysanthemum flower painted under the pilot's side window. We stopped here for a moment as if my escort were paying some sort of special respect. The plaque next to the craft read simply, 'Donated by an anonymous American and used by Wing Commander Stewart Falstaff as his personal transport through the end of WWII. It served the RAF through the Berlin Airlift and was retired the following year'

After this, the young lady opened a normal door within the larger hangar door and led me out onto the tarmac where I saw a Spitfire sitting as picturesque as ever it was. We walked the fifty yards in silence and she stopped right behind the left wing where the pilot would mount up. The small side door was down and the cockpit Perspex rolled back as if the airplane were actually waiting for my arrival.

"If you will climb up to the cockpit, sir, there is a package behind the seat that Henry left for you. Once retrieved it might be easier if you climb in. I believe there will be a note of explanation."

Following her instructions I found the package and then eased myself into the cockpit. My feet automatically found the rudder pedals and I adjusted the seat forward a bit to better suit my height. Looking at the package, I found my name written upon it in Henry's handwriting. She was correct as inside was a note.

George,

Before I forget, and because I am presently in the company of some very old and dear friends, I thought I would jot down some instructions for you. You will need to confirm some of it with my solicitor who will be awaiting your phone call.

My wish is to bequeath to you the Egham Spitfire. She is now your charge and when the time comes, which it will, I am sure you will do likewise to someone you know will take good care of her. Along with this, I am also giving you my war time diary. Although it was strictly against regulations to record mission details and some other such things, I did it anyhow. That's just my nature I suppose. Most of what is written inside no one would believe in any case; the same as they would say it was impossible that you ever flew for the Germans during the war.

My best to you and your darling wife.

We shall meet again.

Henry

Looking back at my escort, she nodded to me as if already aware of what was in the note. That was when I remembered I didn't even know her name.

"I'm sorry, but who exactly are you?" I asked.

She smiled a sad yet beautiful smile. "Flight Lieutenant Archie Corn wrote a poem for me," she said in explanation. "It was the most delightful and yet saddest of things I'd ever heard. The ending stanzas go thus;

'We will be but ghosts of what went before then,
Remembered for a generation or two
Until even that is taken by oblivion.

And yet we both shall ever hear the music of children's voices
Pretending they can fly.' "

She saluted in a good RAF manner and told me, "I am the Egham
Spitfire, sir."

That said she was gone as if she'd never been there at all.

Standing in the cockpit I watched where she'd been for a good
few seconds and then finally turned my eyes to the sky and the setting
sun. In the fading light I saw but a single contrail stretching across what
was left of the blue and for a moment my mind boggled at the thought of
hundreds of them corkscrewing and converging across the expanse of that
sky as they battled.

I understood then that the thought processes of modern times
could never fully grasp the absolute sacrifice made by an entire nation in
doing what it took to turn back the Wolf at the door.

It didn't matter that you were undergunned and undermanned. You
went.

It didn't matter that mistakes were made. That happens.

It didn't matter that your family and chums would miss you when
you were gone. That was the cost of freedom.

You were fighitng for the very survival of your country and your
people.

And that was all that mattered.

Reaching for the sky I held the small package aloft and uttered the
only words I could think to say.

"Thank you."

About the Author

Vixyy Fox is not exactly human; to know her is to see her as a Fennec Fox. Most people would not understand this but mankind, through the ages, has always associated themselves with the animals.

In reality, she is, of course, human; but you should see her in your mind as the creature she is.

Vixyy has been writing for most of her life but it was not until the turn of the century that she discovered who she was. Thus the style of her art form was born and has ever since flourished.

Weasel Press

Weasel Press is a new independent publisher still figuring things out in the literary world. We're dedicated in seeking quality writers and helping them get a voice in an already loud world. We're a little rusty at the moment since things are still under construction, but we hope to build a great reputation!

Our first publication was Vagabonds: Anthology of the Mad Ones. This is a literary magazine which is still printing and still growing.

This past year we've released two issues of Vagabonds partnered with Mind Steady Productions to bring an electric issue of Open Mind., moving deeper into the dark world with The Haunted Traveler.

We've got a lot of plans for the near future, so stick around and watch us grow into something awesome!

Please view our Current Publications to get a better feel for what we'll be doing in the future!

We gladly accept all questions, comments, concerns through email at:

systmaticwzl@gmail.com
http://www.weaselpress.com

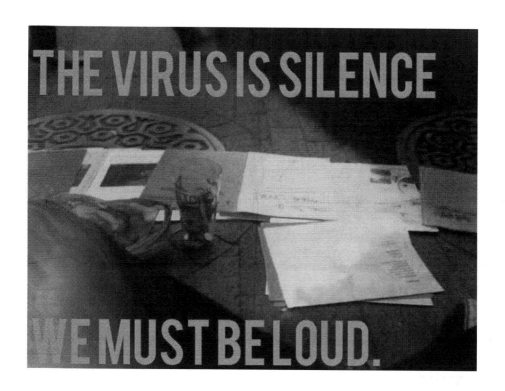

Spreading Poetry Among the Masses

Poetry has immense power in the community, however it is generally thought of as a dead art. One of the goals of Weasel Press is to help push poetry into a larger light. We have never needed poetry more than we do today. But we are not the only ones bringing poetry to the masses.Books and Shovels are preading poetry and other literary genres to the world thorugh more unorthodox publishing methods. They're traveling across country, pakc of books in their car and flashbombing the world with words of great and sometimes unheard of writers. To find out more information, visit the website below!

http://undegroundbooksandshovels.wordpress.com/
http://www.nostroviatowriting.com/
http://www.undergroundbooks.org/

14328556R00231

Printed in Great Britain
by Amazon.co.uk, Ltd.,
Marston Gate.